GONE TO POT

Is this story for you?

This story is a daring view into the underbelly of the sixties and seventies. For all of you who survived these tumultuous times, this account will serve as a recollection. This story is also for all of you who weren't there and may wonder if you could have survived. In either case, this story is a revealing adventure.

The characters in this story come alive in telling ways—their altruistic ideals, their efforts, their misguided expectations, their successes and failures are distinctive in crazy ways and hit a nerve in all of us.

To say this period of American culture is anything less than pivotal is an understatement. The effects this era's fallout has had on values, morality, and politics have become no less than worldwide.

To my beautiful wife: Carolyn,
for her immitigable patience and...

To my parents:
Richard and Aristine Manke

GONE TO POT

Karl Manke

author of

AGE OF SHAME

UNINTENDED CONSEQUENCES

SECRETS, LIES AND DREAMS

THE PRODIGAL FATHER

& THE SCOURGE OF CAPTAIN SEAVEY

Alexander Books

Alexander, N.C.

Publisher: Ralph Roberts
Cover Layout: Ralph Roberts
Cover Art: Jeffery Gulick
Interior Design and Electronic Page Assembly: WorldComm®

ISBN 978-1-57090-284-0

Alexander Books—an imprint of *Creativity, Inc.*—is a full-service publisher located at 65 Macedonia Road, Alexander, NC 28701. Phone 1-828-252-9515, Fax 1-828-255-8719. For orders only: 1-800-472-0438. Visa and MasterCard accepted.

This book is also available on the Internet at **Amazon.com**

GONE TO POT

1967-1977

CHAPTER 1

"Get her the hell out of here before she barfs her guts all over my apartment!" The voice behind this imperative is a twenty year old college sophomore with shoulder length hair. He's a skinny shirtless young man with a fringed leather vest covering a muscle-less chest and a pair of bell bottom jeans gracing a similar complement of a skinny butt and legs. He's obsessing about an imminent mess. He's pleading with another girl to throw the over-inebriated girl from his apartment.

"You're an ass Phillip, you're just an ass. Can't you see she needs help?" says her equally stoned friend.

"Yea, I see she needs help—that's why I want you to help her out the door and down the street."

The time is 1967. The place is Michigan State University campus. Change is everywhere. Longtime social and moral norms are in a nearly indefinable state of flux. There is an overwhelming desire by the young to remain free of any restrictions that reflect the values of a previous generation. Sound reasoning is giving way to a self-serving subjective model that promises freedom from constraining, calculated religious and moral standards. Many of these old parental values have been rehearsed and practiced since birth. All this effort is carried out in the hopes of extending these values into the lives of their children. Unfortunately, the previous generation is seeing their time honored traditions quickly crumbling.

Phillip Grayling Hampton is hardly an exception. It's his efforts bringing this party to fruition. There's plenty of pot, cocaine and alcohol to satisfy this heisted Saturday night gathering of college students.

Over the span of the evening, Deidre Lueker has gratified her desire to get high, eventually indulging herself into a comatose state. To describe her as anything less than typical of this belligerent age would remove her from a whole generation of young people.

She has a wholesome beauty about her. Her hair, adorned with a Navajo head band, is sun-streaked blonde ending just above her waist. The neat style of clothing showcased by the women of her mother's generation and worn with panache has given way to wearing a braless T-shirt paired with an ankle length, paisley peasant dress accented with socks and sandals. There is an aspect of wild and crazy to this mingled look. It lends itself to the spirit of a poor Polish immigrant just stepping off the boat along with a carefully crafted sophomoric appearance designed to bring shock to anyone over the age of thirty. It's the look chosen by the burgeoning feminist movement to underscore a drastic departure from what is referred to as "a repressive woman's role" within the American culture.

Dutifully, her friends half walk and half drag her to a tent pitched in a small wooded area behind a dorm on campus along the Red Cedar River. It's here a group calling themselves SDS short for "Students for a Democratic Society" have stationed themselves as protestors. The naiveté of this group is typical of middle-class young people raised by parents in an ordered, safe community. They are straightaway choosing to cast safety aside as unimportant in favor of a communal lifestyle. The expectation is that this divergence will be based on each being given over to the protection of the other, therefore no more need of repressive law-enforcement. Love and flower power will win the day.

Anxious to return to the party for more free pot and booze, Deidre's friends feel they've fulfilled their role as her caretaker, leaving her alone to sleep off her excesses. Little do they know their departure is paralleling an unseen interloper lurking in the brush.

Soon Deidre finds her near comatose state is far from tranquil. She senses a weight on her, but in her drug and alcohol induced haze is not aware of the cause. It's accompanied by a mixture of pleasure and disturbance. In her semiconscious condition, she's aware of an unsolicited sexual stimulation, but hardly conscious of its origin. It's producing an agitation causing her to involuntarily thrash about digging at her attacker. This, in turn, stimulates the intruder to orgasm. Using Deidre's dress, he quickly cleans himself and disappears into the night as mysteriously as he appeared. Within the hour the intruder returns. Again making his way into her tent, he obliges himself as before, taking advantage of his victim's helpless condition to repeat the same vile act. With the amount of drugs and alcohol ingested, it's not strange that Deidre's brain remains unable to connect all that is happening. When he has finished, he once more leaves his hapless dupe victimized and bleeding.

It is morning. Aware that all is not well, but not sure just what it is that's out of sorts, Deidre makes a shocking discovery. Her dress, along with her sleeping bag, is crusted with dried blood and some other substance. Her head is muddled as she tries to grasp something out of her confused thoughts. It's clear she's struggling to explain her odd dilemma. What comes to mind right away is the remembrance of someone on top of her. She recalls their panting breath. The luminous body paint she had happily decorated herself with the night before is the only bright thing adorning her this morning.

With her mind forcing a connection, it relates itself to the source of her pain. She hastily examines her chafed vagina. It immediately reveals what her body has been attempting to tell her. She's sore and bruised and bleeding. Her mind continues racing in the hopes of landing on a satisfactory explanation. It's obvious she's undergone trauma. The how and by whom remain a mystery.

Reluctant to share this quandary with anyone, she quickly changes out of her soiled dress into a pair of jeans. The first person she encounters sitting alone at a smoldering campfire is Shelly Parks. She's her closest friend and one of the females that helped her get back to her tent the previous night. Not wanting to alert anyone to her predicament, she glibly sits down next to Shelly trying to be as cool as possible under the inner strain of her growing confusion.

Shelly is a dark-haired beauty, taller than Deidre and more statuesque with well-developed proportions. She's the first to speak.

"Well, well chickee do look at you! You look clanked."

"I am. I had a bum trip last night."

"You're not tellin' me anything new. I helped carry you from the party to your tent. You were stoned out of your gourd."

Deidre stares intensely, as if she's waiting for Shelly to tell her the rest of the story.

Shelly is puzzled by the stare, as though she may have left something out. "What?" It's all she can come up with, still wearing the same perplexed look.

"Is that all that happened?" asks Deidre still staring. It's obvious she's trying hard to choke back tears.

Shelly's whole demeanor changes in response to Deidre's strained behavior.

"Deidre you're not telling me something. What are you leaving out?" With tears making their way to her cheeks, she begins to shake. A simple explanation appears to be even more distant than before. Taking her hand out of a clothing bag she unfolds its contents. There on the ground in front of both of them is the evidence of what could have been the results of a beating.

Recognizing it as the dress Deidre had worn to the party, Shelly immediately notices the stains. "What the hell did you do to your dress Deidre?"

"I was hoping you could tell me!" exclaims Deidre, crying desperately.

Shelly can do nothing but look in disbelief at what is rapidly becoming more and more evident. Still wanting to believe what is lying before her is the simple result of consensual sex, with a slight smirk, she slowly forms the words, "Did you get balled last night?"

With her face twisting into what can only be described as a show of panic, Deidre wads up her soiled dress and buries it back in the bag hoping with this gesture her unhappiness will depart along with the entombed dress.

"I don't know what happened, but I don't think it was very good," says an obviously fearful and shaking Deidre.

Shelly is beginning to grasp the full measure of Deidre's trauma. Forming the words in her mind that she has only read in newspapers, Shelly swallows hard. "Do you think you were raped?"

Deidre reels at the sound of these words. "Yes!"

In her mind to say more than this is to give it a reality she's unwilling to grant such an unseemly exploit.

"Do you think we should get the police involved?" asks Shelly.

This question snaps Deidre to attention.

"Hell no! Those pigs would just say I had it comin'. You know damn well they would," angrily sobs Deidre. It's obvious the anger and hurt are fomenting in her words and actions.

"What do you think we should do?" asks Shelly, allowing herself to become more involved with the plight of her friend.

"I don't really know," says an increasingly beleaguered Deidre. The gloomy look on her face is morphing her from an energetic, vivacious twenty year old feminist into a weak, defeated, needy little girl.

Shelly has been her best friend since they met in kindergarten at St. Micheal Lutheran School. They have continually supported one another throughout their short lives. They are college roommates and now have become involved with the anti-Vietnam War movement. Although Shelly's family has been torn by divorce, they both nonetheless come from middle-class families who have done their best to instill the traditional Christian values.

Both girls have committed themselves to the growing student led anti-war SDS crusade. The stated mission of the SDS, according to its leaders, is to disrupt U.S. government-led foreign or domestic policies wherever possible.

"I'm not sure either, but I think we should report this to Phillip," says Shelly. The positive tone in her voice is the kind of support these two young women have unselfishly lent to one another for the better part of their young lives, leading each other out of seeming perilous situations.

Phillip Grayling Hampton II is the son of a wealthy automotive executive. He has led a typical self-absorbed life emblematic of spoiled rich kids. Having the financial freedom that lends itself to a lot of free time, Phillip has been appointed the local SDS organizer. His business classes at the university have been replaced by a social awareness curriculum led by proclaimed Socialist and Communist professors. He considers himself a "social progressive" dedicated to the overthrow of the United States government. But at the same time, he's willing to enjoy the financial freedom provided by a wealthy father. Personally, he's neither thrifty by inclination nor economical by necessity. His father considers his own peace of mind well worth the money it takes to support this son, providing the young man will agree to keep his unconventional lifestyle away from his father's attention.

Together, Deidre and Shelly make their way to Phillip's off campus pad. It's a loft-style flat shared with an eclectic montage of motley-haired twenty-something males and females self-describing themselves as "hippies." The musky odor of marijuana permeates the air as the two make their way up the well-worn industrial-style stairway to the third floor. In the truest representation of trust, the door has been removed allowing free access to and from this bastion of innovation. Their hope is that their free ways will be considered as the leading edge of a utopian community where trust and honesty prevail. This, of course, is in direct contrast to the perceived rut of failed trusts shared by their parents' generation.

Entering the smoke filled room, they spot Phillip sitting on the floor surrounded by a circle of males and females all garbed in paisley, or tie-dyed shirts, and bell bottom trousers. The group is passing a joint between them the size of a man's thumb. After each inhales the weed's rough textured smudgy smoke, the gasping sound of "WOW!" is followed by the equally grating word "HEEHEER!" as the reefer is passed to the next waiting set of fingers. The joint makes its way around the room and back to Phillip. He takes his awaited hit and merrily passes the giant joint to the two newcomers. Torn by wanting to address Phillip on a much more serious note, Deidre and Shelly, nonetheless oblige his generous offer and spend the next two hours so high neither are able to recite their entire name in a single sentence. It's late in the afternoon before anyone is ready to have a conversation pertaining to any reality within their physical world.

Shelly and Deidre have finally pulled Phillip aside long enough to talk about what may have happened to Deidre. The question is, whether her rape is the result of stoned behavior among the partygoers—and by whom? Phillip seems to be affronted by the thought that any of "the good people" could be capable of such a dirty trick.

"Phillip this is more than a prank. This is a violation of Deidre's natural rights and especially to her as a human being," comes back Shelly, throwing the soiled dress in Phillip's lap. Deidre is in tears again.

Realizing these two ladies are not going to let him off the hook, Phillip takes a more retaliatory tone. "I bet it was some of those frat guys hanging around looking for an opportunity to take advantage of one of you girls willing to give him a little free love."

Without waiting to see what kind of reaction this proposition has on the two ladies, he slams them with another hypothetical he hopes if not a home run turns into at least a center field hit. "That hit and run tactic is typical of their kind."

Allowing this thought to take root, he's quick to ask, "Did you get a good look at any of the violators?"

Still sobbing, Deidre merely shakes her head.

"This is sure as hell a bummer. Give me a few days and I'll try to get some satisfaction for you. Meanwhile chill and let's see what falls out."

Shelly takes the unexamined dress from Phillip's lap and redeposits it back into the small laundry bag.

"One more question Phillip," says Deidre.

"Sure. What do you need?" asks Phillip.

"Can I use your shower?"

With what seems a sympathetic gesture, Phillip gently wipes a tear from her cheek with his thumb. "Be my guest, Deidre."

CHAPTER 2

As usual with the human species, and especially the young, the urgency of Deidre's problem soon gives way to more immediate concerns.

Phillip, along with several others in his circle, is quick to move on to what is considered to be their self-declared vocation to "comfort the afflicted, and afflict the comfortable". This mission statement has a lofty tone and is readily adapted by these self-proclaimed reformers. It's problematic in that the "afflicted" and the "comfortable" are most times discerned by subjective prejudices. As lofty as this statement may resonate among the great unwashed, in most cases merely freaking out the squares is sufficient action taken.

Phillip has gotten word that some of the SDS national leadership is organizing an assault on Wall Street. The local chapter is being asked to show support by rallying the troops to New York. These are the very missions they spend hours discussing in the hopes of bringing the nation to its knees. Or at least get the press to cover the mayhem. As is the usual method of operation, the hard core instigators of these causes are usually much more committed to the success of their movement than the rank and file supporters who are more concerned that the rally develops into a good party with plenty of sex, drugs and rock and roll. This convocation is not to be an exception. Phillip and his cohorts, despite the political overtones of the national leaders, are all hoping for a full blown party.

Phillip and his band of merry men are heavy on the mayhem, but weak on the differing brands of communism, socialism and anarchy building behind much of the so called unrest. In the simplest terms, when push comes to shove, they will become supporters of nearly any cause providing there is a ready supply of women supporting the sexual revolution, LSD, hashish, or pot.

This is common ground for many of the student run newspapers within universities across the country. It's no secret they are hungry for anything that protests against the existing establishment, or what is generally referred to as "the military-industrial complex." When asked what exactly this means, varying answers are forthcoming depending on what forces influenced their latest rhetoric.

Phillip is readily campaigning for the cause. He has already convinced his inner core of disciples to prepare for the trip to New York. The conveyance of choice utilized to transport the growing number of willing dissidents is a ten year old school bus that's been transformed into a brightly painted psychedelic traveling party pad. The seats have been pulled out and replaced with bean bag seats neatly arranged along the walls beneath the windows. Welding the rear emergency door closed allows for the entire rear of the bus to be outfitted with bunk beds. Curtains have been added. These certainly create a sense of mystery, but are utilized more for the prevention of prying establishment eyes hoping to sight a dope smoker. The total capacity is for a dozen comfortably.

Manny Meitzer is part of Phillip's inner circle. He's the son of Jewish immigrant parents from Hitler's Germany. His father is a jeweler and during WWII had been able to hoard enough gemstones to buy his family's way out from under the ever prevalent eye of Hitler's SS Jew hunters.

John "Breezy" Yoder is another of Phillip's main confidants. A true peacenik, he's a twenty year old male from some Amish place in Indiana. He left the Amish because of their repressive lifestyle, showing up at Michigan State University after hearing about the tent community. He never enrolled in school but stayed in the tent village to fulfill his obsession with Phillip's "ban the bomb" efforts.

Breezy's girlfriend, Zan Tribblefurt is a farm girl from Idaho. She is an anthropology major and her main interest is urban cultures. None of her family has ever gone to college and they are never without a word of praise for this eldest daughter matriculating at a top ten rated university. None of the family has a clue what an anthropologist does, but they are willing to fork over the tuition, trusting this career will provide her with a living. She has opted to stay at Michigan State this summer by convincing her parents she's doing an independent class project that will look good on her resume. Of course this requires they continue her monetary support.

Deidre and Shelly have let it be known they also want to be included on this expedition. It's typical of the young to never resolve a past issue, if it means postponing the next adventure. For Deidre, this may be a way of putting the rape she's sure she suffered out of her mind—moving on to the next escapade in the hopes the hazy memory will fade into obscurity.

In typical carefree fashion, Shelly and Deidre have pulled up stakes, showing up with baggage in tow. With enough excitement and dope, the hope is these problems and all their effects can be left behind. They believe a geographical change will—at least for the moment—fill the bill.

After three days on the road with two flat tires, a failed fuel pump, and a ticket for improper equipment, they finally arrive at their appointed destination—New York City's East Village. The buildings represent an earlier era of progress, but for the most part no longer answer the demands of modern living. They would be all but abandoned if it were not for a whole new group of the underclass willing to fill them. It's regarded as the hippie capital of the east side of the continent. Previously this area around St. Marks Place was the Beatnik/Bohemian neighborhood. It's now being invaded by a horde of young people looking for their own cultural identity.

These young political activists are apart from the much more settled poets and artists who have been here for years and have developed a counterculture centered on the arts, thus becoming more or less apolitical.

In the abiding predisposition of this aging counterculture's "live and let live" philosophy, the old time Beatniks are giving way to an influx of new and somewhat effervescent youthful naivety. They are willing to tolerate this change partly because of their desire to keep a perpetual vigilance on their own fading youth and partly because it's the hip thing to do. Many of these senescent Beatniks are realizing their own youth has been very temporary.

Nonetheless, these cultural bottom feeders have a wealth of information to exchange with this new breed of wageless advocates. The old shepherds safeguarding rewards through hard work have been summarily branded as capitalistic and are therefore regarded as an enemy as contemptuous as a leper. The new trusted leaders guide their sycophants in the communist/socialist art of ripping off the government for free food and rent. The process is generally as simple as going to the nearest government sponsored welfare office and filling out the paper work.

The East Village attraction is cheap rent to start with. But as the Bohemian artists and hippies continue to pour into the area, much to their chagrin, the real estate developers are beginning to chase the lucrative attraction. Surreptitiously, these people with their strange counterculture lives are creating a whole new capitalistic market.

Not wanting to exhibit a Midwestern demeanor, these new arrivals are all very self-conscious and hope they will not be perceived as uncool. All the people out on the streets are young—late teens to early twenties. They are all doing something that appears to be groovy. Some are clustered together passing a joint. Some are playing guitars with an open guitar case to receive tips. Others are just plain panhandling from smooth shaven tourists who come just to gawk. There appears to be an atmosphere of brotherhood and good vibes in this hippie world.

Consequently, individually, each of the newcomers is paying close attention to how these New Yorkers perceive them. Their main strategy is to fill their verbiage with plenty of anti-Vietnam, anti-cop, anti-establishment expressions. This is thought to be a sure bet to let these people become aware of where their heads are. It seems to be working well as they find they have some common ground with these much more cosmopolitan freaks.

Having assumed his role as spokesman for the group, Phillip is acquainting himself with a rather eclectic looking man on the street. "Hey man, WOW! I'm diggin' all you far out freaks. You guys are beautiful man," declares a smiling Phillip leaning out of the bus window to a young man looking like the portrayal of Christ seen on prayer cards.

He's bearded; his hair is dark and curly resting on his shoulders. His demeanor is a mixture of open trust and guarded retreat. It's difficult for anyone to tell who are the flower children and who are the opportunistic outlaw predators; who are the pacifists and who are the violent revolutionaries. But in general, the point of congruence between all of these disparate groups is they have the police as their common enemy. In this accord they find a meeting ground to consort with the others—at least superficially.

It's obvious the man is looking over the psychedelic paint job covering the bus. The expression on his face indicates these are people he also would like to trust. A big smile of approval sweeps across his features as he flashes an approving "V" shaped peace sign.

"This beast is outta sight man! What can I do for you, Dude?" responds the man looking back at the haggard driver behind the wheel.

"We're just getting into town for the 'Wall Street' happening. I want to know where the action is."

"You're closer than you think. Let me come aboard and I'll lead you to a good spot for your bus."

With a trustful sweeping hand gesture, Phillip waves the man aboard. Grasping each other's hands in the traditional hippie handshake of locked thumbs, they quickly get about their business as traffic is backing up behind this behemoth.

"Phillip Hampton is my name," declares Phillip with one nervous eye on his passenger and the other on his giant rear view mirror displaying a traffic jam behind them.

"Mine is Abbie, Abbie Hoffman," says the bearded stranger. Realizing the angst the bus is creating with all the honking taxicabs and truck horns, Abbie flips an obscene finger gesture in the general direction of the pile up behind them.

"Screw 'em, let 'em wait. They don't own the road," says Abbie in an attempt to pass along his present attitude toward seeming straight people in a hurry.

Without a doubt, the self-proclaimed hippie moniker of being "The Beautiful People" doesn't always hold true or there is a persistent warped concept of "beautiful." The conventional attitude of hippies is the idea that their own personal civil rights trump common courtesies. They are prepared at a moment's notice to be ready, willing, and able to demonstrate their individual rights. This is more often than not done with the intention of delivering a message; hell bent on making their point regardless of the cost to all others' rights. Emboldened by their own sense of "rightness," many of these new guardians of the American social order will rise up with the certainty of gods to wage war using their personal raging to denounce any opposition.

Holding true to his purpose, Abbie guides this green, Midwestern driver through the labyrinth of this big city maze until they come to rest in an alley behind a six story building. This back street alley is littered with anything that can be disposed of. In this process, discarding cans, bottles, broken furniture, unusable television components, and any part that can wear out on an automobile is the norm. Much of it has been picked through by other residents. This is done in the hopes of finding useful items promising to make their lives more comfortable.

The back entrance to the building serves more uses than merely providing access. Lining the walls of already narrow hallways is an overflow of bicycles, mattresses, and furniture in questionable stages of usefulness, all gradually working their way toward the alley.

One by one, the tired and weary travelers abandon the magic bus. It had held such a strong allure just a few days ago, but poor diet, amphetamines and a lack of sleep has taken its toll. Following their new friend, Abbie, into the building, the pungent aroma of pot hangs in the air along with the head banging beat of acid-rock. The distinct sound of crying children interrupts an otherwise surreal happening. It's apparent the melodic line of free-love has successfully serenaded its way into the lives of these young people. The promise of "free" sex without consequences has proven to be anything but *free.* Subsequently, their crying progeny refuse to resign without a fight. They did not ask to be brought into this world, but now that they're here, they're hell bent on getting attention.

Deidre, in particular, is in need of real rest. She is trying her best to put the unsettling events of a few days ago far behind. Unfortunately, there's a terrible haunting hanging about this incident that's not about to loosen its grasp. For all of her recent inclinations to embrace the burgeoning philosophies of the free sex movement, she still finds herself pulled by a deeper value that leaves her feeling cheap and used. She has never completely abandoned herself to the notion of sleeping around for the mere experience or a seeming thrill. Instead, in her young twenty years, she has tried to use discretion, although not 100% successfully.

For the moment, her ready access to drugs seems adequate to remove her immediate inhibitions, but a deeper seated value of respecting her personhood charges back with sobriety. Ostensibly, each of these indiscretions only returns to plague her conscience. It's as though she finds "sexually freeing herself" merely a liberating idea, but more often it's a reminder of her pious Christian guilt. Adding to this, the fear of going to sleep lest she experience another encounter she can't control makes for a very uncomfortable situation. Now, she finds herself in the midst of this latest happening. It's proving to be physically and mentally exhausting.

Abbie makes his way through this maze of debris with the stealth of a cat. It's as though getting around each obstacle has been rehearsed often enough that it's completed without thought. At last they arrive before an open door on the third floor. His gait does not slacken as he marches through. Waiting on the inside are a half dozen or so people engaged in various activities. Among them is a young man not more than twenty years old and a young woman approximately five years his senior. Simultaneously, they pass a joint while amusing themselves with the antics of a two year old toddler. Another bearded youth is holding his arm while letting out a stream of epithets, cursing everything in sight as he has just banged his elbow. Another is staring off into space, grasping at things only he can see. Another is watching the sun come up despite it being in the afternoon on a cloudy day. He seems to be content with the experience as he recites "WOW!" over and over.

Disregarding the perpetual haze of marijuana smoke, the overwhelming odor permeating the apartment is the unmistakable smell of ammonia. Its origin is quickly tracked to an overflowing cat litter box across the room. The two provocateurs can be seen restfully lounging atop a cupboard satisfied they are safely out of range of these new arrivals. There are no two chairs even similar in design or of the same period anywhere in the room. When more people show up, things get ramped up. To accommodate them, a search is begun throughout the hallways for more castoff furnishings.

It's apparent Abbie is not taken back in the least by the antics of these roommates. Careful not to bring anyone's hallucinations to a bad ending, he begins with as many introductions as can be safely made with those still in various stages of tripping.

The unspoken fascination held by these new Midwest arrivals for these seeming eastern analogues is a welcome source of comfort. As is the custom of this generation, judgment is withheld for each other, reserved only for those in the straight community. The most striking thing that can be said of this whole event is that in spite of all the altered minds that are scattered throughout the building, there is nonetheless a sense of compatibility. It's as though each of these participants dramatizes a desire to be totally self-absorbed within themselves while still desiring to remain in the community of others.

Abbie's hyperactive movements make it clear he has a personal agenda in dealing with issues. He is undoubtedly calculating in his thoughts. They're concise and lack even the remotest hint of compromise. Causes always need dreamers to lead and leaders only need followers who are willing to live vicariously through the dreams of their leader. He possesses the qualities of a natural born organizer whose dreams are so large his adherents only need to grasp on to his coattails to find their nirvana.

In this setting, young men like Abbie consider themselves to be revolutionaries. They have cast aside what they perceive as the failed order of the world's rulers in favor of a new anarchy of disorder which they see as producing a fresh new form of freedom. A live and let live philosophy is threatening every corner of society, from its religious institutions to its economic policies and everything in between.

Dropping out of mainstream America through the use of hallucinogens is the prevailing action taken by these self-described revolutionaries. This phenomenon can only be supported through a burgeoning wealthy middle to upper class, whose children now possess the luxury of an economic system willing to supply food and shelter for their romps.

By the afternoon, a motley crew of bearded, long-haired young men and a few young women with equally bizarre modes of hair and dress styles has made its way to the third floor flat. The music has a nearly primal, animal beat, designed to free the spirit and bring about a sense of belonging. Abbie is noticeably in charge. It's apparent nothing can get started without a half dozen joints being passed around. There should be no doubt in anyone's mind of Abbie's power over this crew of would be revolutionaries.

Abbie is sure he has enough of the attention of this band of willing radicals to lay out his plan. "As things measure up, if we all stand together we can create history. The press is more than willing to hang on our every move. They can't get enough of our capers. Tomorrow we will give them all they desire. The more people we piss off, the more the press eats it up.

"Tomorrow we lay waste to the Mother Goose of Amerika! We are going to attack their golden egg—Wall Street! Capitalism will never die unless we meet it with what it understands best—violence! It's only direct action that will change the captains of capitalism. We want to force them to show us their repressive side, how they deal with people who oppose them, so expect them to start cracking our skulls."

Abbie spends the next hour going over each detail of how they expect to glean every last bit of the press they can squeeze out of this event. To bring as many people as possible out to demonstrate, each person in the room is asked to phone ten people and ask each of them to phone ten people. Every person crammed into the room has pledged their support. They expect to have a thousand freaks in the streets by noon tomorrow.

A follower comes back with, "Right on Abbie."

"Death to the Wall Street pigs," says another.

Small groups break off with nary a scarcity of arm chair demagogues. Any scheme to bring down the establishment can readily find a listening ear as though its originator was a social order genius. There is no denying those involved with Abbie readily accept any notion brought to change the current social structure of America is going to have to be done by force. It's almost as if they have an unconscious hope that if they protest loud enough, their protestations will serve to dislodge them from their own overlapping connections to the social order of their parents.

Deidre, not fully acquainted with the politics of this movement, has made her way along with Shelly back to the bus. They hope this move to be a reprieve from the general hubbub of this ramped up revolutionary activity. Both of these young ladies are trying their best to cast aside what is being described by many in their generation as "repressive baggage." The problem with that thought is we are all the sum of our experiences. These two girls have had a parochial upbringing and the old proverb "as the twig is bent, so grows the tree" holds them both tightly in its grip. There remain many overlapping values that prevent anyone, including these two, from claiming to be a displaced person.

Nonetheless, they have resolved to set aside old thoughts and to play a role in the next day's demonstration as best they can.

CHAPTER 3

Phillip has been totally mesmerized by Abbie. In spite of the hippie movement being described as ageless, Abbie seems to have a few more years on him giving the impression he's been around the block a couple more times. Phillip has always yearned for a more substantial leadership role in this new youth movement, but has lacked the passion and charisma. Abbie's passion is infectious. It has a compelling allure. People are taken in by his seeming aptitude for spewing contempt toward the establishment. When he erupts into a disparaging denunciation of the authorities, he does it with such flair that it has been described as poetic.

Wanting Abbie to become aware of his complete agreement, Phillip feels more and more obsequious in the presence of this popular leader. There is no doubt Abbie is his superior on so many levels. Phillip can only hope he is able to sufficiently disguise his anxiety as he comes into Abbie's presence. He's looking at him with all new eyes. He's no longer merely the helpful stranger who guided them to this back alley rendezvous, but rather a leader of epic proportions.

"Hey man, I want to let you know you can depend on my posse. We'll have your back for sure," says a noticeably pumped up Phillip.

Abbie stops and stares for a moment not sure what this Midwest contingent can bring to the table. "Thanks man. With a little luck, we'll bring these Wall Street pigs to their knees."

Phillip, as well as the rest of the Midwest gang, returns to the bus. Breezy and Zan are stoned past any semblance of coherent conversation heading instead straight for their bunks. In taking his cue from Abbie, Phillip has been instructed to prepare to use their bus as the lead vehicle in tomorrow's advance on Wall Street. Abbie and a contingency of his inner circle are to be guests on board. This is to include another known leader, Jerry Rubin.

Growing up can mean many things, depending on the frame of reference. Jerry Rubin was once heard to say, "Growing up means collecting garbage. Staying young means throwing out as much garbage as you collect." He further believed those growing up before 1950, because of living in a mental world of economic depression, Nazism, Stalin's twisted version of communism, and concentration camps prevented that generation from realizing its dreams. He senses dreaming has returned to his generation and is enhanced through drugs.

Jerry and Abbie are more inclined to describe themselves as the "political" wing of the youth movement. They are more political activists rather than merely concerned with personal liberties. Jerry presents himself as more whimsical in his pranks against the establishment as opposed to Abbie's intense desire to see the whole establishment implode.

They both agree that the romance of the revolution is the main attraction that brings a steady stream of children from the working class into the movement. Once there, the promise to guarantee a steady supply of drugs, sex, and rock and roll will keep them there.

They're both aware not all of their followers share their intensity for political action. Both also agree they need these marginal folks to ramp up their demonstrations. In reality, neither of these new ideologues is much different than the old ideologues, who find that in order to support their personal agendas, they need to employ people who champion the idea of belonging to a cause. The glue that holds them all together is their common desire to protest the values of the establishment. Any rules of order—social, religious or civil—despite their long history of being tweaked, are readily rejected as oppressive and to be cast out with distrust.

Both of these burgeoning zealots, along with other counterculture advocates, have found common ground in a general distrust of money. It's been wisely agreed by all parties involved that this protest against Wall Street will be underlined as a protest against money in favor of the more important ingredient of love.

The day has at last arrived. The different captains of the planned demonstration have reported in. They are assured they will have nearly the thousand they had hoped would join them. It's demonstratively organized where on each block of St. Marks Place they will pick up several hundred young demonstrators instructed to fall in behind the lead bus. Happenings like this take on a life of their own. This one is not to be an exception. Soon everything is underway. There is a holiday giddiness about this undertaking. The bus is resplendent in the mid-morning sunlight with all the psychedelic paint bursting out of its old rusted body.

Phillip is in rare form as he maneuvers the behemoth down Second Avenue. The sight of a thousand tie-dyed, long-haired hippies on foot behind him lends him the exhilaration of a true leader without being one.

Suddenly from this mayhem a spontaneous chorus of voices bursts in unity. They have begun to sing Bob Dylan's song "The Times They Are A-Changin'."

Come mothers and fathers
Throughout the land
And don't criticize
What you can't understand
Your sons and your daughters
Are beyond your command.
Your old road is rapidly agin'
Please get out of the new one if you can't lend a hand,
For the times they are a changin'.

Abbie and Jerry are in the back of the bus carefully going over their script. Phillip feels a bit left out of this inner circle of planners. He secretly wishes he had a more commanding lead in this demonstration. They have delegated a freak named "Sparrow" to guide the bus on the proper route.

He has a distinct New York accent to the degree Phillip has had to ask him to repeat himself several times.

"We gettin' close man. Be ready to paak."

"Be ready to what?" asks Phillip.

"Ta paak! Ta paak!" repeats the noticeably irritated guide.

"Oh, you mean to park."

"Dats what I been tryin' to tell ya, ta paak!"

The trip is only a couple miles and it's been done without incident. The whole affair has caught the police off guard. No permits were asked for, much less issued. In short order, they have arrived at the New York Stock Exchange and are "paaked."

There is no way Phillip is going to miss this event. He instructs Breezy to stay with the bus. Abbie and Jerry have moved to the front of the bus, ready to exit along with a dozen lieutenants. Not to miss this opportunity, Phillip attaches himself to the last man out. Boldly and with purpose, they all enter the building going directly toward the stairs leading to the balcony. They are summarily stopped by an official looking middle-aged man in a dark blue suit, spit-shined Bostonian shoes, and a red tie.

"What can I help you with?" he asks in a somewhat sardonic tone.

"What else man, we're here to see the New York Stock Exchange," says Abbie with the blunt tone of one who does this every day.

"I'm sorry I can't let you see the Stock Exchange," says the man in his most official and authoritative voice.

Feigning shock, Abbie clutches at his chest. "I'm aghast! Why do you say that?"

"Because you're damned hippies and up to no damn good. Now I'm going ask you to leave or I'll have the authorities escort you out of the building."

Still feigning shock, Abbie shouts at the top of his lungs, "We're not hippies, we're Jews and we've come to see the Stock Exchange."

This last verbal exchange has left the official dazed. Realizing the repercussions of alienating Jews at the Exchange, he relents. Word of this confrontation has quickly spread across the floor. All trading has come to a halt as the long-haired troupe makes its way to the balcony edge. All eyes are turned upward. There's an obvious mixture of curiosity and wonderment at the presumed boldness of this motley crew. A few of the younger pages applaud this audacious move while most of the members stand in astonishment. At a signal, everyone on the balcony begins to toss dollar bills in the air, watching them float to the Exchange floor. The first reaction is to begin to pick them up to examine them. Most are one dollar bills, but nonetheless real and are making an impact. Before much more interaction between the floor and the hippies, the police have made their way to the balcony and begin to physically escort the demonstrators out of the building.

Once outside, they begin to party on the steps of the Stock Exchange. They have begun to dance to "Ring Around the Rosie," all the while tossing currency into the wind and taunting the cops and every straight person on the street. Abbie can't resist the opportunity to light his cigarettes with five dollar bills in full view of several short-haired, dark-suited men sporting long ties and carrying briefcases. They appear to be the kind taken aback at the thought, much less the very sight, of someone actually burning money.

Others are taking advantage of the attention they're getting especially from reporters on the scene by burning their draft cards. All this is orchestrated with the firm intention of gaining the attention of the press.

"They eat this shit up. The more outrageous we become, the more we're makin' headlines," Jerry's been heard to say with a knowing smirk.

The police have finally organized themselves and are making their way through the throngs of revelers. Now that the hippies have accomplished what they came to do, and don't have the need for excessive violence, they begin to peacefully make their way back to St. Marks Place. Each is content with what Abbie describes as "makin' a commercial for the revolution."

CHAPTER 4

There is no question that Phillip is captivated with this kind of bold, big city happening. The Michigan style of protesting has been relatively tame compared to the ramped up, brazen, in your face style practiced by Abbie and Jerry. Soon they've all arrived back at Abbie's crash pad reveling in what they all perceive to be a victory of sorts. Abbie and Jerry are beyond giddy over their seeming triumph. An outsider would probably have a different take on what they sensed to be a significant turn of events in this happening, but then in true hippie form fantasies more often become their reality.

"Damn man, did you see the look on that straight dude's face when I lit that cigarette with that five dollar bill?" Not waiting for an answer, he chortles on. "I think he shit his pants right on the spot."

In the background can be heard the distinct words to Bob Dylan's song *"Something is happening but you don't know what it is, do you Mrs. Jones?"* Lyrics like these have become the scriptures for this generation. They revere these artists as one would a religious prophet, as a spokesman from God.

Phillip and his bus load of Michigan hippies are soon anxious to move on to new endeavors. The New York experience has been an invaluable eye opening happening for this wandering band of would be revolutionaries. To imagine there is a single cause bringing all of these young people under one umbrella would be a false premise. Some, like Abbie and Jerry, have found themselves buried deep in the anti-establishment movement as adamant reactionaries. They have separated themselves from the mainstream low intellectuals and placed themselves above as a higher radical intellectual unit.

As much as Phillip finds these New Yorkers intriguing, he and the other Midwestern variety of hippies have found both Jerry and Abbie a bit elitist for their taste. Regarding Phillip and his crew, it's a matter of finding their place in this ever-changing tide of rebellion. One thing is certain, whatever brand of insurrection is chosen, the common bond between all of them is that it will be directed against their parents' brand of government, religion, and morals. To be more succinct, they're against the direction America has historically taken in its overall development.

As in most cases with reactionaries, it becomes much easier to rail against the establishment than to develop a comprehensive replacement. This thought is reflected more often than not in a utopian sentiment that all one needs to do is drop out of society and stay high. At this juncture, this opinion is said to be brought to the forefront by a "feeling brain" rather than a "thinking brain." This judgment is not a new perception. In a previous age Winston Churchill recognized its bearing in his own development as reflected in his statement, "When I was a young man had I not been a liberal, I could have been accused of not having a heart, but now that I'm a mature man had I remained a liberal, I could be regarded as not having a brain."

"All we need is love, love, love" as stated in the Beatles' song. This theme could never be argued against, nor could it ever be argued that the people in hell don't need ice water, but in neither case is one to presume it will happen because it's desired.

This crew has grown beyond merely being an alliance of like minds. They have more or less become a pseudo-family of sorts. In trying to escape the fast paced values their parents are trying to prepare them for, Phillip has assumed a leadership role, to lead these willing followers out of their parents' rat-race. It's not that he has needed to aggressively pursue that part, but rather he has filled a vacuum deliberately left open by the rest.

It's been several days since the Wall Street happening. The party that ensued afterward has pretty much wound down. Abbie has disappeared out of their lives as quickly as he entered. The bus is still parked in the same back alley off St. Marks Place. Now, with the Wall Street happening behind them, it is time for the Michigan people to pull up stakes and move on. Phillip is holding an open forum of sorts. Each of them yearns for another adventure and a growing aversion to the fast paced life of these city dwellers is beginning to creep in on the psyches of these free spirits.

What makes the Midwesterners different from the New York people is they don't have a particular feeling or need to destroy the technological world. After all they have a bus. This alone gives them the freedom to merely drop out—to leave a world they choose not to live in. Traveling becomes the drug of the moment. This means, unlike so many of the city freaks stuck where they are, they can freely move about the country. Many of these city folk have never learned to drive and have no intention of ever owning a car or leaving the city. There is also a strange kind of kinship among these New Yorkers. Even as they rail against each other over life matters, they choose to live and fight on the inside.

Half of the Michigan people that arrived on the bus have chosen to stay. They have blended in quite well with the city happenings and have taken their things and moved on. Of the original dozen that left Michigan a week ago only Phillip, Manny, Breezy and his girlfriend Zan, along with Deidre and Shelly are left.

It's apparent from the satisfied look on Phillip's face, he is ready to move on. Looking about for any opposition, he is only met with looks of approval.

The question remaining in the minds of all is *"where do we go from here?"*

"California!" says Breezy.

"It's settled! We're headin' for Californy," says Phillip with a whoop. The only thing left to do is for him to bring this whole plan to fruition. He contacts his father for money and within an hour Phillip's father has wired $500 in cash. He has given the old man a cock and bull story about the bus breaking down and needing repairs to make it back to Michigan.

"We got the bread," he says with a triumphant boast returning with a fist full of bills. "It's show time kids. Let's fire this beast alive and blow this scene!"

Within twenty minutes they are heading out of New York. Looking out of the bus's curtained windows, the city sights come alive. For this contingency of Midwesterners, every action seems strange and is worthy of their attention. Panhandling appears to be everywhere. Recently it's become more and more difficult to separate the panhandling hippies from the hardcore city panhandlers. Many dress alike, are long-haired and unshaven. Both are beginning to succumb to the same addictions and diseases. Age may be the only distinction separating these two groups as the hippies remain, at least for the time being, a bit younger.

A growing number are a lost generation of high school drop outs who have run away from home. Some are psychotics who have avoided overrun institutions. Nonetheless, many are reasonably mature people who are college drop outs. They were thought to be the next generation of professionals. Others are people who have become disillusioned with the competitive business world. Though many of these have chosen this less productive lifestyle, they originally came from upper middle-class families and will readily take a taxpayer handout. For the most part they are renegades from middle-class America.

Deidre has opened her guitar case for the first time in a week. "I love to sing Joan Baez's folk songs. I feel peace and contentment when I play her melodies," she admits while fondly strumming each chord.

Unaffected by her melodic tunes, Phillip wheels the big psychedelic behemoth through snarls of unfamiliar traffic. He finds himself anxiously leaning ahead nearly touching his nose to the windshield. His body language suggests he is more than just a little uptight. Within the hour the city begins to thin out. As the colorful bus unrolls the highway before them, the asphalt parking lots, concrete buildings and bumper to bumper traffic begin to give way to green lawns and cornfields. As much as Phillip admired Abbie and Jerry, he has to admit to himself that big city life is not for him. Speaking to Manny, who has chosen to take the front seat closest to the bus steps and nearly across from the driver's seat, Phillip tells him, "Roll me a doobie, Dude. I need to chill out."

Manny dutifully reaches under his seat, pulling out a paper plate along with a bag of weed and rolling papers. He can roll a joint tighter than the rest of them under nearly any conditions. In less than a minute, he has the fully packed reefer in his mouth, lit and ready to pass to Phillip. The rest of the bus's coalition, smelling the pungent aroma from the freshly lit marijuana, quickly gathers at the front of the bus as anxious as baby birds awaiting their next feeding.

The bus, not able to reach speeds beyond 50mph, continues its westward trek while gathering a line of angry motorists. Of course none are ticked off enough to risk passing this unwelcome self-appointed traffic controller against the oncoming traffic. Having a heap like this leading the pack is bad enough for these regular folks without the added realization it's full of dirty hippies. Often the middle index finger is thrown in the direction of their slow moving colossus. Those inside gleefully respond by pressing their fingers in a "V" shaped peace sign against the windows returning the token. Far from accepting this gesture as a sign of peace, it's viewed as further proof of this generation's belligerence.

These marijuana fuddled brains take great delight in pissing off all straight people as a way of passing the time. In spite of the bus's seeming ability to raise the ire of hurrying motorists, its occupants consider their lives and their jalopy to be a magnificent dysphemism.

CHAPTER 5

The energetic wave of youthful idealism reflected earlier in the decade by the presidential election of forty-three year old John F. Kennedy, and a growing commitment to such endeavors as the Peace Corp, has all but given way to the much more somber reality of death and war. The shock of President Kennedy's assassination followed by the escalation of the Vietnam conflict has put a different face on "Camelot." As casualties continue to mount in Vietnam which, in spite of the carefully crafted daily updates, seems to have no purpose, the folksiness of Kennedy's successor, Lyndon Johnson, does little to regain the confidence of the young people. After all, they have the most to lose—their lives.

With no end in sight, disillusionment soon sweeps across the entire country. America is experiencing an uneasy cohesion. Political parties, which in the past overlapped, are now more divided. Everyone's life seems to be threatened either by change or, as in the case of the young, the threat of changes not coming fast enough. The fine promises of the Great Society are crumbling in the face of angry Negroes demanding an equal portion of the American dream. The press is having a field day fueling the fires of "Black Power" slogans with the burning of Watts, Los

Angeles, Cleveland, and Chicago. To add even more to the already growing mistrust of the Johnson administration, he appears on national TV and assures the nation all is well. The enchantment of an earlier Camelot is disintegrating into deep disenchantment. The mood of many across the nation is definitely bitter and angry.

This little family of freaks, for better or for worse, is gaily beginning the trek to California. Their hope is that each will continue to free themselves from any latent hang-ups created by the nation's history and in the process discover their personal nirvana.

Deidre is in a weird mindset. For much of her life she has remained somewhat indifferent, learning to survive in her own ways. But for the moment there are many things going on that are creating hang-ups for Deidre. She has recurring paranoid brain flashes of her grandmother being hurt by her waning regard for her Lutheran legacy and disregarding their proud German heritage. After all, it was her grandmother who comforted her when she felt lost as a child. Not that her parents had shut their eyes to her needs, but they weren't as cognizant to her distresses as her grandmother. "Oma" was always able to share her simple faith with Deidre in such a way that it never came across as judgmental or preachy. In the simplicity of a grandmother with less than an eighth grade education, she would explain to Deidre's young spirit that there are two angels in everyone, a good angel and a bad angel. In the closet of her own mind, she can't help but ponder which of these spirits is gaining now. What would this now departed saint of a woman say about her seeming dilemma? Would she think I have gone mad? It's as though she's begging her soul to stop torturing her.

So far Deidre been able to avoid sex with Phillip. He has had his eye on her since the first time he met her. She has never shown any interest in him despite his persistent attention toward her. There's something about him that inwardly chafes her. She is unable to place her finger on exactly what it is, but she nonetheless finds it awkwardly unattractive. He is well-built though a little on the thin side, with fine features now covered by a thin dark beard. It's been said the eyes are the window to the soul. His eyes are dark and empty, not possessing a happy spark. She perceives some weakness in his character. *"Maybe I just don't trust him,"* she muses to herself, *"he's a little too self-absorbed for me."* Phillip senses this haunting distance between them. He's used to manipulating his family to get what he wants, this quiet rejection makes him want to try all the harder. Despite his efforts to close the gap, Deidre remains cold. When his awkward attempts fail, it only makes him want to get drunk, or stoned. For Deidre, it simply makes his lurking advances more uncomfortable.

Deidre and Shelly have shared the ups and downs of each other's lives for most of their existence. What holds them together is sketchy. Of the two, Shelly had a much more wounded upbringing. When her father chose to desert the family in favor of a much younger woman, Shelly was already nine years old. Her mother never forgave him, resulting in a bitter and angry life. Shelly's defense against both her obviously dysfunctional parents has been to create her own brand of dysfunction. In part, it has resulted in indifference toward any kind of future. She lives only for the moment.

Shelly and Deidre find themselves sharing a bunk near the back of the bus with no one else nearby for a change. With the aid of a noisy exhaust system, it provides them with enough privacy to air a few grievances.

Deidre is the first to share her anxiety. "I know I chose to come on this trip but I'm getting more and more uncomfortable."

Shelly is all ears tilting her head, accompanied by a little frown. "What's goin' on kid?" she questions. She has noticed a shroud of bleakness surrounding her friend.

"I know Phillip would like to get somthin' goin' between us. I can feel him gettin' bugged about me continuing to blow him off," says a much more agitated Deidre.

"I know you're really ragged by him. He doesn't know I'm watchin' him, but I catch him starin' at you while you're sleepin'," says Shelly.

"Well that creeps me out! Now I probably won't get any sleep."

They both sit quietly for a moment. A shirtless Jimmy Hendricks pumping out a tune stares down on both of them from a poster on the ceiling. Next to him, Frank Zappa is also vying for their attention.

Deidre says, "I hope I can keep my head together long enough to get to California."

With a true look of concern for her friend, Shelly assures her, "Don't worry about it, Deidre. We'll make it like we always do—together."

The weather is turning hot. The road is shimmering ahead like a basin of hot tar. The worst thing that can happen happens—BANG! A front tire blows out. The bus begins to careen back and forth across the road. Phillip is losing his battle to keep the behemoth out of the ditches running along either side of the highway. In seconds they find themselves being propelled backwards through a strip of barbed wire fence on the opposite side of the road. The bus has twisted completely around presenting its rear end to 150 feet of barbed wire and accompanying fence posts spearing their way through the broken back windows.

It happens way too fast for anyone's mind to discern the sequence of events. They're all struck like a deer in the headlights with no choice but to see the escapade to its conclusion. To this crew, what spanned thirty seconds may as well have been thirty minutes. It couldn't come to an end soon enough. Once stopped, everything is quiet with the exception of a half dozen red winged blackbirds scolding and dive bombing the unwelcome bus invading their territory.

Phillip's hands are fastened to the wheel as though to let go will cause the bus to go out of control once again. He hold his frozen posture, waiting for his struggling mind to convince his body he can at last loosen his grip.

The twisting of the bus has left its cargo strewn from one end to another. There is loose stuff covering nearly every inch of floor surface. The people are jammed under bunks, and on top of one another. Some are trying to stand. Breezy is near panic as he examines Zan's bleeding forehead. She is alarmed after discovering it's her own blood staining her hands. Even in all the confusion, Manny has managed to regain his composure enough to come to the aid of these fallen companions. He quickly recalls his Boy Scout training and attempts to cleanse Zan's wound. The only immediately available materials are a canteen of water and his own headband. With the deft hands of a trained Boy Scout, he wipes the water soaked bandanna across the wound only to bring about a howl of pain from Zan. He soon discovers there is a shard of broken glass embedded in the cut. With the compassion of a Civil War surgeon, Manny insists it has to come out immediately. Without waiting for confirmation, he opens the blade of his pocket knife. Glancing around for seemingly something in particular, he grabs a half full bottle of wine. In the time it takes to blink, he has the bottle uncorked dumping its contents across the blade. The next flash is the steel tip flicking a scarlet red quarter inch piece of bloodied glass free of the wound.

This commotion has caught the attention of everyone on the bus. When it's clear there are no more injuries, the attention quickly turns to the fate of the ditched coach. Phillip is clearly shaken to his very core. The last time he had crashed a vehicle was back in high school. Then he could depend on his father to keep him out of trouble. At this point, he's on his own. Looking around and away from the crash scene all he sees is a hay field. He's in a bit of a muddlement. They have enough LSD, pot and hashish to send them all to the pokey.

"Before the pigs get here, we have to get all our dope stashed somewhere!" pronounces Phillip.

All hands are scampering to gather as much contraband as they can quickly sort out. Placing it all into a canvas backpack, Phillip spots a cement culvert at the end of the ditch. "Perfect," he muses quietly under his breath. Snatching the bag over his shoulder, he makes a beeline for the twelve inch orifice. Slapping the pack with both hands, he attempts to shape the bag into a plug that will fit the hole and forces it into the opening. It can't come soon enough. By the time he arrives back at the tilted bus, a farmer driving a John Deere tractor is making his way toward this stranded assemblage of tattered ruffians. Arriving, he has the troubled look all older adults possess when encountering these bands of hippie marauders. He's a man in his fifties wearing a pair of bib overalls and a cap that also says "John Deere."

"What in tarnation you folks do ta yer bus?" he wisecracks.

They are all standing around without a clue how to rectify their situation, completely out of their element. Long before the group does, he comes to the realization of just how big a predicament this group has gotten themselves into. The blown tire is torn completely off its rim leaving nothing but a strip of mangled rubber with no purpose.

"Sposin' you folks gonna need a lotta help getting outta here an back on the road?" He says this with the full understanding of how damn helpless this crew of "dope smokin', commies" can be.

As usual Phillip is the first to step forward. "Yes, sir. Any help you can give us will be deeply appreciated."

"Oh I spose I can help ya alright, but it ain't gonna come cheap," says the farmer.

Now looking a bit grimmer, Phillip pauses for a moment before finally forming the words, "What do you figure it's gonna cost, sir?"

The farmer strokes his beard for a moment as though he's pondering the question at a deeper level. "I'm figurin' a couple days labor in this here hay field otta cover it."

The closest Phillip has ever been to a hay field was once when he had been drinking with a friend, they stopped to pee in one.

"What exactly is it you want me to do, sir?" he dares ask.

"It ain't particuary sompum I want just *you* ta do. I want the whole damn bunch of you out in that field tomorra mornin' at dawn. By the way, my name ain't sir, it's Joe Smith. You can call me Joe." He says this with a sly little grin—the kind of grin that overtakes farmers when they know they got city slickers by the short hairs.

They all stand looking at each other for a moment trying to digest what price this agrarian has just charged them to get them out of their mess.

Again Phillip takes the lead. "Bright and early, sir—I mean Joe. Just come by and we'll be ready."

With the negotiations done and over with, Phillip turns around to face his crew. They all stand quietly dumbfounded staring directly at him.

"What?" he says, staring back. It's the only word he can come up with. He's well aware without asking, that his crew has never even peed in a hay field much less worked in one. Their only response is to shake their heads in disbelief at this seemingly ridiculous contract and walk away.

By morning the conscripted crew is up and waiting as agreed. There hasn't been a lot said among them as no one really knows what to say.

Suddenly a strange noise breaks the silence. Producing this cacophonous resonance is a lumbering machine making its way down the road. They all stare at this oncoming apparatus pulling a barge behind it as if it were some kind of an alien craft. It's nothing more than a tractor pulling a wagon. But for these city dwellers it may as well have been from some planet beyond the sun.

"Get yer lazy asses on this wagon, we got work ta do!" says Joe with the same impatient imperative as yesterday.

There is something of the unknown in his command. Something strangely intimidating, suggesting they don't ask too many questions. Without a word, they all pile onto the wagon with feet dangling over its edge and gripping anything that promises they won't be thrown off its back. For better or for worse, they will spend the next ten hours learning the finer points of baling hay. At noon, they get a brief reprieve when a gong sounds. On a farm this can only mean one thing—it's dinner time. Joe Smith calls a welcomed time out while leading the near exhausted troop to a well shaded grove of hardwoods. It's mowed and laid out with picnic tables.

Pointing to a lady clad in a simple flowered house dress with an apron flapping in the breeze, Joe introduces her. "This here is Ella Mae, she's my wife and today she's your chef."

With no more introduction than that, she smiles modestly and points them to a picnic lunch laid out on an adjoining table. None of them need a second invitation. Within fifteen minutes they have collectively devoured enough food to be well on their way to earning the by-name "Thrashers."

With dinner over, they are given a short respite. Joe, on the other hand, doesn't seem to need more rest. He's having no problem finding things that need to be fussed with on his tractor. Soon they're all back in the field throwing bales of hay on the wagon. Joe is beginning to like this crew. After being told what their next task is, and because of their lack of farm experience, they are hardly in a position to have short cuts.

Each of these new born agrarians finds themselves taking the measure of this strange bucolic lifestyle. They are carefully weighing the pluses and minuses of this nearly Gothic way of life. Not seeing the complexities that accompany the farm world, they are creating an iconic picture of a simple way of life that promises the nirvana they all long for.

Back at the bus after a long, hard day, they take the opportunity to discuss their new experiences. They have retrieved their pot stash and are all kicking back with their thoughts on this side trip.

Manny is the first to open the conversation. "Hey man, I'm really diggin' this farm trip. This is somethin' I can see myself getting' into."

In response to Manny, everyone is taking their individual experience and theorizing it into their own journey.

"We could get some land and sell vegetables," says Breezy with a big, pot-smoking grin.

"Yeah man and some chickens. We could sell eggs, too!" adds Shelly.

Zan and Breezy are the only ones with any previous farm experience. She sits quietly listening as one after another shares exemplary descriptions of what they believe farm life to be. Finally she speaks up.

"You guys must be nuts. I couldn't wait to get away from all those shit kickers and now you wanna take me back."

"It don't have to be like that, Zan. We can make it different. We're a new generation. We know what's happenin'. It don't have to be like it was when you grew up," assures Breezy.

Soon the pot has its way and they all begin to drop off for a much needed night's sleep.

The sound of birds serves as an alarm clock the next morning. A small clutch of young blue jays is filling the air with their protestations over a hawk perched in a nearby tree.

The crew scrambles around, somewhat disagreeable over the lack of food. None of them ever eat before noon, but the calories burned the day before are screaming to be replaced. It's not long before the now familiar sound of a tractor makes its way down the road. Within a few minutes, and with very few unknowns, the crew begins what they had so well-rehearsed in the fields the day before all over again.

As sure as the sun is ready to set, the work day finally comes to an end. Joe has kept his word. He has arrived with a new tire, a jack, and a tractor large enough to pull them out of the ditch.

"Oh, and before I forget, Ella Mae sent this here with me. She seems to think you all look underfed." His next gesture is to produce a box full of groceries with bread and lunch meats. Thanking Joe for his help, the rag tag crew couldn't be happier. Having scored food and a new tire, they're soon on the road again.

CHAPTER 6

The success of the Protestant Reformation during the 16th century came about in a large part because of the Gutenberg Press. That newfangled contraption made written opinions available to thousands of people within a very short time. The success of the whole hippie movement came about in a similar way through the underground newspapers making their way into even the smallest of towns. They kept all readers aware of upcoming festivals, love-ins, demonstrations, or just cool things in general. The traditional mainstream press had no interest and usually reported on counterculture events only if they turned violent.

Unrest seems to be popping up in every facet of American life (i.e. civil rights, unjust war, inequality among the rich and the poor). Many of these underground opinions remained mostly unchallenged by a mainstream press unprepared to do battle with this unseen, unknown enemy lurking in what by all accounts are uncharted waters. Much of the immediate pressure the young are feeling centers around being forced to fight a war they disagree with. This alone is enough to lead the charge to drop out and into something perceived to be a kinder way of life. They're in agreement to begin to put their ideas together to build a commune around something meaningful. If nothing else, they are ready to drop off the path they perceive their parents have selected in favor of the nirvana they are convinced can be theirs. It almost seems to center around rewinding themselves back to a simpler frontier life with the certainty they will get it right this time.

Breezy continues his rave about getting some land. It's interesting to watch Zan sticking her finger in her throat in a gagging gesture over his seeming naiveté toward farming.

"Breezy, I love you, but your head ain't right. You don't know shit about what you think is goin' ta be a great life. It's either too much rain or too little, too late. It's either too damn hot or too damn cold. If you got some crazy idea you're gonna drag me back into some kind of shit-kickin' life, you can forget it!" says a more than disgruntled girlfriend.

"Babe, you're just pissed at your parents for making you milk cows, but I promise—no cows," continues Breezy hoping for a coalescence. Zan's response is a look of utter abhorrence.

Looking around at the rest of the pack, Breezy hopes they are more in tune with him than with Zan. After all this farming thing is so great a concept he can't get it off his mind, much less imagine the others not sharing the same exuberance.

"Hey man, I'm just sayin' we really need to check this whole thing out," continues a more than insistent Breezy

Manny likes the idea of starting their own commune, but as usual, he hesitates until he sees if Phillip gets down with the whole thing.

Phillip is beginning to realize this whole "hippie thing" is more of an individual exploration of mind and soul rather than a group quest. He finds his head lingering around their New York experience. He's discovering the people he is particularly drawn to are political activists and not so much the drop out crowd, but at this point, he is willing to go along with the pack.

"I think what we need to do is to crash in on one of these communes and see what they're about, spend a few days psychin' 'em out," says Phillip with an air of caution. "No sense in committing to somthin' that don't fit who we are."

Within a few seconds Breezy has rifled through his duffel bag producing a handful of underground newspapers.

"Here's a whole stack we can look through," he says. The excitement of this new adventure is evident by the response from eager hands sorting through this pile of psychedelic news rags from all over the country.

After a bunch of "way out" comments about nearly each of the commune descriptions, they are in a quandary considering where to go first. By this time a few days have passed and the bus is making its way across northern Indiana. Wanting to more or less table the whole "commune" idea for a while and hoping it will go away, Phillip recalls a summer vacation spot in a northern Lake Michigan coastal town. It's a place where he spent time as a youngster along with his family. The name of the village is Elberta. It's a small village of around 750 people of mostly Norwegian or Swedish lineage and left mostly undisturbed by the modern ways of the downstate metro areas.

"Before we do anything we wish we hadn't, we need a vacation to get our heads on straight. I know the grooviest place in the whole universe to crash 'til we can get it together," he says. "It's hotter than the hubs of Billie blue hell travelin' in this bus and we gotta have a break."

With a quick accounting of funds and a full vote of "hell yes," they turn the big psychedelic behemoth to the north. With every wheel turn the fast paced expressway traffic vanishes along with the Gary, Indiana smokestacks and everything they stand for. All left behind.

Making their way up the eastern coast line of Lake Michigan they find themselves under its spell. Each feels a dream which could be built on. They begin to sense how Columbus must have felt finding the new world. Michigan's glacier carved beauty nearly cries aloud that this is the garden to build a world around.

These are the types of experiences screaming to each as to why they can't go home again. St. Joseph, Benton Harbor, South Haven, Holland, Grand Haven, Whitehall, Montague, Ludington, Manistee, Arcadia and finally their long awaited destination, the tiny village of Elberta. The gentle southwesterly breeze whispers there's magic in the air.

The streets in this tiny village seem to be painted in their own sunlight. Who knows what they'll find? These kinds of romantic moments seldom happen. They feel like explorers coming upon something so simple it is awestriking. As in most cases, the hope is that perceptions will meet reality. Nonetheless, it's easy to give one's heart to the natural beauty of this part of God's country.

Without question, the sight of a psychedelic painted bus lumbering its way through the main street has caught the attention of everyone who sees it. Being somewhat of a closed community, this sight certainly provokes a strong reaction of suspicion.

Burl (his last name is never used and seems to be lost), the village marshal, makes special note of this ponderous phenomenon. Burl takes his responsibilities as the town's chief law-enforcement officer very seriously. His uniform consists of a typical policeman's hat with a huge badge gracing the center that says "Marshal," a navy blue coverall of the type that could also be worn by a garage mechanic with the moniker "Burl" stitched across the right breast. On his hip, he carries a holstered 45 Colt draped down his thigh and tied off to his leg with an abandoned shoe string.

"What the hell!" are the only words he can come up with reacting to this ostentatious conveyance transporting an even stranger delegation of long-haired shirtless males and T-shirted, braless females.

Phillip is also analyzing the reception they're getting. He remembers Burl from his earlier days as the kind of law-enforcement officer that could always be found at the Mayfair Tavern holding court for any community problems that needed attention.

As they pass through town, Phillip quickly takes stock of Burl's early 60s Nash Rambler with the red light attached to the top. It's sitting in its usual parking space alongside the Mayfair. Its owner is standing, hat in hand, scratching the side of his head in wonderment at this intrusion. Out of deference, Phillip gives a "V" shaped peace sign to this obviously bewildered peace officer creating yet more suspicion.

The village is not on the way to any other place, so it has always remained somewhat isolated. Most of the villagers are related in various ways through marriages or as cousins so many times removed no one remembers quite how. Either way, they are all curiously suspicious of these strange looking interlopers.

Coming into the area of the Betsie Bay, Deidre closes her eyes, romancing the moment. It's like magic to behold the huge car ferries in the harbor all preparing to make another trip across the huge inland sea. Clicking and clanging sounds emanate from a diesel-driven yard engine pushing waiting boxcars into the ship's belly. There is also a distant whishing sound of a steam-operated dredging barge working in the harbor. It's the kind of community where time, in many ways, has stood still.

Recalling an area behind the large dune that protects the town from the ravages of Lake Michigan, Phillip continues his quest. He has in mind a rather secluded area down the beach. It's in a region that can only be reached by traveling a rough eroded sandy two rut track that weaves three quarters of a mile down the shoreline. As precarious as this questionable route proves to be, he manages to reach an outcropping of scotch pines that are stubbornly clinging to life in spite of the lifeless soil in which they find themselves.

"Here we are boys and girls, our new home!" announces Phillip.

There is a sense of anticipation as one by one, they exit their herculean carrier. The breeze off the lake is cool and refreshing. Despite the open windows, it's a welcome change after being confined for several hundred miles in the blistering hot tin jitney. It takes a minute for each of them to work the kinks out enough to begin the hundred foot trek to the beckoning shore. The synchronous gentle sound of small waves lapping at the sandy beach is drawing them into its gentility. With hardly a second thought they all plunge headlong—clothes and all—into its alluring spissitude. The shock of the near glacial waters has them scrambling for shore in seconds. That's all but Breezy, he's determined to savor every second of its coolness he can bear.

Their next step is to prepare a makeshift camp. It's something each of them have had experience with at some point in the past. Within a few hours they have hammocks strung in every tree that will support one, a latrine dug, and a campfire cooking the last of some slumgullion someone has thrown together. All in all, life on the beach is proving to be wonderful.

That's in stark contrast to what is brewing back at the Mayfair Tavern. The psychedelic bus is all the buzz.

"I couldn't believe my eyes. I thought I was lookin' at a pack of bearded ladies with all that long hair," declares a man wearing a flat top haircut.

"I heard these here hippie types take some kinda drugs that make 'em wanna stare at the sun 'til their eyeballs burn out," declares another.

"The truth is they ain't nothin' but a bunch a draft dodgin' commie pinkos and that ain't no shit," says yet another man slamming his beer glass to the bar. His bulging paunch won't permit his T-shirt to meet his belt buckle exposing a six inch stretch of red pimpled belly fat.

The discussion picks up as more and more begin to congregate. The bar maid is a middle-aged women hoping her pulled back hair and gaudy red lipstick will keep the "middle-aged" thing at bay. She's chompin' at the bit to get her two cents in.

"Well believe you me, if one ah my kids showed up lookin' like any ah them, they'd be lookin' for another home. You can take that to the bank!"

"Ain't none of 'em got ah job that's for damn sure. When I was their age I was pickin' cherries out ta Smeltzer's orchards. These ain't nothin' but a bunch ah rich kids livin' off their ole man," says yet another.

"One thing's for damn sure, they ain't none of 'em belong in this town!" says a grizzled man with a missing row of upper dentures.

So far Burl is sitting quietly, puffing on a cigarette and sipping a warm beer. He's being attentive to the conversation without entering into it. It's his way of monitoring a situation as to whether it dies of starvation or is fed enough to begin to take a life of its own. It seems everyone but Burl has spoken his or her piece. Now the natural way things proceed in Elberta is at some point everyone turns their attention to Burl. He's still puffing on a non-filtered Lucky Strike and finishing up the last swallow of beer. It seems like the time to get him involved.

A man by the name of Gilroy is the first to turn directly to Burl with a challenging look. "What say you, Burl? You gonna let this kind walk around like they own the place? Or you gonna do somethin' about 'em?"

Burl purposefully takes his time with a last drag from his Lucky Strike, then simultaneously blows the smoke out his nostrils while butting it.

"Ain't no law I know of they broke yet." He says in his most official tone.

After a pause to let this statement settle in for a moment, he adds, "But if any ah you gentlemen wanna do some surveillance and report back to me—have at it. Just make damn sure none ah you get the idea ta take things inta yer own hands."

Looking at each of them about the room, while lighting another Lucky, he adds, "You do understand that. Right?"

Their silence is all the affirmation he needs as he orders another beer. They know that he knows that they know not to do anything extralegal on their own. What emboldens them is the fact that a few years earlier Burl had deputized them along with a group he has come to refer to as his posse. They were to be rallied in the case of village emergencies. So far there has been only one time they needed to be employed. Four year old Richie Stratten went missing. A posse alert was sent out. They combed the hills and swamp to no avail. He later awoke from his nap and crawled out of the dog house.

A man named Fred is quite perturbed at the whole situation. He lives directly over the dune where all these persona non grata have squatted. He has singled out another young guy named Buck along with his brother Bogie (who gained the name for no other reason than having a funny lisp similar to Humphrey Bogart). The three of them consider themselves dedicated to the past time of drinking anything that contains alcohol. Certainly this raises them several notches above those pot heads down on the beach. What can be said in defense of these local yokels is they do hold merchant marine jobs on the car ferries. They generally work twenty days on and have eight days off. This event happens to coincide with their off time.

"What say we get us a case ah beer and *surveillance* 'em as Burl said?" suggests Fred, and then adds, "I know just the spot up on the bluff."

He's gained the attention of the other two, especially when an important job such as this can be done with the assistance of a case of beer. It doesn't take long before this coalition in all seriousness approaches Burl with their plan to surveillance these guys from the top of the bluff some three hundred feet above their camp.

"Since me and the boys are doin' village work, Burl, what say you put this here case ah beer on the village tab?" asks Fred in his most serious tone.

Burl doesn't say a word. He doesn't have to. Fred already knows what Burl's reaction will be before he even asks. Knowing full well he had pushed the envelope to the limit, Fred quickly takes out his own billfold depositing the $4.89 for the beer on the bar.

The trio heads back to Fred's trailer at the bottom of the dune on the village side. Even before they open the door, three bottles from the case of Old Milwaukee are already in the hands of the three surveillance volunteers.

"We got us ah lot of plannin' ta do ta make this come out the way we want it to," says Fred while slapping his two compatriots on the back.

The evening wears on. The planning never really gets started before it's pitch black and the case of beer is nearly gone.

"No damn sense in tryin' ta get anything done ta night. We may as well finish this beer off and get started on it tomorrow," says Buck.

He finds he's already talking only to himself since Bogie and Fred are already passed out. This is far from the first time this trio has found themselves in a similar situation.

CHAPTER 7

On the other side of the dune, Phillip and his band of confederates are oblivious to the stir they have created in the village. The next afternoon, they are busy doing the things hippies do when they feel they are outside the focal point of the law—taking drugs and going naked. The southwest wind provides a steady breeze across the water creating the perfect wave conditions for body surfing or mindlessly bobbing in the currents. It is beyond this crew to imagine that they can merely enjoy the natural conditions without the enhancement effects of LSD. They are all in various stages of undress and drug influence.

On top of the bluff taking in all the aspects of this debauchery is the hungover, but recovering surveillance team. They have equipped themselves with binoculars and enough beer to assure they will overcome any chance of a drought.

"Looket 'em sons-a-bitches. They all runnin' around neked. They must be drugged out they minds," says Fred not stopping to put his binoculars down since they've arrived.

"I can't say for sure what kind of drugs they're on but them three chicks sure as hell got some nice knockers!" says Bogie.

Not able to pull themselves away from their voyeurism, they spend the rest of the day drinking warm beer, peering through their binoculars, and commenting on every aspect of Shelly's, Deidre's, and Zan's anatomy. As it goes with voyeurs, they feel safe under a blanket of concealment. As the day wears on, they become empowered by the control they have over their unsuspecting prey. With the setting sun and the promise of impending darkness on the trail, they are forced to make the decision—as painful as it is—to pack up their surveillance equipment, amounting to no more than a few unopened beers, and make their way back down the razor-back ridge leading to Fred's trailer.

They begin discussing what their surveillancin' has brought to light. After an afternoon of warm beer, Buck takes a long pull on a freshly opened cold one. He's the first to put into words the conclusion they have all come to. "How in the hell can fine looking chicks like these get tangled up with the likes of those assholes they're hangin' out with?"

"It's the way it always goes—good lookin' chicks end up goin' for the dumb asses," further laments Fred.

The decision is soon made to get with Burl some time the next day. Meantime, as is usual with this trio, they pass out rather than fall asleep. Mornings are not good for some in this village, and especially not for those who flirted the night before with John Barley Corn. That includes more than a few. Nonetheless, much of the work that gets done in this community is done by folks who are either tired or don't feel good.

"Sometimes I think my body is trapped by an idiot's brain," laments Buck as he attempts to fill a glass with water. His hand is shaking so badly, he spills more than he gets over his lips. Regardless of how they feel, they have an obligation to meet with Burl at 10:00am at the Mayfair. Burl's Nash Rambler is sitting in his habitual parking spot. He's already seated at his regular table having what he routinely refers to as breakfast. It consists of two raw eggs and a dash of Tabasco sauce, all deposited into a glass of beer.

"Bout time you boys showed up," says Burl with a wry grin, nursing his breakfast.

Fred's the first to speak. "Well, you can bet your sweet ass, we been busy. Them hippies ain't nothin' but a bunch ah psychos all drugged up prancin' around buck ass neked, starin' at the sun."

Burl gives Fred a wary glance. "How'd you figure they was on drugs?" he asks.

"Well, hell man, anybody dance around naked for hours all by his self gotta be on somthin'," returns Fred with an authoritative voice.

"What else you see 'em doin'?" inquires Burl. He's noticeably more interested.

"They was runnin' around neked out in the lake!" says Fred with even a stronger voice.

"You boys willin' to swear to what you're sayin' if I go get a warrant?" asks Burl with a very official air.

"Hell yeah man. We seen it all through binoculars from the top of the bluff up above Fred's place," says Bogie pleased he's able to report such vital information to Burl.

"I guess you boys done your homework. All I have ta do now is convince the prosecutor over in the courthouse we got us a menace on our hands."

The trio gives each other knowing glances of having moved up a few notches in importance around town.

By late afternoon, Burl has made the twelve mile round trip to Beulah, the county seat, and back to the Mayfair Tavern with the proper papers in hand. The trio of surveillancers has utilized their time spreading the alarm concerning the pack of dirty hippies practicing who-knows-what, maybe witchcraft, down on the beach. Word travels at lightning speed in Elberta when they perceive a threat to the town's values—real or imagined. The tavern is filling with tobacco smoking men eager to hear what may be going down with these here "hippie types."

"We gotta get these vermin outta town. God only knows who's gonna follow 'em if we don't do somethin' now," says a portly man named Ed, smoking a cigar. He says this with a set jaw that indicates he's been through this kind of situation in the past.

Burl is confident his deputized posse can respond to this menace. "Okay boys, I want you all at the bottom of Anderson Hill in an hour. We're gonna go over and take a look at what we're dealin' with."

Within the hour, the appointed meeting place is packed with trucks and cars. Men emerge with pistols strapped to their sides. The look in their eyes says there will be no retreat in this emergency situation. For them it's a one way street—get the job done. Burl is at the forefront of this cavalcade of mostly ordinary overweight, middle-aged men preparing to defend their town against this uninvited bunch of city dwellers.

"I don't want any of you men actin' like a bunch ah lawless cowboys.

That's why you're all gonna wait for orders from me." Burl says this with a firmness that can't be misunderstood.

With that said, Burl takes his place at the lead as the twenty or so minions fall in place behind him. The trek up the hill is exhausting for young men in good physical condition much less for this constabulary of beer drinking, tobacco smoking, and overweight workforce. They haven't quite reached the halfway point before most of them need a break to catch their breath. Coughing is heard everywhere as this troupe, still determined to finish, is left exhausted. The group begins to thin out with Burl and the trio of Fred, Bogie, and Buck well ahead.

"Maybe it's time to say good-by to these guys for a while. If we wait on them we'll never get this job done," says Burl placing one foot in front of the other as he plods up the giant dune.

Finally reaching the top, Fred takes the lead. From here on there are many trails cut into the thick forested dune by a team of loggers back in the early 1900s. It's easy to pick the wrong trail if one isn't familiar with them. Fred and his two compatriots know these hills like the backs of their hands. After all, this was their playground growing up. Fred points to a sandy trail leading into a thick, dense forested area. This is a much easier trek and they begin to put even more distance between themselves and the rest of the still struggling posse.

It's only a quarter mile to the bluff overlooking their quarry. There's not a sign of anyone other than the tracks and empty beer cans left by the previous day's surveillance crew.

"You boys make this mess up here?" asks Burl kicking a discarded beer can across the sandy surface.

Noticeably embarrassed, the guilty trio glances at one another searching for an alibi.

Buck takes the lead. "These were already here when we got here. We figured those hippie pigs left 'em up here while scroungin' for fire wood."

Burl moves to the edge of the bluff, overlooking the still stationary psychedelic painted bus. Placing his binoculars to his eyes, he begins his own surveillance. What he sees pretty much substantiates what he has already imagined.

Using a phrase he has heard hippies use, he mumbles something. "Looks like they're all feeling groovy alright."

Unbeknownst to Phillip and his band of free spirits, their every move is being watched. They have spent the last few days tripping unmolested on LSD and some mushrooms they acquired in New York. They have no reason to believe this is going to be anything but another wonderful day with the same security. They are all in some altered state of being. Each is absorbed into themselves, alone with their individual highs.

Suddenly from out of nowhere, they find themselves accosted by a group of screaming men with nightsticks ordering them to the ground. Burl watches from the bluff with horror as this group of men begins to club these docile, compliant, maverick, drugged, nonconformists. He quickly realizes these men are part of his out of shape posse. They obviously took a different trail, leading them directly to the beach. He begins shouting for them to desist, but since he is 300 feet above the fracas he cannot be heard over the sound of the breaking waves.

"Come on boys we have ta get down there before somebody gets hurt," says Burl, already making his way down the steep embankment.

By the time they reach the bottom, the mob has taken on a life of its own. With the full intent of getting this mayhem under control, Burl seizes the raised nightstick from the hand of one Louie Webber. Louie's a thick-necked lout who would beat his grandmother if a crowd led the way. He's truly enjoying the havoc. The mob is dragging the girls by the hair to what they intend to be a corral for the whole lot of them. The young men aren't faring as well. They're being kicked, cursed and beaten before being driven to the same locale.

In the time it takes Burl to grab, shout and push his pack of so called deputies into some semblance of order, Phillip and the other five are in various stages of consciousness—partly from the drugs and partly from the thrashing they've just received. For Burl, this is exactly the scene he was trying to avoid. To even pretend this group of hippies deserved this kind of treatment at the hands of this legally deputized mob would never sit well with the judge. Nonetheless, Burl attempts to play out the hand he's been dealt. Facing this gypsy-like group of free spirits, he waves in his hand a writ from the court. "This here is an order for the likes of all you to appear before the judge on charges yet to be determined."

Burl pauses for a moment to let this declaration settle into their still somewhat befuddled minds. The disturbed looks on each of their faces indicates he is making the desired impact. As soon as he's satisfied he has their attention, he continues, "Or if you pack up and hit the road this all goes away."

The bewildered look on the faces of Phillip's crew is a strong indication they are all still reeling from the ambush they've just suffered.

Phillip takes his ad hoc position as spokesman. "We'll be out of here within the hour, sir. You can count on it."

Deidre is sitting wide-eyed, staring straight ahead. Her immense blue eyes and beautiful blonde hair are a stark contrast to the fear reflected in her tanned face. She has not been feeling well the past couple mornings. This fiasco is hardly setting well with the nausea she has been experiencing. It's been intensifying since they arrived on the beach days before. Now to have some beer-soaked goon drag her across the sand by her hair is a hassle she can easily do without. As the cretin loosens his grasp, she turns her eyes up and spits at him. He in turn raises his hand to pummel her yet one more time, but catches Burl's mean eyes giving him the hard stare that he knows is a strong suggestion he better think twice.

Having said everything that needs to be said, Burl and his posse along with their overdeveloped sense of justice begin their trudge back toward the bluff they had fifteen minutes ago bolted down like kamikaze. On the other hand, Phillip and his merry band are struggling with putting everything that has taken place in that same fifteen minute period into some kind of perspective. The struggle is to make a decision that puts them all on the same page. A mixture of adrenalin and a throttling has its own way of bringing to light a new attitude toward survival. In this case it's become apparent that all agree "getting the hell out of here" is their chief priority. With very little having to be said among them, they begin their exodus campaign.

Within the hour they are making their way back down the same two rut track that only days before had been so beguiling. As their bus lumbers back through town, they are suddenly met by a cavalcade of pickup trucks and automobiles falling in front and behind them serving as an escort to the village limits. As is common among such village predators, they smell blood in the water. Cat calls and a few eggs, as well as the middle finger are thrown indiscriminately toward the escaping bus.

Having been insulated on their college campus for the past few years with like-minded people is hardly the kind of experience that's needed to face conservative middle America. Phillip is at the helm with his hands gripping the wheel in nearly a death grip. Sweat runs down his scrawny neck as he frantically grinds through the gears wondering how he's going to get this assault behind them. Finally they reach the village border and the cavalcade breaks away. The results look much like when the worker bees are expelling a giant queen as this multi-colored giant breaks free and travels down the road uncontested.

No one breaks the silence as each of the participants reflects on their individual trauma. A certain part of each of their lives came to a halt on that beach. It's as though there has been a strange kind of termination to an innocence they had been taking for granted—believing what they held would never end. Their next step remains unclear.

They head south. Phillip finally pulls the bus to a stop near a wooded area along the highway. Breaking the silence, he asks, "Anyone gotta pee?"

This is a welcomed break. From their reaction, it quickly becomes obvious everyone is ready. Nonetheless each of them exits the bus with a wary eye on the road behind them. There's a lingering fear of a real possibility of an unforeseen adversary lurking about. What comes to the forefront is how much they are going to need one another as a community. Rather than entering the woods singularly as they have in the past, they now find themselves going in groups as an unspoken precaution. None of them can remember a time they felt this vulnerable on the Michigan State campus or even in New York. This is the first time any of them has felt this alone. There is definitely a looming horizon of change slamming its way in their direction.

CHAPTER 8

The temperatures have been hovering in the 90s across the Midwest. Driving this bus at 50 mph with all the windows wide open is doing nothing more than creating a blast furnace of hot air. Shelly is flapping her braless T-shirt allowing a cascade of air to flow across her overheated breasts. Deidre's sickness concerns everyone because of her recurring nausea. She'll seem fine and then suddenly be sick again. Phillip has accommodated her more than once by stopping alongside the road to let her settle her stomach.

Shelly ponders what in the world could be wrong with her friend.

"If we could cool off, I know damn well we'd all feel better," she says still flapping her baggy top forcing the hot air across her sweating chest.

The patron saint of the young regardless of era continues to be Methuselah. The fountain of youth however is proving to have its limitations. Up until now there have been very simple challenges to a youthful self-delusion of Shangri-la outside the establishment of their parents. But with Deidre's undiagnosed malady, something has to give. Try as they might, none can come up with a solution. The situation has trumped their limited expertise. As long as she remains in her bunk, to some extent, she remains out of sight, out of mind and the perception is she's getting along okay. It seems by afternoon Deidre rebounds only to relapse with the same old symptoms the next day.

While Deidre is forced to stay in her bunk, the rest of the group has recovered from their Elberta fiasco enough to begin a new plan. Breezy is happy as can be that his whole idea of starting a commune is back in the realm of consideration. "I have to say the New York happening was a great eye-opener," continues Breezy in his quest for verification of the great contrast between the strung out urban hippies and street people in the city with the counterculture envisioned by this bus load of Middle America hippies. "We can start our own thing. We can get away from the madness and get back to the earth, man."

Frequently seen reading B.F. Skinner's book, *Walden Two*, Breezy has quietly become an advocate of many of its tenets. This is far from Breezy's first encounter with what is being more and more portrayed as a counterculture movement among the country's youth. Bitten with the freedom bug after reading about a group of German youth from the late 19th century called the *Wandervogl,* he quit school after eighth grade at the age of fourteen, as all Amish children do. Always restless, he next said goodbye to his parents and left home to travel around the country, hitching rides and hopping freights. The world began to open in a new and different way.

"I experienced its underbelly." He will quickly share this tale with anyone who cares to listen. "I was at the mercy of every predator on the road. All they did was drive around all day lookin' for somebody ta queer. I had ta jump, run or fight at some point practically every day.

"You don't how many times I asked myself, 'what the hell am I doin' out here?' I knew the sun had to be shinin' somewhere. That's when I hitched a ride with a couple of beatniks in an old beat up pickup outside San Francisco. It was late in the afternoon and I had no place ta go. They started tellin' me about this place they were stayin'. They called it a commune. I had no clue what a commune was, but I figured there's nothin' ta loose by goin with them and findin' out.

"An hour later we drove into a compound of military tents, old buses, and shipping containers. The men and women were mainly writers, poets, artists and out of work actors. I was only sixteen and they seemed like they were all real smart. I asked one what they were doing there. She said they were 'distilling out the exploitation of the proletariat.' Anyway, I hung out there for a few days. It was the coolest place I've ever been."

The rest of his compatriots always find themselves fascinated when Breezy unwraps his earlier exploits.

"Why'd ya leave these people Breezy?" asks Zan, still suspicious of this whole farm thing Breezy thinks they all need to do.

"I don't know, maybe cause I never felt smart enough ta stick around people like that," says Breezy, with a simple transparency he seems to naturally possess. "Besides, there were way too many queers hangin' around to suit me."

Manny is a bit more pragmatic than most. He always listens with little to say, but when he does, it's worth hearing. "Where in the hell do you think we can get the money to do all this?" Whether he likes it or not, these are the very words his father spoke about nearly everything that came his way.

Regardless of how much anti-capitalist rhetoric they spout, it always came down to how they were going to get the money to live the capitalistic-free lifestyle they have chosen.

Breezy is once again falling back on his Amish roots. "We don't need ta buy it. We can start out by rentin'. I know old run down farms in Indiana we can get in to cheap. They got old beat up houses they'd be happier than hell to be getting somethin' for 'em."

Phillip is listening with a careful ear. This agrarian life is not something that immediately appeals to him, but he can see where he could begin to build a political base for his own ambitions.

"You know Breezy, you may be on to something. You lead the way and we'll follow," adds Phillip with a noticeable degree of affirmation.

With a few hundred dollars left between all of them, they decide in a matter of minutes to begin the trek to southern Indiana. With a little luck and a bus that stays together, they can be in the area tomorrow.

Meanwhile they are not above shoplifting for food. The process is to stop at a grocery store along the way to ask directions. While the clerk is distracted trying to help, the rest load up with whatever can be hoarded into bags or pockets. But to remove suspicion, they always buy a can of something.

****

It's 1967 and Bob Dylan is the big rage across the country. Dylan is definitely doing what churches have hoped they could accomplish but failed to do—he's uniting a whole generation of youth under the one umbrella of music. The result is every kid with a guitar is another Dylan wannabe. There may be some ethnic differences between households or even within households. There seem to be grandparents in many American families that speak English with varying European accents. Nonetheless, the great phenomena remains that the offspring of these immigrants have more in common with their peers as Americans than with the ethnic heritage of their parents. The connections are generally a shared interest in music and the ties made between each other in public schools.

With a new quest and a few "forbidden fruits" from the Harris country grocery store, they are on their way to "The Promised Land" in an Amish section of Indiana. Deidre is feeling much better and is willing to pass off her illness as a summer virus. She is becoming more excited about the prospect of getting their own commune. The miles roll by. The Michigan dunes soon give way to the smokestacks of Gary, Indiana followed by the farm belt in the central part of the state.

Breezy wants to reach Martin County around the Loogootee area. He was raised there before abandoning his Amish roots. Within the Amish tradition once a baptized person turns their back on their religion, the church will shun that person until they repent and return to the church. Not being baptized yet, Breezy is referred to as sowing his oats or "Rumspringa." He left before he was old enough to officially join the church so he cannot be shunned, but he's definitely considered suspect. He will be even more of an oddity now that he's returning with a bunch of

"English" as the non-Amish are called. Nevertheless, he has maintained contact with some of the other unbaptized young men.

One of these is a cousin, a young Amish man named Albert Stahl. Both his parents died leaving him a 280-acre farm. Albert has been struggling to work the farm and pay his taxes. Were he both baptized and married the whole community would be more than ready to lend a hand. Being neither, he is not given the same consideration by his Amish neighbors. Before he left to live among the English, Breezy lived with Albert for a brief time helping him with chores. Now Albert's left alone except for an occasional burst of compunction on the part of his single friends to give him a hand.

Seeing this psychedelic bus loaded with English hippies stopping in his yard is enough to give him pause. Giving way to his Pennsylvania Dutch German dialect, he bursts out, *"Mein Got im Himmel, was ist das?"* (My God in heaven, what is that?) Before he can form a second thought, he catches a glimpse of a familiar form coming across the lawn. He immediately recognizes this long-haired, bearded reprobate as his long lost cousin. They break into a spirited exchange speaking in their familiar Pennsylvania Dutch.

Since this whole affair is on Breezy's turf, he's eager to take charge. Soon introductions are made to bring everyone into a first name basis. Breezy then begins to query Albert about any available vacant farms. Albert is deep in thought as Breezy explains why he's asking.

"Well, I want to tell you, cousin, if I don't get some help around here, I'll be joinin' ya!" laments Albert nervously running his hands through his hair.

"Wadda ya tellin' me, Albert? You losin' the farm?" asks Breezy.

"I'm gonna, if I don't get that hay in. I got the tax people standin' in line ta get their hands on this farm. They know it's worth a lot more than the taxes owed on it," says Albert with more than enough concern in his voice to reveal that his situation is dire.

Breezy is more than attentive. Changing to German, he informs his cousin he may be able to help him. Turning next to his gang, Breezy makes an appeal.

"You guys heard what he said, and all you bein' experts at hayin' are you gonna let him swing in the wind or we gonna help him out?"

Phillip, recognizing an opportunity to get himself back in the game, is the first to speak up. "Hell yes we're gonna help!"

Within a matter of seconds, Albert's worries have been reduced to something manageable as the rest of the crew follows his lead and jumps on board.

Albert's home is typical of the Amish in this part of the country. Its original builders were early settlers from the late 1800s. They cleared the land, built a home and barns that were purchased by Albert's father and mother long before he was born. The old coal and wood burning furnace has never been replaced. Power is from batteries and gas rather than a public power source. There has been no need for updating anything as it fit the chosen lifestyle of this Old Order Amish family. After inviting them into his sparsely decorated home to a lunch of home canned beef and potatoes, they begin to plot their course of action.

Phillip quickly analyzes the situation. He has become accustomed to his leadership role and is angling for ways to keep it in spite of being a complete foreigner to this whole agrarian scene. To add to his confusion, Albert has no modern farm machinery. At least when they were on the Smith farm, they had modern tractors. On the Stahl farm, they're introduced to what the Amish refer to as an Amish tractor. It consists of a flatbed farm wagon carrying a diesel engine attached to a sickle blade all being pulled by two giant draft horses. It's the Amish farmer's way of keeping intense labor to a minimum while adhering to the bishop's ban on pneumatic tractor tires.

When Albert's parents died within a year of each other, his two older sisters had already married and moved with their husbands to an Amish settlement near the small village of Ovid in central Michigan. This left Albert with the responsibility to maintain the farm by himself. This gang of hippies showing up is an answer to his prayer in a form he had never imagined. He couldn't be happier with the division of labor. He's in charge of Barny and Moe, the huge plow horses. Breezy runs the sickle connected to the flatbed. Manny rides and positions the huge rake dragged behind the wagon pulling the hay into windrows. Phillip, Zan, Deidre, and Shelly are all on the ground with pitch forks. They are left to clean up any loose hay left behind. The only commonalities with the Smith farm are the heat, the sweat, and the sweet smell of fresh cut hay. It's a balmy day and they are all amazed how much work they've accomplished by the end of it.

Phillip has used much of his time while in the field analyzing the farm's topography. He's noticed it has a natural bowl shape on one end. It would be a perfect place to handle a good-sized crowd sitting above the bowl peering down at some event below. *"This whole damn set up is full of promise,"* he muses to himself.

After a full day in the fields, they're all ready for a meal and a good night's sleep. There is no running water, so an improvised bath house in one of the outbuildings is the best that can be done. It's amazing what can be accomplished with one pail of cold water since each person is responsible for pumping their own bath water.

They've built a campfire more for comfort than warmth, besides it keeps the mosquitoes away. All have gone to bed except Phillip, Manny, and Breezy. Phillip has been waiting for a time like this all day to pull these two compatriots aside to run a thought by them. He sits there poking a stick at the glowing embers. They have known him long enough to know he's got something on his mind.

Manny breaks the ice. "So what's up, Phillip? You've been quiet all evening," he says looking him straight on for his answer.

Phillip is excited at the prospect of getting this idea into words. "You know ever since we pulled in here, I've felt some really good vibes about this place."

He's definitely gotten their attention as his face begins to break into a very familiar facial expression that he only has when he's about to explode with some new idea. It's a mixture of a sordid grin and an intellectual smugness.

"I think we all have," agrees Breezy. "Helping Albert is a righteous cause."

Manny's not so ready to let Phillip's statement pass as some form of altruism on Phillip's part. He rightly suspects there is more below the surface of his words. "Wadda ya got in mind, Phillip?" he asks.

"Have any of you noticed the hill in that field we were working in and how it forms into a bowl at the bottom?" asks Phillip. There is a distinct tension to his voice.

Both Manny and Breezy are attentive but noticeably puzzled as to what their friend may be getting at.

"So?" says Manny still waiting for clarification.

"I'm thinkin' rock concert!!" Grinning from ear to ear, Phillip gets these words out as if they were on a rubber band pulled tight way back inside his brain that suddenly lets loose.

Manny looks at Breezy, who is looking back at him. Soon all three begin to look at each other with a very knowing look that says Phillip is definitely on to something. They spend the next three hours going over various aspects of such a plan. It's near midnight before they finally turn in.

The next morning brings with it the question of how to present such a project to Albert. Breezy knows better than the rest what trouble this could cause Albert if the bishop catches wind of such a worldly design. On the other hand the Amish have always been quite inventive when it comes to circumventing the bishops. The three of them have decided to keep quiet about their proposal until they can have a meeting with the girls as well as Albert.

The day wears on with nothing more problematic than a few expected minor muscle aches. Albert is particularly jubilant at the prospect of getting all the hay cut, baled and in the barn. The seller's market is strong enough to assure him he can get out from under the tax lien that's been placed on the farm in short order.

This evening around the campfire the three of them decide to announce their idea to the girls. Like all ideas when first presented, there is usually a lag between hearing what has been said and the brain processing what has just been heard.

"Are you guys sure you can handle a project that big?" asks Zan. She is usually the most pragmatic when the boys come up with what she oftentimes labels as "hair-brained schemes."

"Not without your support. It is going to take all of us working hard to pull this off. But the payoff can be great and allow us to get the land we need to begin our dream of a commune." With a few more questions and a few more tentative answers the decision is made to present their plan to Albert.

The last thing Albert knows much about is a rock concert. The closest he has ever gotten to anything even remotely resembling such an event is the young people's hymn sing on Sunday evenings. The fact this is his only frame of reference and in deference to Breezy for saving his farm, he agrees to let them do whatever needs to be done to bring this escapade to life. Breezy is more sensitive to what may have to be done to ward off the wrath of the bishop.

"The first thing we have to do is have some paper agreement that Albert is renting the farm to a group of English. This should satisfy the church there is no Amish involvement in this caper."

At this juncture Phillip jumps in. "The next step is to make sure your diesel engine can run a generator large enough to put out the kind of amps required to run everything."

To suggest Albert is dumbfounded at all this rigmarole would certainly be an understatement. However, he's noticeably excited about what these English may be concocting.

CHAPTER 9

Everyone begins to express an opinion on how they believe such an event should proceed. Excitement is in the air. It's a brand new adventure. Phillip quickly realizes he's going to have to get control of these doings early on or risk chaos. He is well aware, probably more so than the others, things are changing fast. The wild and crazy things that are coming at them are permanent experiences changing each of their lives in inexpressible ways. Seldom do anyone of them think of their home or loved ones. The adventure has become everything.

The excitement is catching up with Albert. He's been more of a quiet observer than a participant. The Amish life is a full life in the sense that it gives meaningful values in an otherwise corrupt world. They have used the Bible to proffer answers to all their life problems. Watching this crew of English buzz around holds a curious fascination for Albert. Being separated from the world as the young Amish are doesn't mean they are any less fascinated with the sinful world. Within their communities the seven deadly sins do exist, just as in the rest of creation. The difference is the Amish have limited the number of circumstances in which to practice.

Albert has managed to have a phone installed in a small phone booth outside his barn. It doesn't raise the ire of the church so long as it's used for farm business. Non-business calls are considered frivolous and worldly, therefore sinful. Also because he has not been baptized, much of his behavior remains outside the scope of the bishops. This has also enabled him to have a car which he keeps hidden in an old buggy shed out of sight behind the barn. It's a 1952 four door Ford sedan. The thing runs as good now as it did the day it came out of the showroom. For having a supposedly limited contact with modern machinery, the Amish have proven themselves to be able mechanics.

Having this phone has enhanced Phillip's ability (with the aid of an illegal blue box and a black box that emulates the signaling thus allowing free long distance) to contact every underground newspaper in every state across the country. Literary rags with names such as *Ramparts*, *Fifth Estate*, *Distant Drummer*, *East Village*, *Helix Seattle*, *Kaleidoscope*, and *The Last Times* to name just a few. He has each paper advertising a *Love In* with music by bands such as The Who enabling like-minded people to come and be part of a Fall Happening. Phillip does not have The Who booked but is hopeful when they see the interest generated by the event they will want to be part of it. He has spent long hours ensuring they will have plenty of acid, weed, mushrooms and of course a medical tent manned by like-minded med students who share in the free lifestyle of hippiedom.

He finds himself continually tracing his finger over and over across his lip as he tries to keep up with the details of this escapade. He can't help but think of how he is emulating his father as he recalls his father's demeanor while buried deep in some corporate challenge. The words he remembers his father muttering are the same words he finds himself muttering, *"Plan the work and work the plan."* This is much more pragmatic than he is willing to own—much less admit to in the presence of any hippie. What he's discovering is with the hard effort he and all his compatriots are putting into this project, he is becoming more jacked by seeing it to its end. Like many men of vision that have preceded him, he is finding the journey exhilarating.

"I love this stuff," he tells Manny.

Manny is truly Phillip's right hand in this whole enterprise. His own exuberance is fed as he is stimulated by Phillip's trust and dependence on him. Until the next few weeks conclude, they will not know whether the plan is successful. But for now, the two of them are content to act in concert as Phillip serves the part of an executive and Manny is in the role of managing all the actors.

This means Manny is making sure that much of the physical labor is in Breezy's hands and is getting finished. Breezy in turn has attempted to stay under the radar of the church. He has exploited the labor of a few of his young cousins without informing them exactly what they are doing. Phillip is trying to keep what is going to be happening here quiet. It's growing so fast and so haphazardly he's hoping it will be over and done before the Amish bishops or the Martin County councilmen can put together a comprehensive bunch of guidelines. In a closed community such as this, that is a challenge. Compound this with a suspicious Loogootee citizenry and it becomes apparent that more and more eyes are turning toward the activities of this group of freaky-looking intruders.

"What's this I hear 'bout them hippie guys plannin' some kind of orgy out there at yer place?" asks a townsman while pumping gas into Albert's car. Breezy is riding along with Albert to pick up a few more supplies. Hearing this question from someone not in any way connected to any part of the project prompts him to step in.

"Nah! You know how wild somma' them Rumspringa boys can get this time of year. I wouldn't put anything past 'em," answers Breezy hoping to dispel any rumors.

Meantime Phillip is in his glory. Instead of tiring under the strain of all this organizing, it's fed his exuberance. It is as though his soul has found its expression in haggling with bands over how much he's willing to pay them or what food vendors will pay for a spot or how many port-a-johns they'll need for the five thousand people he's expecting.

With only days to go before Martin County will undergo the invasion of an army of dirty, sweating hippies, Phillip has called a meeting of all his crew to update where they all stand.

"If we plan to stay ahead of any rumors that may be getting legs, we have to keep the momentum moving," says Phillip. "With a little luck, we can have this happening well on its way before the bishops and the county officials know what hit them."

The tension is mounting and everyone is sharing Phillip's hyperactive mode. Breezy and Zan have for the most part abandoned the bus. They have found a private spot in Albert's haymow. The hay is inviting to this would be runaway farm girl.

"I can't help it, I still love the smell of new cut hay," she admits as she digs her buttocks in a bit deeper. "I find it therapeutic."

Even though Breezy is no stranger to the farm life he abandoned at an early age, he is much more interested in Zan's wiggling buttocks than he is in any conversation concerning hay smells. Snuggling in a bit closer, Breezy realizes this is not her sexy snuggle. Zan is making it clear to Breezy she is much more interested in having a conversation than she is in having a roll in the hay. If he wants any chance for a future roll in the hay, he had better get into a conversational mode pronto. Like all males, he finds it physically and mentally confusing at first, but soon is calmed down enough to go through this perplexing form of foreplay.

"Breezy, do you think you will ever return to being Amish?" she asks.

This question catches him completely off guard. It's not as if he hasn't mulled the thought around privately, but to have it come from outside puts it in a whole different perspective.

"In all seriousness, I don't think I could. It's not that I don't believe they have some legitimate fears concerning the outside world, it's that I see as many flaws among the Amish that are equally damaging."

Zan indicates her acceptance of Breezy's response by snuggling a bit closer with yet another question. "Did you have an Amish girlfriend?"

Breezy's first thought is to dismiss the question as foolish, which always gets him in trouble. He can sense immediately she is a bit more than merely curious. A second thought strongly suggests he give this question a serious answer.

"You have to remember, I was only sixteen and yes, I did have a girlfriend I had known my entire life."

Breezy can tell, that in spite of Zan's seemingly relaxed tone, her body language is telling a different story. Her snuggle has relaxed enough to be more of an indicator of her attitude toward this new revelation.

Her next question is even more pointed. "Do you think of her now that you're here?"

Breezy knows from past experience there is not going to be a satisfactory conclusion to this questioning. Whatever romantic designs he imagined could develop out of this liaison are quickly evaporating.

"She married my cousin, Aaron, and has two kids," he says, hoping this will be enough to put the proper distance between himself and this old paramour. He can feel her snuggling with a bit more intention, making him believe he may be adequately out of the woods on this one.

She pauses for a second, satisfied there is not a contender for Breezy's affections. She then poses another question. "Do you still think the commune idea is a good one?"

Pondering for a moment, he says, "I think it will give us a lot more freedom to live a lifestyle without the hassles."

"I sure hope you're right. My parents aren't going to believe I'm heading back in that direction again, after the big pile of grief I gave them about getting off the farm," reflects Zan with a tinge of guilt in her voice.

Breezy is quiet for a moment preparing himself for more discussion. Instead he feels Zan's snuggle changing from her chat snuggle to her sexy snuggle. *"Well worth the wait,"* he thinks to himself as things take their course.

CHAPTER 10

The morning of truth arrives, bringing with it a nice cool breeze. It's one of those rare weather patterns making its way down from the Great Lakes. It has all the hallmarks of a great weekend. Phillip has been up since the crack of dawn. There are already a dozen vehicles parked on the road with sleeping hippies sprawled in every direction occupying every square inch of empty space. Within the hour there are several hundred vehicles beginning to file through the gate into the parking lot. Several buses arrive carrying bands with such names as The Kinks, The Monkees, The Association, Paul Revere and the Raiders, and The Who. Soon the headliner, The Morgue, with an entourage of hearses arrives. By afternoon there is hardly a spot in the parking area that is not occupied by a tent, van, bus or human body.

The pungent aroma of marijuana flows through the air with every breath. The whole event takes on a very festive mood as hippies from various parts of the country engage with one another.

"Where ya from, man?"

"Owosso, Dude. Where you from?"

It's apparent every corner of the country is represented. They quickly discovering how much they all have in common, especially in attitudes toward the Vietnam War and the whole corrupt Washington, DC power structure.

By mid-afternoon the bands begin to play. The Amish boys are manning the huge diesel generators with a skill equal to any accomplished sound engineer.

Phillip shows up all over the place. He's chauffeured in an Amish buggy by a young lad named Chester. Chester couldn't be prouder than he is today to be a part of this English event. Picking up on the English phrases, he is unrestrained in using expressions like "Out of sight, man!" or "This is groovy!" These are hardly phrases that he will be using with his Amish family, but for the present, like young people everywhere, he is basking in the excitement of being a small part of this happening.

The food vendors have all prepared themselves to add LSD laced Kool-Aid to their menu. The attendees are also unrestrained in the variety of colorful costumes they have opted to wear. There is every color in the rainbow of tie-dyed apparel including combinations of colors never before seen. Beads, flowers, and feathers are all interwoven into each hippie's outfit in such a way they hope will set them apart as unusual, however they have become uniform in the non-conformity.

Bursts of whooping applause accompany each band as it makes its way to the platform. Drug addled hippies are dancing everywhere—some with clothing and many without. The pond at the back corner of the farm is full of naked bodies. Each moment is lived as though there will not be another. Songs applauding a drop out world turning on to drugs is the mind set of these young adventurers.

Phillip is working his way through the various vendors collecting owed rent. Other than a few drug overdoses, everything appears to be coming off on schedule. A group described as the Amish Insurance Providers are affording security for what is proving to be a peaceful event. This organization is mainly made up of unbaptized young Amish tough guys with an emphasis on enforcing the Amish traditions among their community and also providing protection and care from catastrophic calamities affecting their people. They are somewhat out from under the bishop's watchful eye because of their unbaptized status and are also known to hire themselves to outsiders to manage security during English events.

A light flashes as The Morgue, a band from a small Michigan town named Owosso, makes its way to the stage. A howl from the crowd exceeding five thousand greets them. They respond by nearly bouncing to the platform. In seconds they begin blasting out their signature anthem *"Goin' to the Barber Shop."* The woofers in all six amplifiers are reaching their blow out capacity. Nonetheless, the group answers the demand from the roaring crowd to maintain this gratifying decibel level.

The energy is flowing in harmony from performers to audience, from audience to performers. For these young people, the performers are god like and their voice is in the enlightenment of their music. The pounding rhythm of the electric guitars along with the beat of the drums and the nearly trance like strobe lights flashing across the sweating bodies of drug soaked brains are all intended to create an Arcadian ambiance not to be rivaled anywhere in the universe.

The grand finale is a psychedelic light show. Continuing to answer the demands of this insatiable crowd, the band continues to play long after their set is completed. After a half dozen curtain calls finally both performers and audience are exhausted. The performers take quick advantage of this seeming end point and make a bee-line for their vehicles leaving their road crew to finish the task of packing up. Such is the life of rock stars.

CHAPTER 11

By the next morning the grounds give the appearance of a tangled mass of human Zombies all twisted in with those attempting to make their exit. It's obvious the mood is much more subdued than the night before.

Phillip's mind has not stopped churning. The impression Jerry Rubin and Abbie Hoffman had on him in New York is firmly imprinted on his mind. But now he's carving out his own agenda. It prompts him to work the crowd like a vote hungry politician. Soon he spots a young man with a prosthetic foot. Not wanting to be crass and yet driven by his curiosity, he engages the fellow in a conversation.

"How'd we do man? Did ya enjoy the show?"

The young man's smile broadens. "Outta sight, man. This is the grooviest happening I've had since leaving Philadelphia," confesses the young man.

Seeing he has penetrated a barrier with their common enjoyment of a rock concert, he delves further into the young man's opinion on the war. "Looks like ya been ta Nam, man. Wadda ya think of it?"

The young man's demeanor suddenly takes a more depressing expression as his gala spirit is quickly replaced with a distinctly defensive attitude. "If ya like getting yer ass blown up, it's a great place. But if ya ain't inta that kind of crap, it's a shit-hole!!"

"That how ya lost a foot?" Phillip inquires further.

"A big 10-4 on that one," says the young man lifting his footless leg as though to examine it yet one more time. "They warned us about land mines but failed to tell us where in the hell they put 'em!"

This interaction has caught the attention of several more sunburned, bedraggled, blurry-eyed concert goers. The tone has definitely changed from the lightheartedness of the past twenty-four hours to an angry defiance. Another young man gracing his head with a red bandanna formed into a headband speaks up. “We need more love not war, man!”

“Right on, man!” comes from another voice.

“Hell man, I burned my draft card back in ’65!” answers yet another protesting voice.

Phillip is getting the type of feedback he has been hoping for. Manny is listening and watching intently, waiting to see where Phillip is going with this. Soon Phillip shows his hand.

“You all sound like good people. We’re planning on starting a commune and are looking for the kind of visionary people that are interested in sharing that experience.”

Phillip has now caught the attention of several more flower people.

“Wow man, that really sounds groovy. Where we gotta sign up?” says a dude wearing a broad-brimmed Amish hat he had traded earlier for a beaded necklace.

There are also several young, hippie peace women with eclectic costumes varying from resembling pictures of Pocahontas to looking like southern Spain’s Andalusian Gypsies. Some have long braided hair and brightly colored jewelry, but none with make-up or shaved legs. Many have an earthy quality about them and could be described simply as “earth women.”

Many of these youth yearn for a simpler life than the highly competitive lifestyle their parents were hell bent to pass on to them. There is a mysterious longing for a slower life than that of the previous generation who when they were the same age were adamant to build the greatest and wealthiest economy the world has ever seen and proudly accomplished it. A number of the younger generation see the obsession to get ahead as insane and have become adamant about stopping the world of commercialism—and if they can't do that, they'll at least get off the course by dropping out.

The few people Phillip was engaged with minutes before has now swelled to more than twenty. More are lingering around the edges struggling to catch a hint as to what can be so enthusiastically holding the attention of so many of their compatriots. Soon word has spread around for those interested and who want to take a shot at this opportunity to hang around and help clean up.

The exodus of the five thousand takes the better part of the day. It's been a bittersweet experience for the local merchants. None of them have ever experienced the onslaught of so many raggedy people. It seems they all needed everything from food and gas to auto parts for the many beat up motorized vehicles of every year and make trying to get another mile down the road.

"Never in my life have I ever smelt so many stinky kids all at one time as I have this weekend," says Millie Turnwald, the owner of Millie's Diner in Loogootee. All the same, she is happy to have gotten the unexpected bump in business. She isn't the only one to have experienced a windfall in profit.

William "Billy" Barnes' garage sold out of anything that even resembled an auto part.

"Them kids was keepin' us operators overtime sendin' home for money ta get 'em ta hell outta here," chuckles "Toadie" Bila a matronly women working part time at the local Western Union office.

The Martin County supervisors have finally figured out what has just happened. They've called a special emergency meeting. It's being given the same priority as if it were a nuclear attack. "Them little weaselin' sons-a-bitches got no damn business comin' down here without permits to pull off a stunt like they done," says Arlie Hampton a lifelong resident of Martin County and a county supervisor.

"They all need ta be prosecuted and sent out on a chain gang for a year," says Normal Kiergaard, the head supervisor.

"Ya start talkin' like that Normal, we jus end up havin' 'em hangin' around. Then we gotta feed 'em. Jus let 'em get the hell outta here like they doin'," says Earl Snowdon, the Martin County Sheriff. He's a big burly, cigar-smoking man with a flattop haircut. He retired as a sergeant with twenty years in the military police and is in his second elected term serving the people of Martin County.

"What happens iffin they don't all leave? Wadda we gonna do then?" adds Arlie carrying a definite note of concern in his voice.

"Don't worry yerself about it Arlie. We got our ways a handlin' them kind of stragglers," restates Sheriff Snowdon with a firm bit of irony in his tone. He's instructed his deputies to do all they can to move this horde out of their county.

"What happens to any of them once they cross the Martin County border is no concern of ours," he says taking a long slow reassuring pull on his cigar. With the smoke swirling around his head, he adds, "Jus like this here smoke tryin' ta disappear, these here critters gonna be doin' the same. By this time next week they gonna prove ta be only a temporary headache." With a big grin he slaps Arlie a reassuring smack across the back.

CHAPTER 12

Phillip could not be happier. After all expenses are paid, they end up with $10,000 profit. Albert is also very grateful all this hubbub on his farm is winding down. The Amish have their own internal ways of handling dissidents. It usually begins with gossip. If that doesn't bring about the desired results, a committee of several church neighbors calls on the person warning them of the consequences of their behavior. Since Albert is yet unbaptized, their influence on him is limited. Knowing he's pushed the envelope beyond a safe turning point, he doesn't feel the need to kiss the devil good morning unnecessarily. However, after conferring with his inner circle, Phillip has one more offer to make Albert. Taking Breezy and Manny along with him, they get Albert aside and begin to feel him out a little as far as what he expects out of his farm.

"Wadda ya think about us helpin' ya get that hay off yer fields?"

"Boy you don't know how relieved I am to have that done and get those tax people off my back."

Stepping in a bit closer, Phillip rests a hand on Albert's shoulder, "How'd you like ta have some permanent help around here, say like year round?" asks Phillip, with a much more patronizing tone.

Not quite sure how to answer Phillip's question, Albert takes a tentative moment to process what Phillip may be asking. "I'm not sure how that's gonna happen. But yeah, the more help I can get around here the better."

Sensing a lack of hostility, Phillip zeros in on laying out his plan. "How'd you like to lease a hundred of your least productive acres to us in exchange for all the help you need with taxes and labor to keep this place goin'?"

It's obvious Albert has been blind-sided. He stands unblinking for a moment. He has grown accustomed to fretting about the farm and now to have an offer that will remove that anguish is like removing a foe he's having a love affair with.

Finally Albert's mind and mouth agree long enough to begin to form some words. "What in hell you wanna do all that for?"

Phillip's face breaks into a broad grin. He senses things may be going in his direction. "We want to start a commune where we can live off the land. You know, like grow some vegetables, maybe have some pigs, er...cows and chickens and stuff like that." Phillip senses he has quickly left his area of expertise and nervously looks to Breezy to pull him out of the situation.

Breezy catches on to Phillip's self-conscious uneasiness and takes over speaking with Albert in their common German dialect. "We took in enough on the concert to keep us going through the winter months and get started with a garden and a few head of livestock in the spring. There'll be about twenty of us. I'm pretty sure things'll work out okay."

Albert in turn responds in German leaving Phillip wondering where all this may be going. "I'm fine with this, but I wonder what the church will do when they find out."

"I doubt they will have much to say as long as you're merely renting your ground and not involved with the English lifestyle," assures Breezy. All this German talk is leaving Phillip uneasily on the sidelines. Still not sure where this conversation is going, he can't help but exhibit his anxiety. But as all things end, so does his wait.

Albert is the first to drop the German. "Okay Phillip ya got a deal as long as the bishop don't give me grief."

Phillip's demeanor quickly changes from anxious to relieved. Manny has a penchant for legal jargon and soon begins to draw up an agreement on a piece of paper. By afternoon everyone is of the same mind. They all sign and Phillip, Manny, and Breezy return to the assembly of the new co-op with the good news.

"We got us a commune boys and girls." Phillip announces as one would winning a lottery.

By late afternoon, the original crew of six is joined by fourteen others deciding they'd like to stay on and help bring a commune to life. The first few days are lived as politely as possible with each person going the extra mile to assure harmony. But as all things go among God's creatures differences begin to appear. It's a simple fix in the beginning. Those who are of one mind stay together, those of an opposing mind also band together. This is all in the hopes of still maintaining a core attitude.

This problem brings Phillip to a point where he feels the commune needs a mission statement. It begins one evening around the common campfire when Phillip instructs Manny to have each person write out a summary of what they hope the commune will become. Over the next few days the group works on this thought. By the end of the week, they have hammered out enough consensus to put together their common mission statement. It's based somewhat on B.F. Skinner's *Walden Two*, but most are unaware of this. (Breezy's really the only one who's studied Skinner.) They all sign, but as is true with humans, one young man couldn't agree and decided to leave.

The area they have chosen to live on is around the pond. It's in the agreement with Albert that the pond will remain a common source of water for any livestock owned by either party. Soon the area between the pond and a wooded area is beginning to take on the look of a tent/shack village.

It's clear they are going to have to do something about sturdier living quarters than the tents. With colder weather around the corner something more permanent and easy to heat is needed. There is an old, abandoned hip-roofed barn from an earlier owner near the pond. It's in need of a roof and the interior walls need insulating. Repairs are soon made and it is quickly adapted as a community room.

In the natural way of things, many of the single women seek the aid of the men to provide them with some kind of living quarters other than the pup tents they had brought to the concert for what was expected to be only a weekend jaunt. This need gives rise to the idea of building quarters around the exterior of the barn saving on construction by utilizing the barn's walls. Scrap lumber is foraged from every shack and abandoned unguarded building found anywhere in a ten mile radius around the farm. Albert has also agreed to allow them to clear enough of the thirty or so acres of woods to supply logs for needed structural beams. Some of the young men have had a little experience with hammer and nails but none have enough building savvy to bear the distinction of carpenter. Much of what is built has to be tweaked and reinforced as mistakes are inevitable with this determined but inexperienced crew. With all hands and minds nearly on the same page, they are able to cobble together enough living space to accommodate all of them.

There is an eclectic assortment of individual personalities and skills in this new tribal commune. Quinton Baze is an example of both eclectic talent and personality. He is from a small town in Maine where he quit high school to pursue his interest in the blacksmith trade. He's now twenty years old with about seven years of experience welding everything from farm machinery to art objects. With the kind of engineering mind he has, it's mainly by his direction that these buildings are still holding together.

Audra Cummings has become the ad hoc health care provider. She is somewhere in her mid-twenties with several years working experience as a homeopathic nurse. Her abilities vary from herbal remedies to midwifery. Her free spirit tendencies assisted her decision to join this *Walden* type experiment.

Their original concept of everyday being a "joy day" is taking on a different meaning. Where in the beginning days of communal life, it meant getting stoned all day, every day. Now the giant garden Breezy and his crew put in is more abundant than expected. The piglets and calves bought from Albert are turning into pigs and cows and are constantly hungry. Without Breezy's expertise, this whole "let's get back to the earth" idea would have been over long ago.

Out in the woodlot, Quinton and his crew are making certain there will be enough fire wood to heat each apartment through the winter months. They are also refurbishing fifty-gallon barrels collected from the many scrap yards throughout the area. When these metal contrivances are turned on their side, fitted with a door and supported by a couple rows of cement blocks, they become an excellent wood burner for cooking and heating.

Another crew is busy digging a huge root cellar. As a group they have come to the conclusion that if things go according to plan, they can thrive through the non-growing months with a proper storage facility.

Zan is teaching the city girls what canning vegetables is all about.

Every day is becoming less and less a "let's get stoned day" and more of a "work day." This mindset has become a reality within every facet of the commune. That is not to say the holy sacrament of LSD doesn't continue to be a major part of the spiritual life of this community. But at least for now, it is reserved more for recreational times rather than work days.

As time hurtles forward, the various differences in individual personalities begin to clash. There are those, such as Phillip, who attempt to methodically plan a course of action. Some others are content to wake up in the morning and allow the day to begin with no plan in mind—sort of the "if it feels good do it" philosophy. Since it is Phillip's profit from the concert that is supporting these newcomers, they usually quickly become compliant to his line of order. Of course, each person is expected to contribute what monies they have to the common cause. If that includes getting more cash from home, then that too is to be placed in the common kitty. Phillip is sure his course of action will insure a utopian society. He truly believes the country's establishment is corrupt and therefore has no objection to taking their wealth and redistributing it to his own cause. In other words the ends will justify the means.

All the same, it is becoming apparent there needs to be an improved governance system—at least one that will meet some of the rising discontent. Phillip, along with the rest, hopes to establish a family-like atmosphere where personal freedoms prevail, while not infringing on the rights of others. Central elements are carefully crafted to insure the continued use of marijuana, psychedelic drugs, and sexual preferences as a matter of personal freedom. The expectation of Phillip, together with the other males and a few of the females in this burgeoning commune, is that free sex among them is a healthy lifestyle. Of course, this moral principle always appeals more to males than females. Some of the women, like Deidre, are less comfortable with this belief.

"I want to pick who I want to sleep with. You guys say you want free love but the way I see it is you want free sex," laments Deidre.

"Ahh Deidre, you're so damned uptight—you need to work on yourself," counters Phillip. He views the moral certitude of his parents' generation as a malfunction and Deidre, in his estimation, carries too much of a residual from her formative years. Deidre is aware of the seeming attraction Phillip has for her, yet she recoils at the thought of having sexual intercourse with him. Only a year ago, she had a relationship with another boy in the unfulfilled hope it would be a lasting alliance. Since that time she has been very haphazard about taking birth control pills which also serves as a deterrent to any sex life.

"You guys all think it's so cool to have sex, but what are you going to do if one of us gets pregnant?" challenges Shelly. She is on birth control pills as are the rest of the young women and not quite as reluctant as Deidre to pass herself around.

"You girls are supposed to be on the pill so that kind of shit don't happen," says a now visibly testy Phillip.

"That's not the question Phillip. The question is 'What are the plans if one of us becomes pregnant'?" reiterates Shelly with a bit of testiness in her own voice. This confrontation has also caught the attention of the others, male and female.

Phillip has never enjoyed anyone confronting his decisions or for that matter lack of decision. It often results with him storming out of the room in a pout. In this case, he has a second thought.

"What's *your* proposal if one of you gets lax and you find yourself knocked up?" he asks. From the tone of the question it's clear he wants to throw the ball back in Shelly's court.

"I may be misunderstanding you Phillip, but are you intimating we're on our own if we should happen to get pregnant?" questions Shelly.

As his eyes dart around looking for a way out of the corner he seems to have painted himself into, it's obvious Phillip is not prepared to be quizzed at this level. Giving himself a moment, he wipes his mouth with a piece of his shirt cuff in the hopes of coming up with something that negates his unmistakably chauvinistic attitude. Deafening silence is his only answer. No one has seen him so completely disarmed. It's obvious he doesn't care to have the world as he's beginning to view it disturbed. Still searching for a way out of this conundrum, he attempts to regroup in the hopes of a smoother ride.

"I, for one, will be the first to support any one of you in getting an abortion," he crows thinking he's hit a home run.

Linda, one of the new girls, asks the obvious question, "What happens if I don't want an abortion?"

The question is again directed to Phillip. Again there is an uncomfortable pause. All the other males are just as uncomfortable and are happy the questioning has Phillip on the hot seat, instead of them.

"You saying you'd want to have the baby?" he asks, somewhat surprised at her question.

"I'm not saying anything. I'm merely asking," she returns.

Again Phillip finds himself at a loss for a satisfactory answer.

"I suppose we could vote on something like that," he says stumbling with the words.

"Vote on it! What the hell are you saying? All you guys are getting free ass and you're gonna vote on it? For you guys, free love just means free sex and ta hell with what we may want!" she blurts.

Her last words have hit home with a few more of the other women. These are thoughts they've had but tried to snuff for fear of appearing uptight. They are in various ways beginning to realize free love doesn't necessarily give them parity. Their role in this communal society hasn't changed much from that of mainstream America—except maybe for different table manners. They're realizing that sexual freedom doesn't mean they're liberated and regarded as equal with men.

"It sounds to me like the primary position we women are expected to have here is on our backs," further states Linda.

Some of the other females are feeling awkward with this discourse. As usual with females, they share a feeling of not wanting to rock the boat. Nonetheless, this diversity in thought is a hefty indicator to Phillip of the need to include women and the needs of women in any council placements.

Later that evening, Deidre and Shelly return to their shared apartment. Deidre is being exceptionally meditative. Shelly has known her long enough to realize she has something going on that's causing this pensiveness. After a period of time, she is still un-talkative and Shelly has had enough.

"Okay Deidre, let's hear what ya got goin' on in that pin head."

Looking up Deidre gives Shelly her *what the hell you talking about* look.

"You know damn well what I'm talking about. You got your panties in a twist over somthin' so let's hear it!"

Deidre pulls her knees up to her chin, lets out a long sigh and says, "Shelly, I haven't had a period in months—I think I'm pregnant."

Shelly's whole demeanor is suddenly reduced from that of assured confidence to stunned diffidence. She struggles for a meaningful response. "How can that be? You don't screw any of these guys!" she blunders.

"You're right, I don't, but that doesn't mean I haven't been screwed," she says in a near whisper.

Shelly is desperately trying to follow her friend's words. "What are you saying, Deidre? One of these guys raped you?"

"Not one of these guys here, but somebody back at school. Remember when you helped me back to my tent and the next morning the dress I was wearing was covered in my blood and some guy's cum. I know that's the night it happened."

Shelly is looking at her friend with a befuddled gaze as she recalls that incident and then the morning sickness Deidre had later on.

"Oh my god. I hope you're wrong!" she says in a strained whisper, as if whispering will change the inevitable.

"I'm positive I'm right. I hadn't had sex since I broke up with Charley the year before and I haven't been with anyone since," says Deidre throwing the bag with the semen and blood encrusted dress down. "So I know it had to have happened that night."

Shelly is looking at this object as one would roadkill. "Why in God's name have you kept that disgusting dress!!?" she says, kicking the bag across the room.

Deidre retrieves it as one would a valuable heirloom. "I don't know why I've kept it," she says, "but I can't bring myself to throw it away until I can confront my attacker. I want him to see how sick and depraved his mind must be."

Listening to the hurt in her friend's voice brings with it a wave of compassion. "What are you gonna do, Deidre? And let me say whatever you do, I'm with you," expresses Shelly in her most assuring words.

"I don't know yet what I should do. What would you do?" asks Deidre.

It's clear neither of them is prepared in any way to deal with this new development. Shelly doesn't answer. It's not because she doesn't want to. She desperately wants to, but has no words to give. She can only give herself silently. Enveloping her friend in her arms seems to be enough for now.

CHAPTER 13

Phillip is starting to realize that if he wants to stay in the forefront of this commune he better be prepared to become much more mindful of its parts. This truth has been evident in humans since Adam and Eve. There is a very selfish self-centered factor in both males and females. When either sex dominates, the other usually feels as though they've been kicked to the curb.

Phillip's nascent need to be in the vanguard of this commune's policy making is unquestionably keeping him on his toes. He is finding that if his personal ambition is to be in a dominant governing position then it must be tempered to allow a democratic council to emerge. To be in the forefront, the best he can hope to achieve is to be its greatest contributor and advocate.

On this particular summer morning, rain is keeping nearly everyone inside. The community room is busy with activities. An assortment of stray dogs and cats has found a home here and become a point of entertainment. A few of the guys have set up a target and are amusing themselves with a knife throwing competition.

Phillip has other things on his mind and seeks Manny out to discuss how they can establish order, while remaining free from order.

Manny is becoming his only trusted adviser. With the mindset of an accountant, Manny is always calculating, but lacks the personality to become an effective leader. He is more than willing to see his policies come to life through Phillip's more charismatic persona. Phillip, on the other hand, finds Manny's thought processes continue to be a necessary asset to him.

Now with strong overtones of urgency Manny says, "I believe you need to take control of the governance. It's necessary that you come up with a name, draw up the bylaws and a manifesto and then present this to a council for approval. I'm sure this move will keep you in a governing position for some time."

Giving Manny's insightfulness only a moment's thought, Phillip says, "Manny you're a genius. I don't know what I'd do without you. How about you give me a hand with all this?"

Within seconds Manny has pulled out his Smith-Corona typewriter ready to go to work. For the rest of the week the two of them hammer out a combination of *Walden Two*, and various Libertarian Socialist ideas. For good measure they include the guidelines from the Hindu *Kama Sutra* dealing with attempting to place virtues above money, a secure life, and a proper place for pleasure. With this Hindu work included, it gives the whole project a spiritual bent that wouldn't normally be there.

In their final draft they have initiated a Board of Planners as the only government. It's to consist of three men and three women. Their job is to make policy, pick managers, and then oversee the results. Manny worked out a stratagem that he feels will keep the comprehensive power in Phillip's hands.

Manny goes on to further explain, "Because of our small size, we'll make planners managers and the managers planners. This will keep them busy enough with their own department and less likely to have a handle on the overall operation thus leaving you with a general overall view of the entire inner workings of the commune. This will give you a definite leg up as we grow."

While Manny continues to run through all the advantages of this manifesto, Phillip thumbs through the pages to be sure everything is in order. He hopes to reduce the number of opposing points of view by anticipating objections. This is a tactic he learned in a pre-law class.

Understanding Phillip's concerns with the finished document, Manny also anticipates some of Phillip's points.

"If you notice, I've offered to continue my services as secretary and treasurer. We're proposing this as a non-elected post, but an appointed position selected by the general manager. So in the event you are not voted in, I'll still maintain a level of influence for a while."

Phillip is totally engrossed in reading. Finally finishing, with a confident grin, he slaps the document to the table.

"You've done a damn good job, Manny. We now have a brotherhood that I believe we can all trust. With a platform statement like we've come up with, we'll definitely touch the soul of our emerging youth culture. I believe with all my heart we've separated good from evil," affirms Phillip.

"Good! I say it's time to have a group meeting and get this show on the road," declares a satisfied Manny.

The two of them are more than ready to present what has taken them all week to put together. By the evening meal, the news has spread to the entire assemblage. As usual the mental attitude of this group is laissez-faire. They are prone to agree with anything that doesn't interfere with sex, drug use, race relations, or with their burgeoning new religion of love and freedom. For the most part, they are content to be followers. Letting people like Phillip make policy is no problem as long as he can assure them they will have a community that has very little control. But at the same time insure stringent control regarding the overall acceptance of differing behaviors. This is especially true concerning non-monogamous relationships. (The overall opinion is the acceptance of this practice reduces the fear of isolation among them.)

Although there are as yet no children in this community, in the event this should happen, the overall consensus is these children are to live and be raised in common.

Phillip is convinced that communism as the establishment explains it has lost its context. He feels exhilarated to be a part of a burgeoning youth movement that openly and willingly espouses many communist components. This group, as well as nearly every other youth movement, is satisfied with any idea that is against the stodginess and intolerance of the establishment. To these young activists, their parents' generation has become complacent cowards toward issues that matter to their future such as the cold war, the bomb, civil rights, and universal authoritarianism. Hence, they believe they must take the world into their own hands if they are to survive.

Within a short time, the document is approved, managers and planners have been selected and all that's remains is to give this commune a name that can be attached to this pseudo-legal document. In deference to Karl Marx and their Amish host, they finally agree on a German name *Die Landarbeiter* (farm workers). It has a nice non-American avant-garde, leftist sound about it. Everyone agrees it also has a very cool sounding ring to it.

CHAPTER 14

It's midafternoon. A car with Michigan license plates cruises down the main street in Loogootee. Millie is placing chairs on top of tables preparing to clean the floors of her diner after the lunch rush. Interrupting her routine are the four occupants from the late model Ford, two middle-aged men along with two middle-aged women.

"How do you do ma'am? We're looking for something to eat. Are you still open?" questions a fortyish looking man with graying temples and a pleasant demeanor.

"We're always open for payin' customers," chuckles Millie at the same time preparing to make these newcomers welcome by putting chairs back around one of the tables.

"We sure appreciate it. We've been on the road all day," pipes up one of the women. Further inquiring, she asks, "By the way, do you have a motel in the area?"

"Yes, we do. It's actually a motor court about a mile out of town—Wesley Trimmer runs it. He's got about a half dozen cabins—rents 'em by the night or week," says Millie with an air of authority. "Actually, he's my brother-in-law," she goes on, "I can give him a call if you want."

"That would be great. We'd like to have five cabins, if we can," says the gray-haired man.

Millie finds herself doing a quick head count. "Did you say four or five?"

"Five. Yes, five will be just what we need," continues the man without a hitch.

From the tone in his voice, she decides not to question any further. After taking their order, she gives Wes a call. The last time he had so many rooms occupied was during the rock concert. He is more than delighted with this opportunity to have them filled again.

Millie is typical of small town people. She wants to learn all she can of these strangers' business without appearing to be prying. They are also interested in learning everything they can get out of Millie without coming across as snoopy outsiders. The process begins with the gray-haired man, who Millie overhears referred to as Mike, asking about the hippie commune.

"I can't tell you much about it other than they do a lot of naked stuff out there," describes Millie doing a little hoochie-coochie wiggle with her hips.

"How many would you say are living out there?" questions one of the females.

"I couldn't tell you for sure, but Emil Rothstedder is an Amish neighbor. He claims there's at least a couple dozen."

"Do they ever come to town?" asks Mike.

"The only time I ever see any of 'em is when they come in to get a wire from Western Union with money from their parents," informs Millie.

"How do they know they've got money here?" further pries Mike.

"Ole Sam over at Western Union sends Billy Barnes' boy, William, out to the farm and fetches 'em back."

Sensing they have probably pushed their questions hard enough, they spend the rest of the meal making small talk about the weather. They definitely learned more than Millie.

Within the hour, the four have finished eating and made their way to Wes's motel. He has half a dozen cabins situated in a row behind the building and couldn't be more accommodating. Usually he's content with a couple of feed salesmen taking a room every so often, but having five cabins rented at one time is a windfall he hadn't expected.

****

It's a Monday morning at Die Landarbeiter Commune. After the weekend, everyone is busy getting themselves back into a work mode. There is a crew making their way to the woodlot to finish cutting up some tree tops left over from the logs they had harvested earlier for construction projects. Another crew is attempting to make a few more repairs to the barn's roof.

Audra Cummings, the ad hoc health provider for the commune has examined Deidre and verified her suspicions. Audra is happy to be a part of the experience. She spent much of her life as the daughter of a missionary to the Navaho Indians. It was there she gained an interest in Indian healing arts, applying a more holistic discipline to the sick. She also assisted in many midwife undertakings. At best these involvements can be very satisfying but risky.

"You are indeed pregnant my dear," she says with a big smile.

Deidre has had nothing but restless nights trying to wrestle through this labyrinth of confusion. Now to have it confirmed brings out a spiteful hatred. *The monster that did this to me will have to answer to you God and I hope you send him to hell!* is her most prevalent thought.

Her next thought is how she can expediently get rid of this problem. With tears in her eyes and shaking at the prospect this news has spawned, she asks in a trembling, nearly inaudible voice, "Can you get rid of it for me?"

Audra stares intently at her for a moment with unblinking eyes. "Why?" is her one word response.

Still trembling Deidre nearly spits the words from her mouth, "Because this is the bastard child of a monster who raped me!!"

Seeing how distraught Deidre is getting, Audra takes her by the hand and leads her to a chair. Sitting across from her, she affectionately places both her hands around Deidre's.

"I can do that but I'm going to ask you to give it a couple weeks, for both our sakes." Audra's eyes begin to moisten as a look of desperation overtakes her usually cheerful demeanor.

Both of them show the other a quizzical moment of confused attention.

Seeing how Deidre is buried in her own despair, Audra decides to go on in spite of her difficulty.

"There is something I want to share with you, Deidre, and I hope you'll listen. I was in your shoes when in I was your age. There I was the daughter of a missionary and I found myself knocked up—not just knocked up, but knocked up by the chief's son who was married and ten years older than me. Of course I panicked. He also panicked when he heard about it. He immediately made arrangements to have a midwife discreetly give me an abortion." The tears are running down her weather-roughened cheeks as she continues, "I saw my baby, Deidre. His little mouth was gasping. He died in less than a minute." Letting out an unforgiving sigh, she tightens her grasp on Deidre's hands. "Don't make the same mistake."

Both sit for a while silently. Their minds are churning—one with what has happened and one with what could happen. Rising, Deidre wipes her nose while walking to the door and standing in the opening, she turns and nods agreement to give it a couple weeks. Closing the door behind her, she quietly leaves.

Audra gives Deidre a light working schedule. Today, Deidre, Shelly and Zan are digging up a few ginseng roots they discovered in the woods. When dried they bring big money on the Chinese market. The three have just returned when young William Barnes arrives from town looking for Deidre Lueker.

Surprised to have anyone asking for her, Deidre warily asks, "Who wants me?"

"Ole Sam from the Western Union sent me out here to tell you, you have a telegram," replies William with an official air.

"Who would be sending me a telegram?" questions Deidre, directed at anyone listening.

"Don't know nothin' about that," says William matter-of-factly. "Alls I do is deliver the message."

With that said, he jumps on his bicycle and heads back toward town leaving the relationship between message and messenger a mystery.

Deidre's mind begins to attempt the process of reasoning through this strange phenomenon. *Who knows where I am to be sending me a message? Is this some kind of an emergency about my family?*

The more she tries to dissect its curious factors, the more the mystery intensifies. Shelly and Zan are both as intrigued as Deidre with this conundrum. After an ineffective attempt at solving the enigma, curiosity wins. Together, they decide a trip to the Western Union office in town will ultimately work out the dilemma. Wasting no time, they approach Phillip about using one of the cars held in common by the commune. Phillip is fine with this since it's been his experience that these Western Union affairs usually bring money from a parent. Now with one of the few cars available to them, the girls make the trek to Loogootee.

On arrival, they waste no time reaching the Western Union office. It's located in an old building that in better times had served as a boarding house. Ole Ajax Bila and his wife Tillie better known as "Toadie" still make their home in some of the living quarters. The bright yellow sign is the only updated effort on the entire building. They find an available parking space in front of the building behind a new, dark colored Ford sedan. In spite of their recent commitment to a vow of agrarian near poverty, they can't help but be drawn to its sleek lines. They are about to enter the Western Union office, when the window on the black Ford rolls down and a kindly-looking lady asks, "Which of you young ladies is Deidre Lueker?"

To say the three of them are surprised at this turn of events would be an understatement. Looking at one another with a *what in the hell is going on with this?* look, Deidre approaches the sedan. Suddenly the doors fly open. Two men grab her and fling her into the back seat. In seconds the car is speeding down the street leaving the other two girls behind speechless and frozen to the sidewalk. By the time they gather their wits, the sedan is nowhere in sight. The reality of what has just taken place turns into panic and they begin to scream. This of course, attracts the attention of Ole Ajax in the Western Union office. Running into the street, he demands in a commanding tone, "What in tarnation you two screamin' about?"

By the time the two of them manage to get their story out, Ajax is dumbstruck. All he can do at this moment is stare at them with a quizzical expression.

"I never received no telegram for that girl and I sure as hell didn't send that kid clear out there on a wild goose chase," says a bewildered Ajax.

After a few more people emerge, someone suggests they call the sheriff's office and get Earl involved with this. Meanwhile, Toadie appears. Despite her suspicions of all the goings-on with these hippies, she puts a motherly arm around both these hysterical young women and brings them inside off the street.

"You girls pay no never mind ta all this horse shit. Earl will get ta the bottom of all this in a hurry. There ain't nothin' goes on in this county he don't get to the bottom of sooner or later."

Earl is Toadie's cousin and she has every confidence he'll have the problem solved before this goes to twenty-four hours.

****

In the meantime, the back seat of black Ford sedan is chaos. Deidre's whole body is exhibiting a fearful and violent reaction toward her horrid circumstances. Her mind is tumbling over itself trying to gain even the slightest perspective as to what is happening to her. Meanwhile, she is frozen to her seat in fear and cannot stop shaking. Her captors are doing all they can to calm her.

"You're going to be alright! We are not here to harm you!" says the lady who had called Deidre to the car before the men abducted her. The only organs seemingly functioning in an escape mode are her eyes as they dart around seeking any outlet. She finds herself caught between two middle-aged women she has never seen before, while two middle-aged men equally as strange occupy the front seat. So far the men have remained silent. They are more intent on reaching a predetermined destination than dealing with Deidre.

The other lady speaks for the first time. "We are friends of your parents. They are very concerned for your welfare and have asked us to intervene on their behalf."

These words increase Deidre's confusion as she tries to make sense of her horrendous situation. Deidre only half hears what they are saying as more and more of the reality of her powerlessness makes its way into her mind. She's trapped in a speeding sedan, after being strong-armed into the car by two strange men and seated between two strange women who are trying to convince her of the good they are doing.

The second lady continues, speaking in a calm reassuring voice. "Your parents are concerned that you are being held by strong cult personalities that are dominating your will."

As Deidre listens to this woman's words, her thoughts begin to turn her fear into anger. Her anger increases as she struggles to imagine her parents doing this to her.

Shortly, the sedan stops in a concealed area behind a cabin in a wooded environment she is not familiar with. The two men exit the sedan looking around for anyone that may be lurking in the area. Satisfied things are okay, they nod to the two women. They in turn, continue the back seat dialogue with Deidre to assure her they are not here to harm her, but only to be assured she's not being held in this commune against her will. Deidre has calmed her fear and anger enough to believe she is not going to be physically harmed.

"All we are asking is that you assure us that you are not being brainwashed by some cult. Your parents deserve this assurance. Are you okay with this?" questions the soft-spoken woman.

Realizing her predicament seems to be less threatening, she agrees to co-operate. With that settled, the man called Mike opens the car door, the women exit and lead Deidre into the empty cabin. It's a typical overnight cabin containing a bed with a patterned quilt, a kitchenette, a small table and chairs, a worn mohair couch and easy chair with a shaded reading lamp, several curtained windows and screens, and a bare plank board floor with a throw rug in the center.

Mike seems to be in charge, at least he's the one giving directions. "My name is Mike, Deidre," he begins.

Pointing to each of the others, he introduces them individually. "This is Sue. She is a clinical psychologist. This is Marcia. She was exploited by a group which she later discovered was not always acting in her best interest. George here is my assistant. I think you're getting an idea of why you're here."

"Not really," says a truly perplexed Deidre.

"At the request of your parents we have agreed to intervene," leads off Mike.

"Intervene in what?" sounds off Deidre with a boldness she has not had the need to display in some time.

"Your parents are concerned for your welfare. They haven't heard a word from you in a few months and are worried sick you're being held against your will in this cult," concedes Mike in a very earnest tone.

Gaining more courage, Deidre decides to do a bit of questioning herself.

"First off, it's not a cult and how do I know you're telling me the truth about who you are?"

Anticipating this question, Mike reaches into his inside jacket pocket and produces an envelope. Staring directly at Deidre without saying a word, he hands it to her. Across the face of the covering, she immediately recognizes her name scrawled in her father's handwriting. Cautiously opening it, she begins to read silently. By the time she finishes reading the letter her temperament has changed to reticent stoicism.

After a few minutes of silence, she says, "They have no business doing this. I want you to take me back to my friends now!! I can't believe you're doing this to me...you have no right."

Mike immediately raises his voice—not in an abusive mode—but loud enough to attempt to take control of this conversation.

"Do you honestly expect me to excuse myself from this pursuit and dishonor your parents in the same way you have? Do you?"

Not waiting for Deidre to answer and more concerned with her reactive body language, he continues with another barrage of accusations.

"These are the people who sacrificed to give you the education and the advantages they were never privy to and now you actually believe you owe them no explanation for your divergent behavior? What the hell kind of person are you anyway?"

Deidre is noticeably struck by Mike's seeming forthrightness. He is a seasoned deprogrammer and is cognizant of any change in the demeanor of his subjects. Without a moment's hesitation, he lowers his voice to a gentler, softer tone.

"All your parents want is for us to reassure them that you are not being brainwashed by this group you've become involved with. I don't think that's asking too much, is it?"

Leaning forward in his chair, he presses Deidre for confirmation. He's expecting Deidre's acquiescence to his last question to reinforce his expectations. To his satisfaction Deidre agrees with his assessment. All four adults are pleased to note her voice is becoming less hostile. Mike is sure things are turning in a more positive direction for his team.

Sue finds Deidre's softer tone more to her liking and doesn't hesitate to begin her leg of the program. "Tell me about your leader...ah Phillip, I believe his name is," she questions, conveying a portrayal of concern.

Deidre is willing at this point to co-operate, get this assessment over with, and dump these people out of her life. "I wouldn't say he's the leader. Sometimes he acts like he is but we have a democratic form of government. He usually makes a strong case for himself, but if we don't like what he wants, we can vote him down."

Putting her fingers to her lips in a pensive pose, Sue continues, "How often does he get voted down?"

This question noticeably gnaws at Deidre. "I don't remember every circumstance, but I'm sure it's happened," she says, straining to make her answer convincing.

Still holding her lips, Sue sharpens her questioning. "I don't mean to berate you on this but I believe it's important for all of us to know how many times this man's authority has been challenged and successfully defeated."

Deidre is not able to hide her discomfort. This question has her eyes darting about the room looking for that elusive escape route that doesn't seem to be materializing.

Sue can sense Deidre's growing hostility toward this last question. "Okay, let's leave that question alone for the moment and focus on your words 'sometimes he acts like he is.' This was in response to me asking you to tell me about your leader Phillip. I sense some hostility toward him at this point—true or untrue?"

Deidre lets these words bounce around in her head for a moment before she answers. “I wouldn’t say hostility, exactly. He likes to impress me with his leadership prowess. I think he hopes it will be enough for me to become his woman...but I’m not interested in him that way.”

“So if he annoys you so much, why haven’t you left the commune?”

Her thoughts seem to wander off for a moment before she pronounces, “Honestly, I like it there. I feel safe there.”

“Safe? Or just afraid to leave and think for yourself?” interrogates Sue.

Deidre would just as soon this line of questioning stopped. She would like to sidestep this kind of inquiry. It’s becoming obvious to her that she is very uncomfortable with this close scrutiny.

“Can we take a rest from all this crap? It’s starting to give me a headache,” she asks in her most disgusted tone of voice.

Ignoring her plea, Sue keeps the questions coming well into the night. Then Marcia returns and picks up with her own line of questioning, giving Sue the opportunity to exit without notice back to her own cabin for some sleep. Deidre is becoming so exhausted that all she wants is sleep. It becomes apparent as Mike arrives with the dawn that a new battery of questions is making its way into the interrogation process. By this time Deidre is so weary and exhausted from lack of sleep, she finds her defenses crumbling. Regardless, Mike hammers away for the rest of the morning. The relay team of interrogators continues, reducing Deidre’s thoughts to unreliable speculations.

CHAPTER 15

Sheriff Snowdon has begun investigating. He doesn’t appear to be as alarmed as the rest of the townsfolk. He carefully interviews Ajax and Toadie as well as young William Barnes, allowing the story to unfold.

"Them people offered me a buck, iffin I'd take that story about a telegram out there ta that hippie place," says William in near tears when he discovers what he has unwittingly been involved in.

Millie heard from a restaurant patron about the buzz down the street. Removing her apron, she makes her way to Earl's patrol car. He appears to be busy making out a report. Tapping on the window, she gets his attention. "Just ta let you know, I think I know where them people you lookin' for may be."

Earl rolls down his window with a look of surprise. "Wadda ya got, Millie?"

She spends the next few minutes telling him about the strangers who had lunch and then she sent them out to Wes's place.

"I know these is the same folks yer lookin' for," she adds.

The stories Earl is getting from each of these witnesses are facts well-spiced with each of their opinions as to what may be going on in this case.

Returning to her restaurant, Millie picks up on some of the continuing local opinions.

"I got a sneakin' suspicion that girl's been kidnapped ta sell as a sex slave ta one ah them A-rab fellers. They pay any amount ta get one ah them blonde-haired, hippie girls," says a toothless patron nursing his third cup of coffee at Millie's.

"Ah hell, you jest upset you ain't that A-rab feller ain't cha," comes back another grizzled old geezer. Both of them slap each other on the back in their attempt at humor.

The day has finally spent itself. Shelly and Zan have returned to the commune only to share their unresolved anxiety with the whole commune. Earl has seemingly wrapped up his interviews and left town.

****

Back at Wes's cabins, Mike is concluding his session with a worn out Deidre when his assistant George calls him aside.

"Someone here to speak with you, Mike. I think you need to see him real soon."

Mike reads a sense of urgency on George's face. Indicating for Sue to resume Deidre's deprogramming session, he follows George to a waiting sedan parked behind the cabin. The figure behind the wheel motions for Mike to enter the passenger's side where he finds himself confronted by Sheriff Snowdon dressed in civilian clothing and driving an unmarked car.

"What's the crisis?" asks Mike.

Mike hardly gets the question out before Earl begins. "You know when we met I told you my sympathies lie with you and the work you're doing to get these kids straightened out. Things are changin' fast since yesterday. People in town are aware of the strangers askin' for a place to stay. They're startin' ta put two and two tagether figurin' they can solve this kidnappin' problem themselves. I don't need no vigilantes risen up so I'm askin' ya to get whatever yer doin' done and get out of my jurisdiction."

Mike considers his options as he gets out of the car. He charged Deidre's parents $20,000 to take care of their problem and the process can't be rushed. He returns to Deidre's interrogation and without explanation secures a handcuff to the bedpost and places Deidre's wrist in the other cuff. Motioning for Sue to follow him, they exit the cabin leaving this mind weary, distraught soul alone.

Immediately after the door closes, the first sensation Deidre's war torn spirit becomes aware of is the dead silence. Soon she realizes that for the first time since her ordeal began, she is totally alone within this cabin turned prison. Looking around, she attempts to clear her muddled mind. Next to the bed on a nightstand is a bottle of hand lotion. Stretching her untethered arm across the bed, she coaxes the resistant bottle across the night stand. Success! All at once it's in her hand. Quickly unscrewing the top she dumps the whole of the contents on her manacled hand and twists until her small wrist is free. The knowledge she must move quickly kick-starts her adrenalin. Like a cat she moves to the unlocked door and slips out unseen, just in time to see another man she doesn't know leaving.

The whole team assembles for a panicked meeting in the cabin next door and Mike quickly spells out the new development.

"Start packin' up we gotta move quickly. This location's been compromised."

After packing his part, Mike finally makes his way back to the deprogramming cabin only to find the handcuff still attached to the bedpost, but with no Deidre being held. It's obvious she has managed to slip the cuff and escape.

The situation is rapidly moving from a manageable state of affairs to a seemingly unmanageable chaos. Panic quickly spreads throughout the whole team. With the woods surrounding them, they have no idea where to begin a search. Weighing their options, they conclude it may be time to cut their losses and move on.

Deidre is no more than a few yards away hiding in an abandoned shack, watching as her panicked nemeses pack up to leave. Not sure what is transpiring, she spends the next few hours watching to see if they will return. The shack is full of garden tools giving off a warm earthy smell that reminds her of an old aunt whose house had the same odor. By late in the day, her adrenalin has worn off and fatigue is having its way. She is suddenly aware of the life growing in her womb along with an unexpected surge of concern. She finds herself wondering if this little baby is as anxious as she is. She finds she is not thinking of this child as the "rapist's monster" but as *her* child.

Another unconstrained thought suddenly erupts into her psyche. It is an understanding that they belong to one another and neither of them is alone—they have each other. Not able to control her weariness a minute longer, and still unconsciously holding both her hands protectively around her womb, she falls into a deep slumber.

****

Shelly and Zan are not about to give in to this trespass against their friend. A near sleepless night has passed. Morning arrives with a cavalry of adamant female militants hell-bent on getting one of their own returned. Zan and Shelly are in the forefront of the campaign. Phillip is trying his best to appear as though he has things under control. It's agreed to take the bus and one car so as to accommodate any situation that may arise.

Phillip is struggling to fit the pieces of Shelly's and Zan's account of yesterday's events into a comprehensive strategy as they caravan toward Loogootee. Speaking to both girls, he questions them once again about what they heard in town.

"You say you heard that Millie's brother-in-law rented his cabins to a group of strangers driving a dark colored, late model Ford with Michigan plates?"

Both women nod their heads at this repeat of their accounting from yesterday. As usual, Phillip assumes the lead in this probe. He makes the call to bypass town and make their way directly to Wes's cabins outside Loogootee. He quickly forms a consensus as they take a detour to save some time. Phillip finds little or no reason to surrender the reins of command to any challenger since he's the only one voicing a strategy.

When they are close, Phillip issues an order to pull off the highway and have a small contingent headed by Manny make their way through the woods and come in behind the cabins. Several volunteers disembark and begin the trek while Phillip and the rest of the crew boldly park the bus on Wes's two track driveway leaving little room for anyone to get past.

Aware of the deal the sheriff made with the team of deprogrammers, Wes suddenly finds himself facing the band of hippie freaks alone. Peeking out from behind a curtained window, he's terrified to see so many. Grabbing his loaded shotgun from behind the door, he decides to drive the horde off his property, even if it means shooting them all.

"Get the hell off my property for I commence ta shoot every damn one ah ya," he yells from an open window.

Seeing the peril they may be in, Phillip holds up his hand as a commander would halt a column of troops. "Okay sir, we're not here to cause any harm. We only want to ask you a few questions."

Phillip's voice has taken on a strange new mixture of a pleading bargainer on one hand and a commanding general on the other. The forest behind the cabins suddenly comes alive with distress calls from a family of blue jays. One look and they know the cause of the uproar. Manny and his crew are coming up the two track. He has his arm wrapped in a supportive way around what appears to be a bedraggled waif of a girl.

The group had discovered their terrified missing member hiding in the old shack behind the cabins on the edge of the woods. She had at first thought it was her captors returning. The fear of falling back under their control had her shaking uncontrollably, but when they threw the door open, she recognized her liberators and burst into tears.

Seeing Deidre reduced to this state causes Phillip to want to take her away from the crowd and have her all to himself. This is as close to a feeling of love as Phillip has ever felt. He's much more acquainted with lust as are many of his generation.

Now Wes is becoming even more agitated as this throng of bearded, long-haired, unkempt hippies is seemingly invading him. He suddenly throws caution to the wind and touches off a shot above their heads. Phillip is the first to run. Seeking shelter behind the bus, he recomposes himself long enough to yell back at Wes.

"Please don't shoot, we're out of here!!"

Within seconds the whole crew is loaded into their vehicles and making their way back out to the road where they are met by Sheriff Snowdon. He is in his cruiser now. With lights flashing, he indicates for them to pull the bus to the shoulder. He slowly and purposefully makes his way to the bus's door. With a simple silent hand gesture, he indicates he wants it opened. Phillip is visibly shaken by this sudden change of events and nervously fiddles with the door lever before finally getting it open. With the confidence that only comes with superior authority, Earl steps into the bus.

After a cold stare at every individual on the bus, he breaks his silence. "There ain't ever gonna be no vigilante uprisen' in this county as long as I'm the sheriff. I want every one of you hippie sons-a-bitches out of my county by the end of this week. If you ain't gone, you'll all suffer the consequences of your decision."

He departs the bus and with one last gesture, shapes his hand into the configuration of a pistol. He points it back at the bus's inhabitants and with his mouth forms the word—BANG!

As Snowdon drives off, the unanticipated impact he has made on these young protesters is obvious in their demeanor. Deidre sits spellbound as she immediately recognizes Earl as the man she had seen leaving the cabins.

Phillip's major concern for the moment is to return to the commune where there is a perception of safety—at least for the time being. For the rest, their attention turns back to Deidre.

Shelly is the first to rush to Deidre's seat. "My God girl, you look like you been through hell and back. What in God's name did they do to you?"

All Deidre can muster up is, "Thank you all! Thank you! Thank you!"

Her eyes are dark rimmed and puffy. Her hair is sweat soaked with what little moisture she has left in her body. She has an odor about her that always accompanies a shower-less, anxious situation. Nonetheless, with her safety assured, she couldn't look more beautiful. Each comrade gathers around her for no other reason than to give her a reassuring touch. These bracing moments are shared by the whole commune bringing an outpouring of love and concern for their stolen sister.

"My God, I thought I lost you! Are you hurt? Is there anything you need?" continues Shelly, nearly pleading.

"A hug will do," says Deidre, forcing a grin through her tears.

Shelly silently holds her just as she has so many times in the past. There is an almost surreal atmosphere as the rest of the crew sits quietly reflecting on the disorienting happenings of the last couple days.

There is a sense of relief when the bus pulls into the communal compound. It's at least a temporary reprieve from the lurking outside establishment. The impending threat from Sheriff Snowdon is fresh on everyone's mind. Each has had experiences with knee jerk reactions from a nervous uptight citizenry.

Audra leads Deidre aside to take her blood pressure and give her as complete an examination as she knows how. Privately—save for Shelly—and out of earshot of the rest of the crowd, Audra dauntlessly asks the question that so far no one has wanted to ask.

"Did those bastards rape you, Deidre?"

"No. All they did was try and convince me to leave you guys. They believed, along with my parents who hired them, that this is some kind of cult and that I am being held against my will," reports Deidre, sobbing with a lingering fear they may still be lurking for her somewhere. Stopping long enough to recover from her sobbing, she continues, "And that prick of a sheriff is in on the whole affair."

Phillip has managed to lurk undetected outside Audra's apartment in an attempt to catch some answers surrounding her painful ordeal. Now, hearing the sheriff was part of this whole kidnapping affair brings a renewed fear of the power this man holds over their welfare. Not given to bravery, Phillip returns to his apartment.

Phillip is a coward by nature, but hides his reaction as a man who prefers peace over war. When fearful situations arise, his makeup tells him to run where a man of courage will stand and fight. Others, who also prefer peace may see the need to stand one's ground against an abusive bully and convincingly defeat him at any cost in order to bring about peace. Phillip is not this man. Like so many men who yearn for power, he lacks the courage that would set him apart. The men in Texas refer to this type of cowboy as "All hat and no cows."

Calling an emergency meeting of the entire commune, Phillip lays his cards on the table. "I hate to say this but I believe we are facing an intractable enemy. I don't see how we can successfully fight against this man without taking injuries we don't want. As a man of peace, I recommend we move on to a different location."

Quinton Baze, the blacksmith who nearly single-handedly designed and built Die Landarbeiter, is visibly taken back and incensed at Phillip's lack of courage to stand his ground for his beliefs.

"Man I can't believe you're ready to cut and run over this asshole sheriff! We built this place as a haven to live our lives the way we choose and now you want us to pack up and run? You can count me out, I ain't goin' nowhere!"

The rest of the assembly is quietly contemplative. This is actually the first time anyone has so rigorously opposed Phillip's leadership. He also finds himself struck quiet for the moment without an immediate answer.

Manny recognizes the potential threat that can grow out of this one dissenting voice. Before this crises gains momentum, he quickly jumps to the floor with an alternative suggestion. "Emotions are getting out of hand right now, we're all exhausted. Why don't we sleep on this tonight and give some thought to our alternatives? We can gather again tomorrow and generate more reasonable ideas."

No one disagrees. Everyone is tired and hardly in any condition to begin a debate. Shelly and Deidre are especially in favor of getting some long overdue sleep.

CHAPTER 16

As has been the case since anyone can remember tomorrow becomes today arriving on schedule. The general way policy problems are approached on the farm is to assign the work agenda for the day, get what chores need attending all accomplished and then confront any troublesome issues in a general assembly.

Quinton is chomping at the bit to get this whole procedure underway. He has spent much of the day campaigning for his position to hold their ground at Die Landarbeiter. "I know we are much stronger united than we realize. I know damn well that sheriff is like all bullies—he'll cave as soon as he has a strong opposition."

The attraction for many of the members is to have a peaceful existence at *any* cost, much like the surrounding Amish. However, standing up for something is not the same as aggression. Pacification frequently just encourages more bullying.

Phillip has also had time to reconsider his plan to abandon Die

Landarbeiter for a less stressful location. Manny has pulled Phillip aside and hopes to convince him there is another option.

"If you decide to leave Phillip, we may split the commune into unnecessary factions of those in favor and those who aren't. I know there are folks here, like Quinton, who will throw themselves into the heat of the fire for a worthy cause—that is, if you manage them correctly. I believe we can beat these pigs at their own game, if we plan it right."

Phillip has also had a night and a day to realize his weakness is often to run rather than fight. The hippie mantra of love, love, love is usually sung by those less inclined to exhibit any aggression. This is a personality trait requires no effort from him. Pacifism is what attracted him originally to this whole notion of "the anti-war movement." There is an almost primitive innocence to this notion and if left to its own, one will act accordingly. Leaders like Phillip need advisers like Manny as a check on their impulses.

"I'm all ears Manny, what have you got?" questions Phillip.

Manny has been an ardent student of men like Saul Alinsky, who perfected the art of community organizing. "I think you need to take command of this situation by fanning the hostilities that already exist against the establishment. There is no question these pigs are going to try and bully us. It won't be much of a stretch to whip up a hatred for them."

Leaning forward in his chair, Phillip is listening with renewed interest to his trusted confidant. Taking another sip from his coffee, he pauses for a moment to assess what Manny is getting at.

Manny, in turn, continues with his prescription. "I know once we get these guys whipped up, it won't take much to get them into a public confrontation. This is the kind of shit the press eats up."

"Damn Manny, you've done it again," says Phillip. "Let's get this done!"

They make their way into the large common room prepared with a solution they hope will bring the sheriff to his knees. The room is packed.

When the meeting begins, Quinton is surprised to find very little opposition. Phillip agrees with Quinton in principle and then steps out in front with a plan. Once again, by being multidimensional, Phillip has skillfully managed to retain control of the operation.

The plan is to mobilize for action in such a way that the press will be ready to report on every crazy happening. The idea is to convey a stark contrast between what appears to be a peaceful agrarian commune unfairly brutalized by an oppressive sheriff. If done correctly, the sympathies will be in the direction of the protesters. The commune is not particularly interested in gaining adult support as much as gaining young sympathizers. The universal mantra among the counterculture movement is "don't trust anyone over thirty."

Phillip is once again in his element organizing the event. He still has all the radio and newspaper contacts that made his rock concert a success. Before the day is over, all media outlets in the country are aware of the ensuing struggle going on in Martin County. By the next day, a steady stream of hippies in every kind of conveyance that can make its way down the road is finding their way into the area. Big vans full of media people are filling up every available hotel and motel in a twenty-five mile radius. Phillip holds a press conference across the street from the (once again) startled Martin County Sheriff's Department. This is the second event in a month that has caught the sheriff on his blind side.

This is evident when reporters question Sheriff Snowdon on his policies regarding the accusations made against him regarding his restricting the freedom of movement by members of the Die Landarbeiter commune and possible complicity in a kidnapping. His frustration over what he considers to be the business of Martin County and no one else is evident in his hostility toward the reporters. He attempts to demonstrate this by ignoring them. But after being hounded for most of the day by the press for an official statement, he is finally cornered on his way out of the building, attempting to get into his car.

"I consider this to be a question for Martin County to take care of. We sure as hell don't need a bunch of outside meddlers stickin' their damn noses in ta our affairs," says Sheriff Snowdon, slamming the door and nearly taking a reporter's fingers along with it.

Across the street, Phillip is continuing to entertain the press, energized by the attention he's managed to bring to their cause.

"This Sheriff is a bum trip. He's no different than Hitler's SS. We're going to have our own Nuremberg trials and fry his ass," he tells reporters, while continuing his emboldened rant against the established law enforcement.

"Is your group planning on taking the law into your own hands?" asks a well-meaning reporter.

"Law! What law? These pigs don't follow any law. They believe that might makes right. We're here to demonstrate what might is. We'll have thousands of freaks here tomorrow ready to live free or die," says Phillip using much of his SDS rhetoric for this occasion.

Die Landarbeiter is the main host to this event inviting enough "barefooted, dope smoking, commie pinkos," as described by the mayor, "to nearly double the size of Martin County."

Loogootee is a small American town with a revolution about to erupt. The locals have just recovered from the rock concert fiasco and are being invaded again with another horde from the outside. For the most part, the local citizens are all John Birch sympathizers ready to grab their guns.

"But only iffin we hafta," adds Early Wallace the pot-bellied, bald headed mayor of Loogootee.

Most of the opposition to this onslaught of demonstrators is the usual knee jerk reaction of a community caught once again with its pants down.

Manny is spending much of his time working with Quinton's group designated to be the steering committee. Quinton, along with the other commune members have done as much as they can to fan the flames of discontent and bring the throng up to speed concerning the kidnapping escapade as well as the threats spewed by the sheriff. There are enough diverse of viewpoints in play to allow each person their own demonstration for their own personal cause. Nonetheless, their goals are to try and keep the herd on track with the major chant LIVE FREE OR DIE!

The schedule for the next day is to bring the protestors into Loogootee by noon and begin a planned demonstration concentrating on the Sheriff's Department. There are enough tie-dyed, bearded, long-haired hippie freaks to last Martin County a lifetime. The female demonstrators are no better. Many of them are dressed in cast off military clothing representing nearly every war our country has fought in.

Sheriff Snowdon is determined to keep this a local issue and not to be interfered with by state police or the governor. In an effort to become proactive, he has lined up his entire department around the perimeter along with his own special sheriff's car.

"When these little pecker-heads see this line of law enforcement it'll serve as enuff of ah deterrent ta cause them pee squatters ta run like baby girls," says Snowdon, biting on the stub of a cigar. His deputies are prepared with nightsticks and teargas. It's evident they are nervous about this strange development. Many of them aren't much older than the demonstrators. Even so, they have the law on their side and are determined to hold their positions.

The throng begins to move forward with Phillip and Manny positioned in the very front. The deputies are resolute and hold their ground until suddenly a rock crashes on the sheriff's windshield. All chaos suddenly breaks out. The deputies begin to indiscriminately swing their nightsticks.

Blood has been spilled. Several of the protestors have bloody gashes on their heads. The protestors are moving forward causing the deputies to retreat. Now they are swinging their sticks more as protection for themselves rather than as a deterrent against rioting.

The sheriff's car is surrounded by at least a couple hundred protestors shouting, "DEATH TO THE PIGS!" Those surrounding the car begin to rock it while others stomp on the roof. It's all the sheriff can do to protect himself from serious injury while helplessly bouncing from floor to ceiling.

Deputies attempt to arrest a few of the least active of the group until some of the more aggressive protestors pull them free. It becomes a full blown riot in minutes. Suddenly the tide is turning and the protestors are becoming the government, holding the sheriff a prisoner in his own upturned car.

For the rest of the afternoon, different groups within the throng use the overturned car's underside as a stage to tell everyone what is going down with the war, civil rights, the feminist movement and anything else that is anti-establishment. Meanwhile, the mayor is trying to get through to the governor's office. There are people having picnics on the department lawn. Others are playing guitars, dancing or sitting in the lotus position chanting "Oomm, Oommm." The deputies have retreated and are watching through locked doors and windows from inside the sheriff's office, leaderless and helpless to rectify the situation.

Phillip suddenly sees things through new eyes. He is becoming conscious of the power they're able to muster against these old institutions. It's certainly emboldening him. He's duly impressed with how favorably events are unfolding. A whole new culture is bursting forth in Martin County.

As Phillip recalls how he himself had cowered at the sheriff's hands only a few days earlier, it is very satisfying to watch that same sheriff cowering now. According to Phillip's wristwatch, the poor wretch has been trapped in his overturned vehicle for nearly six hours. At this moment, Phillip suddenly has a delightful thought, *"I hope he's pissin' his pants."*

Like all things, time mixed with action changes the dynamics. By early evening the mayor has successfully reached the governor and the state police have taken charge. With a sea of big men wearing broad brimmed hats and black and blue uniforms, they have successfully freed Sheriff Snowdon. He is definitely the worse for wear. The police force seems to be more inclined to keep order than attempt to break up the party. People are publicly smoking reefers, drinking, and openly urinating on every lawn in Loogootee, all with no penalties.

Despite their inability to sustain the advantage they had earlier, Phillip and the other protestors are reveling in the mayhem they have created. By sheer numbers, they temporarily became the biggest political force in the state. For a brief period, the sheriff along with other authorities got the message. But outside of Martin County, the courts, the police, and the politicians still hold all the cards. They are much more organized. They hold a sustainable amount of force at their disposal, and when it's challenged, they are prepared to meet the resistance with superior force.

At least for the time being, the commune is out of danger. Within a day, the great exodus has begun once again. All that remains are a dozen or so broken down vehicles abandoned throughout the county and a lot of garbage. As a show of community consciousness, Phillip has volunteered the entire commune to clean up the leftover debris in Loogootee.

Sheriff Snowdon is keeping a low profile. He's caught in a crossfire—on one side for not doing enough to prevent the havoc and on the other for being so arrogant as to create the situation in the first place. All in all, it's hoped he is rethinking his position on Die Landarbeiter.

CHAPTER 17

Things are beginning to take on a calmer flavor at Die Landarbeiter.

Phillip and Manny avoid most of the manual labor portion of communal life. They are more inclined to busy themselves with scrutinizing political activity around the country. They consider giving weekly updates sufficient for their contribution—along with acting as treasurers for the commune's monies. Since they don't spend much, their surplus should get them through the winter. By all establishment standards, they are well below the poverty level. Nevertheless, in spite of being poor, they believe themselves to be much freer than their mortgage enslaved parents.

All in all, things are going relatively smoothly for a commune as unaccustomed to the rigors of survival as this conglomeration. Most of this crew is upper middle-class young people who by and large have glamorized "getting right with the earth" as something that happens with no effort. However, in spite of the clumsiness with which some of these hardships are met, each day is considered a soul-building experience. Even a dumb fox will get a chicken once in a while, so with the tenacity of dumb foxes, they still manage to get things done.

By using the profit from the rock concert frugally, along with an occasional stipend sent by a concerned parent, Manny is able to make these small amounts of money carry through the basic needs of the commune. On so many different levels, he is proving to be a talented manager.

After his Bar-Mitzvah, he started working in his father's jewelry store. Manny learned quickly what business is all about. He and his father worked well together for a number of years. The clash between father and son didn't come about until after Manny went off to college and began to come home with left wing socialist ideas. Irving Meitzner had his fill of leftist European politics in Poland and readily welcomed the freedom he found in America. To have his son espousing a near communist rhetoric was a setback to the old man causing a near mortal blow to their relationship. After his estrangement from his father, Manny finds the rejection too difficult to deal with and very seldom goes home.

Manny thrives on supporting a leader that can adequately portray his ideas. He has very seldom stood alone and fought for anything. He's proving to be the perfect chief of staff for a determined leader whom he can vicariously live through.

Phillip's yearnings for a larger personal political presence have caused him to be in covert contact with Abbie Hoffman and Jerry Rubin. Without informing Manny, he's planning on pulling this game plan out the following spring. Manny is an invaluable asset to Phillip's ambitions, but until Phillip is sure he can be brought into Abbie and Jerry's inner circle, he's keeping his aspirations close to the vest.

Considering the people in Die Landarbeiter weren't born and raised to it, they are adjusting surprisingly well to the communal way of life. It is difficult to even imagine that after living a spoiled middle-class American life of modern conveniences one would cheerfully bask in using an outdoor commode, or a common hand-pumped water supply, or bathing in the small pond. All this is certainly more than any of their parents would have considered them capable of handling.

Turning their backs on the material facets of modern life is only half the battle. One is expected to meet the material needs of the commune before one considers their own concerns. This proves to be easier when the warm euphoria toward sharing and belonging are induced by alcohol or drugs, but these altruistic actions fall short as the chemistry wears off.

Of course this is only the material portion of communal life. The more rigorous part is to give up the self and embrace a non-violent Gandhi kind of life. In each of these blended facets of life, the individual egos are finding living and sharing with one another is an ongoing challenge.

The personal struggles these individuals are undergoing shape the religious needs making up this community's mixture of beliefs. Most attempt to discount the pervasive faith taught in American Judeo-Christian circles in favor of a Buddhist, Zen, or Hindu religion buried in Asian mysticism. None of the members of Die Landarbeiter have gone much deeper into any of these Eastern religions than to wear the clothing, do some meditation, eat mainly vegetables, and practice a bit of yoga. If the intent is to merely separate oneself from mainstream America, this will indeed do it.

Audra is not only the health care provider, but she has also assumed the role of spiritual adviser. She holds weekly rap sessions where participants can express their spiritual insights—often under the influence of LSD, mescaline, pot, or mushrooms.

"Our spirituality is nourished by our coming together to share our memories and hopes. A sense of community will arise from sharing common visions and common goals," she reveals.

As much as this statement rings true, what is often brought to the table are bits and pieces of disconnected thoughts from an assortment of religions. Because much of what is expressed is never understood, the perception is it must be too deep to comprehend. Manifestations like "Wow man, that's really deep" are echoed around the room by drugged minds.

Even so, the commune manages to struggle on. Now and then a few leave in search of other experiences, only to be replaced by new seekers.

The focus of most of this generation seems to be a search for meaning. Earnest Hemingway referred to the generation raised through WWI as the "Lost Generation." This depiction could just as easily apply to this new generation of wandering souls.

CHAPTER 18

The summer of '67 has left only its memory in the minds of those who lived through it. Fall is also well on its way to making itself into a past tense. Deidre's is the only pregnancy in the commune.

"You're progressing quite satisfactorily," assures Audra, as she examines her.

"Good! I'm really beginning to feel a lot of movement," says a nearly gleeful Deidre.

Coming face to face with a much more confident, aspiring mother, no one can miss the surprise in Audra's expression. She has been watching for any changes in Deidre's attitude toward the fate of this unborn child. Earlier Deidre wanted to abort the baby, but after the kidnapping she seemed more settled somehow. Audra's secret desire is for Deidre to go full term and then give the baby to her to raise. She is still seeking some kind of redemptive act that will remove the stain on her conscience after aborting her own child. *"Could this possibly be the cathartic I'm hoping for?"* is her innermost thought. Instead she is confronted with this turnabout in Deidre's attitude.

It is time to stop wondering and discuss it. Trying her best to cover her disappointment, Audra takes a moment to assume a more fitting demeanor.

"It sounds like you've had a turn around. What, may I ask, brought this about? Was it something I said?"

Deidre considers the questions for a second. "No, I don't think it was anything we discussed. I believe I've come to the conclusion that for the present this child is all I have that's mine and I don't want to lose that certainty. The thought gives me peace."

Audra is taken back by this change of heart and tries to hide her disappointment. Her surprise over Deidre's plans to go full term leads her to probe further. "So are you saying you're going to keep the baby?" she further investigates.

"That's my plan," says a still upbeat Deidre. Smiling, she then adds, "I think the commune will be the perfect place to raise a child."

Audra is left speechless. Clearing her throat, she manages to add, "If there's anything I can do to help you, let me know, okay?" With that, they part for the time being.

No sooner has Deidre left, than Phillip makes an appearance. It seems he has been quietly shadowing Deidre's ongoing pregnancy. At this point, he feels compelled to inquire of Audra what Deidre's status is. Audra is not aware of the romantic interest Phillip may have toward Deidre. She asks, "What is it you're concerned with?"

"After all she's been through, it's just a general concern for her well-being I guess," he replies.

"She's cool, she's doing good," states Audra in an assuring voice.

Still hanging in the room with a bewildered gaze, something prompts him to ask one more question, "Has she ever revealed who knocked her up?"

Finding this question to border between nosiness and genuine concern, Audra measures her answer. "No she hasn't." Letting her answer float in the room for a moment, she adds, "Why do you find *that* important?"

"Oh no particular reason, just curious," he responds. Willing to take his chances with yet another question, he continues "Is she planning on adopting the kid out?"

The look Audra gives him without an answer is enough for him to sense he may be treading on a private issue. He says his good-bye and leaves.

Back at his headquarters in the bus, he's quizzed by Manny. "I noticed you leaving Audra's. Are ya feelin' okay?"

"Oh no, it's not me, I was checkin' on Deidre," chuckles Phillip.

Manny knows Phillip better than anyone at Die Landarbeiter. Phillip's chuckle is a nervous chuckle that he only uses when he is undergoing some emotional trauma.

"So you still carryin' a torch for Deidre?" questions Manny with a little knowing smirk.

"Naw, I don't think I want to be takin' care of some squallin' kid right now. I think she should have gotten an abortion and got on with life," says Phillip in a sarcastic tone.

This attitude is in nearly direct opposition to their mission statement of Love, Peace, and Tolerance. Manny knows Phillip well enough to understand Phillip's different faces. Integrity is not always at the top of the list. When love, peace, and tolerance fit his ambitions, he quickly embraces all of it. When it doesn't, he can become quite cynical. Phillip is the type of leader who believes very strongly in whatever advances his own well-being. Persons displaying this form of dishonesty rarely see themselves as anything other than truthful.

Because Phillip is inherently blind to his own flaws, he is quick to point out those of others. His tendency is to get on his soapbox and explain how the world needs to be. It's not his inclination to give others a lot of room for opinions that don't conform to his. This attitude has served him well thus far because the folks at Die Landarbeiter are laid back enough not to want the responsibilities of handling the commune's affairs and are content to give him a free hand.

Phillip decides he has spent too much time on this Deidre crap and changes the tenor of the conversation.

"Manny I've been waiting for the right moment to discuss something with you."

Manny's attention also changes to a look of curiosity. "Well, I'm here and I'm all ears."

"I've been in contact with the New York people about getting with them this spring in an all-out effort to end this stupid Vietnam bullshit war. They're plannin' somthin' big and I think we should be part of it," says Phillip with an enthusiasm Manny hasn't seen since they raided Wall Street. This is just the kind of stuff that continues to feed their youthful appetite for hullabaloo.

Manny looks to Phillip to come up with the daring ideas, which of course then Manny expects to play a major role in getting them to work.

"Out of sight, Dude. I think that'll be the grooviest thing we've taken on yet," responds Manny with an equal amount of exuberance.

CHAPTER 19

The winters in southern Indiana are not nearly as brutal as Michigan. They start later and by the grace of God, they end sooner. It's well into December. So far the amount of snow and cold weather has been mildly tolerable. For the most part, the day to day chores are being tended to. Albert is satisfied with the work the commune has helped him with and the bishops have turned a blind eye toward his involvement with the English—at least for the time being.

Breezy has taken on the task of butchering one of the pigs. It's a good sized hog—somewhere around 250 pounds. For most of the commune, this is a graphic introduction to where their ham sandwiches come from.

Phillip and Manny are seldom seen around the farm. They seem to be spending much of their time sending telegrams or using Albert's phone booth to call New York. Not everyone is on the same page as Phillip and Manny. By involving themselves with east coast political programs sponsored by Abbie, they have become much more political.

"Capitalism is going to destroy our country," preaches Phillip at the open rap meeting on a blustery Saturday in December. The common area of the barn is scattered with picnic tables filled with commune members. They have come to rap about anything that may be on their minds. Fifty gallon barrels redesigned as wood stoves are radiating enough heat to make everyone comfortable.

Phillip continues to dominate much of the discussion with his declamation against the police. On the other hand when the subject of the Vietnam War comes up, he can be just as verbal.

"It's the bloodthirsty military industrial complex that corrupt politicians continue to propagate, *that's* what we need to destroy," he continues to harangue.

"They're the bastards that keep the war goin'."

"Hey man, I've dropped outta all that bullshit. I don't give a damn what they do, I'm just gonna stay stoned," says another.

"I think the whole system is tied so tight together that it'll take a flaming, bloody revolution to bust it up," says Quinton.

"I think we can work things out peacefully," says Zan.

"That's pie in the sky sister. Violence has always been the American way," says Quinton taking another hit on a fat joint making its way around the room.

Phillip has added a new drug to his repertoire—moonshine whiskey. It is often reflected in a much more belligerent attitude. Even he admits in a rather cavalier way he often can't tell if he's drunk or high. At the moment, he seems to be saturated with the more aggressive effects of moonshine.

"Come '68, one way or the other, we're gonna get things happening!!" says Phillip raising an exuberant fist in the air. Most of the commune is tolerant of Phillip's frequent non-directional rants toward the establishment. Zan along with a few others listen with a critical ear in the hopes of giving Phillip's grandiosity some substance.

"We're gonna make damn sure we get out of this war, and then we're going to get a man in the White House that will make sure everybody is provided with enough food, a place to live, education, medical care, heat, electricity, all this as a matter of course," says Zan.

Out of the entire commune, Zan remains the biggest peacenik. She often wears her emotions on her sleeve.

"If we don't bring the stupid world together, what's the sense in going on? Who wants to merely exist? It's gotta be love and peace," she continues.

"Because of this damnable war, there are going to be a lot of people whose dreams are never going to come true," adds Manny. "What happens if we're among them? That's why we need to fight."

Breezy is sitting pensively and quiet. At last he decides to add something. "I recall last summer, we made the decision to drop out of all the hullabaloo and find a place where we could live and find our own peace away from the world. Now you're talking about starting a revolution." Without recognizing it, his Amish roots are showing.

Zan is sitting next to Breezy. She pulls herself closer. She too has found solace and a renewed meaning to life at Die Landarbeiter. The idea of disrupting the peace they've come to enjoy and leave the farm to create some distant agitation doesn't appeal to either of them.

Phillip on the other hand continues his grandiloquence against the establishment with the zeal of a TV evangelist. "The scams of the military-industrial complex will continue until we the people pull them down. It's in our hands. If we want success, we have to wage a revolution against their greed."

The commune is beginning to undergo an internal change. It's taking on the flavor of the tower of Babel. There are those voices who are finding this lifestyle of communal sharing regenerating. Then there are those in Phillip's and Manny's camp who are restless with this kind of peace.

"I don't find this to be peace," says Manny in his most philosophical voice. "I find this to be stagnation! Real peace is a sense of well-being in the middle of a shit storm!"

Deidre and Shelly are more listeners than participants at this juncture. Without a real existential awareness of the changes that are looming on her horizon, Deidre is willing to sit and contemplate how much her life is about to change and how it's going to affect her decisions. Playing with the bulging elastic band on the peasant type skirt she's wearing, her thoughts are more pointedly on what's going on beneath it.

"You're going to have to count me out, Phillip. I can't be haulin' a kid around while we're wagin' havoc," states Deidre patting her pregnant belly in defiance.

Before Phillip's brain can stop his tongue, he blurts out, "You coulda got rid of that kid a long time ago."

As soon as he says these blazing words, he knows whatever chance he may have imagined he had with Deidre has come to a screeching halt.

Looking him square in the eyes, her lips become pinched as she takes on an angry squint with a middle finger in his face. He blinks a couple of times expecting next to feel her fist in his mouth. Instead, she turns on her heels and heads back to her apartment. Shelly, observing what has just taken place, runs after her. She knows her friend well enough to know the tears are going to come. As the door to their lodging closes behind them, the water begins to flow. Shelly has been through these kind of downturns with Deidre many times. She has always been there when situations in her life have been the darkest. Shelly possesses an ability to see a situation and analyze it, where all Deidre sees is darkness and doubt.

"Don't give Phillip so much of yourself to trifle with. You and I both know he looks at you as damaged goods because of your pregnancy. Don't give him the satisfaction," says Shelly trying to pick words that have the right balance to dismiss Phillip.

"You don't know how much I loathe his attitude toward me," says Deidre through her tears.

"I don't believe there is anyone in this commune that has a better idea what you're going through than me," she says handing Deidre a towel. "After all, I know you better than anyone else."

Deidre manages to dry her tears and blow her nose several times. At last she is composed enough to express a heartfelt thankfulness for her lifelong friend. "You can't believe how much you've helped me these past several months. I honestly don't know what I would do without you," confesses Deidre in a much more solemn tone.

"You don't have to try and explain. Unlike blood family members, you and I have chosen one another as sisters. I know you would not hesitate to do the same for me," acknowledges Shelly.

Deidre has calmed enough by this time to take on a much more earnest demeanor. "Shelly, you know I love you and trust you with my deepest secrets."

Hesitating for a moment, indicating what she plans to say next is something she considers profound, she continues, "If anything should happen to me after this baby is born would you consider taking it as your own?"

Taking Deidre's hand and with tears forming in her own eyes, she submits, "What would ever make you think you had to ask? Of course I will." With tears streaming from them both, they hug one another as a seal of this new and special bond.

CHAPTER 20

Phillip and Manny spend much of their time catching up on the history behind protesting the Vietnam War. After all, they were still high school students at the time of the Gulf of Tonkin incident. Nearly the entire nation was behind the decision LBJ and Congress made to teach Ho Chi Minh a lesson and prevent the Domino Effect from occurring in the event we ignored this growing Asian crisis. (The theory postulated that if one nation in Southeast Asia fell to communist aggression, the others would follow.) It wasn't until the draft increased from 3,000 a month to 33,000 a month that it got the attention of America's youth.

Phillip and Manny, along with all the other male commune members, had long ago burned their draft cards as an open protest to the LBJ administration. The nationalism the previous generation felt resulted from winning WWII. It's more than waning in their offspring—it's nonexistent.

Voices in the news media, more often than not, are causing confusion by not supporting the war effort as they had in WWII. People are much more befuddled, while politicians dodge straightforward questions about why we are involving our youth in a war we refuse to win.

Critics of the so called "draft dodgers" claim that these young people lack a sense of courage. They, on the other hand, maintain they will refuse to give their lives for the advancement of some ambiguous political agenda.

"This is what really bothers me about this war. Sometimes I feel like one of the bad guys. After all, WWII was clear cut—the Nazis on one side, us on the other," says a returning Vietnam soldier.

Many Americans reflect a sense of pride in what is being done to free the Vietnamese people from the threat of an unwanted communist aggression. America's sense of responsibility calls for it to take the side of the vulnerable underdog, especially when being menaced by a despotic bully. There is an overwhelming sense this is a justifiable war leading to a confidence of right actions. To think otherwise seems unpatriotic as well as unreasonable. The result is a definite lulling effect on the American psyche.

The youth maintain they see through the idea that South Vietnam is a brave little democracy. Their misgivings are bolstered by reports there is a 15% desertion rate by South Vietnamese soldiers and that 50% of American foreign aid money ends up in the hands of black marketers. This kind of information (usually withheld by government forces and only clandestinely leaked to the news media) and other leaks made to the press, all aid in reinforcing the counterculture position.

Phillip can quite easily see himself aligned with the latest movement, providing he has a chance to rise to a leadership position. He half-jokingly has stated, "I'd be willing to be drafted, if I could go in as a general."

Eugene McCarthy, the senator from Minnesota is openly rallying college students behind his anti-war bid for the presidency. His agenda has caught the attention of Phillip. This is the quality of protest Phillip imagines he can glean the most attention with.

It's remarkable how quickly Phillip can switch gears. He believes he's succeeded in bringing the commune's energy levels to the point needed to accomplish his objectives. Now he feels confident enough in his leadership skills to move beyond the Die Landarbeiter. Phillip definitely feels he is headed toward his ideal destiny of leadership and power. *"If I stay here, I know I'll never make it big,"* he fears.

"Manny, I believe we've about run the course here. Doors aren't gonna open for us as long as we hang out in a commune. Wadda ya say we pack up and make ourselves available ta this senator guy, McCarthy? I'll bet we can gain some valuable experience with these guys," says Phillip.

It's been obvious to everyone, Phillip is restless and ready to move on. This apple didn't fall far from the tree. Phillip's father possesses the same penchant for leadership but in the world of corporate business. There is no doubt he is his father's son.

Manny is always ready to follow Phillip's lead. "Right on, Dude! When?"

There is a deep sense of companionship that neither of them ever imagined they would share. Barely looking out of the corner of their eyes for the other's reaction, they nevertheless know they're on the same page.

"As soon as we can unwind ourselves from this place," says Phillip in a somewhat condescending tone.

The conversation soon makes its way back to the Minnesota candidate.

"Everything I hear about this guy is good. There is a guy named Sheldon Green that's running his campaign, he insists anyone coming on board has to cut their beard and hair and wear a suit," adds Phillip.

This last statement stops Manny in mid-everything. "Who in the hell is this guy 'Green'?" he questions.

"I don't know who he is, but evidently he runs all of McCarthy's campaign stuff. It makes me wonder what the hell we'll look like in a suit and tie," laughs Phillip.

Phillip knows he's leaving the commune in good hands. Zan and Breezy are the *go to* people for most of the farm questions and Quinton is the repair guy. Audra has the answers for most of the day to day health issues. Adding to this, their crop plan included making sure they grew enough pot to last through the off season. The harvest turned out to be a bumper crop. The addition of a moonshine still further insures the commune can stay stoned nearly indefinitely.

Over the next week, Phillip and Manny concentrate on getting the bus in good running order. After all, it will probably be their home through the winter somewhere in America.

The fall rains are pelting the area pretty good. Phillip and Manny have gone into town to have some tune up work done on the bus. They are making their way back through a greasy mud-slicked country road when the headlights hit on what appears to be a road block. It's a fallen tree stretching across the entire road. Quickly applying the brakes, Phillip puts the bus into a skid as he stops.

Manny is the first to realize what this road block is all about as several hooded men surround the front of the bus. They're dressed as Klansmen. One of them is wielding a tire iron. He makes his way to the bus door. CRACK! It's the sound of breaking glass. The bus door window has been broken. Several gloved hands pry the compromised door open. Phillip and Manny are jerked out, thrown to the ground, and handcuffed. While being restrained, they feel the sensation of cold steel. They suddenly realize their clothing is being cut off with buck knives.

In yet another maneuver, they feel a burning sensation and a stench of creosote. Before they can develop a clear thought, they find they're completely at the mercy of these marauders. In less than five brutalizing minutes, they find themselves covered from head to toe in hot tar and chicken feathers. In spite of their painful screams, the assailants wordlessly continue their heartless ministrations.

Without comment, they're both set on a rail and bounced until the pain in their balls forces them to let go, whereupon they instantly find themselves plummeting to the ground. Their energy begins to give out as they are dragged to their feet and placed back on the rail, only to have the whole process begin all over again.

In all of the mayhem, Phillip notices a brown pant leg exposed beneath one man's Klan robe. There is a black and gold stripe running down the side. Despite the extreme discomfort he's being subjected to, his brain tells him these men include a man he is well-acquainted with. His suspicion is confirmed by the smell of chewed cigar breath through the mouth opening only inches from his face and a voice that has been indelibly fixed in his psyche.

"You pecker-heads is slow learners and fast forgetters," says the unmistakable voice of Sheriff Snowdon. "Now maybe y'all will pay a little closer attention to what I'm tellin' ya. GET YER HIPPIE ASSES OUTTA MY COUNTY!"

With that, the attackers gather themselves into several vehicles and leave their victims to their doom.

A cold rain continues falling causing the chicken feathers to smell as only wet chicken feathers can and also causing the tar to harden into dense clumps on already raw, blistered skin. There isn't a soul in sight who can say they witnessed this. Nor is there anyone to come to their aid. They are pitifully left to survive as best they can.

Manny is the first to crawl to his feet. The bus is still running and the headlights illuminate Phillip lying in the mud, nearly unconscious.

"Get up man!" shouts Manny trying as best he can to bring Phillip to his feet. It's obvious they are both in great distress. "We've got to get the hell outta here before those madmen return for another round," continues Manny.

Phillip responds slowly. Finally on his feet, they look at one another in disbelief. With only a primordial urge to survive, they make their way back to the bus. It's the only refuge they have in this wilderness. Fumbling with tar-covered hands, Phillip manages to grind the bus into gear. The rear wheels of the bus spin, sliding the monster from one side of the road to the other as they make their way around the fallen tree. The wheels finally catch in a solid spot of stone and gravel, causing the bus to lurch forward and nearly throwing the hapless passengers from their seats.

Struggling with the last bit of their physical strength and youthful determination, they finally arrive back at Dic Landarbeiter.

Albert is at the driveway entrance working on a piece of farm equipment as Phillip brings the bus to a halt. Albert looks up and freezes as two tarred and feathered aliens stumble out of the bus and fall at his feet.

Still not able to discern what exactly is before him, he continues to stare while his hand still holds a wrench that has suddenly forgotten its purpose.

"Albert, ya gotta help us," says Manny, trying to get to his feet.

Albert's sight and brain finally snap back. Dropping the wrench, he grabs hold of Manny and pulls him to his feet and then does the same for Phillip. Albert knows immediately what this is and who is responsible.

"You guys met the Martin County Ku-Klux-Klan!"

"Ya, and I think we got on their bad side," Phillip says in a barely audible voice.

Quickly assessing the situation, Albert leads them to the machine shop. After grabbing some large rags and a can of turpentine, he soaks a rag in the solution and begins to wipe first one, then the other.

"We gotta get this shit off you as quick as we can," he says with the voice of one on a mission.

Reinvigorated by Albert's helping hands, they both begin to help scrub off the muck.

This episode has produced an emptiness in both Phillip and Manny. Never in their collective life experiences have they felt such defeat. It's a lonely sense of powerlessness.

The garage door keeps opening as word has gotten around.

"Whoa! What the hell? What the hell happened to you guys?" is the usual reaction to each person's first glance.

With streaks of black tar coloring his naked body, Phillip tries to make light of his humiliation.

"Sheriff Snowdon lost his sense of humor," says Phillip with a forced smile.

"Wadda ya think we outta do about it?" asks Quinton. From the look on his face, he's ready for war.

Manny is next to speak, "We need to think this through and decide if this is a battle we can win."

"Manny's right, Quinton. We have to choose our battles. We need to live to fight another day," says Phillip in a tone of earnest reservation.

Their whole demeanor turns back to sullen as they continue their scrubbing vigil.

Just as it is in all communities a diversity of thought begins to separate its people into factions. In the present case at Die Landarbeiter, most are content to be close to the land. Others like Phillip and Manny are much more politically motivated with issues surrounding the war and less concerned with environmental involvements.

Phillip and Manny said their good-byes several weeks ago. The last news was they had allied themselves with the Eugene McCarthy people in his bid for the presidency. That wasn't much of a surprise as everyone in the commune has come to learn of their political ambitions.

CHAPTER 21

Phillip couldn't be happier. He and Manny have accomplished what they set out to do. Both are part of the McCarthy bid for the presidency. Phillip is making the transition from a radical hippie, whose goal is to turn everyone on that can be turned on and turn off everyone else, to being a reasonable voice of protest. Their leftist politics and the McCarthy politics fit like a glove. The young people are on fire realizing a candidate as important as Eugene McCarthy is taking a serious stand against the war. They have shed their beards in favor of sideburns and mustaches, both well-trimmed. A suit and tie have replaced the bell-bottomed jeans and tie-dyed shirts. The idea is to give the public at large the impression of a more legitimate movement and not some crazy minority. The top people have strongly indicated the anti-war hippie movement is not helping their cause.

The slogan "Be clean for Gene" is catching on with hundreds of young volunteers.

Sheldon Green is coordinator for the door to door campaigning. This gives him a perfect opportunity to inform the American public in a face to face discourse.

"Hi. My name is Sheldon Green. I'd like to get your opinion on the war in Vietnam, and tell you about Eugene McCarthy." He does this with the zeal of a Jehovah's Witness.

"Are you aware this war is costing us, the taxpayers, an arm and a leg in more ways than we can imagine? We're more often taking higher casualties than the people we supposedly are there to free," asserts Sheldon in a well-crafted set of talking points all designed to raise the public's ire against the Johnson administration.

Phillip and Manny catch on to this technique fairly quickly. They have found they need to set aside the more radical front of Abbie Hoffman and Jerry Rubin that alienates many people in favor of creating a dialogue of understanding with America at large.

"Unlike our allies in the counterculture, we want a revolution of minds brought about by persuasion rather than body bags full of our opposition," states Sheldon at a training seminar.

"On the other hand, it's important we don't alienate the hardcore protesters. They can get a thousand freaks out in a day to do the dirty work on the streets. The problem is they can't be controlled. So we have to be careful on what points we collaborate and where we have to stay on the sidelines," further states Sheldon.

It's becoming increasingly obvious to Phillip and Manny they are going to have to figure a way of financing this escapade. The safety net the commune provided is no longer a viable option. The small amount of cash they had in their pockets when they hit the road is being eaten by fuel costs to keep their home away from home on the move. Nonetheless, the bus provides a place to get out of the weather and have some sense of security. The local campaign committees are willing to pay partial fuel costs and offer sack lunches, but only for campaign related work.

The obvious next step for them is to contact their families for additional support. Phillip is the first to do this. His father is a no nonsense top Chrysler executive. Phillip hasn't talked to his father since he called for money to get out of New York. Reaching his father's office, a familiar voice answers, "Mr. Hampton's office, Mildred speaking. How may I assist you?"

"Mildred this is Phillip Jr..."

Mildred has been instructed not to transfer a call from Phillip Jr. until she clears it with his father first.

"Well how are you Phillip? We haven't heard from you in months."

"I'm doing fine," he says, more than a little anxious to get past any unnecessary salutations. "Is my father in?"

"He's in the building, but I'm not sure where. Let me put you on hold and I'll try and locate him." Her next step is to gently knock on Mr. Hampton's closed office door.

"Come in Mildred. What is it?" says the elder Hampton, busy at his desk and peering over the top of his glasses.

"I have Junior on the phone asking for you. Do you want to take the call?"

Taking a moment to digest this disruptive announcement, the senior Hampton motions for Mildred to leave and picks up the phone.

"Hello Phillip. How are you doing? We haven't heard from you in some time."

"I'm doing fine, Dad. How are you and Mother?"

"We're fine. Say I'm glad you called. I haven't received a bill for your fall tuition. Are you not enrolled?"

This is the very conversation Phillip had been hoping to circumvent, now it's coming at him full force.

"Yeah, I know, Dad. Some other things have come up." Knowing his father's conservative political views and the fact he had served in WWII as a major is quickly overshadowing the importance Phillip has placed on this whole anti-war movement.

"What the hell could come up that's more important than you getting your education?" the old man is quick to ask.

Trying to measure his words, they begin to sound very shallow when measured against his father's world of getting things accomplished.

"I've taken a year off to work for the Eugene McCarthy campaign," expresses Phillip in his most official voice. There is no immediate reply from his father. It's dead silent for what seems like time out of mind. Without warning there is a sudden explosion on the other end of the phone.

"Did I hear you say you're campaigning for that left wing communist, nut case McCarthy?" screams his father from somewhere down deep in the bowels of Phillip's phone. It's enough to cause Phillip to react. Jerking the phone from his ear, he attempts to compose himself. Before he can make his mind and mouth work together, his father beats him to the draw once again.

"That gawdam commie would sell this country out in a heartbeat. Chrysler finally got a contract to supply troop trucks and that pecker-head tried to block a vote to budget the project."

Phillip knows better than to try and interject anything that will oppose his father's political perspective. Instead he hopes his father will believe his silence means he's being swayed.

It's another fifteen minutes of listening before Phillip is asked what's on his mind. Phillip Senior knows exactly what is on his son's mind without the annoyance of asking. The only time Junior is in touch is when he needs money.

"I hate to ask you, Dad, but I'm living on a shoestring. I'm wondering if you could advance me a couple thousand out of my trust to help me out."

"You know damn well that trust is set up to support you while you're in college. Now you're asking to draw money out to campaign for this gawdam commie, pinko, who would gut the military right out of this country."

"Well, it's not like this experience isn't educational in a lot of ways. I never could have learned as much about our political system sitting in a classroom," says Phillip hoping this conversation will end quickly. He understands his father's temperament well enough to realize the longer the conversation extends, the deeper he may get pulled into having to debate him. This exercise never ends well for Phillip.

"If the bullshit this McCarthy guy is throwing out were concrete, there'd be enough to circle the world," says the senior Hampton with the confidence of a man who understands his world.

Phillip can feel the palms of his hands beginning to sweat. This always happens when his father challenges the ill thought-out parts of what his father describes as his "disconnected" political opinions.

Phillip has seldom had difficulty connecting with his peers because they rarely ask for more than one line talking points. His father, on the other hand, always challenges his son to a depth he's not willing to go. Phillip falls back on his listening response not born out of genuine interest, but rather out of an unwillingness to be buried over his head. As long as he sprinkles the conversation with..."You're probably right Dad," or..."I'll be sure and check that out" or..."That sounds reasonable," he knows his father will believe he's made headway and get off his case. Phillip much prefers the excitement the counterculture offers rather than some staid old guy making his decisions. But his patience eventually pays off as his father detects what he mistakenly perceives as humility in his son. The senior Hampton is of the opinion this trait promotes teachability. With a sufficient amount of obsequious behavior, Phillip manages to convince his father to wire the two thousand dollars.

Manny has had similar success. He's convinced his father that Eugene McCarthy is a righteous man to Jews and supports a righteous cause. He hasn't convinced him two thousand dollars' worth, but has managed to get half.

With a pocket full of cash, "It's time we find some new digs," says Phillip.

"Yer definitely on to something. This bus sure as hell ain't cutting it anymore. I'm beginnin' ta feel like I was born and raised in this damn thing," replies Manny. Minneapolis's snowy streets give a sense of urgency to their quest for off street living. By afternoon, they are able to find a furnished pad in a downtown section near the McCarthy headquarters.

It's not much, but it's warm and it's above a deli. The aroma of fresh baked bread wafts through the natural ventilation gaps in the hundred year old building. It's enough reason to spend the rest of the day slurping hot coffee and eating fresh bagels. Besides there is a hot babe behind the counter that Phillip has taken a liking to.

Her name tag reveals her name is Katt. He finds himself imagining how easily he could fall in love with this girl. In the midst of their flirtations, she tells them about a party around the corner in an old warehouse loft where she shares an apartment with two other girls.

By 7:00 that evening, the snow is blowing so hard outside that it is difficult to tell how much is new and how much is carried by the wind. Either way it's become too boring for these harum-scarum pilgrims of action. With the address supplied by their new friend, Katt, they battle their way through drifts of packed snow entertaining visions of making it with some of these McCarthy chicks. In Phillip's case, he is envisioning a liaison with Katt. She has a wild Nordic look that has always enchanted him.

The party is huge. People are pouring through the storm from every bar in town. There is a live band echoing the sounds of the age. Competing with it is a din of voices coming from every corner of the huge open warehouse/apartment. There are faces from all over, almost everything life has to offer has found a place in this timeworn old building. It could easily be mistaken for a used furniture store. There are old couches, chairs, tables, beds of every age and description spread around like a cockeyed art project gone awry. Albeit, the cultural integration of these furnishings is perfect, each is being used for its distinct design.

A dude named Woody something or other seems to be the host. He's decked out in army fatigues that are beginning to take on a battle worn appearance. His long hair is pulled back in a ponytail. His eyes contain a wild untamed something—maybe it's a non-compliant flash as he looks about through a beard as wild and defiant as that "something" reflected in his eyes. The story is he's an army deserter who had survived a tour in Vietnam. When he discovered he was going to be sent back again, he decided to go AWOL.

It's difficult to discern whether he has a healthy defiance against an unpopular war or if it's just his nature to be a rebel. Either way, he is an accomplished entrepreneur. He has at least a hundred people packed into his digs and has enough drugs for sale to keep this party rolling 'til the sun comes up.

Phillip and Manny are welcomed and immediately made aware of the LSD, reefer, heroin, and cocaine available. It only takes a moment for them to decide on a couple hits of acid and a handful of pre-rolled reefers. There is an atmosphere of released stress throughout the room. It's about a frantic desire to escape the everyday vicissitudes life is throwing their way.

Looking about the huge room, one would gather an orgy was taking place. Some people are openly copulating on the beds barely made discrete by flimsy room dividers. Others are in various stages of undress. Others are content to release a manic behavior not acceptable in the straight world, with flailing arms and legs dancing to a tune only they may hear. There is no impending warring voice warning of the consequences of any display of behaviors. The overall concern is only for the moment. If it feels good, do it.

Phillip suddenly spots Katt. His heartbeats are running into each other as he makes his way toward her corner of the room. She is with a group discussing the war. Phillip arrives in time to include himself in a joint being passed. Spotting Phillip, Katt lends a bit of an appreciative grin to see him show up. She's loose enough to include a warm hug. The drugs and the unrestrained atmosphere have loosened her inhibitions. He is as ready to receive as she is to give. Leading her off to a couch where they can be alone, she is all over him. Whatever contained emotions she may have had earlier at the deli, she is willing to throw off in this environment. He, in turn, is ready to follow her lead.

There is no thought of love, they simply find each other attractive. It's crazy but that's what seems to make it okay. For the moment there is no fear, no regret, just raw, unfettered, youthful passion. There is nothing beyond this moment for either of them. There is no war, no future and no past, only the moment. There is no notice of the sweating body each is presenting to the other. Pure lust has no restraints. There is no resistance to where this liaison is taking them. It quickly culminates in a shared moment of sexual release. It's only then they find sharing the afterglow rather awkward. There is a common sense of never meeting again, a sense of sharing an intimacy that had been lost in the fray. Every breath becomes an inward sigh as an inner darkness overtakes them.

Love is forbidden here. This is more a self-satisfying, reckless use of emotions. These moments have a mood that can't be sustained. Both find themselves ready to adjourn after the climax. They go their separate ways. Was this to be merely some sentimental liaison? They have had a stolen moment of intimacy that made them one for that moment. The haunting thought is always of some sense of guilt in stealing something from the other they didn't have a right to. This is hardly the kind of closeness that shares any concern for the other, rather it's a blatant theft of a piece of the other person.

The evening progresses with Phillip and Katt intent on going in their opposite directions. After all this is the consensus of their generation; sex is casual recreation. But there's something that didn't quite slip away between the two of them. Maybe it's the beginning of each desiring to find that someone with that "something."

The next day Phillip finds himself going downstairs to the deli. There she is behind the counter, blonde hair pulled back revealing big hoop earrings and an elegant elongated neck. Her eyes are the kind of blue that has a wet glisten, making them more stirring.

"How ya doin'?" asks Phillip, attempting to be glib without a presumption.

"Not bad. Didn't expect to see you," Katt replies. There's an equal amount of flippancy in her answer.

"That was one groovy happening you led me to, girl. I appreciated your hospitality," says Phillip.

"I'm glad you had a good time, it's always crazy at Woody's," says Katt, revealing a smile in her voice.

"What say we get together again?" throws out Phillip, nervously stroking his chin.

"I spose it'd be okay. When?" responds Katt.

"How about I come this way after you close this evening. We'll go get a bite to eat," proposes Phillip.

The upshot of this meeting suggests they may have left something out on their first encounter. There remains an equal amount of curiosity as to what that "something" may be.

CHAPTER 22

It's late December of 1967. Die Landarbeiter is in full swing with the various religious observances symbolically represented by everything from Christmas trees, to Hanukkah bushes, to Yule logs.

Audra, aside from being the health provider for the commune also considers herself a Wicca. She honors the Yule time Winter Solstice as a rebirth of the great god, who is regarded as the newborn solstice sun. She particularly likes to wear her blood red and pitch black dresses during this season.

Deidre and Shelly discover this time of the year brings with it a yearning for the familiar. They have cut and decorated a Christmas tree both in their shared apartment as well as in the community room and are discussing whether or not to make a crèche.

"Wadda ya think Deidre, should we?" questions Shelly.

Pondering the thought for a moment, Deidre replies "I dunno. It sure would blow some minds."

"Yer right, most of these people will figure it's too establishment and probably freak out," determines Shelly. The decision is finally made to place the disputed manger scene outside their door.

****

Sheldon Green is the go-to person for the big Presidential Primary push in New Hampshire. Finding himself looking for diligent lieutenants who are able to organize, he is actively scouting among the local dissidents. Phillip and Manny have been in Minnesota long enough to have caught Sheldon's attention. They have successfully entrenched themselves into the inner circle of Sheldon's governing body. Phillip has arranged to bring a bus load of campaign workers from Minnesota to New Hampshire in February.

Phillip had invited Katt; whose comfort zone would definitely be stretched on a trip such as this.

"Why do you want me to go, Phillip?" asks Katt. Her tone is on the simple side.

"I think it will broaden your horizons." He firmly believes it's one thing to talk passionately about ending the war, but another to be actively involved.

"What makes you think my horizons are too narrow?" She is clearly agitated by Phillip's condescending attitude.

"Well, look at your life. You and your friends sit around getting stoned talking about the war but that's as far as you go. You do nothing to end it."

Hearing himself, combined with the look on Katt's face, Phillip realizes he has probably sabotaged any further relationship with her.

Listening to Phillip's pontification, Katt can feel a hostile response chewing its way from her brain to her tongue. As it gains momentum her hands go to her hips, her jaw juts forward, and her mouth goes into gear. "Well Mr. Asshole, you were happy enough to do the same as long as you could get in my pants!"

Phillip is aware that his attraction to Katt at this juncture is purely physical. He made an attempt to get to know her better, but soon realized his first estimation of her was out of whack. He quickly realized she is a simple hippie girl and that's it. He regards her as a mental light-weight. "A nice distraction on a stormy night," he's been heard to say.

Katt on the other hand finds Phillip to be "a self-absorbed and arrogant prig." It's obvious this relationship has hit a dead end. Katt is content to stay in Minnesota while Phillip continues to dream big dreams for himself. Neither of them is devastated over the end of something that never really got started.

Manny has been busy scrounging in junk yards. In his preparedness, he has been vigilant to take into consideration possible breakdowns. In the event of some mishap, he's used the few available resources they have to stock the bus with a couple of extra used tires, a water pump, a few spark plugs, etc. He also has furnished the bus with enough emergency food and water to last a couple days. Things are looking promising as the hour of departure approaches.

By the end of the week, Phillip is ready to head out with a bus load of college students to make the pilgrimage to New Hampshire. It's bitter cold. The temperatures have been plunging into the sub-zero levels. While Manny was getting the bus ready, Phillip handled the details of where they will stay once in New Hampshire. Phillip has managed to use his network of SDS chapters to find housing in the Dartmouth College dorms. They plan on being involved there for at least a month. The McCarthy campaign has agreed to supply food for only one meal a day and gas to get to New Hampshire. Facing these obstacles is just another outlet for the adventurous spirits of the young. There is nothing this crew doesn't think they can do. Schemes and dreams go hand in hand. For this caper, the fear of risk is buried under a blanket of adventure.

The summer tie-dyed clothing has given way to army surplus winter fatigues, lined boots, fur hats with ear flaps, gloves and scarfs and last but not least a sleeping bag. "Be Clean for Gene" has resonated throughout the whole campaign resulting in a cleaner public presence. This bus load consists of a dozen hard core McCarthy anti-war adherents. They're all seasoned demonstrators. Most have been arrested on various charges of civil disobedience.

The sense of championing something important rings loud and clear within this group. "We're gonna get this war done!" is the prevailing mantra.

"There's got to be more love on this bus, roll some more reefer!" shouts someone.

"Right on!" is a unified response.

This group, as most of the young of this age, still yearns to have family. They gather themselves around common interests such as music, dress, far out religions, a relaxation of sexual codes, and a disdain for authority. In many ways this age has become its own religion; the religion of what's happening now.

At any rate, this busload of non-compliant agitators is convinced they can energize the world enough to bring about a revolution. They are composed of disillusioned students, teachers, a couple social workers, a lawyer, a dog groomer, a news editor for a newspaper, and a nursing home worker. Another thing they all have in common is a strong sense of urgency toward changing the country. All in all, there is plenty of commonality among them to bring about a sense of oneness in life and purpose.

Phillip has taken the first shift behind the wheel. The roads are fairly clear despite the threatening snow clouds. These are forever prevalent in the region this time of year. It's not unusual to have winds blowing snow so hard it creates whiteout conditions. Nonetheless, if people paid that much attention to the weather they'd never leave the house. Caution and readiness are the key words for the day. Because of weather and the fact this aging bus can deliver no more than 45-50 miles per hour, this trip will last three days at best.

Manny has ingeniously hooked up a kerosene burning stove to keep the bus warm against the defunct heater. The bean bag chairs can be positioned for naps or arranged for conversations. People are getting to know one another better whereas some had been only vaguely aware of each other. This is what's loosely described as a "Be-in."

The conversations settle around grievances against the authorities. Everyone has a story of how they have been mistreated. These conversations come to the same conclusions; all their rebellion is warranted and reaffirmed through their common experience with the "pigs." This is in direct opposition to the thinking of their parents who held stricter moral values and a nearly blank check was given to the trusted actions of the authorities.

Phillip relates an incident when he was in private school. He got himself into some trouble with the administration when he and a fellow student decided to get even with another student who had offended them in some way. They decided to break into this student's room, steal his money and burn it. When they ultimately got caught, they were expelled. When his father heard about the incident from the school administrator, he dismissed Phillip's explanation of initiating the violation as a justifiable retribution. "He automatically took the side of those dickheads who couldn't wait to expel me!" laments Phillip.

"Come the revolution, we'll know who's with us and all those against us," says a former school teacher named Clarence.

"We gotta free all our brothers and sisters rotting in some establishment jail cell and replace 'em with the judges that put 'em there!" says a student named Lyman.

"I know we're scarin' the hell out of all these establishment pricks," adds Sid, the attorney among the group, "When one of us becomes involved with the courts and I start throwing a first amendment defense in their face, they know the case is going to get dicey and more than likely catch the attention of the press. That's when they start shittin' all over themselves. I love every minute of it."

Manny listens with interest. "I know damn well if it weren't for you lawyers on our side, we'd all be sittin' in some pig's pen."

Another student named Charles lends his opinion. "We gotta take every case to the Supreme Court!"

The grievances mount with each account. The initiators, as well as the listeners of these conversations feed off each other's fearful suspicions surrounding the establishment, each adding more and more fuel to the fires of opposition.

The lone newspaper reporter has been silent 'til now. His name is Virgil. He was let go from his position when he insisted on writing a story exposing the fraud committed by a well-respected city councilman.

"I know why these politicians are dishonest," says Virgil.

This statement alone is enough to get the attention of the rest of the bus. Their faces all turn for the awaited account.

"They have no money of their own to run a campaign, consequently they rely on contributors. The larger the contribution, the more beholdin' the guy becomes. Before he knows it, he's in in the pocket of people with whom hc has no political commonality."

These conversations continue to grow more intense with each contributor vying to produce a more dramatic story.

Going unnoticed thus far by the passengers is the deteriorating weather conditions. About midnight, the decision is made to stop in the next town and replenish their supply of kerosene. They have crossed into Michigan's Upper Peninsula near a community named Ironwood. They find the streets bare of traffic with ten foot piles of snow on every corner. The wind is whipping about with no regard for life of any kind. The temperatures are plunging into single digits.

Added to this, the windshield wiper blades are gathering large clumps of ice preventing the snow from being adequately scraped off—resulting in a windshield nearly encrusted with ice.

Looking up and down the lifeless streets, the consensus is to continue heading east on Highway 2 toward Bessemer, a small town a few miles down the road.

"I don't think we should chance it," says Virgil. His is the only dissenting voice.

Phillip is still behind the wheel. He agrees with the others. "I don't know what the cops are like around here. They may not take to a psychedelic bus loaded with a bunch of hippies parked on their street, especially with all the dope we got with us. I think we need to keep on moving as best we can."

Having been behind the wheel since the afternoon, Phillip relinquishes control. "Manny, I need to get some shut eye. You take over, but for God's sake keep her between the ditches." Manny has driven this behemoth thousands of miles. He's as proficient a driver as Phillip. But after looking out the frosted windshield, he's not eager to jump behind the wheel.

On a clear day, Highway 2 is a straight flat shot between Ironwood and Bessemer with clear markings of white and yellow paint. At night, in the middle of a blizzard, it turns into an indiscernible blanket of white snow—a broad white, crystalline path of part road and part ditch separating a thick growth of ominous timber. Nothing more than a trench between piled snowbanks at best.

Every bit a man on a mission, Manny slowly starts the trek to Bessemer. The poor old worn tires are grasping for anything on this snow packed road that will give them traction. This causes the bus to sporadically lurch in unpredictable directions. Manny finds himself gripping the wheel with an iron grasp. The wind is producing a sideways wall of white with a backdrop of a black moonless night. Now with eyes that are too fearful to trust taking the chance of blinking, he notices the headlight on the driver's side is burned out. This leaves him at an alarming disadvantage. He's fighting to stay in what he perceives to be the middle of the highway.

Anyone driving in these conditions, regardless of how skilled, more often than not finds themselves at the mercy of powers outside of themselves. There is little to trust outside of pure luck. Ordinary wheel fluctuations become magnified perils. Each carries with it a potentially deadly outcome. The hum of the motor along with the single headlight reflecting off streaking lines of white snow creates a mesmerizing phenomenon. There can be no margin of error. Manny must stay alert beyond anything he's ever experienced.

He's very aware of the eleven other people he's carrying. At this point he doesn't want to risk the ire of any of them by causing a disruption in the planned agenda to get to New Hampshire. Any thought more devastating than that is too horrific to contemplate.

Phillip has just dozed off when he senses something going awry. It's the feeling one gets when being pulled sideways. This odd force is accompanied with what is unmistakably the sound of Manny's panicked voice clearly expressing terror. "Oh shit!" is all he can press out in the moment.

Out of nowhere the bus is suddenly being pulled to the left. It seems the front tires on the blind side of the vehicle have dropped off the road's hard surface onto a much different surface along the shoulder. In a split second gravitational forces are in charge of the consequences on twelve lives.

Manny's knee jerk reaction only exacerbates the situation. He yanks the wheel and jams the brakes. The laws of gravity are clearly winning. Manny continues the struggle as the bus fights to stay right side up. The trajectory sends the huge transport plunging full force off the road and through a plowed snowbank. If it were not for the four foot high mound acting as a stabilizing force, the bus would have surely rolled. Not quite finished, the lunging monster continues to plow forward a short distance, finally coming to rest in a tangled mass of brush and snow.

Manny is clearly shaken. His hands are still on the wheel, his eyes are focused straight ahead. He appears to be gazing through what looks to be a cracked windshield.

The rest of the crew on board is in various stages of disarray. They had all been sleeping and are waking to discover themselves thrown around and as defenseless as the dead.

Within seconds all are on their feet, truly alarmed at their situation. The usual yawns and stretching have given way to terrified faces all pressing against the windows in search of an explanation for the disconcerting awakening. One by one they begin to grasp the seriousness of the situation. The common pronouncement being, "What the hell!"

On closer inspection, the nose of the bus has plowed up enough snow to prevent it from going forward. Also the door is leaning against a large tree they had narrowly missed. The position of both prevents anyone from exiting.

By more of a reflexive reaction than thought, Manny slams the gears in reverse. The engine roars, the tires spin without moving the bus an inch. If the power of "wishing" could move a bus this size there is enough wishing going on in here to move ten buses.

Phillips natural reaction is to take charge of the situation. "Is everyone okay?" Not waiting for an answer, he makes his way through the tangle of sleeping bags, bean bag chairs, and packs of belongings, all strewn about the floor.

Satisfied no one is hurt, Phillip continues with a litany of orders. "Somebody check the stove. The last damn thing we need now is a fire. Manny shut the motor off. We need to save as much fuel as we can."

Instantaneously a voice from the back of the bus communicates, "All's well back here."

"How much kerosene is left?" further questions Phillip.

"About three quarters of a gallon," returns the same voice.

"Stay in your sleeping bags and turn the stove off until we need it back on," further orders Phillip.

The internal lights are still glowing, giving a dim eeriness to the whole affair. Further assessing their situation, Phillip orders Manny to turn them off as well and save the battery.

Attempting to sleep is sporadic at best. Morning breaks with the storm relentlessly continuing its attack. More than a foot of snow has already fallen since their fateful brush with disaster with no hint of letting up.

There is a curtained off area toward the back directly across from the stove that serves as a toilet. It's not much. Quinton had engineered it before they left Die Landarbeiter. It's basically an outdoor toilet set up to dump its contents onto the road. They use it infrequently, usually waiting for fuel stops to make use of the stations' more agreeable bathroom facilities. But now it is the main facility servicing a dozen trapped inhabitants.

Phillip is on his "A" game as he organizes a breakfast brigade. For the most part everyone is co-operative in trying to stay out of each other's way.

Suddenly Clarence notices something no one else has. Tammy, the pet groomer, is apparently still sleeping. On closer inspection, he notices what appears to be dried blood coming from both her nose and ears. She also has taken on an ashen appearance. Her breathing is labored and she is non-responsive. The huge ten gallon glass water jug fell on her head.

What at first has been considered to be merely a pain-in-the-ass delay has quickly turned into a full blown emergency. They're now finding themselves facing what appears to be a life and death situation.

Phillip's mind and eyes dart around attempting to calculate their options. Meanwhile the storm outside along with the tree and brush covering is continuing to keep the bus interior dark. "*The damn door is blocked! How we gonna get her outta here?*" becomes his ultimate concern. They had the emergency rear door welded closed in order to place bunk beds across the back. It now occurs to him that regardless of the doors, there's no place to go.

Manny always recognizes when Phillip is out of ideas and attempts to fill the gap. "I think we need to bring the help here. There is no way we can move her," Manny exclaims.

Quickly attempting to regain his leadership, Phillip chimes in. "You're absolutely right, Manny. That has been exactly my thoughts." Not yet able to get his head around a solution, Phillip stalls long enough for Manny to resume his thought.

Taking this pause to be his next cue, Manny continues. "I don't believe we can be more than a few miles out of Ironwood." Contemplating yet a step beyond he adds, "I think some of us should go and bring help back."

Assuming his rightful return to the leadership throne of his own making, Phillip once again joins with Manny's assessment offering to assist in getting things together for anyone who will volunteer for such an arduous task.

Clarence and Lyman are the first to step forward. Phillip is relieved this undertaking is quickly resolved—especially in view of it not requiring him to be one of the volunteers. Visibly back in command, he gets a few of the others to put together a support pack of food and water.

It's agreed the only way out of the bus is through a window. They slide one open only to find it barely accommodates a full grown man. Clarence and Lyman realize the fuller impact of this undertaking only after both have made their way to the ground. The snow is much deeper than expected. They struggle just to make it to the road. The blizzard is the worst the region has experienced in some time. Nonetheless, their resolve to get the needed help drives them forward. It's one of their own whose life is depending on their success in bringing back the needed medical assistance.

The storm rages on. The visibility is less than a few feet. By the time they reach what they perceive to be the road, they can no longer see the bus. There is no sunny side to this street. With no idea where they are, or how far they are from help, the two of them begin what they hope will be a successful undertaking.

This task is much more difficult than either of them had imagined. The wind is so fierce that the blowing snow is actually capable of cutting exposed skin. The drifting snow is waist high in some places. Forcing their way through these drifts has no reward other than confronting another of the same and then yet another and then another. In some places it's difficult to tell if they're still on the road. The tracks left from their bus are but small indentations.

They trudge on for what seems like several hours but in reality was probably only about one. Despite their youth, neither of them is even remotely prepared for this kind of battle. The temperature is ten degrees Fahrenheit, nevertheless both are soaked with sweat. Nearing exhaustion, they simultaneously come to the same conclusion.

Clarence is the first to confess, trying to yell above the howling wind, "I've had it man. I don't think I can go on."

Lyman is hardly in any better shape himself. "I'm with ya, Dude. But we don't have a lot of options right now," he shouts back.

Neither have ever felt this alone and desperate. This moment is overwhelming. Looking around only intensifies their growing fears.

"I don't have a clue where we are or how far we have to go yet," concedes Clarence. "If we don't pull ourselves together, they'll find us lying in the road froze solid."

"I was expectin' we'd see some traffic out here—at least a snowplow," bemoans Lyman. Both of them have grown up surrounded by conditions like this, but never gotten themselves in a situation this dire.

Just as they are discussing their next move, Clarence suddenly drops to the snow covered road. "AAARRRGGG!!" he yelps.

Seeing Clarence fall, Lyman also drops to the ground in reaction. "What the hell happened?" Lyman shouts out above the fray.

"I've turned my goddam ankle," shouts back Clarence still rolling in the snow holding his leg. With his other hand, Clarence feels around trying to discover some hidden nemesis. It's a deep pothole. It had remained undetected by a covering of fresh powder.

Struggling to get to his feet, Clarence readily accepts Lyman's help. Once up, Clarence discovers he can barely place any weight on his right ankle. He is going to have to depend on Lyman to save them.

Between Clarence and the weather, Lyman is in a near panic meltdown. He's been thrown headfirst out of his comfort zone into high stress anxiety. For the moment Lyman sees no happy ending for this catastrophe. On the other hand this misfortune is causing Lyman to think outside the box. His immediate concern is to find some shelter. A warm house for him and an attentive medical team for Lyman and Tammy would be perfect. But then the people in hell would also like to have ice water. In neither case does it appear either is going to readily happen.

With Clarence leaning heavily on his shoulder, Lyman's focus is centered on a darkened area barely visible through the blowing snow. Lyman's concentration has abruptly been enhanced by adrenalin. His fear is burying itself beneath his need to survive. In contrast with the blandness of the blizzard, this oasis gives the impression of snow sculpted by some outside agent. Continuing to look straight ahead his focus sharpens.

"Just in time. I found you just in time," Lyman exclaims recognizing the darkened area as a stand of pine trees.

Supporting Clarence with his shoulder, he leads into what he is trusting to be their sanctuary. The upper boughs lay heavy with the falling snow creating a cave like condition beneath.

With agonizing effort, the two of them manage to reach what turns out to be their promised land. Once under the canopy, the ground is nearly bare but for a bed of fallen needles, and the wind is at a minimum.

Lyman's first task is to get Clarence comfortable. Leaning him against a tree trunk, he finds several dead branches that are easily broken. His mind is racing with what now seems to be an enhanced level of concentration. It's something he's never experienced in his young life. He senses this phenomenon as a genuine happening.

His next concern is the chill he's beginning to feel. The sweat they have worked up has soaked their shirts beneath their parkas and now it's beginning to cool. Lyman as well as Clarence recognize the potential for hypothermia and frostbite.

As if on cue, Lyman begins to break dried dead branches from the trees. Meanwhile Clarence is clearing an area as best he can for a fire. Neither of them smoke cigarettes, but both carry Zippo lighters in the event a joint should happen to show up.

Within a half hour of Clarence's disaster, they have managed to get out of the storm into a semblance of safety with some measure of comfort.

They have a fire going. This alone is a huge advantage over the raging elements. Clarence has a pocket knife that has never cut anything other than chunks of hashish. Now it's put to use in a more proletarian line of work cutting pine boughs to build a less drafty shelter.

With both of them warmer, their attention turns back to Clarence's injury. After pulling his boot off, his ankle doesn't appear to be broken. Even with the uneven flickering of the fire, the yellow-orange-black ring encircling his ankle evidences broken blood vessels. This always accompanies a severe sprain.

After examining the puffy, swollen skin, he exclaims, "I damn near wish it was broken. That only takes six weeks to heal. This damn thing'll be six months."

Scrounging around in his pocket, Lyman finds the remnants of a bag of pot complete with papers. Not expecting this little surprise, he wiggles the bag in front of Clarence, exclaiming, "See here Clarence, there is a God!!"

"I can sure as hell use a little self-medication right now," declares Clarence.

As always, the pot gives them a sense of contentment despite their present predicament. In time the pot has mellowed them and the fire into one. They're perfectly content to sit staring at the flames, eating dried jerky, and sipping on water. The thought of going back out into the storm to seek help has become remote.

Soon the day is sucked into history. What got done today will pay forward in their tomorrows, what is left undone will remain in the world of the misplaced. Darkness comes early this time of year.

Meantime, back at the bus the mood is somber at best. The skies are as gray inside as outside. The wind continues howling with an unrelenting determination. Tammy's condition is somewhat confusing. No one here has had any medical training and can only respond to her symptoms with a sense of peril. She has regained consciousness but is having difficulty communicating. Her words are garbled. At best, they can agree she's had a serious concussion, but from that point on they're at a loss as to treatment.

By late afternoon amidst the darkness a sense of boredom once again completely overtakes them. On the one hand this confinement assures them of protection, but on the other hand, it produces a claustrophobic condition. It's sheer misery for these energetic youths to be confined for this long. It's far from what anyone would describe as a cozy bunker. The crash has left the vehicle tilted enough to make standing a dizzying challenge. There is no escape unless one wants to crawl out a window and risk being unable to crawl back up the six foot drop to the ground.

Phillip has little forbearance for these kinds of reversals much less with the screw-ups of others. The people surrounding him are rapidly losing any qualities he finds appealing. It's easy to have a high regard for people under smoother circumstances. How one reacts when things go awry and circumstances run counter, is what divides strong and weak leaders. Phillip doesn't seem to realize his weaknesses. He believes whatever reaction he chooses is the correct one regardless of its effectiveness.

For most of the day Phillip has been nursing a bottle of Boone's Farm wine. He's getting muzzy with the reality that he can't control his environment much less the people surrounding him. Continuing to find himself in a funk, he returns to his spiraling thoughts. *"What a great show this could be, if only Manny hadn't run off the goddam road."*

To say Manny's happy with the situation would be silly but as usual, he is endeavoring to keep people optimistic. Regardless of his efforts, the rest of the crew is far from happy with this state of affairs. Stuck all day in a sleeping bag in the dark with very little heat is not what they signed on for. He is also concerned with how Clarence and Lyman are faring.

Secretly, Manny had been hoping Phillip would have been brave enough to volunteer. This would have unquestionably proven him as a selfless leader. Manny imagines how the two of them could have been the ones to bring help and how much this would have added to their status.

CHAPTER 23

The weather patterns remain precarious throughout the region. Highway 2 has been closed until further notice. These kinds of weather conditions are frankly accepted by the locals. They're remarkably competent in their preparations to be snowbound for several days at a time. The various first responders are prepared to answer in all emergency situations—usually among folks caught outside their safety zone. The difference between life and death hangs on these effective and efficient response teams.

For the past twenty-four hours the State Police Post in Wakefield has been abuzz. Their jurisdiction includes the storm beleaguered area between Ironwood and Bessemer. The entire post along with every other law-enforcement agency is on high alert. The local road commissions are also working overtime. The storm, as of yesterday, has dumped thirty inches of snow and is still not finished. Cooperation between agencies is a must to maximize the safety of the citizenry.

By morning it's determined the snow fall is beginning to wane, but the wind continues to menace any hope of reducing the drifting. Even so, the highways need to be re-opened. The plows are out in full force.

The Gogebic County Sheriff Department is also gearing up, carrying extra blankets in the event they are faced with stranded motorists found suffering from hypothermia. In this part of the world, if extra measures aren't taken, Mother Nature will have her way.

Two young deputies are paired together today. Neither has more than a few months service. Both have fathers who retired from law-enforcement.

The driver in this instance is Tyler Cassidy, his partner riding shotgun is Malachi Maloney. They have been instructed to be on the lookout for anyone stranded and stand ready to assist.

"When I was little, my Dad would come home after one of these storms and tell me about people he had helped," reports Malachi. In spite of the number of years passing, the pride can still be heard in his voice.

"Yeah, I know what you mean. I still call my Dad for advice when I get stuck with a problem," says Tyler. In sharing these small moments of admiration for their fathers, they have a common bond. They freely admit their parents' role in their decisions to go into law-enforcement careers.

The huge V-shaped snowplow they're following is parting the snow, creating its own tangled storm within a storm. It's impossible to see anything except the billowing white crystals surrounding the whole truck, all sparkling in the sunlight.

Seemingly mesmerized with the truck's strange changing art creations, Tyler reflects, "Looks like an exhibition of Michigan-style Swirling Dervishes."

Concerned with how close Tyler is following the truck, Malachi makes a nervous gesture, "If you get any closer, we may end up Ditched Dervishes."

****

Clarence and Lyman find themselves awakening to the unmistakable sound of a plow truck. A shot of adrenalin shoots through their bodies, rushing thoughts through their brains of someone coming to their rescue. Reviewing the reality of their situation nonetheless creates a cruel anxiety. It's a mixture of hope and despair. The two of them are some 100 feet from the road. For Clarence it may as well be 100 miles. Overnight his ankle has swollen to twice the size of the other. Adding to this whole debacle is the fact the distance has waist-deep snow. The temperatures are hovering in the low teens making it imperative they keep a fire going.

Torn between attempting to make his way to hail down their possible rescuers or rekindle their fire, Lyman realizes the truck has made its way down the road and is long gone. It's times like these where the brutalities of life meet a nearly unbearable sense of loneliness. For now, he turns his efforts to increasing the perimeter around their camp in his wood scrounging project. Soon the fire is hot enough to take the stiff coldness out of their limbs.

Taking stock of their dwindling food supply, they quietly divide what's left. Neither is very talkative in trying to deal with the letdown dashing their hopes of a prompt rescue.

Contemplating their situation while chewing on a piece of jerky, Clarence expresses his thoughts. "I know we can't get out to the road fast enough to hail a passing car, but I think we can bring attention to where we are."

Listening attentively, Lyman asks the obvious question. "What you got in mind, Clarence?"

"We gotta set one of these damn trees on fire," he says very matter of factly. "Somethin' like that is bound to catch somebody's attention."

For the second time this morning, Lyman's spirits rise. "You're onta sompthin' Clarence." says Lyman envisioning Clarence's idea.

With that agreement, Lyman picks a tree closer to the highway. After clearing the snow off the boughs and around the base of the tree, he piles kindling beneath it.

With the aid of a small tree stripped of its limbs and used as a crutch, Clarence makes his way to Lyman's project. His first reaction is "Holy shit Lyman! You plannin' on burnin' the whole damn woods?"

****

Meanwhile, a mile down the road, the crew on the bus awakens to their second morning of frigid temperatures. Phillip has a horrible headache from the wine he spent the day before drinking. Manny is refilling the kerosene stove, ever conscious of the decreasing amount left in the container. The mood overall is not good. It's a mixed bag of impatience—of being stuck in the snow, but also with one another.

Phillip's impatience has surfaced in anger with his apparent powerlessness over his state of affairs. He's finding people, places, and things simply will not cooperate.

"Where in the hell is the help we sent for?" he vents. "They should have been here yesterday already."

He has a situation with an injured girl, a marooned bus, diminishing kerosene, confined quarters and people looking to him for direction. Every breath is a sigh. Cabin fever is unhesitatingly and in various ways working its way into everyone.

Virgil, the newspaper man, is writing in a note book. It hasn't left his hand since this escapade began. It seems to be his way of dealing with adversity.

Sid, the attorney, is pacing as best he can among all the bodies and belongings. He's older and more independent than the others; maybe late twenties. He is obviously looking for some kind of escape route. He decides, *"I need to get out of here even if it's for only a few minutes."* Before anyone realizes what's going on, he has slid a window open and is forcing himself through the opening. The clatter along with the cold draft has brought everyone to their feet. Some are prepared to follow him, others are annoyed he's wasting the small amount of heat they are trying to conserve. All in all, no one is at their best. Sliding down to what he perceives to be the ground, he sinks into snow way beyond his ability to maneuver.

His thoughts immediately begin shouting a message into his brain, "*You've royally screwed up this time.*" Seeing how deep the snow actually is, no one follows. Those remaining inside are unwilling to leave the window open and waste their heat. Dashing his hopes he can find a way back up the six foot side of the bus, he's left to his own devices.

"*If I can get to the road, I know I can get a ride,*" he thinks. The blowing snow soon envelops his getaway. Within minutes, he has become so disoriented he has no idea where he is.

****

The patrol car carrying the two young deputies has been busy all morning rescuing stranded motorists. Deputy Maloney and Deputy Cassidy are responsible for getting each of these folks safely off the road. Some were forced to sleep in their cars until the plows arrived. Others required a wrecker after sliding off the road into the bush.

It's late afternoon and the two law-enforcement officers are retracing their earlier road patrol when they spot a blazing tree on the side of the highway.

"What the hell!!" says Deputy Maloney. "Tyler are you seeing what I'm lookin' at?"

Deputy Cassidy is just as startled as his partner. Bringing the patrol car to a stop, they both exit to get a better take on the cause of the fire. What they see is unmistakably a man frantically waving his arms.

"Are you okay?" shouts Deputy Maloney.

The lone man is shouting back, "I have an injured man back here," all the time pointing behind him.

"Do you need medical assistance?" becomes Deputy Cassidy's first concern.

"Yes," is Lyman's only reply.

Meantime Deputy Maloney is snowshoeing across the crest to make a better assessment of the situation. Lyman couldn't be happier to see these two uniforms if he had won a trip to a warm island paradise. It's a stark contrast to the diatribe they were spewing about cops being pigs only a day before. Upon his arrival and with the tree still smoldering, Deputy Maloney immediately makes his way to Clarence.

"What happened to you, sir?" is Deputy Maloney's urgent question.

"I twisted my damn ankle," replies Clarence while peeling down his sock. It's clear his foot is swollen to the point his boot won't fit.

Their smoke-smudged faces give the deputy the impression they have been here for some time.

"How long you fellas been stuck here?" asks the deputy.

Clarence and Lyman explain how they slid off the road and one of their friends was injured. The reason they are where they are is due to them going for help.

"Where are your friends located now, sir?" Deputy Maloney continues to press.

"Back toward Bessemer, but I can't tell you how far—maybe a mile or two," reports Lyman. "But I don't think they can be seen from the road. We slid into the bush pretty good."

With a few more questions determining which side of the road the bus is on and what kind of injury the passenger sustained, Deputy Maloney leaves them to radio for an ambulance.

Meanwhile another sheriff's car arrives. Deputies Maloney and Cassidy leave these new arrivals to attend to Clarence and Lyman while they begin the search for the crashed bus. While bringing Cassidy up to date with the information he had learned, they set off on yet another rescue mission.

Creeping along at a snail's pace Maloney and Cassidy keep a vigilant eye peeled for the elusive bus. Suddenly Deputy Maloney cries, "Look over there Tyler!"

Stopping the patrol car, both are looking at what possibly appears to be their bus. Without a close scrutiny it could easily be passed off as a painted billboard of sorts half-covered in snow and abandoned in the brush.

"Let's take a look," says Deputy Cassidy.

The wind has stopped blowing and the skies are that deep blue when nature has cleared out all the debris allowing the sun to make diamonds of every snowflake. The world looks sweet again.

Still standing on the road, Deputy Cassidy points his bull horn in the direction of this strange single panel of painted designs. "ANYONE HERE?" he calls.

In a moment a waving hand appears in an opening on the top of the painting. It's clearly a human hand.

"Bingo!" shouts Deputy Maloney at this pronounced sign of life. "We've found our bus."

On board, Manny is trying to wake Phillip out of his stupor. Phillip has used every drug and drank everything available rather than face what appears to him to be an impending defeat. The stormy clouds are lifting for everyone as they prepare to be freed from their ostensibly endless confinement.

There is actually some laughter of relief as the reality of their rescue sinks in. Soon the smiles and giddiness spread. The irony in this part of their debacle is their appreciation for these previously declared enemies in law-enforcement. As with Clarence and Lyman an hour before, not one word about "The Pigs" being here to rescue them has entered the vocabulary of anyone.

Back on the highway, the two deputies have radioed for the next available ambulance and wrecker. While they're waiting, Deputy Maloney notices some obvious boot tracks leading away from the bus and running parallel with the road. He follows along the highway to a point where they seem to wander off into an open field. Returning to the patrol car, he retrieves a pair of binoculars. Making his way back to where the prints wander off, he places the glass to his eyes and peers out into a white abyss. At the end of the footprints, lying against a lone tree is the form of a man. His head is slumped with his arms appearing to be loosely folded across his chest. He gives the impression of having fallen asleep. Maloney knows better.

At the same time he hears the wail of emergency vehicles. In short order, the ambulance attendants are out of their vehicle and conferring with the deputies, on their heels are the wrecker personnel.

Deputy Maloney directs the attention of the medical team to the lone man in the field. Meanwhile, Deputy Cassidy discusses with the wrecker crew how to get the bus out of the brush and back to the highway.

The ambulance is staffed with three team members, two males and a female. She's a big, blonde-haired Finnish girl from Ironwood. There is no question she could put the two males to shame in any kind of strength contest. She is already pulling out a flat-bottomed skid with side rails along with several pair of snowshoes. Within a couple of minutes they're making their way across the snow-blanketed field toward the victim.

The wrecker crew hardly needs any directions. They work together like their well-maintained truck. One is positioning the truck to run a cable the hundred or so feet to the disabled bus. Meanwhile, the others are arranging various chains, tire blocks that will discourage the truck from sliding, and various tools no one but them can readily name. All three of these teams have employed themselves in work that benefits the well-being of their fellow citizens.

Phillip is beginning to come around. The hangover cobwebs are still plaguing him, as well as the shakes. He scrounges around until he finds a quarter-filled bottle of wine left when he passed out. Unscrewing the top he chugs the remainder. Shortly, he is able to get a grasp on what is transpiring. Watching the efforts of these men and women who have come to deliver him from his misfortune, his drug and alcohol-fogged mind begins to twist their efforts.

"Look how much these guys enjoy making their living off the misery of others. They can't get enough of it."

Some of the others are also finding themselves convoluted. Their first reaction of joy and relief with being rescued is short-lived and replaced by a return to their more cynical attitude of suspicion and near paranoia.

Manny is the first to recognize another possibility turning into a major problem. "We gotta get rid of the dope. If they decide to search the bus, we're shit out of luck."

The normal way would have been to dump it into the toilet a let it spill down the road, but conditions have changed.

"How we gonna do that, they're right outside our door?" questions Virgil.

Manny has already retrieved a bag and is passing it around to each person. Half-heartedly each is depositing their stash which includes everything from LSD, to speed, to pot and mescaline.

To answer Virgil's question, Manny simply states, "I don't know yet."

Tammy is recovering. Her mind has cleared enough she does not think she needs medical attention.

Outside the bus, the well-ordered mayhem continues. Without warning, the bus suddenly lurches. The creaking sound of strained metal resonates throughout the vehicle. Slowly, purposefully, the bus begins to crawl from its snow cave.

As soon as the vehicle has cleared the tree that blocked the door, Manny spots an opportunity. He quickly assesses where the deputies are. Seeing that they're busy with the retrieved body of Sid, he slips out the freed door, around to the front of the bus and out of everyone's sight. He quickly deposits the bag of dope under a layer of snow.

From this moment on everything begins to go quickly. The bus is soon back on the highway. More police cars have arrived due to Sid's demise. He's lying on the sled frozen solid in the same position they found him. He resembles something you'd expect to see in a National Geographic exhibition.

Among the deputies, a sergeant has assumed command of this whole operation. He begins by asking Sid's relationship to the rest of them. Working his way through the confusion, the sergeant asks if he can come aboard to finish his questioning regarding Sid. Phillip's suspicion is correct this is a ploy to get aboard and begin a search with the expectation of finding contraband drugs. With the questioning concerning Sid over with, the sergeant moves into the next phase of his investigation. "You folks have any illegal drugs?"

Manny is the first to speak up, "No sir."

"Do you mind if I look?" is the sergeant's next question.

"I'm going to presume if I say no you'll find a way of searching anyway," says Manny now a bit more rigid.

"You're right, it'll just take longer. We'd have to wait for a search warrant to be issued and all of us would be sittin' around for the afternoon, but then we'd search anyway—so we may as well get it over with now," says the sergeant.

"Why do you think you have to search us? We haven't broken any laws," further questions Phillip jumping into the fray.

Giving his shoulders a slight shrug the sergeant in his most polite, but official matter of fact voice declares, "Because you fit the profile, sir." Pausing for a moment as if waiting for his last statement to sink in, he continues, "So how do you want to do this—the hard way or the easy way?"

Phillip is again ready to regain his leadership role. "Yeah, go ahead. You won't find anything."

With a slight hand signal, the waiting deputies enter the bus. They methodically frisk everyone. Satisfied no one is carrying, they begin to search belongings. Soon they're finished and come up dry, thanks to Manny.

Phillip believes he sees signs of disappointment crossing the faces of these public servants. On the one hand he can't be grateful enough for having been delivered so masterfully by this group of professionals, on the other hand he isn't ready to give up his predetermined opinion that they're all "Pigs."

One by one the different agencies are leaving. The wrecker driver wants to be paid up front, even though Phillip has assured him if he sends the bill to his father it would get paid. He ultimately has to dip into the small amount of cash he has left to avoid having the bus impounded.

The ambulance is also leaving. They have returned Clarence and Lyman after wrapping Clarence's ankle. Poor ole Sid is another story. No one got to know him very well, but they all counted themselves lucky to have a lawyer on board. Now they consider themselves fortunate not to have to pay for his final expenses. All they had to do was hand over the few belongings left in his sleeping bag and let the ambulance team deal with the rest of it.

The police are soon on their way to other calls requiring assistance. The crew on the bus is beginning to settle back into the idea of moving on. When the last police car leaves, they have only one thing left to do.

"Manny, get the bloody dope and let's blow this hole!" shouts Phillip. He's once again back in the driver's seat ready to roll.

Not having to be told twice, Manny leaps from the bottom step to the snow-packed ground, nearly slipping on his keister. He brushes away the covering of snow to retrieve the bag of dope and hops back into the waiting bus. The entire crew breaks into applause. The bag is passed around with each repossessing what they had earlier placed in it for safekeeping. As they ramble down the road, the pungent smell of pot along with its joyous effects are enough to cause the group to break into a Bob Dylan song.

CHAPTER 24

With no more than one flat tire, a broken fuel pump, too many extra quarts of oil for anyone to remember, and nearly a week on the road, they finally pull into the Dartmouth dormitory parking lot. Phillip and Manny are fumbling with notebooks containing scribbled names and phone numbers. Their contact person is a student named Amy Pentwirth. She's the designated student coordinator for this Minnesota contingency of McCarthy campaigners.

The parking lot is speckled with every kind of hippie conveyance one can imagine; including curtained Volkswagen buses and outdated step vans, all with different categories of art work adorning any area that could be painted.

Speaking to Manny, Phillip is back to normal and expresses the most positive statement he's said in days, "I know this is where we belong. I got a good feeling about all this."

The atmosphere of this student/intellectual community is more agreeable to Phillip than the communal life where they were content with merely grubbing around in the mud and getting back to nature.

Manny is just as geeked as Phillip about getting involved with the national political scene. "Right on brother! This beats the hell outta bein' a goddam shit kicker. We're gonna be the future of this country."

It's the beginning of March, 1968 in New Hampshire. The weather hasn't been this cold in anyone's recollection. The student teams "For

Gene" have for the most part been well received by the Democratic voters. McCarthy is gaining against incumbent President Lyndon Johnson in every poll. It's all due to these young activists going door to door. They're all hyped up with unfettered enthusiasm, always ready to give tongue to their anti-Vietnam War rhetoric to any and all willing listeners.

If people didn't know better, they could easily believe many of these overly-enthusiastic, motivated students are running for office themselves. They're on fire on every front. They spend much of their time listening to each other's rants. Their minds soon meld together forming a single opinion that has been hailed by the movement as "thinking for ourselves."

The press has become a willing sycophant for any headline involving the anti-culture youth movement. They hang on every word these students supply providing they radically oppose the Washington establishment. It's almost as though the press corps is vicariously living through the daring antics of these rebels. Something many of them had always wanted to do, but were too cowardly to pull off.

Along the way, Phillip and Manny are privy to meeting a few of New Hampshire's old Beatniks. One in particular stands out. He's an old reprobate named Ed Grisswald. Over the years he's come to be known as "Grizz." He's totally bald on the top portion of his head, but wears the remainder of his hair in long white tresses below his shoulders. His back has also rounded into an arthritic hump. His face is weathered and covered with a beard that has never seen a trimmer. To brand him merely as an old reprobate would low-ball his impact on his generation of dissidents. Grizz was born in 1888. He likes to consider himself old-fashioned. By the time he reached his twelfth birthday, he had already become well acquainted with opium, morphine, cocaine, and heroin.

"Hell man, we lived wild and free back in them days. I could buy all this shit in a drug store. Don't get me wrong, we had our share of do-gooders even then, but nobody paid 'em no mind."

Over the years Grizz has seen the do-gooders erode his freedom. His chief hate for all them "damn Washington people" is taken out on the cops who are hired to enforce "their goddam repressive bullshit laws."

He has spent time in prison for drug possession, spending much of that period in the prison's library studying law, particularly those that pertained to his individual rights. By self-educating himself, he has now become a nuisance to the courts by showing up smelly and unkempt on behalf of young people caught up in the legal system. To his delight he's often referred to as the "Dartmouth guru," willingly spending time counseling young people on how to beat the system and on what the cops can and can't do.

Phillip and Manny discover him holding court in an underclass hangout called the Taproom. People make their way in and out. Most are there because their lives are drab and drink too much hoping to fill the hole in their spirit. For many of these folks the party seems to be over. They're hoping for some action, maybe a fight—anything but the same uneventful, predictable boring evening.

They serve 20-cent draft beer, appealing to students as well as old renegades the likes of Grizz.

"My rap sheet's so goddam thick, they use it ta stand on ta change the courthouse light bulbs," he boasts with a broad smile portraying only a single pair of eyeteeth in an otherwise toothless mouth.

"I been arrested for everything from drug possession ta drunk and disorderly and for somethin' they referred to as 'inadequate compliance'... oh yeah there's another one about bein' an instigator ta somethin' I don't even remember what it was."

Grizz likes to keep his community on their toes. About the time some think they have him figured out, he changes all the questions. It's not unlike him to suddenly take up a new religion. When he does, he'll show up wearing togas or kimonos or feathers, burning weird incense and some things he just makes up as he goes. If there's a program on the edge of lunacy, he's all in.

The amazing thing about Grizz is he never went to college, but there's not a subject he doesn't seem to have at least an hour's worth of in depth knowledge, or at least opinion, about. What he probably knows the most is how to irritate the community fathers. To say people don't learn from him is hardly the truth. He always seems to have a twist that baffles those who profess to be in the know.

"If I can't dazzle ya with brilliance, I'll baffle ya with bullshit," is his favorite expression.

"They wanna know where the bear shits in the briar patch, I tell 'em," he rants on.

The problem is most people can't tell when he's serious or just toying with them. On this particular occasion, Grizz has a belt full of cap pistols—maybe a dozen. He's pulling them all out one by one and laying them on the bar.

"Nobody messes with a man with a gun," he declares using the same dead pan expression he uses to tell you "the Pope ain't no Methodist."

Grizz has a female companion. She's a mousy woman; blinking a lot and constantly clearing her throat. Her name is Madge. She's a drab fifty-something woman that has only one feature that is capable of holding a person's attention; her hair is missing on top. She looks more like Grizz's brother than his female companion. It's rumored she had been a school teacher at one time. Seems her family had her committed to a state mental hospital in Pontiac, Michigan due to chronic schizophrenia. Apparently due to overcrowding, the state had released her. Grizz noticed her hitchhiking through town, unable to get a ride and took her in. That was nearly ten years ago, she's been with him ever since.

"She's okay most of the time. Occasionally she goes off and I gotta chain her up for a few days. Ain't much different than when she was in the state hospital. Besides she ain't a bad lay."

Old Grizz is mistrustful of anyone who claims to be an "expurt." Much to the consternation of these folks, he carries his own description of them and loves to point it out. "An 'ex' is a has-been," he illustrates with an impertinent impunity. Then adds, "and a 'spurt' is a drip under pressure."

If this weren't enough, he's sure of at least one more thing about this kind, preaching it to anyone willing or unwilling to listen.

"Those folks that think they got a cure for everything will usually kill ya with the side effects. I'm willin' ta take my chances. They ain't nothin' a good bottle ah Boone's Farm Apple Wine and ah big doobie of Jamaican Red can't cure."

Because this is the Democratic Party's New Hampshire primary, they appeal to the many differing faces within the party. They include everything from Gay Bikers for Christ to John Calvin's Mystic Order of Comanches and too many in between to mention except maybe the Union Democrats.

The Union Democrats are a voice that must be heard by any Democrat that hopes to hold a political office. They hold more than a mere handful of votes. In this particular scene, Grizz has also added unions to his list of "good-fer-nothin'-sons-a-bitches."

"They ain't nothin' more than big business stylin' themselves off as peasant stock fightin' for bread crumbs from the master's table. They ain't ah one of them flab-asses that ain't double dippin' makin' more money than God!"

Phillip is more than attentive to this fount of wisdom. "Are you saying the unions are no good?" asks Phillip. It's clear he's attempting to separate Grizz's facts from fiction.

"I'm sayin' none ah them union people is good. It's just that some are worse than others. Mostly it's they damned greedy leaders that's linin' they own damn pockets posin' as poor thwarted victims of greedy capitalists. They makin' damned sure they ain't gonna be left behind even at the cost of they rank and file goonies."

"What you are tryin' ta say Grizz is unions are no good?" asks Phillip again. There's more than a little perplexity in his voice.

"Well at last my young unlearned friend, you're catchin' on. I remember back in '39 when the big strikes at the car plants was hot stuff. Them folks was all strikin' fer good workin' conditions. I ain't sayin' they's perfect today, but they ain't nothin' like they was when I was there in '36. Most ah them all been fixed. Today all these unions is worried about is gettin' more money."

Manny is just as attentive as Phillip to what their new friend is trying to tell them.

"You sayin' money runs the unions?" Manny digs a bit deeper into the psyche of this free thinking foot soldier for independence.

"Makin' plenty ah bread, that's what America is all about my friend. It don't make no never mind whether you union or captalist, it's makin big bucks that's the main concern," answers Grizz with an air of authority.

Manny is satisfied with Grizz's assessment, but finds himself pushing in deeper. "What about all the good people that have dropped out and are livin' in communes where money doesn't mean anything?"

Grizz doesn't miss a beat. "From what I can see of them folks, they's freed from lovin' a bunch ah material things but they sure as hell ain't free from themselves. They jus as greedy about gettin' one more potato or bein' a big shot in the commune. Ain't a lot ah difference, everybody got somethin' goin' down."

Phillip is listening with curiosity. Something about his outspoken friend has him stumped. "Do you mind if I ask you a personal question?"

"All depends, but I'll sure as hell let ya know."

"Are you a progressive democrat?"

A big grin comes across Grizz's face exposing his two lone eye teeth. "Hell no! I wouldn't belong to anythin' that wants to make the goddam government my boss. Those progressive pecker-heads ain't nothin' more than a bunch of wimps. If I tell you what I am, will you promise not to tell anyone?"

Both Phillip and Manny are all ears. Together they take the pledge. "No, hell no, we won't tell anyone."

Grizz looks first to his right and then to his left to check out who may be eavesdropping. Satisfied they are not being monitored, motioning with his first finger and leaning over the table he moves them forward. Phillip and Manny both respond in sync leaning into Grizz. Without a warning Grizz blurts out in his loudest voice, "I'M A GODDAM ANARCHIST!!"

As a consequence, both jerk back in alarm. Grizz also feigns alarm. Then bursts out laughing as only Grizz can do. He's delighted how he has pulled these two trusting, unsuspecting initiates into his vortex of near psychopathy.

Seeing how they had so easily been taken in, Phillip and Manny recover quick enough to laugh along with Grizz over their faux pas.

Still not willing to release their old miscreant, Phillip pushes forth with yet another question. "Grizz you been around a long time, what's your take on this war?"

Grizz muses for a second. "Gotta get rid of the coffee breaks." He says this as matter-of-factly as one would talk about ridding one's house of rats.

As usual with Grizz, he gives rise to still more questions. Following Grizz's answer, Phillip remains perplexed. "How so Grizz?"

With the same matter-of-fact demeanor, Grizz simply states, "That's where America sits on their do nothin' ass." Waiting and watching for this straightforward, simple solution to sink in, he follows through with, "'Til you get 'em out the goddam coffee shops where they jus talkin' and inta the goddam streets this war ain't ever gonna end, and that's a goddam fact. Americans gotta get out in the streets and declare war on all them city halls across the country."

The night wears on with Grizz tirelessly spewing odious rhetoric against any and all governments around the globe.

CHAPTER 25

Winter soon passes into spring.

One day, Audra makes her way to where Deidre and Shelly are talking. She's carrying a chart with a grouping of what appear to be constellations.

"The stars and planets are aligning themselves in a way that if your baby is born in the next few days it will greatly benefit the child. The chance of a strong reincarnation with a soul that is highly spiritually developed is in the stars," she says with the firm conviction of one who has a special link to the *Summerland* (Wicca heaven).

Deidre has no idea what Audra is talking about, but wants to be with it. She simply nods her head in agreement, while exclaiming, "Cool! That would be very cool!"

Encouraged by Deidre's seeming delight, Audra's face lights up with yet another revelation, "And if it's a girl, she'll be a great achiever."

Audra's heart is politically in the Feminist Movement. She hails her prophetic penetration into the future as a triumph for a cause close to her heart.

Deidre, aware it's not cool to be too Christian, tries to fake exuberance over this insight, exclaiming, "Oh Wow! Far out!" Clearing her throat reveals a rattle deep down in her chest that draws Audra's immediate attention.

Having been so excited to bring this Wicca prophecy to Deidre, Audra had failed to notice until now Deidre's physical condition. "That cough doesn't sound good. How long you had it?" asks Audra. The concern is written all over her face.

"Maybe a week," she confesses. "Why do you ask, it's just a cold?"

Putting a hand to Deidre's forehead, Audra exclaims, "You got yourself one hell of a fever girl. You're going to bed now!"

Over the next two days Deidre's condition deteriorates. Her fever is well over 100 degrees. Audra would much rather use natural homeopathic solutions, but because of the direness of Deidre's condition, she is giving her some of the black market penicillin she has hoarded for just such an occasion. Unfortunately it doesn't seem to be helping. As Audra is considering getting Deidre to a hospital, she begins to go into respiratory failure. Audra knows full well the baby is already suffering from oxygen deprivation and some drastic measures are going to have to happen soon or both mother and baby will die.

"Deidre we have to get you to a hospital. You're not getting any better and I don't want to take the chance of you losing the baby," bemoans Audra.

In a clearly weakened voice, Deidre says, "I don't think I can make it."

"Oh don't worry kid, *we'll* get you there." Audra's voice is firm and reassuring.

Coughing several times, it's obvious Deidre is trying to say something. "I mean I'm having contractions *now*," she manages to get out between gasps for air.

Audra isn't prepared for this kind of life and death happening. All of her deliveries have been with healthy young women. Still keeping her wits about her, Audra measures Deidre's cervix.

"You're definitely dilating,"

It's more than obvious to Audra she's into this situation—way beyond the point of no return. Leaving Deidre for a moment, she goes outside to give Shelly an update. Before she can say a word, Shelly has already read her whole demeanor.

"It's not good, is it?" asks Shelly.

"It's as bad as it can get. She's already in labor. It's too dangerous to move her now." Pausing with deep concern, she adds, "I think she's too weak to make it."

Suddenly a coarse, guttural moan comes from the adjoining bedroom. Without a word, both Audra and Shelly immediately return. Deidre is sitting up holding her stomach. Her hair is soaked with sweat as well as her face and hands. There is no question what is happening here.

Audra wastes not a moment before she has Deidre on her back with legs apart to discover the child's head is already visible in the birth canal. Her focus now is to complete this birth as quickly and safely as possible.

Shelly is instinctively holding on to Deidre's grasping hands, trying to comfort her as best she can. What started as a difficult situation is now progressing to its own end. Within minutes, Audra has the child safely out and railing against its forced liberation. It's a girl. Deidre lets out a long gasp of air and her eyes suddenly fade to a blank stare. They wait anxiously for her next breath—it doesn't come. Once more the irony of life plays its end game of taking one life and replacing it with another.

The next few weeks reflect a mix of feelings with no distinct names. Joy and sorrow are simple words without a descriptive word in between. The responsibility of contacting Deidre's parents and having the local funeral home ship her remains back to Michigan falls on Shelly. Now with a fuller realization that this child—who is named Katherine Shelly by Deidre's choice—is not going away any time soon, the entire commune welcomes this newcomer. Fulfilling her promise to Deidre to parent this child, Shelly assumes this undertaking with the fervor only a loving parent can exhibit.

Day by day her sadness over the loss of her friend is overshadowed with the delight this little girl now called "Kate" brings. She has all her fingers and toes along with a small red birth mark on the back of her neck gracing her hairline. It's rather distinct in its shape and brightness.

Audra is a great help. She is happy to be at least a part of this child's development. At her insistence, she managed to find a wet nurse among the Amish, who is secretly supplying breast milk.

"Breast milk is the only sensible food for this child," insists Audra.

Shelly is happy for the help the entire community is offering, but as it goes with these things, there are always more chiefs than Indians. Everyone has an opinion as to what needs to be done with this child. Shelly sees each of these well-meaning people wanting to use this child as a science project to meet their own ideas of life.

As Shelly grows more accustomed to the daily rigors of child rearing, she takes on more and more of the decisions concerning Kate's welfare. One morning while bathing Kate, the thought of baptizing her crosses her mind. She recalls from her catechism class how, in emergencies, one could baptize another. The thought lingered throughout the day. Digging around in the old box of books she hauls around with her, she digs out that ancient book. Thumbing through the pages, she comes across the remembered formula.

Looking out the window for any disapproving visitors, she fills a pan with water. Putting the ancient text next to the water, she takes little Kate in one arm, with the other she pours the water over her tiny head, all the while pronouncing the words of baptism.

Satisfied she has done what Deidre would have wanted, Shelly sits with baby Kate in her rocking chair. An inexplicable sense of peace settles over her. In the midst of this harmony, she realizes how terribly she misses Deidre.

CHAPTER 26

Deidre's parents were never made aware that they had a grandchild. In their attempt to caution Deidre, they had made it clear when she came of age they would not take on the responsibility of rearing any illegitimate children. Deidre was rightly concerned they would put her child up for adoption should she ever become pregnant.

Audra co-operated with the deception by filing a birth certificate listing Shelly Parks as the birth mother and the father "unknown." Shelly is more than willing to take on her new motherly role. Her days and nights are changing very rapidly. Her nights are interrupted by feedings. Her days by more feedings, diaper changing, and baths. The days race by. In Shelly's life, little Kate is becoming more and more conspicuous by her presence as Deidre becomes more and more conspicuous by her absence.

"I feel so alone without you," sighs Shelly. Nearly every day her thoughts turn to Deidre. Things will remind her of an event they shared or Kate will do something she wishes Deidre was there to experience. There is an emptiness in her without her friend. But this mood quickly passes with the squeal of a contented baby. Kate is an unusually happy child. They look at one another in the way only a mother and daughter can. She and Shelly have truly bonded as mother and child.

Shelly finds herself lying awake wondering where life is going to take her and Kate. To stay on at the commune only lends itself to her lonely memories without her friend. But there is also a sweetness in all this. Looking fondly at Kate, Shelly knows why the skies have become bluer, the birds' songs prettier.

"Katie girl, we gotta make a move one of these days," says Shelly as she puts her on the floor to roll around. Kate quickly finds a corner of her blanket, tasting it and finding it to her liking she squeals in appreciation.

Shelly is considering getting back in college. Her mother has been divorced from her father since he found "Miss Wonderful" at work. Anyway it's hardly an option to go back home. Too many questions would arise. Michigan State University, on the other hand, has on-campus apartments for families.

In talking to Audra, Shelly says, "I think I'd qualify for something like that. I just have to get back there and see what kind of help is available for us." The decision is soon taken out of her hands.

An official looking car makes its way down the lane. Quinton is working on the road which has turned to mud with the heavy spring rains. The car stops and a gray-haired, middle-aged woman dressed in business clothes gets out and speaks with Quinton. She seems to be persistent in her quest to make her way to the living quarters around the barn. Her determination is met by a ribbon of mud. Nonetheless, she carries on, leaving her car behind, hell-bent to make the trek afoot. By the time she has made the journey, the suit pants she's wearing are covered in mud clear to her knees, and her shoes have been sucked off her feet. With Quinton directly on her heels, she is definitely exasperated. It seems she has already identified herself as a representative of the court. Her interest is with Shelly Park and particularly with the well-being of baby Katherine. Quinton has words with her about her authority.

"The Martin County Court system has jurisdiction over any child born in or living in this county, sir," says this lady with a curtness to her voice. "You're within our jurisdiction and I'm here to assure the safety of our children."

Quinton is definitely caught on his blind side by this lady who has identified herself as one Winifred Spencer, officer of Probate Court.

"Well I'm here ta tell ya you may be all that, but that ain't goin' ta get ya far out here, lady," counters Quinton.

"Mr. Quinton or whatever your name is, you may bully others but rest assured you don't bully me. Now I suggest you find it in that pea brain of yours to make Miss Parks aware of my presence here and that you all begin to find it in your best interest to co-operate!"

"Well Mrs. La-de-da or whatever your name may be, you've wasted your time and a good pair of shoes comin' out here. Shelly Parks ain't here and ain't been fer a week," says Quinton with a straight face. He doesn't consider any untruths he may tell any establishment person as a lie. He refers to it as "tellin' the truth even if I gotta lie ta do it."

"Well I hate to differ with you, sir, but we have it from very good sources that she is indeed here. It is not going to sit well with the judge if I have to bring the sheriff into this," adds Winifred.

Quinton's arms are folded tightly across his chest as he holds to his position.

Seeing she is not going to get any further, she gets a last word in. "This is not the last of me you're going to see!"

Turning on her heel she begins the long muddy trek back to her car. Quinton gives her about a fifty foot lead before he opens the door letting loose two Australian sheep dogs.

They immediately spot a new playmate wallowing her way through the mud. In as much time as it would take to say "scat" the dogs have jumped on her to show their appreciation for coming to play with them.

Predictably, she quickly loses her balance and lands face first in a muddy rut. Quinton can hardly contain himself. The louder Winifred squeals, the more excited the dogs become and increase their burgeoning hyper-active sport. Finally reaching her car, she can't get in, start it, and get out of there quick enough.

Watching all this from the privacy of the common area, Shelly and Audra wait until Quinton makes his way inside to discover what had brought this woman to their doorstep.

Openly pensive, Shelly finally says, "I've had an uneasy feeling that something like this was gonna come creepin' in on me over this. I think my idea of getting back to Michigan is the best for Kate and me right now."

Audra and Quinton both agree.

"I got a sneakin' suspicion these do-gooders are gonna regroup and swoop in on us over this. Probably the quicker you get outta Dodge the better off you're gonna be," says Quinton in a matter of fact tone.

This sudden change in events is the kind of decision in which Shelly believes she needs to trust her gut. Before the day comes to a close, Shelly has packed her few belongings and prepared to go north. Trying to keep her focus on being as efficient as possible and leave anything that can be easily replaced, she comes across the symbol of Kate's conception. It's the dress Deidre was wearing the night she was raped. Why Deidre insisted on keeping this article of soiled clothing will forever remain a mystery. It's almost as if Deidre hoped she could hold it up to her rapist someday and he would claim it. Deciding it's too much effort to analyze, she throws the small bag in with her belongings as well as a ready supply of diapers. With Kate already weaned from her wet nurse and now on formula, she feels they're both ready to make the trip.

By the end of the day the two of them are on a bus heading for Lansing, Michigan. With no plan other than to avoid any Martin County officials, she arrives in Lansing with the clothes on her back, a suitcase with a few more clothing items for the two of them, and a second hand baby stroller. Getting off the bus into a dark Michigan night is a sobering experience. Nevertheless, there is an immediate feeling of familiarity with her Lansing surroundings. It's three o'clock in the morning and no longer having any connections to her old friends, she makes her way to the Salvation Army. In spite of being exhausted, Shelly has a sense of relief.

The Salvation Army is prepared for these particular varieties of human needs and gives her a voucher for a nearby motel. This motel would have been fine for her alone, but now that she has Kate, she finds herself much more particular about their surroundings. As it turns out this facility is filled with hippies and street people strung out on everything from cocaine to heroin. In spite of all this, once the warm air from her motel room envelopes her, and her door is locked behind her, her worries are set aside in favor of a long awaited rest.

The next morning she's awakened by a loud pounding on her door. Looking at Kate sleeping soundly in the bed next to her, she cracks the door open, but only as far as the chain allows. Outside peering in is a toothless man with a grizzled beard and bloodshot eyes and the distinct smell of alcohol making its way through the three inch door opening.

"They's a lot ah haryion round here. You people all needs the Lord," says the toothless man with the seriousness of a snake handler.

"Thank you, sir. I'll repent," says Shelly closing her door in the man's face with one hand while re-locking it with the other.

All the commotion has awakened Kate. The bus trip has disrupted her normal schedule resulting in a cranky baby.

"Ahh sweetie you're so hungry, Mommy will get you a bottle." Scrounging around in her bags, she finds a half-full bottle. Running a bit of hot water into it to take the chill off, she puts the nipple into Kate's eager mouth. Aware they have to get settled somewhere soon, Shelly begins to pack things up and prepares to make her way to MSU. She's confident she'll be eligible for student housing.

Forty-five minutes later she is standing before the counter of the housing office waiting on a clerk to round up her records as a student. The middle-aged lady attending to her reappears with a dossier. The look on her face is already telling Shelly things aren't looking too good.

"Miss Parks, our records show you've missed a couple of terms indicating it disrupted your student loans. You're going to have to catch up on those before we can consider reinstating you."

Shelly's heart and mind froze. *"Now what the hell am I going to do?"*

With no other options and only a five dollar bill left, she makes her way back to the Salvation Army. To say she's defeated is a little premature, but she's definitely concerned for Kate's well-being. *"What the hell will they do with us if I can't care for Kate? I can't bear the thought of losing her."* This uninvited thought begins to force its way into her consciousness. By the time she makes her way back and explains her situation, a nice lady, wearing a Salvation Army uniform consisting of a skirt and jacket with a bonnet adorning her tightly bunned hair, is assuring her they will help her with food, nursery care for Kate and housing as long as they are able. All they require is she volunteer in their retail store if she's capable.

Letting out a long sigh and looking at Kate sleeping innocently through all this with the simple child-like faith that all children are blessed with, Shelly agrees with her terms. Unquestionably, Shelly is grateful and relieved she and Kate are not on the streets.

Shelly's mother lives in a small rural community nearby. She is very reluctant to contact her with this surprise homecoming. The last thing she wants to do is move back home under the jurisdiction of her mother. She feels she has made great strides in freeing herself from her familial past.

In her attempt to become her own person, Shelly is quick to see herself as a victim of parents she feels were so intensely wrapped up in their own personal dynamics they ultimately failed her needs. In the hopes of releasing the chains trying to pull her back, she is willing to let sleeping dogs lie—at least for the present.

"We'll get by Katie girl," says Shelly giving her little girl a kiss. "You and Mommy are going to be fine."

Lansing is churning with students finishing exams and heading out for the summer. Simultaneously, Shelly has been miserable with her life lately. She is working at the Salvation Army store while trying to figure out a way to catch up on her missed classes. Sometimes in her thoughts she wonders, *"How did I wind up like this?"*

Conscious that her life is far from where she wants it to be, one day she skips her ride back to pick up Kate at daycare. Her plan is to stop in at an old college drinking hole named "Dagwood's" off Harrison St. She feels her life has been joyless and hopes the diversion will snap her out of her funk. After walking in, she immediately spots an old acquaintance.

"For God's sake it is you, Arnie, Arnie Pinsetter!" she exclaims. They were acquaintances in the anti-war movement the year before. Since this is the only face that's familiar, consequently he has moved up her ladder of importance.

"Shelly? It is Shelly isn't it?" he asks looking her over in the hopes he's got her name right.

"Yeah, I'm still Shelly," she says hoping to appear lighthearted.

"Haven't seen you around lately. You still in school?" he asks.

Without going into details, she hedges the question. "I'm just gettin' back in town. I got a few things to work out, but I'm hopin' for next term."

In passing this new perspective along, she's suddenly aware of how far she's drifted from her previous life. Attempting to regroup and deflect attention away from herself, she feigns an interest in Arnie's life.

"What have you been up to?"

"I'm working as a photojournalist. I sell a few stories along with consequential photographs. So far I'm gettin' by."

Simple as this outing is, Shelly finds it more stimulating than anything she's done since her return. After a few drinks, she becomes unmindful of the time. She's got it in her head the day care will keep Kate until she gets there regardless of the time, and she's sure it won't be that much longer. *"I'll think of an excuse,"* she muses to herself. Another couple of drinks and Arnie is becoming a closer friend than he previously had been.

Time is no longer of the essence. She's discovering an ache she hasn't experienced in some time. Without analyzing it and finding less in her life to believe in, she lets Arnie know she's available. They step out through the backdoor and light up a joint before making their way to Arnie's room. He lives in a four bedroom house which had once served as a family sanctuary, now it houses four students, each with their own room. It's a house that has definitely lost its charm and become a bastion of spilled beer and raging hormones. However, it is still willing to supply a solitary refuge for a one-night stand without totally abandoning its primary purpose as shelter.

Under a drug and alcohol induced passion, and to have no incapacitating encumbrances, the two of them paw at one another until they have removed enough clothing to fulfill their goals.

The night wears on with more drinking and unbound Eros. It's not until Shelly awakens the next morning that the alcohol and drugs have worn off enough to bring her back into reality. She pops up out of bed starting to consider the consequences of the previous night.

"Oh my God! What time is it?" This question is directed at whatever entity is able to supply an answer. Arnie is still lying in bed in the same comatose state he was in the night before. He mumbles something and returns to his snoring.

The full weight of her previous night's escapades crashes down on her with a vengeance. Gathering up her clothing, she continues to ask herself, "What in God's name am I doing? What has become of Kate?" Regardless of her concern, her hangover prevents her from being efficient. She stumbles around the room haphazardly laboring to get her clothing on in the right order.

Once out of the house, it occurs to her she has no idea where she is. Frantic now, she searches for something familiar. It's not until she notices the heavier traffic two blocks away that she has a clue. It's Michigan Avenue. Still realizing she has at least an hour's walk, she sits at a corner bus stop in hopes a bus will be going her way. In spite of luck always having its own way, her prayers are answered. Within twenty minutes she is at Kate's daycare. Trying her best to appear sound and sensible, she rehearses a cock-and-bull story that she hopes will get her off the hook. So far all she's been able to devise is a half-truth she hopes will sound convincing enough to redeem her.

She's met at the door by a Mrs. Willoughby. She's a grandmotherly type along with being a no-nonsense lady that can spot a phony yarn a mile away. Shelly is trying not to be intimidated by the forcefulness of Mrs. Willoughby's persona.

"Oh thank God, Mrs. Willoughby you're still here. I stopped by to see a friend last evening after work. I was so exhausted, I decided to take a short nap before coming by for Kate. The next thing I knew it was morning." Shelly is evaluating her performance by closely studying Mrs. Willoughby's demeanor. She thinks she may have pulled her story off.

Mrs. Willoughby is listening and staring very intently, not saying a word but giving every indication she did not just fall off a turnip truck.

"Well, you're lucky. I decided I'd wait 'til this morning to report you to the Army's welfare agency. Whether your story is true or otherwise, I'll give you this one pass, but mark my words, one more incident like this and I'll report you in a heartbeat. Then it will be up to you to deal with people way over my head."

Shelly heaves a sigh of relief. Aware her lifestyle is in conflict with the Army's protocol for parenting, she realizes she's on thin ice and recognizes she may have to re-evaluate her behavior or make some other arrangements. *"Too much to think about right now,"* she jams it all to the back of her mind—at least for the time being. Meanwhile, her work transportation is preparing to leave. Plucking Kate up in her arms, she hugs her, kisses her, then gives her over once again to Mrs. Willoughby and makes her way back to work.

CHAPTER 27

Things have not gone as smoothly as Shelly had hoped. School is no longer an option but she doesn't consider going home to her mother a realistic choice at this time. Her overnight liaison with Arnie has put her in a probationary status with Mrs. Willoughby. Last, but not least, is the fact she has no money or even a place to go. She's trying very hard to remain optimistic, but a dark cloud has settled over her.

Very conscious of the vigilance of Mrs. Willoughby, Shelly finishes her shift with the temerity of one who realizes her future is hanging by a thread. Gingerly she comes face to face with her seeming nemesis. But as Mrs. Willoughby has earlier assured Shelly, she is withholding any further action providing there is no recurrence of misjudgment on Shelly's part.

Kate's happy face is enough for Shelly to put away any negative thoughts—at least for the moment.

"I don't know what I'd do without you baby girl," says Shelly all the while smothering the child with adoring hugs and kisses.

Relieved to have this rendezvous over with, Shelly and Kate make their way back to their apartment. Sitting out front is a white Volkswagen bus with yellow curtains and peace stickers nearly filling its back side. She is surprised to see Arnie waving to her. Not sure of the purpose for his visit, she waves back. His smile is certainly disarming as he makes his way out of the vehicle toward her and Kate.

"So this is the much-talked-about-Kate, I presume?" says Arnie still sporting his warmhearted smile.

"Yes, it most certainly is," says Shelly. The satisfaction in her heart is telling. "What brings you out this way?" she questions.

Considering the question for a brief second, he smartly responds, "A few things. I certainly wanted to see you again. I wanted to meet Kate... and I have a proposal for you to consider."

Both puzzled and flattered, she says, "Would you come in for a drink and tell me about it?"

Accepting her invitation, they make their way inside.

"I got beer, is that okay?" inquires Shelly making her way to her kitchen.

"Beer's good," he responds.

The nicest way to describe Shelly's apartment is early Salvation Army. Her couch and chair are a dark brown mohair, with spots with no hair. The throw rugs are an early American version of an Oriental copy. The kitchenette is also a mixture of table and chairs from some earlier designs.

Thanking her for the beer, he lights a cigarette and then silently toys with it while contemplating how to say what he came for.

Not willing to wait, Shelly disrupts his obvious pondering. "So what ya got on your mind, Arnie?"

Still continuing to roll the end of his cigarette around the edges of the ashtray, he finally begins to form words, deciding to cut right to the chase.

"You know I'm a photographer. I'd like to take some nudies of you and present them to one of my publishers." Watching for any negative expression from Shelly, he continues. "I think you've got what it takes in looks and attitude to make yourself some easy money."

It would be an understatement to say this proposal has caught her on her blind side. This is a proposition she never would have come up with on her own in a million years and she's not quite sure what kind of response is expected. On the one hand, she feels she should be incensed, but on the other hand, she feels flattered. Still wrestling with her divided feelings, Shelly finally blurts out, "What the hell makes you think that idea is something I'd ever consider?"

"Because I know your look will sell, especially to these downtown guys working in the Capital. They're all spit and polish on the outside but they're leches on the inside—particularly when it comes to hot hippie girls," says Arnie. His conviction for this joint project is distinctly evident in the strength and clarity she hears in his voice.

Listening to Arnie's positive spin on this plan excites a part of her that is beginning to wonder, *"Why can't I do this?"* She takes a sip from her long neck Pabst Blue Ribbon still trying to get her head around such a daring proposal.

"What kind of money can I make doing this?" she asks.

At last hoping he's hit a home run with Shelly, he considers her question. "Since I can't afford to pay you myself, we would have to wait until one of my outlets buy the product. At that point I'd pay you 30% of the net."

"I don't know what all that means, but if I can get a few extra bucks and make Kate's and my life easier, I'll give it a shot," Shelly says, still with a bit of apprehension.

"Oh hell kid, you're a natural. You got all the bells and whistles. I can't imagine not getting buyers," states Arnie with all the confidence of an Arab horse trader. "When ya wanna start?"

"What do I have to do to get ready?" she contemplates.

"For now, nothing. I've got a bit of equipment in my car. We can do a little now—if you're okay with it."

"Let me get Kate fed while you get what you need and then we can go from there," she says attempting to give it some serious thought.

There is something daring, and naughty about this whole affair. Her thinking is beginning to give it a weird sense of risqué legitimacy. Whatever it is, it's getting her juices going. She is already rehearsing a few poses in her mind she found alluring in a recent magazine.

In the time it takes Shelly to feed Kate, bathe, re-diaper, and get her to bed, Arnie has set up a makeshift studio in Shelly's living room. He's definitely done this before. He has lighting, reflectors, tripods cameras, hand held cameras, and an array of backdrops. All he lacks now is a subject in front of his camera.

Shelly is as ready as she's ever going to be. With hands on her hips she asks, "So what is it you want me to do?"

Still arranging and rearranging equipment, Arnie motions her to stand.

"I just want to get a few test shots of you right here. I want to see how much the camera loves you."

Shelly is beginning to feel a nervous perspiration trickling down her sides. It's making her self-conscious. *"This is a lot harder than I thought it would be,"* she thinks to herself as Arnie is tending first to her, then a light, then a backdrop. Finally satisfied, he begins the shoot. Shillik, shillik, shillik, continues the camera as he asks her to reposition every muscle in her body.

"Okay Shelly, you're doin' great. Now, I'd like to get a full frontal view minus the clothing." Finding herself being pulled in by the camera, Shelly follows Arnie's commands.

"Head up, breasts out, arch your back a bit more—good, good." Shillik, shillik, shillik, goes the camera frame after frame.

It's now all about her and she likes it. She remembers the women at the forefront of the Women's Movement declaring that such things as this made women feel demeaned or used. She tests her own experience. "*I'm actually feeling just the opposite. This is exhilarating.*" She has to admit the attention she's receiving from Arnie as he exclaims, "that's great," "oh that's perfect," and "good, good, good!" makes her want to display more of her sensuous side.

As time goes by, and seeing how comfortable Shelly is becoming, Arnie has her pose as a topless Indian princess, a naked hippie girl with a come hither look, and a bare all motorcycle moll with only enough leather to draw in the lustful imagination of any voyeur.

At last satisfied he has enough to get started on a portfolio, Arnie announces, "That's a wrap! Ya done good kid. I told ya you were a natural. I think with what we got here tonight you proved me right."

With little fanfare, Arnie begins packing up his gear. Shelly has put her clothing back on. Not sure where or how this is supposed to end, she waits for a cue from Arnie.

"How do you think your first photo shoot went, Shelly?" asks Arnie while looping a large cord from elbow to hand.

"I'm no pro, but I feel it went okay. I'm not hating myself or anything like that."

"Good! I'm always a little apprehensive with a first timer. Next time we'll work in my studio. I can control outcomes much more closely and you already know what to expect," says Arnie.

"When do you want me again?" she asks. She's out of her element and is more servile than when under familiar conditions.

Attempting to sound as professional as possible, Arnie speculates, "Let me see where these shots can take us. I'll get back with you as soon as I hear from anyone."

Shelly finds herself still yearning for the company of a male and not ready to let him go just yet. Before the words can fully develop in her brain they have sprung to her tongue. "You want to stay and have some supper? I've got a pizza I can pop in the oven."

"I'd hate to put you to the bother."

"No bother, I mean it's not like you're a stranger ya know."

"Let me pack this stuff back in my car and I'll take you up on it," he says maintaining the directness of a professional.

As soon as Arnie is out the door, Shelly applies a much needed swipe of deodorant and brushes her long dark hair from the Indian princess pigtails into a cascade of hair falling down her back. It's not so much that she finds Arnie particularly handsome, but she feels a sense of safety in sharing her sexuality with him. After all, without making any demands, he's the one bringing out her sultry side. Admittedly, she is the one who is leading him to the bedroom.

Arnie finishes packing his photography equipment, and after making his way back to the apartment, he discovers Shelly sitting on her mohair couch. She's still all geeked up over her debut as a nude. Her hands are twirling a joint she has managed to tuck away for just such a special event. Motioning him over with one hand, she places the unlit reefer to her lips with the other. He in turn produces a Zippo lighter.

In seconds the volatile substance is racing to reduce any inhibitions that may have put the brakes on certain questionable behaviors in either of them. The drug is locking them in a kind of primordial abandonment.

Their wordless, wholly ungoverned lusts leave them sexually spent within the next half hour.

In Shelly's case, Arnie is seen as a convenient lover rather than a likely long term prospect. Nonetheless, as they once more use one another, they are unwittingly creating a sense of mutual indebtedness. On the one hand it gives each of them some significance, on the other hand with the lack of commitment it leaves them with a vacancy.

With the onset of the munchies the only thing left to do is to make the pizza.

CHAPTER 28

Eugene McCarthy was emboldened by his extremely close second place to Lyndon Johnson's first place showing in the New Hampshire Presidential Primary. In spite of the initial loss, he has put six primary wins behind him. Phillip and Manny are continuing to support McCarthy all the way to the Chicago convention.

Lyndon Johnson has dropped his bid for re-election, Martin Luther King has been assassinated as well as Robert Kennedy. Civil unrest is being reported in at least a hundred cities around the country.

Phillip and Manny are sure they are making a positive change in the country. The anti-war movement is picking up steam. They are encouraged wherever they go. Unquestionably, the youth are solidly behind their efforts to stop the draft and bring the troops home. They have both adopted a milder, less outrageous approach than some like Tom Hayden or Rennie Davis, who are asking for much more aggressive action.

Phillip is making great strides in presenting a skillful political presentation to church groups, PTA, college fraternities, business groups, and clubs such as Kiwanis and the Lions.

Manny has been appointed the task of getting students as well as non-students registered to vote. The black community is also on the radar for potential voters, especially when it can be shown there is a disproportionate number of Negroes being drafted compared to whites. Most of these non-registered potential voters aren't even aware of the names of the candidates, much less interested in becoming voters.

"Running around door to door attempting to convince these people that democracy can work and that it can be their hands that hold the reins to a new government is not only challenging but a big pain in the ass," declares Manny after a day on the campaign trail.

Phillip is a sympathetic listener as he has his own challenges. "I know what yer up against, but many of the people I'm dealin' with want to blindly follow whatever the government mandates. To these, any kind of opposition is unpatriotic. They look at anyone with an opposing idea as a radical. On the other hand, I got a bunch of highfalutin liberal folks who live off inheritances and give themselves a pass providing they can help the poor with a pittance of their excess. They generally got enough money to keep their kids in some kind of school to shield them from the draft." These are bigger battles than either of them ever expected to face.

Someone listening to Phillip's assessment and familiar with his life of privilege would wonder how he can say these things with a straight face.

"That reminds me, we gotta get our asses back in school before we lose our draft exemption and wake up to find ourselves in some Godforsaken rice paddy," says Manny.

"Let's wait until after the convention in August," says Phillip.

****

Winter campaigning turned to spring campaigning, and now summer is winding down for both Democrats and Republicans. The next big event is each party's convention. The Democrats are the first to hold theirs. Chicago, being a bastion of Democratic politicians is proud to host such an important and prestigious event. Mayor Daley can't be prouder. This is a milestone for his administration. He's bending over backwards to guarantee success for the occasion.

The Democratic Convention is not the only show in town. Rennie Davis, Jerry Rubin, and Tom Hayden are determined to bring the Vietnam War to the forefront of the convention. None are career politicians within the establishment. They are dedicated to bringing every yippie freak, student, and disillusioned Vietnam veteran (some are deserters, some not) into Chicago.

After the King assassination, Mayor Daley sent a memo to his superintendent of police to "shoot to kill any arsonist or anyone with a Molotov cocktail in his hand because they're potential murderers." He also adds, "shoot to maim and cripple anyone looting any stores in our city." The threats made by these radical dissidents to put LSD in his water supply and to burn and loot, will not deter him.

The word is out along with every embellished rumor. This is just the challenge the nation's youth need to test the resolve of such blatant admonitions. Within a few days there are hundreds if not thousands of long-haired hippie freaks occupying Lincoln Park. It is not a park randomly picked to have a melee of unwashed, anti-war protesting hippies and yippies converge and not be noticed. This particular area of Chicago is definitely upscale and certainly not ready to entertain the idea of having this disturbance in their backyard.

So far the protestors are content with running pseudo military drills using Kung Fu tactics as a defense needed in "kicking these pigs in the balls." Some have bo staffs they're twirling around at phantom cops. These tactics aren't necessarily the designs of someone practicing to protect themselves as much as they are aggressive tactics in fighting an opponent.

This group, calling themselves "Yippies," has a disdain for anyone not joining to support them. That includes everyone described as "SDS and the middle-class peace movement."

Phillip and Manny have distanced themselves from this wild-eyed group of protesters. They have volunteered to go out into the streets to reason with these unwieldy anti-war supporters. A strategy is being worked out by Sheldon Green, still acting as McCarthy's lead street coordinator.

"Phillip, what makes you believe you can talk this group into limiting their footprint going into this convention?" inquires Sheldon. Phillip has gotten used to Sheldon's pragmatic approach and is prepared to give him a matter-of-fact response.

"I know many of them from a sit-in we did in New York last year. I think I have a decent enough relationship with their leaders to at least get their attention."

Sheldon muses over this possibility for a moment. "That could be significant if you can get it done. The last thing we need is these guys getting the headlines," says Sheldon. "The press will go wherever the action is and we need them on the convention floor and not in the goddam streets."

"I would like to work with Manny to get this done," expresses Phillip.

Sheldon is trying hard to withhold too strong a judgment against this rogue group of hardcore street protestors, fully realizing they needed each other's support in the past, but for this event, they are causing complications.

"Well, I hope to hell you can get these loose cannons screwed down before the convention begins," he reiterates. "We need every bit of support we can muster if we expect to be victorious."

Phillip and Manny are familiar with Jerry Rubin and his preferred tactics; piss off everybody you can. Faced with the task of getting this job done, they find themselves alone with the responsibility of coming up with a solution. Phillip expresses his concerns, "What do you think Manny, how we gonna manage this?

"I'm not real sure we can get very far. All Jerry talks about is isolating Mayor Daley and killing cops," says Manny. With another thought he adds, "Maybe we should ditch these suits so they don't throw something at us."

After digging around in their old hippie clothing, they deck themselves out in their old preferred dress of tie-dyed T-shirts and bell bottom jeans. Given a free hand to rein in the black sheep, they set out for the Lincoln Park encampment with hopes of initiating a contact.

Making their way through the throngs of dope smoking yippies, they confront a fairly sober looking young man with a headband and studious looking glasses.

"Can you point the way to Rubin's headquarters?" asks Phillip.

The young man points to a tent down the way with a single flag pole flying an American flag upside down beneath a Vietcong banner. Neither of them expected anything less. Jerry has been adamant about honoring "Amerika's" enemies.

Once there, they find Jerry, along with Abbie Hoffman, both tripping on something. They greet one another with the typical hippie handclasp along with a little shoulder bump.

Remembering the New York financial building fiasco, Abbie asks, "Man, you still drivin' that far out psychedelic bus?"

"Oh hell yeah. Can't get rid of that, it's our trademark," answers Phillip realizing they may have found common ground to begin their quest in petitioning Abbie and Jerry to tone down their street protests during the convention.

"What brings you into our tent city? I thought I heard you guys are working with that dickhead McCarthy," asks Abbie.

With this attitude coming at them right out of the gate, Phillip and Manny find themselves glancing at each other with a look of surprise. Both now realize they're going to be much less able to reason with this group than they had originally thought.

"You're right, we are working with the McCarthy campaign. We believe we can win more flies with honey than with vinegar," states Manny trying his best to sound confident. "The SDS and every peace movement in the country is saying 'stay home.' All we're askin' is that your group does the same and let the process work its way through the system."

To make this comment to either of these hardcore dissidents has the same effect as if they'd been hit in the head with a board.

"So your job is to come down here with your nice haircuts and try to convince us to go home? Why?...did McCarthy send *you?* Fidel Castro never sent anyone to do his job. He showed up driving his own tank. Che Guevara always did his own front line battles. If your McCarthy had any balls, he'd be here himself—not sending a couple ah skinny red necks."

Phillip is stumbling for words after this rebuff from his former hero. What was true in New York is true now—he's in over his head. Later as he and Manny are leaving, Phillip is quiet, trying to keep his chin up. Finally speaking out, he says, "We've been taken for fools, Manny. What are we gonna tell Sheldon? I know he's counting on us."

Manny doesn't respond. He has his eye on something else. There is a commotion near the entrance of the park. As they get closer, they realize the Chicago police are entering with large military like vehicles with banks of lights that are lighting up a wide periphery across in front of them. The rock music of MC5 only gets louder as this show of force begins to make its way through the streets. Suddenly a dull sound similar to a cannon makes its way across the park. What quickly becomes apparent is the police are beginning to shoot some kind of projectiles into the crowds of agitators. Manny and Phillip suddenly find themselves facing an onslaught of retreating protestors. They're all coughing and gagging, some even vomiting.

"The pigs are gassin' us," shouts someone. The stinging sensation of teargas is permeating the air.

Directly behind this crowd is a wall of advancing Chicago police all decked out in gas masks. It gives them the sinister look of aliens. Simultaneously, others in the crowd are throwing the teargas canisters back at the police.

Everything is becoming more and more chaotic. Garbage cans are methodically set afire and rolled out into the streets. By this time the mood of both sides is turning toward greater violence resulting in the protestors getting savagely beaten and arrested. Some of the hippies are attempting to pull the gas masks off the police. The police respond with clubs. The yippies return with anything that can be thrown including bags of human waste. This in turn provokes the police all the more, responding with even greater force.

Phillip and Manny are finding it's going to be difficult, if not impossible, for them to escape this melee. They're trapped like rats. Yippies are setting up barricades made of anything that can be pried lose. By this time there is no way the police can tell the difference between militant and non-militant protestors. Everyone is reacting in some erratic fashion. Some are running behind the police and throwing bottles, stones and anything else that can be sent airborne, still others are setting fire to anything that will burn.

There's also no way to tell the difference between cops who are willing to give a break and those who will bust your head for pissing them off. It's total chaos. The war is on.

Being in the wrong place at the wrong time is quickly turning into a battle for survival. For the most part the police are in no mood to sort through all these people to determine which are the bad guys. As far as they're concerned anyone in this encampment is trouble in one way or another and everyone is getting the same treatment.

This, to the consternation of Phillip and Manny, results in sudden indiscriminate blows from a baton wielding policeman. Both are cowering on the ground with their hands and arms receiving most of the strikes as they attempt to protect their heads. Unfortunately for Phillip, he receives a crack to the skull that brings an immediate gush of blood streaming down his face. At the same time, Manny is being dragged away by two burly cops. It's obvious these officers are in no mood to hear reasons why they have made mistakes in wreaking the same brand of law-enforcement on all.

As Manny soon discovers, his protestations fall on deaf ears. He quickly finds himself sitting on a cold, gray steel bench in one of Chicago's infamous paddy wagons. He's not alone. It's packed with dirty, smelly, hardcore radicals from every corner of the country. Most have head wounds giving them a grotesque blood-streaked appearance. It's difficult to discern whether their protestations are a result of the beatings, a reaction to the influence of the drugs they're under, or just general anger. Nonetheless, epithets against the mayor, the president, the Democratic and Republican parties alike, and a special roar against the Chicago Police Department fly every time the door opens.

Prior to this experience, Manny's protesting has been much tamer.

His present experience is with a group who had been warned before coming to Chicago this would be Mayor Daley's reaction. This group occupying Lincoln Park had hoped for 500,000 and was very disappointed with only 2000 answering the near demand for anyone under thirty years of age to be here. They're generally an angry bunch who finds no comfort in anything less than a complete overthrow of the repressive U.S.

government, preferably with one of them as the head of a new free dope smoking revolutionary regime built on drugs, sex, and rock and roll.

Simultaneously, Phillip is left to lie on the ground. He's no longer considered a threat, the police move on to more urgent concerns i.e. those still standing. Hardly prepared to meet these kinds of head injuries a group of volunteers are doing the best they can to bandage up the wounded.

Phillip is barely conscious as he feels the jarring effects of being rushed off on a jerry-rigged stretcher to a makeshift infirmary. It's a tent with a handful of volunteer nurses and a couple medical students. The place is overwhelmed with battered protestors, mostly with head injuries needing stitches, plus a few broken fingers and wrists on those able to stave off the more serious injuries directed toward their skulls. The most that can be done under these conditions is to clean, stitch and bandage their wounds.

As the medics work on Phillip, a news reporter is working his way through the mayhem of tangled bodies getting stories as best he can under the circumstances. The fact that Phillip stands out with his trimmed hair and beardless face draws this reporter closer.

"How ya doin', Dude?" Not waiting for an answer, the reporter continues, "Looks like you took a good one, man. My name is Jenkens. I work for the *Lansing Journal* in Lansing Michigan. I'm covering all this as best I can. Would you mind telling me your story and how you ended up in this tent?"

Still on the groggy side, Phillip nonetheless recognizes the name of the newspaper. With this familiarity, he begins to relate that he went to college in East Lansing at Michigan State University and how he came to work for the McCarthy campaign. He tells how he became trapped while attempting to persuade the protestors to either go home or support the McCarthy anti-war platform and ultimately ended up with stitches in his head.

Jenkens can already picture his exclusive: YIPPIES PLAN TO WRECK DEMOCRATIC CONVENTION!

Meanwhile, Manny is also undergoing a unique new experience. He's being booked into jail on what can only be described as undisclosed charges. It's a robotic type of procedure. The jail people have little time for variety. Those who want to be less than compliant are quickly convinced that it's going to cost much more than it's worth to continue their behavior. For the strictly hardcore, it becomes a matter of pride to continue to hold their ground and receive more physical restraint.

In front of Manny is one of the paddy wagon detainees who was arrested with him. The name he has given is Pigasus. He claims to be the ruler of all pigs including all these cops that have rebelled against him and are trying to overthrow his throne by handcuffing him.

"I will return to take my rightful position in pigland. Come zah revolution vee all drink vodka." With his hands tightly manacled, he nonetheless manages to raise his foot into the groin of one of Chicago's finest sending him to his knees. In less than a split second Pigasus is on the floor. There are at least six men in blue making him aware that compelling force telling him his last move was a good idea was anything but. At least a part of his wish comes true they have him hog-tied with leg manacles. Throughout the whole commotion, Pigasus still manages to get in a few pig grunts.

Manny is happy he's merely a bystander. This status soon changes along with the temperament of the jailers. Trying to keep a semblance of control over this group of mouthy, recalcitrant protestors is like trying to herd a bunch of sixth graders all trying to get away with as much as they can. Even though Manny is trying his best to be compliant, he is swept along with the entire horde toward a holding cell that's already overcrowded.

The smell emanating throughout the entire jail is a mixture of overproduced male hormones and sweat. The cell Manny finally finds himself in is no exception. He's been in a lot of anti-war protests, but none like this one. It almost seems as though most of his fellow cellmates are less inclined to be politically motivated and more given over to the adrenalin rush of fighting cops for any reason, or no reason. With them, fighting cops is not a means to an end rather it's an end in itself.

With no way of making contact with the outside world, Manny feels isolated and more alone than he has in any of his previous protests. *With this mess it could be days before I get out of here*, is his pervasive thought. He tries to find a spot where he can get some rest and collect his thoughts.

With all the hollering, cussing and general discomfort of so many packed into a space designed for half their number, and only one toilet, the tensions are running high. Through the grapevine, they've heard the demonstrators have escalated their resistance to a point the Superintendent of Police has called in his reserve units and put the whole area on high alert.

Meanwhile back at the convention hall, Sheldon is also at a loss for reliable information. He has heard that Phillip and Manny have run into some trouble. Unable to act on such a vague bit of information, he turns back to convention problems he can positively deal with, thus abandoning them both to fate.

Manny is now wrestling alone with an unreliable release system. A part of him is hoping for immediate liberation. He may as well wish upon a star. In this case, he hardly expects his dreams to come true. The catch and release tactic most were expecting is a myth. The powers that prevail have left special orders for anyone arrested in civil disobedience to be held until the Democratic Convention ends. Every cell in a fifty-mile radius is being utilized. Manny's fear has turned to boredom.

The tables have been turned on all those who expected the Chicago authorities to be weak. Many, finding themselves subject to the merciless whims of Mayor Daley, are meeting a stark reality. Those whose drug habits need to be fed regularly are beginning to suffer the effects of withdrawal.

Because of the lack of windows and the policy of removing everyone's wristwatch, it's impossible to know when morning arrives. The only way to keep track of time is by the clang of the food carts.

There is a naked young man lying next to Manny. He had been quite loud and belligerent the night before. The combination of drugs and alcohol soon had its way and he passed out. He's stumbling around attempting to retrieve what articles of clothing he can find. Others are realizing that the masquerade is over. Their drugs of choice have worn off and they're left to deal with the situation at hand with no sedation.

The smell of an overflowing toilet permeates the cell, trumping all other odors. Some are conspiring to find a way to bring attention to their situation. A young man named Irving, who seems to be a ring leader, is busy picking up articles of clothing strewn about and piling them in a corner. Others are soaking their shirts under the single faucet and holding them over their face. Word is traveling through the cell for all to do the same. It quickly becomes evident why. Within seconds flames and smoke are shooting up to the ceiling. Panicked guards are fumbling with the protocol for this unexpected gimmick. Soon, but not soon enough, a sergeant arrives and quickly assesses the situation.

"Get this gawdam cell door open!" he shouts. It's evident this is not a difficulty they deal with every day.

Behind him another guard is ready with a fire extinguisher and prepared to enter the smoke-filled cell. As he enters, the men inside mob the open door. Coughing and gasping, they trample over the poor guard who by this time is having his own breathing difficulties. The whole cell block is in turmoil with guards running to and fro, in and out of unguarded doors. The place is filling with the choking smoke from so many burning polyester hippie garments.

Seeing an opportunity to hurriedly walk unnoticed out an unguarded door, Manny and several other astute cellmates make their way out a back exit leading into a parking lot. Hastily, Manny makes his way to a crowded street. Within moments he has lost himself in the crowd beginning to gather to watch the fire trucks stopping in front of the jail building.

Not wishing to attract any unnecessary attention to himself, Manny slows his pace to a stroll rather than an escape mode. At the time of his detainment, he was stripped of his possessions and consequently, he has no money or identification. He can't hail a cab or get into the convention hall without these conveniences. He realizes the only option he has left is to return to the park; the scene of the crime, in hopes of finding Phillip.

Still in the downtown area and miles from Lincoln Park, he sits down to weigh his options. *I can try and walk which will take me a few hours or I can start panhandling to raise enough for a cab.* He quickly decides to begin a panhandling trade. Catching a glimpse of himself in a department store window, he realizes he doesn't need to dishevel himself any more. Even his countenance has a pale morose look to it. *Perfect. I hope it works.* Looking around, he sees an elderly lady walking a dog. Remembering the effective lines the New York street people used, he begins to ply his new trade.

"Ma'am, I'm a fellow American down on my luck. I haven't eaten since yesterday, would you please be so kind as to give me a half dollar for breakfast?"

Her reaction is typical for this part of the Midwest. Fearful he may be a violent hippie, she quickly gives him what he asks for and promptly trots off down the street in hopes of putting distance and time between the two of them. Within the hour Manny has managed to scrounge enough for bus fare and breakfast.

When Manny finally manages to make his way back to Lincoln Park, the tone has truly changed. It definitely has the look and feel of a war zone. There is trash everywhere. Empty booze bottles lay strewn wherever they were dropped. Trees are indiscriminately cut and used for everything from firewood to battle clubs. In all of the mayhem, some of the police equipment got dropped and left behind so there are yippies with police walkie-talkies. Word has gotten back of the fire and jail break. "Chaos and anarchy are reigning. We've got the pigs on the run," shouts Jerry Rubin pumping his fist in the air. "They can't defeat the free people. People here and people in Vietnam are free today."

This leaves the impression that this whole group is merely playing out their fantasies, much like children.

Manny heads directly toward the tent with the huge Vietcong flag. On the way he passes many other tents. One of them is the infirmary. A familiar voice shouts out and a face appears from its shadows.

"Hey Manny! It's me, Phillip."

He has a joint in one hand and a beer in the other. His head has the appearance of one wounded in battle. Aside from the bandages, the right side of his face is swollen to the point of completely closing one eye. He's struggling to produce a smile. It has a rather twisted, snarky appearance. Passing the reefer to Manny, Phillip motions for him to sit down. Over the next hour they catch each other up on the overnight happenings and plan their next move.

Keeping their voices down, Manny says, "I know we gotta get the hell out of here and back to the convention. We've gotta get to a payphone and get somebody to come pick us up."

Putting down his empty beer bottle, Phillip stands ready to go. "Lead the way, my friend."

CHAPTER 29

Shelly's life is definitely turning a corner from her hippie days of communal life. There, she had a support group to hang onto as life met her with its usual unpredictable ways. Without this reinforcement, she finds herself struggling to make decisions for Kate and herself. Kate has developed a cold that doesn't want to go away. This has kept them both up a couple nights. In spite of this, Shelly has to go to work leaving little Kate with Mrs. Willoughby.

Arnie has stepped in to fill the need for the emotional support she seeks. He has gotten back a few good responses from magazine publishers interested in Shelly's photos. She in turn believes she is gaining ground in securing her independence.

"I don't want to get your hopes up too soon, Shelly. To keep our momentum going forward, I want to do a quick follow up with some new material," Arnie says in a resolute business tone.

Since Shelly is a total stranger to the arena of male magazines, Arnie has assumed the role not only of photographer but also her business manager. With no other ostensible options, she feels she must put her destiny in Arnie's hands and hope for the best.

Nonetheless, Shelly has reservations that come out sideways. In trying to make light of her apprehensions, she tries to make a joke with Arnie. "I hope you're not just hanging these nudies in the men's rooms around campus."

Hearing her tone of misgiving and wanting to maintain a self-absorbed confidence in his own abilities, he would rather she show a bit more trust in his business prowess. "I hope you're joking, Shelly."

With a forced smile of uncertainty, she senses his discomfort with her attempt at humor. She takes a certain pleasure in knowing she has found a chink in his otherwise well-defended persona.

"Well so far all I have is your word you have these wonderful contacts that are drooling over my bare ass."

Not having seen this side of Shelly, he is caught off guard. "This is a process. It can't all be done in one fell swoop. We have to make a brand out of you and that's gonna take time. Your perseverance will be the key ingredient to your success."

Satisfied she has put him on the defensive, Shelly asks, "What exactly is your plan to make me a brand?"

Gaining his confidence back, Arnie clears his throat. This is the opening he's been waiting for. "I want to continue with still photos, but I believe we need to get a bit more aggressive. It wouldn't hurt to do a soft porn film as a promo. There's a hell of a market for new stuff. You definitely got the looks ta make sompthin' like that happen."

This is a step Shelly hadn't even remotely considered. "Now what the hell you askin' me ta do, Arnie? You askin' me ta screw some guy on film?"

Seeing her obvious distaste, Arnie is prepared. "It's not as bad as it sounds. All you have ta do is be a good actress. I can set you up where all you have is have simulated sex. We make it look real."

There is a definite pause in Shelly's response. "You make me want to throw up, Arnie," says Shelly.

"Throw up or not, all I'm doin' is presenting a money-makin' opportunity for both of us. You think about it, Shelly. Hopefully you'll get past your prudishness and look at this as a business proposition," declares Arnie. His tone has changed from defense to offense.

"Damn it, Arnie. I'm a Lutheran girl! Ya don't just start tellin' a Lutheran girl ta screw some stranger on film."

"Take your time, Shelly, but not too much. If you want to push yourself forward ta where you can start makin' some real money, you're gonna have ta make a decision soon." With that said, Arnie turns on his heel leaving Shelly with a decision.

Little Kate has developed a deep, hacking cough that quickly gets Shelly's attention.

"Poor little girl. I wish Mamma could make you feel better. I know you're getting this at daycare, but right now we don't have any other choices."

By midnight, Shelly decides Kate needs emergency medical attention. Dressing her as warmly as she can, she takes her out to wait for the next bus, their only way to reach the emergency room. Within the hour they find themselves sitting in the waiting area of the emergency receiving at St. Lawrence Hospital along with a dozen or more people in various stages of misery.

Shelly is trying to be as patient as she can. Kate's cough is nearly nonstop causing Shelly's anxiety level to shoot through the ceiling. By four a.m. the doctor finally gets to them.

"You have one sick baby, Mrs. Parks," declares the doctor in a tone that can only be interpreted as worrisome. "This baby is severely dehydrated. We need to get an IV started immediately and we're going to have to keep her overnight."

Shelly looks into the blue eyes of her sweet child. Kate's dark curls are stuck to her head in disarray. All Shelly can feel is sadness and despair. *If we weren't so damn poor this never would have happened*, she thinks as an attendant gets Kate's IV started.

It's suggested to Shelly she return home and come back in the morning. By the time she walks into her house, she is exhausted. Going to a kitchen cupboard, she pulls out a bottle of vodka, pours herself a half glass and fills the rest with orange juice, lights a joint and within a half-hour, she has induced herself into a comatose state. Eight hours later she awakens to the realization she has also missed work.

At the same time she hears a knock at her door. Still groggy, she opens the door to Mrs. Willoughby. Shocked to see this formidable, older woman paying her a visit, she suddenly becomes aware of the bag of weed and the near empty bottle of vodka sitting on her table. Attempting to scoop both up in the hopes of neither being noticed, she asks, “So nice to see you Mrs. Willoughby. What brings you by?”

“When you didn’t bring Kate by or answer your phone, I felt the need to check on you,” says Mrs. Willoughby.

“Oh we’re okay—I mean I’m okay. I had to take Kate to the hospital at midnight. She wasn’t getting better. I’m glad I did, the doctor said she was very dehydrated.”

Mrs. Willoughby remains a bit distant as she listens to Shelly. She definitely reflects an air of suspicion as she asserts, “Well, you take a few days off and take care of Kate. I’ll fix it at work for you.”

“I sure appreciate your concern, but I think everything will be okay, Mrs. Willoughby,” says Shelly.

She can’t wait to get this woman out of her apartment. Shelly knows she’s been “busted” as far as the booze and the pot go. What is haunting her is where her standing really is with Mrs. Willoughby.

Within a couple days after getting Kate home, Shelly comes to her own fearful conclusions. *I know that woman is going to be trouble. I have to get out from under her nose before she drives me crazy.*

Fortifying herself with what is becoming her favorite drink of choice—vodka and orange juice, Shelly decides to call Arnie. “Arnie, Shelly here.”

Arnie isn’t surprised to hear from Shelly and he’s happy she didn’t wait any longer. “Hey Shelly, what can I do for you?”

"I've been thinking over that proposal you offered me the other day. Can you give me a few more details?"

Arnie is delighted. "Give me a few minutes. I'll stop by and explain a bit more about it."

CHAPTER 30

The summer in Michigan is nearly over. Kate is starting to exhibit her own personality.

Not without troublesome thoughts, Shelly has accepted Arnie's proposal, thus fulfilling her quest to get out from under the watchful eye of Mrs. Willoughby. She is excited by how well things are going. It seems Arnie has more on the ball than Shelly was at first willing to grant him.

Shelly has discovered she can adapt herself to whatever kind of setting Arnie comes up with to make them money. With a few drinks or an occasional snort of cocaine she is finding it possible to actually find some enjoyment in the diversity.

Lately Arnie has been working on a full length porn film that actually requires Shelly to go beyond the mere simulation of intercourse. The next step is to perform the real thing with a big time male porn star that is actually capable of propelling her career into the limelight.

"Arnie, you know damn well I've drawn a line at having real sex with some guy I don't know," laments Shelly.

Arnie is a little more callous about it. "Oh hell Shelly, you'll probably throw stones at me after this guy," laughs Arnie attempting to play down her reservations.

Still not sure she is ready to throw aside all her moral principles, she hesitates.

Seeing her waffling, Arnie makes a single plea. "At least go with me to meet this guy. If you feel uncomfortable with him, we'll just say good-bye and leave it at that."

Shelly tosses her drink back letting the vodka drift down her throat as her thoughts begin to soften toward agreeing with Arnie's request for at least a meeting.

The meeting is set for the next evening at Archie Tarpoff's restaurant in downtown Lansing. Tarpoff is known for catering to the many dignitaries and celebrities that find their way to Lansing. Archie is in his usual mode of stopping at each table to assure his guests they are never far from his thoughts. He learned the restaurant business from his father and has mastered the art of schmoozing his clients.

Stopping at various tables, he's heard saying, "So happy to have you with us tonight. We've all missed you. Is there anything special I can do for you tonight?"

The recent introduction of the avant-garde dimensions within the porn industry facilitates the speed at which porn stars can establish themselves as true artists. Since this new genre of porn movies is quickly finding a legitimate niche in American filmmaking, Archie welcomes them as high quality entertainers.

In this particular setting, there is an up and coming star who has adopted the stage name Freddie Puddunker. He has an agent who is anxious to find a suitable female counterpart for this new American icon.

Arnie had prepared and presented a very well put together portfolio of Shelly's accomplishments. It is impressive enough to earn this meeting. All that seems to be left is to work out the details. Arnie knows that in this industry the chemistry between the actors has to be right from the get go. To facilitate this, he has provided a variety of wardrobes for Shelly to choose from.

Looking at herself in the mirror, Shelly is beginning to get into the sultry role she's expected to play. Her newly peroxided, blonde hair, makeup, and now her slinky white dress present an enchanting package that from any male's perspective is *outta sight*. A couple lines of cocaine and they are on their way to bigger and better things.

Freddie, whose real name is Orin Rogers, is well-proportioned for his six foot height. As Shelly and Arnie make their entrance, it's evident that Orin likes what he sees. After the introductions, he makes a big production of standing and pulling out a chair for Shelly. It's obvious this man knows how to flatter a woman. To say that Shelly isn't impressed by the special attention, and adding to it, the upscale ambiance of this setting would be an understatement.

As the meeting continues and with the drinks flowing, these two continue to size up each other and the chemistry begins to fit. Looking very demur, Shelly seductively takes a sip from her drink. She is no longer sitting on the fence. By this time, Shelly is leaning forward hanging on every word. She is even in ready agreement that she also needs a name that will draw well on a marquee. They all agree on the name Peaches O'Reddy.

"Oh that's so cool, I love that name," she purrs. Soon all that's left is to arrange for a demo and sign the contract.

To have a crack at the big time in the porn industry is a dream come true for Arnie. In this particular market, Arnie is more than prepared to relinquish the movie making to a more professional group and be satisfied with being Shelly's agent.

The next day when all has settled down, Arnie decides it's time to confront Shelly with a question. Having gotten to know her better, he never assumes he knows her answer. "I gotta ask you, Shelly, before I invest any more time into this project—are you all in?"

Considering the question for a moment, she swishes the ice around her glass of vodka and orange juice. "Yeah Arnie, I'm all in."

Lately her voice has taken on a slight slur with her more frequent use of alcohol.

"I hope you mean it Shelly. The last damn thing I want to happen is to get into this project and have you get cold feet. By the way, can you cut back a little on the booze? It's fine to get in the mood on the set, but you're gettin' carried away."

She returns his concern with a middle finger gesture. "Don't worry about my booze, Arnie. You got a full time job takin' care of your own life."

The days are warm for October. Kate is beginning to crawl. She is thrilled with her new found freedom. Each of her new undertakings is met with an immediate reaction of a smile for like and a frown for dislike. For the most part, she has always been a happy baby. She seems to be adventurous, finding joy and contentment in the newness of her daily life.

Shelly looks at Kate's each accomplishment with astonishment as though this child is the first to ever display these wonders of growth. It often crosses her mind to wonder whether Deidre is aware of Kate. These thoughts are always accompanied with sadness because there is no way of knowing these things for certain.

As her career begins to burgeon, Shelly finds herself withdrawing more and more from her hippie lifestyle into this role of Porn Queen. It's proving to be much more diverse, not to mention much more monetarily gratifying. Periodically, her mind will drift back to her commune days. Finding it too confusing to try and analyze where her head is now compared to that time, she pushes the thoughts behind her.

After taking a financial inventory, she concludes she can afford an upscale apartment and a full time nanny for Kate. A part of her is aware of how little time she is spending with Kate and how much her nanny is filling in. The thought troubles her. *I'll get to it tomorrow*, she tries to tell herself. More often than not if she is not busy on a film set, she is recovering from a hangover and *tomorrow* remains only a vague day, yet to come.

As long as Kate is loved, her little life remains on a steady course. Her blossoming growth and development is monitored by her nanny, Courtney. Courtney's a middle-aged black woman originally from Georgia. She is a lady that has come highly recommended by Shelly's producer whose family has outgrown the need of a nanny. Notwithstanding, Courtney comes with definite ideas on how a child should be raised, at the same time she is careful not to say too much about Shelly's scanty parenting skills. With the child-rearing situation well in hand, Shelly is more and more apt to leave Kate for longer periods of time in favor of her own career concerns.

"Tha' chil' needs her mamma, but it ain't my place ta be sayin' so. I jes do what I can," says Courtney with a sigh. Courtney has also taken notice how much Shelly is drinking when she is home. "Tha' girl gonna kill hersef with her drinkin'," she further laments while busying herself folding another piece of clean laundry.

Arnie has proven to be the perfect enabler. He's well aware of Shelly's struggle between her new career requirements and her parochial school principles that still surface from time to time. Whenever there's a questionable part in a new film that will open new porn markets, he encourages her alcohol and drug use to prevent her from thinking too much about it.

"Just leave it all up to me, baby, and don't worry your pretty head about anything. We got enough big bucks ridin' on this film to make anything you gotta do okay. So get rid of any doubts you may think you got," says Arnie.

Of course Arnie says this about all her films regardless of how perverse they require her to become. Without being able to put the words to her emotions, she falls in line hoping things will get easier. All he thinks about is the size of the market they are breaking into and how profitable it will turn out to be. How bad it may grieve Shelly to continue is something he considers an obstacle to overcome. He makes sure she has plenty of cocaine and vodka in her dressing room to ensure her inhibitions are adequately lowered and at the same time keep her libido highly charged. With her inhibitions drugged, as Shelly moves through each stage of her career each level takes more and more from her persona. Along with this abuse, she is developing more and more alcohol and drug dependence.

Each day it becomes more difficult for Shelly to maintain her sobriety. Along with her new addiction to Camel cigarettes, her voice is beginning to sound raspy, giving her a sleazy sound. It's the kind of voice one would expect from a madam twice her age. Despite this, she maintains a facade she's taken on since becoming somewhat of a cult sensation among pornography fans.

CHAPTER 31

Issues of the day through the 1968 campaign season are mounting. The Vietnam War remains at the forefront of the turmoil, but is soon buttressed by the civil rights movement and the assassinations of presidential hopeful Bobby Kennedy and civil rights leader Martin Luther King. Hubert Humphrey has captured the Democratic nomination and Richard Nixon is the Republican nominee with former Alabama governor George Wallace running as a third party candidate.

The hopes of Senator Eugene McCarthy gaining the Democrat nomination have become ancient history along with dashing the hopes of one Phillip Grayling Hampton II to ride McCarthy's coattails into a political career. Instead, he now finds himself falling into a depression like he has never experienced. Both he and Manny have had to find jobs to keep themselves going. Phillip is pumping gas and Manny is working in a jewelry store repairing watches. They are living at the local YMCA without much of a prospect for something better.

"What the hell we gonna do, Manny? I never expected we'd get beat like this. I feel like I been punched in the gut."

As usual, Manny seems to be much more grounded than Phillip. In his familiar pragmatic way, Manny picks an unlikely rejoinder from the training manual of the United States Marine Corps.

"We will adapt and overcome, Phillip—like we always have," says Manny.

With most political movements, the intellectual appeal is usually trumped by the emotional appeal. This new left, counterculture movement is no exception. What continues to fan the flames of this burgeoning front are a real—or at least in some cases perceived as real—sense of repercussions aimed at this youth-oriented ideology.

Phillip is particularly drawn to this blatant generational unrest. For him the streets have become the stage and he is a leading man. Politics are to be lived not something or somebody he votes for. Taking a deep draw on a joint and holding the exhilarating fumes as long as his lungs are willing, he finally exhales passing the reefer to Manny.

"I know what you're sayin' Manny, but I ain't goin' back to my old man's world. He'd like nothin' better than to have me admit him and his world are gonna be my world. I want a world where we can all be free to be whatever we wanna be and do whatever we wanna do."

Both Phillip and Manny are the same age and have shared many a battle together in their short twenty- two years. They have always been supportive of each other. Up until now, an observer would see this relationship as a somewhat codependent kinship, but in a positive thriving way. Now it stands on the border. Manny is beginning to see a gap growing between himself and Phillip in their ideologies. He's not so sure he's still willing or able to drag Phillip out of his more and more frequent depressive moods.

Taking the passed smoke to his lips, Manny takes the few moments to decide what he's going to say to this latest bummer attitude from Phillip.

"I agree in theory with you about being free to become what we wanna be," says Manny.

Taking the next few moments to let the smoky elixir loosen his inhibitions, he finds a few more thoughts he is willing to let loose.

"But what I'm beginning to question is the hardcore street protesting. We've tried that several times. I don't see us as being able to sustain that effort. The majority of the people joining up are there only for the party, as soon as that aspect wears thin, they abandon the rest of us for the next happening."

Phillip's reaction is immediate. He is suddenly taken back by this crack forming in their relationship. Up until now, Manny has always taken a subordinate role in their partnership, now he seems to be stepping aside.

"What the hell are you sayin' Manny? You think you got a better idea. You saw where that peaceful bullshit McCarthy had us doin' led, so don't expect me to fall for that again. That whole peaceful protesting led to nothin'!" says Phillip.

"Well, I think we can at least sustain a stronger front working inside the system rather than in the streets throwin' bottles," returns Manny.

These are not the responses Phillip's expecting from his long-suffering friend. In spite of the soothing effects marijuana usually produces, Phillip's mood is turning to outright sarcasm.

"I suppose you want us to get used to some bootlickin' job where the sale of your soul will earn your bread. That ain't gonna happen with me. If that's what you're thinkin' you're on yer own," says Phillip.

Recently Manny is becoming less affected by Phillip's mood changes.

After all, he's been through similar episodes with him countless times over the years. But nowadays it's beginning to wear thin. For all of Phillip's assumed leadership gifts more and more of his weaknesses are coming to the forefront. Disappointment is his Achilles Heel.

"You know Phillip, I've stood by you because in spite of all your horseshit I could see a point, but I'm beginning to believe the horseshit's burying you. I'm not sure I wanna take the same course you're on," says Manny.

Phillip is half listening. His curses are mumbled as he rummages through a well-worn duffel bag. His mind is definitely more on what he can't find than on the message Manny is attempting to convey.

"Ah there you are ya little bastard," says Phillip pulling out a half bottle of Boone's Farm. Unscrewing the cap, he takes a long draw.

Manny remains silent as he waves the offered bottle back to Phillip. He's not sure Phillip is hearing much of what he is trying to say—or maybe Phillip's trying to avoid what's being said. Either way, there is a definite shift in Manny's attitude.

"Manny, you know damn well we all gotta live in the real world. As beautiful an idea as it is, non-violence got Martin Luther King and Bobby Kennedy dead. Fightin' these pigs on their own terms is dealin' with what is," says Phillip.

"Revolution isn't always brought about by violence, Phillip. Most people don't want to fight if there's a diplomatic solution," says Manny.

Phillip believes Manny's thinking is a residual ideology left over from the McCarthy camp. For the most part, he feels betrayed, defeated, and abandoned by the whole McCarthy experience. By accepting himself as a victim of these circumstances, his self-centered, selfish thoughts quickly fill the vacuum.

"I suppose you're gonna just roll over and let these capitalist pigs keep destroying the world," barks Phillip.

In his usual pragmatic way, Manny sees the uselessness of this conversation, and changes the subject. "Wadda ya say we go back to Michigan and regroup. I think we need a break," says Manny. By the next morning, they have quit their jobs, readied the bus and are on the road.

Within twenty-four hours, they pull into Lansing still without a plan, but nonetheless, somewhat relieved to be back. Their first stop is Dagwood's. In spite of being absent for a year, they have a sense of returning home.

One of the first people they run into is Roland Wagnar. Roland's parents immigrated from Germany right after he was born giving him dual citizenship. He was their old drug dealer and has successfully managed to build himself a small empire.

"I make people feel better," is his ongoing mantra.

He has an unassuming personality which has lent itself to his success—especially at avoiding arrest. His hair and clothing are plain, as is his personality. Not one of these externals suggests anything about him being a drug dealer. The only questionable outward feature is the cute little Mexican chick he picked up on one of his trips to the border. She is definitely out of his league other than seeing him as a sugar daddy.

Phillip is particularly taken with this chance meeting. "So Rolly, ya got any good shit?" asks Phillip.

Rolly gives him his big dumb look. "What the hell you talkin' about, man?"

"It's me, Phillip Hampton. You remember me don't ya?" says Phillip.

Rolly gives him a second look. "Oh yeah, Hampton. I remember. I gotta be careful. These damned cops are posin' as students. They'd like nothin' more than ta bust me. Where the hell ya been man? It's been a long time."

"You're right, it has been a while. I'm just wondering if I could score some weed?"

"I got some dynamite Panama Red, dude. This stuff'll blow yer head up. How much ya want?"

"A dime bag'll do for now."

Stepping outside to make the deal, Phillip makes it clear he'd like to talk to Rolly about something else. "Ya know if you ever need help, I'd like ta have a crack at the business."

Pausing at the query, Rolly asks, "Whadda ya sayin' man? You thinkin' on cuttin' inta my business?"

"No, no man, I just got back in town. I just need ta be doin' somethin'."

"I dunno man, you think you got the gonads for this business?"

"If I can go door ta door campaigin' for McCarthy, I oughta be able ta sell a little dope."

"I'm not talkin' about sellin' dope. Anybody can do that. I'm talkin' about not gettin' *caught* sellin' dope. That's a whole nother set of skills, dude."

People are beginning to mill around within earshot. Without carrying through the deal, they put the discussion on hold for another day.

****

Meanwhile, Manny is kibitzing about the bar with a completely different agenda. He's looking for one person in particular. Charles Levitt is a young councilman from Detroit who is making quite a name for himself in the Democratic Party. Manny has read about him in just about every left wing news rag printed. He's rumored to hang around Dagwood's.

After asking around, Manny is directed toward a table near the back. The man sitting there is short-necked, maybe thirty, with a pair of spectacles perched on the end of his long pointed nose. With one hand, he's forcing several french fries at a time into his mouth. With the other hand, he's thumbing through what appears to be some sort of document.

Not quite sure how he's going to approach his target, Manny stops short of the table. He stands staring for an uncomfortable moment. It's just long enough to attract the attention of the seated man who lays his document on the table and peers over the top of his glasses. The man does not say anything but his eyes question the reason for the interruption.

"Are you Mr. Levitt?" asks Manny, still hesitant to come closer.

"If you mean, am I Charles Levitt, I am," answers the man. "What can I do for you?"

"My name is Manny Meitzer. I've been following your career and I'm more than a little impressed with your achievements and would like to get some advice from you," says Manny.

Now with both hands free, Charles finishes chewing and wipes his face with a napkin. He stands and extends his right hand to grasp Manny's. With the other hand, he motions for Manny to take the opposite chair. His demeanor is obliging. He's rather diminutive in height but makes up for it in girth.

"You say your name is Meitzer? I've got relatives on my mother's side named Meitzer. They were Holocaust survivors."

"My father's cousin, Louis Meitzer, survived Dachau," replies Manny, happy he has made a possible connection.

"Well, we're probably related. Damned few Jews left in the world not to be," says Charles, adjusting his chair. "So what's pressing on your mind?"

Manny wants to make a good first impression so he pauses long enough to form the right words. "I just got back in town. I worked on the McCarthy campaign, but I'm sure you're very well aware that's over. Humphrey has his own people and is reluctant to take on people he hasn't worked with, so right now I feel like a fish out of water. I'm hoping maybe you have some work ideas for me. I've read a lot about your politics and find your views to be very, very similar to my own."

"Oh so you worked on Gene's campaign. He's a good man. I don't think Hubert is quite the man Gene is, but either of these men is better than Nixon," says Charles.

Manny is trying to breathe and act normally. He's beginning to feel a bit more confident about how this conversation is beginning to play out. "I feel the same way as you. Our party is the only party to stop this damnable war," says Manny.

Charles is paying quite a bit of attention to this exchange, especially to Manny's personality and demeanor. The last thing he wants is to patronize the hot heads. Not to say the party doesn't need them from time to time, but they have demonstrated they are more of an embarrassment than an enhancement.

"What're your feelings about how that gets done?" presses Charles in reference to the Vietnam conflict.

Manny is well aware that Charles could be clever enough to trick him if he isn't cautious. Carefully measuring his reply, Manny wants to be as transparent as he safely can.

"To tell you the truth, I've been all around this struggle—both peaceful and violent. I'm convinced the violent way is not the most effective." Manny then goes on to bring Charles up to date with his anti-war involvement.

When he is satisfied Manny's got a good head and he's not dealing with an Abbie Hoffman, Charles writes a quick note of introduction for Manny.

"You take this note along with you to any Capital Democrat downtown. I believe someone will find a spot for you," contributes Charles.

****

Despite their differences, Phillip and Manny are not ready to completely break this crumbling relationship. There are still areas of mutual aid they share. Financially, neither of them can afford an apartment alone. What they are finding is by giving the other a little space, they can stay out of each other's business. They silently accept their lives are taking separate courses.

The bus has definitely seen better days and the local ordinances are rapidly catching up with any vehicle vagrancy—perceived or otherwise. Parking anywhere in the city is asking for a hassle from the police. Without much of an inspection, this old crate would be sentenced to the nearest junk yard. To continue sleeping in it is only asking for trouble.

For the first few days they find a couple of their old familiar crash pads are still in existence. In some respects they welcome any handout but on the other hand, they are not used to being beholding to anyone other than their upper class families. Both have found their long-suffering families are basically fed up with their shenanigans and have cut them off financially leaving them to fend for themselves.

Life is kicking their asses and they aren't used to being desperate.

"How's that 'adapt and overcome' crap workin' for us Manny?" asks Phillip. Phillip has definitely turned a different corner.

Manny is quietly reflective in spite of Phillip's predicable reaction. He is hoping his meeting with Charles Levitt will open doors for him. He's sure his passion for politics will stand him well in the long run and sooner if he can relieve himself of Phillip.

CHAPTER 32

Phillip's compulsion for running things is kicking in once again, only this time he's without the organizational skills of Manny. They have separated and Manny has moved in with some old friends leaving Phillip to manage on his own.

Phillip has made himself available to Rolly, if for nothing other than running dope to buyers. All the while he's doing this, his mind is telling him he needs to be in charge.

Over the next year the money he has accumulated by selling the bus, along with what Rolly pays him for delivering drugs and what he can steal and resell by slightly shorting people on the amounts he delivers has accumulated into a decent sized nest egg. He continuously plots for the day when he will no longer need Rolly.

A year has passed. It's the summer of 1969. Rolly has taught him well. He no longer sports a beard, long hair and hippie clothing. Phillip has taken on the appearance of a young Mormon missionary: short well-groomed hair, white shirt, black tie, shoes, trousers and the ubiquitous black back pack.

After a year of learning how to avoid police by becoming so nondescript his mother wouldn't recognize him, Phillip has chosen a summer day to branch out on his own. With $2000 cash in hand, he decides to make a bus trip. His destination is Laredo, Texas, a Texas/Mexico border city on the Rio Grande. Being in the drug circles, one can pick up a lot of information indirectly and without asking. As nondescript as these drug dealing guys try to make themselves, there is still a penchant for braggadocio. What he has learned from listening to their self-aggrandizing is how necessary it is to stay on the American side of the border and let the drug smuggling Mexicans make their way across.

Still sporting his Mormon missionary clothing, and after a two day bus ride, Phillip arrives in Laredo toward evening. Renting a locker inside the bus station, he leaves the bulk of his money in the locker for safekeeping, taking only enough for personal expenses. Realizing he must hurry to get a cheap room before the hookers fill them for the night, he manages to get the last one at the Rosalita. It's a flea bitten motel room smelling of mildew but it has an air conditioner and is convenient to Slaughter Park. Slaughter Park is where Rolly makes all his drug deals. He has claimed it is frequented by illegal Mexican drug dealers ready to make a quick deal and seldom watched by the Border Patrol.

Peering out the window through a crack in the curtains, he sees things that are unfamiliar—at least to this Michigan guy. There are vendors openly hawking every kind of taco, burrito, or quesadilla known to man. Phillip's eating has been sporadic over the last few days. Right now anything is welcome. Making his way to the nearest stand for anything edible, he stands out in this crowd. He's way too clean cut for this part of town.

It's not long before he's approached by a twenty something guy with a definite Mexican accent. "Hey man, you wanna buy some good Mexican weed?"

Phillip is taken by surprise by the open forwardness of this man. But he has also learned that these street drug dealers are often undercover police and not to be trusted. Everything he is doing is first time stuff.

"No thank you sir, but I'd like to talk to you about the Bible," replies Phillip.

Looking surprised and at a loss for words, the man is taken back as though he had just been seared with a hot iron. His facial expression would be more appropriate if it were his grandmother asking the same question. Catching himself quickly, the man throws his hands up in a defensive gesture as he mutely backs away.

The whole episode makes Phillip smile. Still not sure whether this was a legitimate drug dealer, he nonetheless enjoys watching his deception play out. The success of this encounter only tends to reinforce Phillip's sense of invincibility.

Before making the return trip to his motel room, Phillip decides to take a walk through Slaughter Park in hopes of getting a better idea of what he is going to have to deal with the next day.

The park is in definite need of some care. There is a whole group of people who seem to have set up more than temporary housing. Some are in tents of all sorts, while others occupy tin and cardboard shacks. The paths are well worn and there is trash everywhere. From what he can tell, this is where all the homeless with mental illness finally land. The Border Patrol tries to get here fairly regularly, if for no other reason than in the hopes of temporarily putting the brakes on unencumbered drug distribution.

Seeing this mess for what it is, Phillip decides to make his way to the river in hopes of avoiding the massive fallout of this LSD generation's self-induced paranoid schizophrenics.

Finally arriving at the shores of the Rio Grande, Phillip is amazed at how close Mexico is. He has listened time and time again to Rolly discussing his method of making contact with "the swimmers." These are unusually strong, young Mexican boys who can swim the distance while carrying an ample supply of marijuana strapped to their bodies. Rolly never went into great detail about how he made the deal with these swimmers, leaving Phillip at the mercy of his own calculations.

All of a sudden, this lack of knowledge makes Phillip feel less confident than before he reached this stage of the game. Looking around in hopes of finding some clue to the process, he notices a group of three young men, somewhere around his age, hanging out near a clump of scrub trees not more than eighty feet away. They seem to have noticed him, also. Being in the drug business for a year has sharpened Phillip's sense of knowing when things aren't looking friendly. This is beginning to appear to be one of those times. Suddenly, he recognizes one of the men at the same time the man recognizes him.

In a thick Mexican accent the man calls out, "Hey Bible man! What you wan heer? You come down here to Preech?" It's the same man that approached him earlier about buying some good Mexican weed.

Attempting to process what may be coming next, Phillip is willing to gamble. Feeling the sweat begin to form in his armpits he shouts back, "I'm only gonna preach if you're a cop. Otherwise, I'm here on business." He holds his breath hoping his reassessment of this guy as a genuine drug dealer is not wrong.

"Hey man no cops heer." Turning to his other friends he prompts them, "Hey Carlos, hey Armando, you guys cops?"

Both answer, "No man, we no cops!"

The man is now looking directly at Phillip. "How bou you preecher man? You a cop?"

Phillip is not sure where he stands with these really, really intimidating men. His sweating hand fumbles around in his pocket for his switchblade knife. He has come to rely on this deadly instrument more than once to get him through a dangerous predicament. Not quite ready to pull it, he opts to wait and see what their next move may be. Robbery among drug dealers is common enough and one can never be ready to react soon enough.

Trying not second-guess himself in this latest quandary, Phillip measures his words. "No man, I'm no cop either and if you're plannin' on robbin' me, I ain't dumb enough to carry cash. So what do you suppose I'm doin' down here?"

The three men glance at each other with a look that suggests they may be changing their intentions.

Not waiting for them to further respond, Phillip assumes the initiative. "What about talkin' ta me about some of that good Mexican weed you were tellin' me about an hour ago."

There is something in Phillip's voice that gets their attention in a different way. They continue to look at one another as though debating whether to move forward with this unlikely demand.

"What you lookeeng for man?"

"I'm looking to do a deal for a half-dozen kilos of quality pot."

The three Mexicans continue looking at one another. Finally the first man speaks. "You talkeeng beeg moanies man. How we know you gots beeg moanies?"

"What the hell other reason would I be hangin' around a shit-hole like this. If you ain't willin' ta do business, I can go somewhere else." With that said, Phillip turns to leave.

"Wayeet man, don leeve. Mabee we do some beesnees, eh?" says the still nameless man.

Phillip stops and notices the man is smiling through his drooping mustache. He's willing to wait giving the man the next word.

"My name ees Tito. I theenk we do some beesnees," says the man now willing to identify himself.

"Okay," says Phillip, "Now I want to ask you some questions. Why should I believe you can deliver that size of an order?"

With a slight chuckle Tito says, "Wha make you theenk I can't? You ass anybodee bow Tito, theey tell you. Nobodee sell anyteeng here less Tito say so. All theese sweemers you see heer work for Tito."

The other two identified as Carlos and Armando are smiling and shaking their heads in agreement with Tito's statement.

Phillip's mind winds up in first gear. He has had nearly every kind of encounter working the streets over the past year and is anxious to begin this new chapter in his life with this untested way of doing business. On the other hand, many negative thoughts are exploding in his head. *What if these guys are playin' me for a sucker? What if they try and rob me? What if they're just settin' me up to collect a reward? What if the dope is scrap weed?*

Nevertheless, Phillip collects himself and his thoughts together long enough to agree to meet with Tito at his motel room the following day during the siesta time. Tito has learned this to be the best time to avoid any Border Patrol. They agree on $150/kilo.

"Just one more thing, Tito—you come alone," establishes Phillip in his sternest tone. "I see you show up with either of these guys and the deal is off," he says, pointing to Carlos and Armando.

Still smiling Tito reaches out to shake hands with Phillip. Phillip grasps Tito's hand drawing him close.

"Tito you screw me over, I'll see that you never get any Michigan business again. You treat me right and I'll bring you more business than you can handle."

Tito stops smiling momentarily with this revelation, and then smiling once again, he vigorously pumps Phillip's hand.

"No need to worree, Senor, Tito know wheer hees bread ees buttered."

CHAPTER 33

Manny couldn't be more elated. Using his letter of introduction from Charles Levitt, he manages to get his foot in the door as a legislative assistant for a Democrat in the Michigan House of Representatives from Levitt's district. As boring as this job may appear to anyone else, to him this is a dream come true. This is the "in" he has been hoping would open up for him. His expectations for his future lie squarely in the world of politics.

This is a full time position in the Lansing office of Michigan Representative Clyde Paderewski, a union Democrat from Hamtramck. So far Manny's exposure to anything political has centered on the anti-Vietnam War effort. Now he is expected to organize an office with all its varying tasks and is in charge of press releases and maintaining positive constituent relations. He is also expected to keep his mouth shut concerning any behavior that could be damaging to his employer's political aspirations. Even though in theory, Manny is supposed to be more inclined to protect the dignity of the office of Representative, in practice, he better damn well protect the reputation of the Representative first.

In wanting to make a good impression on his employer, Manny is adamant about his job. He is more than willing to be the first person in the office each day and the last to leave. His hair is no longer than his employer's and he is content to have his uniform around the office be a suit and tie. Not wanting to risk any confrontation with the law, Manny has purposely curtailed his illegal drug use to the privacy of his own apartment. Careful to listen to his employer's stand on issues, Manny measures his own opinions along the same lines. He is determined to prove to himself and to anyone else he can succeed in politics.

It's not that he could erase his past, even if he wanted to, but he's hoping nothing he's done comes back to haunt him. He's gone so far as to use his position to run a police check on himself to see if that incident during the Chicago convention would show up. Much to his relief it didn't. The only thing he can attribute that stroke of luck to is that nothing got recorded at the time due to all the confusion surrounding the situation.

Leonard Krutz, who goes by Len, is an assistant to another legislator, down the hall. Manny has gotten to know him well enough to begin confiding in him. He's been here for at least the two terms his boss has been elected to. Len is somewhat of a busybody in many aspects. When offering Manny information, he is more than willing to go beyond what needs to be said. He's one of those people who convince themselves that their gossip is information. Manny is open to whatever this seasoned legislative assistant has to say that will keep him on the inside track.

"You may as well know now as later, none of these lawmakers is squeaky clean. Some days it's all we can do to cover their ass," offers Len.

"You're startin' ta scare me, Len," says Manny.

"I don't mean ta scare you, but it helps to come into this job with both eyes open. I'm just sayin' there's more to this stuff than just a bunch of typin'," says Len, attempting to tone down his advice to a low roar.

"You can damn well bet your ass you're gonna be the first one I come to if I need that kind of help," says Manny with a weak nervous smile.

He didn't have to wait long. Barely a day had gone by since his conversation with Len before he was called into Representative Paderewski's office. Paderewski had just gotten back after being out of the office for a week. Today he can't be more accommodating.

"Good to see you, Manny." Pointing to a chair Paderewski invites him to sit down.

"Thank you, sir," says Manny obeying. His manner is rather obsequious.

"I want to tell you what a great job you've been doing getting this office straightened out."

"Thank you, sir," replies Manny again.

"I've just spent nearly a week listening to every five point demand from every union, civil rights, feminist, and anti-war group in the district—including Gay Bikers for Christ. They all think theirs is the only demand I have to deal with. If I dealt with every one of these, I'd never get any work done," says Paderewski handing Manny a pile of papers. "I want you to go through these and assure each of these constituents we have their proposals before us and we will be dealing with each of them personally."

Manny takes a moment to thumb through the stack before addressing his boss. "Yes sir, I'll get right on this," says Manny beginning to rise out of his chair.

Paderewski has more on his mind. Stopping Manny, he points back to the chair indicating he wants him to sit back down.

"Manny, what do you think of marijuana?" he begins.

The question has caught Manny on his blind side. He sits speechless still holding the stack of papers. He takes advantage of a few of them slipping to the floor and uses the time it takes to retrieve them to assess this question.

"I'm not sure I understand your question, sir," stammers Manny still fussing with the documents.

"It's a simple question. I know your generation is substantially acquainted with it and I'm assuming that includes you—or am I wrong?"

Manny's nervousness is unmistakable. Still not sure where this question is leading, he measures his words carefully.

"I suppose for me to say I *never* tried it would be less than truthful," Manny's mind is racing. Not wanting to expose himself unnecessarily, he watches Paderewski's facial expressions for any sign he's gone beyond a simple answer.

Paderewski seeing the discomfort he's causing his young charge interrupts with yet another question.

"Do you think it's something a man my age should try?" Paderewski is old enough to be Manny's father and clearly out of range of them hanging out socially.

Weighing his response, Manny still holds some suspicion as to where this discussion is going and why. He finally finds himself forming the words that are independently coming to the forefront of his thoughts.

"I wouldn't imagine that it could cause you any physical harm, if that's what you mean," answers Manny as best he can. The circumstances are clearly weird and unprecedented.

Paderewski is not finished yet. Now it's his turn to measure his words.

"I've been thinking lately it might be a good idea if I had a bit more exposure to the subject of all this controversy. You know, weigh the good and the bad arguments surrounding the question of its effects. What's your opinion?"

Manny feels very much on the spot. He's only been here a few weeks. To have a question like this posed to him from a man as important as this lawmaker, is heavy to say the least. Again, he hopes to supply an answer that will impress his boss. "I suppose any information you can personally experience is better than someone who has never had the experience, merely giving you their opinion," he says hoping he's on the right track.

"I think that's sensible advice, Manny." Without a second thought Paderewski says, "Do what you can to get me some pot."

Somewhat dumbfounded, Manny considers the request. "How much do you think you'd like me to get?"

"Oh, I don't know, I'll leave that up to you, but make it enough to make a good solid determination. Take the cost out of petty cash. We sure as hell don't need a record of this," says Paderewski rising from his chair. Having given Manny his marching orders, he opens the door and excuses him.

Hardly noticing the skewed armload of crumpled papers he's gripped tightly through this whole fiasco, Manny's mind continues whirling crazily over the strange happenings of the past few minutes. Arriving in his office, he becomes even more anxious over this very beguiling request. After a few minutes of nervous frustration, he bolts from his office and makes his way down the hall hoping Len will be available.

As luck will have it, Len is just coming out of his office. Seeing Manny stampeding down the hall, he stops for a moment.

"Good to see you Manny, what's happenin'?" questions Len. He can clearly see something is wrong.

"Len, you're never gonna believe the conversation I just walked out of with Paderewski," says Manny, hardly able to contain himself.

Considering the ramped up behavior of Manny and not wanting to miss a gossip tidbit, he makes a quick judgment. "Come on down to the coffee shop and tell me about it."

Picking a booth out of earshot, Manny begins to disgorge the conversation he had with his boss. Len is listening with the interest of a gossip columnist. As the story unfolds, a smirk begins to form across his face.

"Well, I'll be go to hell, that old son-of-a bitch is pulling that same old caper once again," says Len. He's clearly taking this much more lightly than Manny and it's obvious he's enjoying every second of this conversation.

Manny's reaction is mixed. He's trying to sort through what Len's unusual response means. It's clear Len is taking this whole episode much more whimsically than he is.

"What's so damn funny, Len?" returns Manny. He clearly does not find this amusing.

"Ole Clyde's been pullin' that marijuana experiment bullshit for years. Get him a kilo. That'll last him awhile," says Len with a clear tone, but dripping with sarcasm.

"You mean he's done this before?" asks Manny.

"Hell yes. I got him a kilo hardly six months ago. He caught me alone one day right here in the coffee shop just as serious as a judge. He said he needed to see what's behind all the hubbub about pot and asked could I help him out," says Len. "So he gives me $400, I got his kilo for $360 and made 40 bucks on the deal," laughs Len at Paderewski's antics.

With this insight, Manny begins to settle down. "I guess I gotta get my head outta the sand," he says, shaking his head at his own naiveté. "That ole fart sure had me goin'."

"How the hell you think he's been elected this many times? If he can't dazzle ya with brilliance, he'll sure as hell try and baffle ya with bullshit," says Len. "And don't worry, there's a lot more to come." Now both are roaring with laughter.

By the next day Manny has contacted Rolly and a kilo of Mexican weed is discreetly left in Paderewski's office in the Michigan State Capitol.

CHAPTER 34

Phillip has successfully pulled off his own first big dope deal. He is astounded at his success. Looking back he is amazed at how easy it was. For the present at least, Phillip is convinced he has discovered his ideal occupation. It's full of intrigue, suspense, danger, and best of all it's a money maker. One thing that's becoming clearer to him is that money gives him the freedom he has always yearned for.

While still in Laredo, Phillip picks up a flier announcing a rock concert in New York State at a town called Woodstock. It promises three days of love and peace. This is just the kind of venue he needs to make some big bucks in his new venture. After spotting a second-hand Volkswagen camper for $500, and not bothering with a bus ticket for the return trip, he quickly makes the deal. Packing up as fast as he can, he next stops by a Church of Latter Day Saints. He strategically picks up as many tracts as they have to give him along with a Book of Mormon. Loading his baggage area with as much of these materials as he can, he's nearly ready to begin his trip.

Next, he utilizes an old trick a drug dealer had shared with him. By removing the inside door panels there's a large enough space inside to safely hide his dope before replacing them. With a bottle of Jack Daniels, which has become his drug of choice lately, Phillip begins his quest to make it to the Woodstock happening. With faith the van will do the job, he merrily begins his 2000 mile trek to this eastern Mecca of drug users.

Shortly after leaving Texas, he notices an unusual cloud formation in the sky. It appears to be that of a bearded grandfatherly type giving a wink toward Phillip as if to say, "You're headed in the right direction" At least this is what Phillip is willing to see in this cloud.

The next couple of days can easily be described as uneventful. That is, until he reaches the Midwestern state of Ohio. Suddenly he discovers himself to be part of a long caravan of similar vehicles full of young people. Concluding it's necessary to stop for gas, he engages in conversation with a carload of college age kids also fueling up.

"So where you people headed?" he asks.

"Hey man, we're headin' for the biggest, baddest, freak show this century will produce," says a shirtless, ponytailed freak taking a hit off a joint being passed from the backseat. In a friendly gesture, he offers a hit to Phillip whom he perceives to be dressed in some kind of "straight insurance salesman" outfit. To his total shock, Phillip accepts, sucking in its vapors all the way to the bottom of his lowest lung lobe.

"Far out, Dude, far out!" is all that can be heard from the entire car as Phillip exhales handing the joint back.

The rest of the trip is reminiscent of this chance meeting. There is every type of vehicle capable of moving forward, all carrying a cargo of the great unwashed, providing they're under the age of thirty.

Just as a van spewing a cloud of black smoke from the tailpipe passes him, two young laughing women each display a pair of bare breasts out the van's side window. Phillip knows immediately this escapade is going to be a sellout moneymaker.

Just as this van speeds out of sight, another familiar vehicle appears behind him. At a glance, he recognizes it as an Ohio state police car. No sooner does this clear, unmistakable realization reach his brain than a red light from the patrol car lights up. He immediately looks down at his speedometer and realizes he is only traveling 35 miles an hour. Reacting quickly, he pulls off the road onto the shoulder. The trooper slowly and methodically makes his way to the back of Phillip's camper. Looking through the back window, he examines the tracts of the Church of Latter Day Saints arranged in neat packages in plain sight across the covering on the bunk bed. He next makes his way to the driver-side window.

"May I see your driver's license, son?" he asks. He's a man much older than Phillip, maybe around his father's age. His air is definitely one of professional confidence. It's a kind of self-confident authority that has always intimidated Phillip. He's fine with his own peers, even arrogantly haughty, but this kind of maturity is ominous. He's never ready for it. As much as he has rehearsed these kinds of situations, Phillip is quivering as he riffles through his glove box. Finally getting his papers in order, he nervously hands them to the waiting patrolman.

"Do you know why I stopped you?" further questions the officer.

"No sir, I don't. I know I couldn't possibly have been speeding," reports Phillip.

"I can readily assure you, you were definitely not speeding. We have a minimum speed limit on our expressway of 45 miles per hour. You were only doing 35. Are you experiencing some kind of engine trouble?" he politely inquires.

Still trying to process this uncertain situation, Phillip had zoned out from the pot he smoked a few minutes ago at the gas station. This contributed to slowing everything down to a crawl. With his mind clearing enough, he finally acknowledges, "No sir, no engine problem other than these Volkswagens only have a 50 horsepower engine. Top speed is 55 miles per hour. I'm a missionary on a trip to New York. I'm on a tight budget and just trying to save on gas."

The officer doesn't say anything while Phillip is explaining his state of affairs, but he is busy looking through all the windows. Finally satisfied, the officer hands him back his driver's license with a single imperative, "Pick your speed up to 45."

"Man there's nothin' like a cop to ruin a good buzz," mutters Phillip as he gets his vehicle back on the road. Out of nowhere, the words of an old song begin to rush through his mind.

"*Oh what a beautiful morning, oh what a beautiful day…everything's going my way.*"

He remains confident he can fall into a barrel of horseshit and come out smelling like a rose.

The rest of the day is uneventful other than a couple hitchhikers he encounters. He doesn't pay much attention to the guy, but the girl is a far-out looking chick. Deciding to pick them up to make the time go by, he soon realizes they're tripping on LSD. They are definitely on a different wave length making it difficult to have any sensible conversation with either of them. Before they have gone more than a mile down the road, both of these interlopers have crawled into the back of the van, stripped off their clothing and begun to dance naked. The next thing Phillip is aware of, the two strangers are freely copulating in the back of his van *on his bunk.* Wanting to remain cool, he tries to ignore them. He doesn't have to wait long. While trying to adjust to their bizarre behavior, the guy demands he stop and let them out. In their LSD tilted minds they have concluded they are being kidnapped and need to escape. Phillip willingly pulls to the side of the highway and lets them out.

On Thursday, he arrives in the town of Woodstock, New York. The town is swarming with hippies. In an attempt to get the scoop on what's coming down, Phillip approaches a group gathered on a street corner. It's obvious they're angry about something.

"Hey man, what's goin' down with the concert this weekend?" he asks.

One of the guys saunters over to his stopped van. "I don't know man, we came here from Colorado. The last we heard is they're havin' stuff happenin' at a town called Woodstock." Pointing his finger, he adds, "Come to find out it's about fifty miles that way in some dude's hayfield."

"Far-out man, thanks a lot for the info," says Phillip anxious to get rolling. Now he is measuring his time in hours. It's imperative he get himself organized. He feels the need to be prepared for unforeseen difficulties he may face in getting his pot to these revelers.

Finding a private place to get six kilos out of concealment and weighed is a challenge. At last he comes across an obscure farm lane and risks pulling off hoping he won't be noticed by the owner. The lane is a two track. It's thick with foliage separating two huge cornfields. Convinced he's alone, he begins his arduous task. Each kilo has to be carefully divided, weighed and bagged. Drug dealers always consider their job worth whatever profit they make considering the amount of work involved, not to mention the risk.

Within a few hours, the task is completed and sleep overtakes him. He awakens to the chatter of crows discussing the meaning of his presence in their domain. The morning is overcast and threatening rain. He takes only a moment to relieve his bladder and then changes from his missionary clothing into his more comfortable tie-dyed T-shirt, bell bottom jeans and sandals. Quickly getting his mind into what he has to do to be prepared for the next two days, Phillip gets himself on the road with a Snickers bar as a breakfast choice.

The road is clogged with every kind of motorized conveyance one can imagine. Many are broken down and abandoned with their cargo of young people making their way on foot hoping to catch a ride like so many pilgrims on their way to the Promised Land.

As Phillip's destination nears, the road becomes more and more crowded. Still several miles from the goal, Phillip makes a decision. *"I'm far enough ahead of the crowd, if I set up along here, I should sell out before the end of the day."*

A suitable spot to stop is just ahead. It's a tractor trail used to enter a field. It's indented far enough to provide another couple cars room to pull off allowing customers an unencumbered shopping experience.

Without fanfare, Phillip unrolls the camper's awning and places himself on a camp chair behind a portable card table. He's ready for business. Just as he had predicted, the traffic has slowed to a snail's pace. He's also positioned to conveniently spot any police cars coming up the road. Between the walking crowd and the cars pulling into his pseudo parking lot, he's selling faster than he has ever experienced in all his drug peddling days.

Man this is like Christmas in August is an honest assessment.

Before the day is over, Phillip has sold every scrap of weed he brought. His choice now is to try and make his way to the happening or get out of there. Just as he is trying to make his decision the sky opens up delivering a deluge. Inside his camper, dry, and with his pockets stuffed with money, he makes another decision. *I'm getting' the hell out of here while the gettin's good.*

CHAPTER 35

A few more years have gone by. Kate is five years old and entering kindergarten. Shelly has enrolled her in a Lutheran parochial school. Since she has been remiss in church attendance herself for years and is reluctant to draw attention to herself, Shelly has decided to keep quiet about her own Lutheran background and enroll Kate as a non-member full tuition student.

In spite of Shelly's daily use of alcohol, she is still managing to keep her career going. Her brand name "Peaches O'Reddy" is voted in the top five nationwide in the "Miss Nude" model contest of the year.

Courtney is still left with much of the child rearing due to demands made on Shelly's time. There is no question Shelly adores Kate, but between her drinking and work, she has little energy left for mothering. Whether because of alcohol or the demands of others, the result remains the same—she's been absent much of Kate's life.

"Miss Kate, you a good lil girl. Courtney makin' sure you stay thata way," says Courtney combing through a mass of brunette curls.

Kate is taking on a look of her own. She has her mother's petite frame, but that's all. The source of her nearly mid-eastern features remains a mystery as does her father. Even though they have no proof, Shelly, as well as Deidre, has always suspected Phillip Grayling Hampton II of being complicit in Deidre's rape and subsequent pregnancy. He has never come forward, but his weird attraction toward Deidre always made him suspect. Kate shares her hair color with Phillip, but that's the only physical characteristic they have in common. Her looks are uniquely her own. Her personality is confident and outgoing. She makes friends easily and is able to remain content in any setting. All in all, she is a well-adjusted little girl.

Kate has no idea when she took her first step, or who was there, or when she first used a real toilet instead of a diaper, or who was present to hear her first words, but Courtney has kept track of who wasn't there.

"That chil' gonna grow up thinkin' I'm her momma iffin her momma don't get herself together soon," says Courtney out loud to the walls, a load of laundry, or anything else she feels is there to hear her concerns. She's careful not to say these things within earshot of Kate for fear she may repeat them. The only ones she *will not* speak to are the authorities. She doesn't trust them anymore than Shelly. Her solution is to handle Kate's circumstances her own way. That means sacrificing a lot of her own private life to oversee where Shelly has left a vacuum.

"I love you, Momma. I love you, Courtney," says Kate. Her affections for Courtney as well as her mother are distributed without judgment.

Kate has an imaginary friend she's named Tweety. She likes to share everything she learns whether at school or elsewhere and she goes into great detail, to make sure Tweety understands what she is trying to explain.

"You sure is a smart little thing ain't you?" says Courtney overhearing Kate's characterizations.

Courtney is one of sixteen siblings. Her parents came north for work. Her mother did housecleaning and her father worked in the car factories. Only a few of her younger brothers and sisters finished high school. Courtney was one of the older children left to oversee the younger ones while her parents worked.

"Ah bin takin' care ah chilin' seems my whole life. Don know how ta do noffin, else," says Courtney. "Beside, Ah gotta say it gimme pleasure takin care some poe chil grown up bad."

Courtney had only one child, many years ago. It was a boy. He died at birth due to the umbilical cord strangling him. Her man never came around again.

"Iffin' I cain't have thatn, I ain't gonna have no mo," she says with regret still lingering in her voice. "Sides tha ma tale a woe. Es me gotta lib wid it."

Courtney is well aware of the kind of work Shelly is involved in and makes no judgments. "It ain't ma place ta be makin somebody job my business. Longs they pays me, ah ain't got no say bout they monies or where they gets it. It ain't none ah ma no never mind."

Courtney is well aware of what alcohol can do to a person. "Ah bin seein' tha tail waggin' the dog aroun this family," she's overheard telling a friend.

She lost her father to the disease. When her father lost his job because of his drinking, he thought he lost all reason to live and drank himself to death in a couple years. The family began to fall apart with the absence of a father even before his death. His lack of parental guidance directly contributed to several of her brothers going to prison and some of her sisters having drug and alcohol problems.

Despite Courtney's lack of formal education, she has a good grasp on life. She's been sharing this advantage with Kate since Kate was a small baby. Her hope is to see the results of sound thinking play out in the life of someone else.

What gives her the most joy is how Kate has learned to sing when she takes her to the Baptist Church. Kate stands waving her arms and swinging her little hips to the rhythm of the singing as if she's been there all her life—but then she practically has.

Kate also has a cat named Muffin. As cats go, this one puts up with all kinds of nonsense including being dressed in doll clothes. What Muffin likes best is to sleep on Kate's pillow.

"Tha cat gimme fits when ah tries ta take im offen that pillow. He stan outside tha room howelin' like he bin scalded," laughs Courtney in retelling the cat's shenanigans.

Courtney knows the day will come when Kate will no longer need her. "This job gots a bitter taste sometimes," she sighs.

****

Shelly longs for something but she can never quite put her finger on exactly what it is. She spends much of her time looking in a mirror examining her body. She is beginning to sense she's walking the fine line between a mature body and an aging one. Trying to determine when she lost herself is just one of the demons that relentlessly chase her, or for that matter whether she ever had a grip on herself at all. Even though she feels her early childhood life was repressive, she finds somewhere underneath it all it must have had some value to feel such a loss. After all, isn't she putting Kate's life on the same track as her parents had done for her?

I feel like I've thrown the baby out with the bathwater—like something's been stolen from me, is her first thought. Her second thought is maybe she's grown ignorant as to what is baby and what is bathwater. She fears somewhere in all the razzle-dazzle of life something has crept in determined to have its way. Trying to discern what is passing fantasies and what is here to stay is becoming more and more clouded. It's at times like these when her thoughts wander back to the seemingly simpler times at the commune. *I miss you, Deidre,* is her reflection when the thundering forces in her life become too loud to bear alone.

Arnie considers it part of his job to clear things up for her. He is the quintessential agent who is riding the wave of someone else's success.

He hopes to be her guru with the simple answers. "Listen babe, sex is here to stay. You're setting a standard that a lot of girls can only hope to reach. You're on top of your game. You may as well ride it out and enjoy it."

Escaping into her work and receiving the accolades of being the best is always short lived. It's not enough to sustain life. It only lasts until it's gone. The year ends with no new contract in sight. Then it's the same every day. Shelly's life is becoming a treadmill of fears and a sense of powerlessness leading to frustrations, followed by drinking until it all goes away. The freedom the new culture promised has also proven to be no more freeing than the culture she is trying to shed. For Shelly there have been no blue skies for a long time.

Arnie is around less and less. Shelly has always known he also promotes other girls, but the looming threat of being placed on the backburner is something she cannot readily accept. As much as she struggles with doing this kind of work, her ego isn't ready for rejection.

When Arnie finally does make an appearance, Shelly can't help but let her anger bubble up to the surface. "So what's goin' on Arnie? You playin' me for one of your bimbos. You get me all hyped up and then you dump me. How the hell you think I'm gonna pay the rent with no work? I feel like you've given me a big slap in the face!"

Attempting to paint a better picture, Arnie plays a different card. Reaching into his bag of brushes, he pulls out his charm brush with a brand new color.

"Rather than seeing this as a slap in the face, let's view this as a new opportunity. We've always talked about beginning a high class escort service. This just may be when the stars are lining up ta move into a new possibility."

"You mean you want me to be your whore?"

"Why do you always have to look at opportunities in the worst possible light?"

"I call it what it is, Arnie," says Shelly taking a long drink from her glass of vodka.

"Maybe if you weren't drunk all the time, our producer might have found another role for you," says Arnie.

This stinging comment has definitely gotten Shelly's attention. Throwing her middle finger in his direction, she yells, "Get the hell out of my house you son-of-a-bitch. It's none of your damn business what I drink!!" Her voice is loud enough to awaken Kate from her nap.

"Mommy, Mommy, what's wrong?" cries Kate, stumbling into the room still rubbing her eyes.

Shelly grabs Kate up into her arms as though she is some kind of security blanket. In her drunken stupor, she continues to vilify Arnie. With tears streaming down her face, Shelly has started a crying jag. It's not something she can turn off at will. The vodka has definitely got a tight hold on her life.

Little Kate is completely at a loss as to what she can do. Holding her mother's face in her hands with tears of fear running down her innocent cheeks, she pleads, "Don't cry, Mommy. Please don't cry anymore!" It's all Kate can express.

Arnie slams the door behind him as he makes his way out of Shelly's apartment determined this is the last time he's going to put up with Shelly's drinking. His intention is to cut her loose and concentrate on other girls filling the vacuum created by Shelly's downward spiral. Fresh new bodies are always waiting to be discovered. There's a new replacement at the drop of a well-placed compliment.

Shelly continues to sob clinging to Kate, rocking her back and forth as though Kate is the only thing that is presently sustaining her life. Kate, on the other hand is terrified at her mother's apparent powerless condition. It leaves her feeling abandoned.

A week passes. For the most part, Arnie has successfully shoved Shelly to the back of his mind. Hardly expecting to hear from her after their wild encounter the week before, he is surprised on answering the doorbell to see her standing on his doorstep.

"Hi Arnie," says a fresh-faced, non-hostile, sober, smiling Shelly. In spite of the smile, there is a sense of desperation enveloping her insides like a caged villain.

"Hey Shelly, what's going on?" he asks. His voice is on the edge of polite. His hand is braced above the door jamb as if to prevent her intrusion.

"I came to apologize. I don't know what came over me, but I want to say I'm sorry."

Arnie is caught off guard. He remains tensely silent for a moment and continues to stare, still not sure how he is going to respond.

Shelly takes the opportunity to speak again. "I haven't had a drink all week. I want to get back to work. I want to talk to you about your proposal. I think it's something I can handle."

Continuing his scrutiny, Arnie moves his hand. "Come on in and we'll talk about it."

These are familiar surroundings. Despite the many times she has been in this apartment, Shelly gingerly makes her way to the same chair she has in the past occupied with confidence as they discussed her prospering career. Now that sureness seems to have slipped away.

With the keenness of a vulture, Arnie recognizes the malleability in this undoubtedly defeated antagonist. "Okay Shelly, we can try this provided there's no drinking and your Lutheran guilt trip stays under control."

With her foot back in the door, Shelly musters up enough security to not sound servile. She's definitely aware of the thin ice below her and restrains her usual combative tone. "I can do that Arnie."

Once again, Arnie remains pensive. He's had enough negative experience trying to manage the behavior of his girls, especially when it comes to drugs and alcohol. He remains somewhat on edge with her outward quick turnaround.

"I want you to know one screw up and we're done, Shelly. This project is too big to let you or anyone ruin it by being stupid. You'll be dealin' with high rollers spending $500 a pop to spend an evening with you.

These guys can't afford to have their indiscretions come to light. So let's see if we can make you, me, and the client happy."

Realizing this is a whole new setting where there is no longer a director controlling a sex scene between two actors who realize much of what they are doing is hard work. Now she's expected to be the director, stage manager, lighting expert and actor all in one in an attempt to fulfill the fantasies of a warped client.

After pledging her allegiance to their new project, Shelly returns to her apartment. Courtney is there tending to Kate. Shelly immediately goes to her room and pours herself a drink. Courtney is a restrained observer. Being black has taught her a restraint that white people are seldom called on to practice. It reflects as a quiet wisdom that catches the attention of troubled people.

Shelly returns and sits with Kate. Courtney has an eye on her without making it apparent. The vodka relaxes Shelly enough to loosen her tongue.

"You always seem to be so content, Courtney. Do you ever feel sad?" asks Shelly, now wishing she had poured a bigger drink.

Courtney is surprised at this sudden and certainly unexpected question. Putting down an armload of Kate's misplaced toys, in a soft tone Courtney says, "Lor' yes chil'. Why you askin'?"

"Cause you always seem to have your head on straight. I mean you seem to be content," replies Shelly straining to find the right words.

Courtney recognizes before her sits a wounded young adult who has lost her way. There are many in Courtney's world who believe that a person's end is determined by their beginning. Being born into poverty or drug or alcohol addiction traps a person into the same life.

"Lor' Miss Shelly, ah gots stuff like everybody gots. Ah jes loosen up on how tight ah grips 'em."

Shelly is heartened by the mere presence of this woman. She shines like a beacon in an otherwise darkened home. "I don't know how to do that anymore," replies Shelly in a voice that contains an honesty Courtney has not heard from her young impulsive employer.

"You ain't never gonna know till ya needs ta know. They ain't no sense wastin' words on a body tha ain't ready ta hear 'em," affirms Courtney with the assurance of one who has survived that test.

"I think I know what you're sayin'. Maybe I'm lookin' for a simple answer," says Shelly.

"They all simple answers Miss Shelly. They jes hard to assept. Maybe you lookin fo da horse's teeff in da wrong end."

"Courtney you're a Godsend. I don't know what Kate and I would do without you," declares Shelly crossing the room to give Courtney a hug. For the first time since she can remember, the mere presence of Courtney is a comfort. For reasons that are not real clear, Shelly sees this little exchange between herself and Courtney as a crossroad. She feels this is the closest human relationship she has had since she lost Deidre.

Courtney gives Shelly a slight nod to acknowledge she heard what she has said but not enough for Shelly to consider that "simple" means "easy." *Oh Lor, give ole Courtney da strenth ta hep this chil' pick up her pieces,* she prays.

The weeks wear on and Shelly manages to keep her drinking out of Arnie's sight. Meanwhile, he has lined up enough high rollers to keep her so busy she doesn't have a lot of spare time. She occasionally has a few drinks with her clients but not nearly as much as her body seems to want.

CHAPTER 36

Spring has sprung in the year of 1975. The fall of Saigon in April ended the war in Vietnam with a clear loss of 50,000 American lives. As much as the government tries to spin a win for the United States it's become clear we've lost to the North Vietnamese government backed by our old Korean Conflict nemesis—China.

It's also becoming clear that more than a foreign war has been lost. A whole generation of American youth has also been lost—lost to drugs, alcohol, substandard values, and mediocre teachers. As much as the politicians are calling for every life to be improved through the feminist movement, the civil rights movement, gay rights movement and many other kinds of social engineering movements, the country is not improving. That's not to say these movements are having no effect. Each change brings with it its own set of problems. Many of these are proving to be more destructive to communities than ever suspected. Trial marriages or bringing children into the world without a commitment from both parents to raise them is becoming more and more the norm.

For Phillip, the more dysfunctional a community becomes the better his drug business is. Since he has become more and more a contender in the underground drug trade, he has managed to carve out a very lucrative living. For a number of years, he and his old boss, Rolly, have managed to successfully grow their businesses without having to engage one another. That ends with a chance meeting this May evening in Dagwood's. The whole campus is celebrating the end of the Vietnam War, or more correctly celebrating the end of the draft.

Both Phillip and Rolly have successfully avoided the draft. In Rolly's case, he had been drafted back in'67. He passed his physical and embarked on a sixteen week boot camp. After graduation from boot training, he was sent home on leave to await orders. His orders soon arrived and he was being sent to Vietnam. On the pretense of wanting to say good bye to his grandparents, he made a trip back to Germany where he held a dual citizenship. Once there, he joined the German Army. They in turn sent notice of his enlistment back to the U.S. Army. The U.S. responded by sending Rolly's discharge papers freeing him from any further obligation to the U.S. Armed Forces. He then deserted the German Army and with his U.S. Army discharge in hand made his way back to the States. Since there is no reciprocity between the U.S. and Germany dealing with military deserters, Rolly was free of any further military obligation in Germany or the U.S. He chose for the sake of his privacy and to avoid any further official action to become a non-person. He lived under assumed names and paid everything with cash, hence leaving no paper trail.

Phillip also had been drafted. When he went for his military physical, he went berserk in his meeting with the army psychiatrist. He began his confrontation by screaming at the doctor that he had to be sent to Vietnam. This unprecedented request, of course, prompted the doctor to inquire why this was such a priority. Phillip's response was, "I NEED TO KILL PEOPLE, DOC. YOU GOTTA MAKE SURE I GO TO NAM, PLEASE, PLEASE! I REALLY NEED TO KILL!!"

The psychiatrist totally rejected him from all military service as mentally unfit.

This chance meeting between the two drug dealers is one of rare congeniality. After all, they have both become quite wealthy capitalizing on the country's youth losing their way. The meeting begins on a cordial note.

Rolly is the first to break the ice. "Hey Phillip, my man. How's things happenin' in your world?" says Rolly, griping Phillip's hand in the familiar hippie handshake.

Phillip's response is equally friendly, "Far out and outta sight, Dude."

After a few more minutes of small talk, Phillip says, "It's strange we should run into each other because I was thinking about getting a hold of you."

Rolly's demeanor changes from one of friendly camaraderie to where he is expecting something not so friendly to pop out of Phillip's mouth. "Yeah? What's on your mind?" asks Rolly.

"I got an opportunity to cut my costs on everything there's a market for, from pot to heroin and everything in between," whispers Phillip.

"So why are you tellin' me?" asks Rolly. He's a bit more defensive than he had been a minute ago.

Phillip motions Rolly to an empty table off to the side. After they are seated, Phillip leans in. "Because this is bigger than anything I've ever dealt with."

"How big you talkin'?" questions Rolly.

"Big! I mean like a hundred fifty grand," reveals Phillip.

"Wow, that's a damn big chunk a change, Dude," replies Rolly. "So whadda ya want outta me?"

"If yer interested, I'll tell you more," says Phillip.

"I might be, tell me what ya got," says Rolly. He's noticeably much more relaxed now that the risk of Phillip raising hell with him for undercutting some of Phillip's prices is not the issue.

Both order whiskey and water. As soon as the waitress leaves, Phillip leans forward across the table, at the same time looking around to see who may be within earshot. Satisfied they're not going to have eavesdroppers, Phillip continues.

"I got a client who buys weed from me here in downtown Lansing. He's in the import-export business. Most of his suppliers have their manufacturing done in Colombia."

Rolly interrupts Phillip at this point. "What the hell is in South Carolina?"

"Not Columbia, South Carolina, Colombia, South *America*!" reiterates Phillip in a more forceful voice.

This immediately gets Rolly's attention. Most drug dealers are aware that much of the illegal drugs ending up in the United States come from places south of the border.

"Tell me more my friend," says Rolly. His enthusiasm is peaking. He's been seeking a more direct southern connection for some time. Anything coming from Colombia goes through Mexican cartels, who take a substantial cut. This information contains a promising outlook.

Phillip begins. "My client buys pottery, statues, figurines and the like from a wholesaler in Santa Barta, Colombia to resell in his downtown store. He avoids import tax by sailing down there himself, loading his boat, and sailing back to a small port in Key West, Florida. I made a trip down there with him as a first mate. I learned a hell of a lot about boating in those waters."

Rolly's wheels are turning a mile a minute listening to Phillip's scuttlebutt. Wanting to hear more, Rolly leans in even more attentively.

Seeing he has Rolly's undivided attention, Phillip lights a cigarette, all the time paying close attention to Rolly's reaction. Taking in a long drag and finally exhaling, he continues, "I figure we can do the same. This guy don't want nothin' ta do with the drug business. He says it's all he can do ta worry about what he's doin' now. He says he can't imagine worryin' about a boatload of drugs."

"Where the hell you plan on gettin' a boat?" asks Rolly.

Seeing Rolly's increased interest, Phillip continues, "That's all taken care of. While I was in Florida, I did a little snoopin' around on my own. I ran into a guy in a bar near the harbor. This guy turns out to be the captain of a boat owned by a Michigan legislator named Paderewski. Just so happens an old roommate of mine works for the dude.

"We got ta talking and one thing led to another. He told me about how they would sail throughout the Caribbean. After a few drinks, he also began to tell me how he charters trips on his own while the boss is in Michigan.

"I listened for a while. When things began to sound like I might be able to take this conversation to the next level, I asked him about drug smuggling in that region. He got a little irate at that point, askin' if I was a cop.

"It took a while for him to calm down. It helped when I told him about just comin' back from a trip to Santa Marta, Colombia and how I helped bring back a boatload of contraband household furnishings. He then began to share with me some of his own experiences along the same lines.

"The night wore on as well as the drinks. When he figured he knew me well enough, we agreed on a price. I checked the boat out. It's a seventy-eight footer, powered by twin diesels. It's capable of carryin' two tons."

Rolly continues to muse. "Why you want *me* in the deal?"

"'Cause I want ta get the lowest price I can. While I was there I found the best price per kilo of pot is eighty bucks. If I buy two tons, that includes packaging and loading the boat."

"So, I'll ask ya again. Why do ya need me?"

"Cause I ain't got the money. I need another fifty grand," says Phillip.

Rolly's business head is clicking into gear. "So what do we have to pay this captain?"

"He takes a third," reports Phillip.

"Holy Mother of God! That's a hell of a lot!" exclaims Rolly.

"It may be, but unless you've learned to walk on water we need him."

Rolly pensively stares at nothing in particular for a moment. Phillip notices Rolly's lips barely moving followed with a slight mumble. Without warning, Rolly suddenly slaps his hand on the table. "You got a deal Phillip!"

With a big smile, Phillip reaches across the table grasping Rolly's hand to seal the deal.

"What the hell were you mumblin'?" asks Phillip.

"I was doin' the math in my head. I figure I can get back around a half mil outta this deal. That's a hell of a lot better than I'm gettin' now," says a delighted Rolly. "When we gonna get started?"

"How about yesterday?" says Phillip.

They both need to tie up some loose ends and agree to begin their dangerous undertaking within a few days.

CHAPTER 37

Arriving in Key West, Florida the following week, Phillip and Rolly go directly to Captain Tony's Saloon. This legendary watering hole is in the same location as the infamous Sloppy Joe's Bar, frequented by Ernest Hemingway back in the 1930s.

Tony Tarraccino is the proprietor. He's a crusty middle-aged transplant from New Jersey having made his way to Key West after a near fatal beating involving a group of gangsters with whom he had a misunderstanding.

"Them dumb asses thought they'd kilt me, left me for dead at the city dump. My ole man was a whiskey drinkin' bootlegger. Hell, them punks din't come close ta whippin' me like he could," says Tony throwing back a shot of his own "House Whiskey." (He had quit school at 14 to manufacture and sell his own and is still doing it.)

Tony's well-acquainted with the drug underworld. He's been involved with everything from fishing to gun running and more recently the cocaine business. He's been married more times and has more children than Georgie Jessel has uncles.

His bar is a well-known hot spot for Caribbean drug deals to be hashed out. This meeting Phillip and Rolly have arranged with Paderewski's yacht captain is no exception. Phillip spots him sitting behind a tree that is situated in the middle of the bar.

The story is the tree is a hangin' tree. It has hoisted the necks of sixteen pirates and a woman who killed her husband and children. But for now it provides the privacy they need to complete their plans surrounding this risky venture.

The captain looks up in time to see Phillip and a stranger approaching the table. He hadn't expected an unscreened guest. From the look on the face of this seasoned seafarer, Phillip realizes he's made a misstep and it's time for some introductions.

"Rolly, I'd like you to meet Captain Paul Rikker. Captain Rikker, I'd like you to meet my partner Roland Wagnar."

Captain Rikker rises and extends his hand, while studying this dark horse.

"You can call me Rolly," conveys the stranger.

Following them is a pretty waitress prepared to take their order.

"Whiskey and water for me," declares Rolly.

"I'll have the same, and bring a refill for the Captain," orders Phillip.

Rolly's eyes are darting all around. He has never seen a bar quite like this. Every square inch of wall and ceiling space is covered. There is in an array of currencies from just about every country in the world. Another tradition is for first time women to hang their brassiere on a rafter. No one can remember how or when the tradition began, but it's been long revered by the male clientele. A montage of license plates from anywhere one finds automobiles is also part of the display.

A bit of uneasy small talk accompanies the initial introductions. Soon the talk turns to a more earnest topic.

Captain Rikker begins with a personal concern. "I'm more than a little uneasy." He looks directly at Phillip and then to Rolly. "I didn't expect a partner I've never met and especially one I know nothing about."

"I can tell you I dig the dude. He's the guy that broke me into the business. He's sold more weed than you and me together. He's also bringin' the other fifty grand to get us the premium price the two of us didn't have," states Phillip. The bluntness of Phillip's tone has given the captain a bit more assurance he's not dealing with a greenhorn.

After an hour of trading war stories, the three of them make their way to the boat. It's a 1970, seventy-eight foot state of the art Stephens Cockpit Motoryacht. It has 5 cabins, 4 double and 1 single, 3 heads with showers, a large salon, modern galley, and twin 475 HP Detroit Diesels. Written in big bold letters across the aft is the name *Polish Princess*.

There is one more aspect to this ship that needs to be considered. It has an arsenal. Anyone sailing in Caribbean waters without defense is dancing with the devil. Many have discovered much to their consternation being unarmed is not an advantage. Captain Rikker is adamant these two must become well-versed in each of these weapons. They range from large caliber rifles to pistols. He insists they at least dry fire each of them. Phillip and Rolly are both issued a loaded .38 Smith and Wesson revolver.

Within twenty-four hours, they have departed Key West and are on the first leg, heading for a fuel stop at Cooper Jack Bay in the Turks and Caicos Islands. The temperature is in the mid-80s. The winds are 10 miles per hour out of the east. In other words, a perfect day for boating.

Captain Rikker patiently acquaints these landlubbers with the finer details of reading a compass, manning the wheel, and learning proper radio lingo. He will cover most of these responsibilities, but there will be times he'll need to sleep.

After Rikker is confident these two can run in open water, they set up eight-hour watches. Rolly will take the first watch starting at daylight, Phillip the second, and Captain Rikker the more precarious night time third watch.

The man at the wheel is responsible for more than merely keeping the ship on course. He is also on the lookout for other water craft—large and small. He is also expected to discern the intent of these other boats (i.e. are they approaching the craft, what side to pass on, are they in distress, are they hostile, are they the coastguard or just another type of recreational boat).

"If any craft looks suspicious be sure and wake me. It will not be a sailing vessel. Rather it will always be a smaller, faster powerboat," says Captain Rikker. "These guys can be pretty creative. They've got a lot of energy and are always scheming. They spend days out here looking for the opportunity to prey on somebody they perceive to be an easy target." With these instructions, Captain Rikker leaves Rolly at the wheel and retires to his cabin.

Rolly experiences a sense of importance he's never known with anything else while standing behind the wheel of this magnificent craft. *Hell man, this is somthin' I could get used to.* He considers he just might get himself a fine boat like this when this venture is completed.

A couple days out of Key West, Phillip is lying in his bunk preparing to take the watch. He's been watching the antics of a less than modern, wooden boat that's been dogging them. He doesn't think too much about the situation until they are less than a hundred feet off the port side. Questioning himself, Phillip says out loud, "I wonder if Rolly is aware of this?"

Leaving his cabin, he makes his way to the ship's wheelhouse in time to hear an explosion off the bow. Rolly is taken by complete surprise by this clandestine attack. Captain Rikker is immediately awakened by the explosion. He is still in his skivvies when he bolts through the cabin door. Just then another explosion blows water onto the ship's windshield.

"Keep those bastards on the port side!" Rikker shouts. Just as he makes his way back out of the wheelhouse, the sound of a voice in broken English comes bellowing through a bull horn above the sound of the wind and engine.

"PREEPARE TO BEE BOARTED. THEES ESS A ROBBERY. ANY RESISTANCE AND I WEEL KEEL ALL OF YOU!!"

Rolly lets loose of the wheel as he unholsters his pistol. Phillip is frozen and unable to move. His mind is attempting to put this into some category that will give a proper response. All the while, the interloper speed boat is edging closer and is now within thirty feet of the yacht. The four man crew looks like they have done this before. One is armed with a machete while another is carrying a grenade launcher. The third is holding a rope with a gaff attached designed to fasten their boat to the *Polish Princess.* The fourth buccaneer is preparing to attach a boarding ladder.

The looks on the faces of these men are similar to any criminal who's intent on getting what he wants through violence. Be it an armed robbery of a high end bank, or that of one homeless person attacking another for some advantage he may gain. The look of purpose with the intent of committing violence is first and foremost reflected within each face.

Rolly shouts at Phillip, "Don't just stand there, draw your gun man!"

Phillip is still frozen. The only thing that's moving on him is his eyes as they blink uncontrollably with no apparent purpose.

Suddenly there is a burst of automatic gunfire. The intensity causes Rolly to tackle Phillip to the deck. Rolly is expecting any minute to have the intruders come bursting through the cabin door. The reverberations of the rapid fire resonate through the very fabric of the ship causing a glass of water to crash to the deck. Phillip has at last drawn his pistol preparing to defend himself. The gunfire continues with round after round of rapid fire shots.

As quickly as it started, it ends with a startling silence. Both Phillip and Rolly remain lying on the deck motionless, but with their eyes glued to the cabin door expecting to be dead in a matter of seconds.

Instead the door from below swings open. Both Phillip and Rolly swing around expecting to go out in a blaze of terror.

"Don't shoot!" shouts the voice of their absent captain throwing his hands in the air.

Still in the fight mode the two men remain frozen with both their pistols aimed firmly at the captain. It takes a few moments before they relax enough to lower their weapons.

"Are you alright?" Rikker shouts with a glancing inspection of both men. He throws open the door and looks out toward the intruders. By this time Phillip and Rolly have pulled themselves together enough to follow. They are just in time to see what's left of their adversaries' boat making a hasty descent to Davy Jones's locker.

Phillip is the first to speak. "What the hell just took place?"

Rolly, just as curious as Phillip, is also waiting with baited breath for an explanation. Captain Rikker motions for the two to follow him. He leads them into the bow cabin where the smell of gunpowder permeates every breath. There before them is what appears to be an automatic gun mounted on a tripod with the barrel clearly sticking out a porthole in the direction of their antagonists.

"What the hell is this thing?" questions Phillip.

"This, sir, is a 50 caliber automatic weapon that at one time bedecked a U.S. Army helicopter," informs Rikker with the voice of a tour guide. "The congressman got it through some back channel only he knows. Nonetheless, this is only the second tıme I've had to use it. The last time was on an excursion with Paderewski. The outcome was the same. It leaves nothin' to report to anybody. It's like it never happened."

Captain Rikker deftly puts the drifting ship back on course while Rolly comes up from the galley with a bottle of Jack Daniels and three glasses. All agree, this single event is enough excitement for the rest of their lives. The three offer a toast to their good fortune.

It isn't until the aftermath when lying alone in their bunks that each is compelled by an inner voice to evaluate their response. Fear has a way of making a level playing ground. Secretly each of them knows their individual reaction gives the true measure of them as men.

Phillip has tried most of his life to put consideration of such moments of cowardice off with the expectation he'll do better the next time. He always gives himself another opportunity to make up for past shortcomings. *I'll do better next time* has become his mantra. Unfortunately for him, there doesn't seem to be a magical aligning of the stars to bring this change about. For the most part, Phillip remains the same Phillip—caught between wanting to do great things and always falling short.

CHAPTER 38

A half day goes by when the chattering on the radio indicates they are coming to their first fuel stop at Cooper Jack Bay in the Caicos Islands. It can't come soon enough as the tank is less than a quarter full. For any yacht captain, running this close to empty in precarious waters is cause for grave concern.

With a problem-free stop, the dilemma becomes history. A clear weather forecast for the next few days is enough to send them confidently out on the next leg of their journey.

The momentary vacuum left after the incident the day before has also become history as new concerns begin to fill otherwise empty thoughts.

Captain Rikker calls a meeting as they leave port. "We've got to keep a careful watch on our compass. The next part of this journey takes us through the straits separating Cuba and Haiti. It's absolutely imperative we don't let the ship wander into Cuban waters or we'll be up a creek without a paddle. We don't want to be close enough to draw attention. The Cubans will take anything as an excuse to seize American boats."

If Phillip and Rolly had any notion this was to be a pleasant Caribbean cruise those notions have been dashed. This whole trip is proving to be as harrowing as any pulp fiction novel. After their last encounter, every sea craft sighted is carefully scrutinized.

When not at the wheel, Phillip and Rolly have taken advantage of the open seas to toss out empty bottles and cans for target practice with the various weapons in the arsenal on board. Both are becoming quite proficient.

"We shoulda been doin' this from the beginning. Just between you and me, Rolly, I don't believe I knew enough about that pistol to have done any harm to those four attackers," confesses Phillip in an attempt to excuse his seeming cowardice.

Rolly listens to Phillip give his rendition as to why he froze up. It's apparent Phillip is attempting to put a spin on his pathetic reaction in a situation that could have resulted in death for all of them had the other two reacted in the same way. Regardless of Phillip's whiny attempt, Rolly has already decided how effective Phillip would be covering his back in a tight situation. *With you Dude, I hope I never have to experience that threat* is Rolly's conclusion. Phillip's lack of response under fire is a real concern. It's eroded any previous thoughts as to Phillip's prowess and exposed his lack of courage.

With the threat of Cuban patrol boats appearing on the starboard side and Haitian pirates on the port side, the voyage continues under a vigilant surveillance. Both these nemeses employ fast power boats to intimidate the sluggish, less maneuverable yachts.

To say that things have gotten tense on board is an understatement.

None are getting much sleep. They've put themselves on short catnaps to keep a wary eye on anything appearing on the horizon. From past experience, being alert to their surroundings is a defense that can't be ignored for a moment.

The day passes uneventfully. This lack of turmoil is enough to lift the spirits of this weary crew. It's in times like these when boring is good. To be sure this particular business is not for the faint-hearted.

The port of Santa Marta is on the horizon. They have entered Colombian waters. Tensions arise once again. It's well-established the government is not in command in this port city. The drug lords are the community policy setters when it comes to insuring a proliferating drug business. Passports are a must on the government side. Once that is taken care of, the government workers, the police, or any other low to high level government official stands in line for "incentives" (what people in the U.S. refer to as bribes) provided to insure these folks look the other way during drug business.

To maintain good relations with legitimate hotels and tourist restaurants and bars, the drug dealers await darkness when the police close the beaches. It's here the "mules" (natives carrying contraband drugs from the cartel plantations) come with whatever they are capable of physically smuggling to this outlet. It's here the boats from the north are lined up to buy as much as they find available.

In order to cater to the American buyer, the harbor owners have provided marinas that will accommodate any size vessel capable of making the trip. The seventy-eight foot yacht is readily berthed in a slip which has been reserved for this occasion. It's a marina controlled by an inland drug lord who caters to American buyers.

What is readily noticeable by a new arrival is the number of armed guards posted at various entry points. Even though Captain Rikker has been in this marina previously, he is nevertheless, wary of any governmental changes which can often occur overnight in these third world countries.

"Keep your pistols concealed, but readily accessible," advises Captain Rikker. "Until we know who we're dealing with, it's wise to keep your eyes and ears alert."

The rule is no one is to leave the boat until the customs people have inspected it. Within a few minutes of docking the *Polish Princess,* a uniformed customs inspector makes his way to the vessel. He's very much taken with his job as he presents himself in a very official, no nonsense manner. He begins by asking for passports. Ten minutes later after more questions and a visual tour of the ship, he concludes his inspection bidding everyone to enjoy Colombia.

He's followed by a much more affable fellow, who Captain Rikker recognizes as the marina manager. "Hey Raphael, *como esta*?"

Raphael answers in English "Good Capitan, how was your trip?"

Without revealing any of the harrowing details, Captain Rikker returns with a similar friendly exchange. "Beautiful weather, beautiful trip my friend."

The fact that everyone in sight is on the take from the drug lords does little to guarantee the ship's safety against pilferage.

"Having one hand on what you wish to continue owning and the other hand on a gun gives the opportunists a second thought," cautions Rikker.

Since Rikker has had the most experience in this region, he continues his commands. "Rolly, you stay with the boat. Don't let anyone on board regardless of what they tell you. This city is full of artful carpetbaggers looking for any advantage they can find to relieve us of anything and everything we own."

Giving a nod of agreement while not in any position to question, Rolly positions himself in a deck chair prepared to take his watch. He is fully aware the stuff they own is the hundred-fifty grand sitting in the ship's vault. With everything that has to be accomplished yet, they all realize their work is far from over.

Turning to Phillip, Captain Rikker asks, "You ready to rock and roll?"

Phillip waves him forward saying, "Let's light this candle!"

The city is full of tourists. People are gathered in groups in front of statues depicting everything from saints and liberators, to Spanish conquistadors. Others pose in front of buildings that date to the time of the explorers, never too shy to ask other happy tourists to take their pictures. The expectation is their happy smiling faces will freeze this event in time forever.

Phillip and the captain pay little attention to these vacationers. They are on a much more arduous mission than a leisurely sightseeing tour. Their destination is the C.O.D. Bar (Collect On Delivery). It's known to provide access to information on where contraband of all kinds can be purchased.

Once there, the place is full of all sorts of people, from straight people on vacation to drug dealers attempting to size up a tourist hoping to score some marijuana, cocaine, or even heroin.

Rikker pulls out a stool at the bar and Phillip follows suit. When the bartender takes their order, Rikker passes a note along with their payment. The barkeeper gives a knowing nod then disappears through a door leading to a back room.

Both are churning on the inside while trying to maintain a level of calmness.

Phillip begins to feel himself freezing under the tension. Excusing himself, he makes his way to the bathroom. He barely makes it to the toilet before he empties his gut. It seems to be the emotional release he needs. After washing his face, he makes his way back to his waiting compatriot.

Captain Rikker takes one look at the ashen demeanor of his partner and makes a quick assessment. "Holy crap, Dude! You look like hawk bait!" Further assessing Phillip's deteriorating condition, he's compelled to get more assurance as to what this is going to mean.

"You sure you're up to this? I mean, maybe you're in the wrong business."

Not responding immediately, Phillip sits back and swallows his entire drink in a couple gulps. Lighting a cigarette, he breaks his silence, "I'm okay. Everything's okay."

The bartender returns in the middle of this discussion to summon the two of them to the back room. Looking at Phillip's deteriorating condition, Rikker quickly makes an executive decision.

"Phillip, stay here and have another drink," he says.

Phillip nods in agreement.

Captain Rikker soon disappears behind the closed door. When the bartender returns, he brings Phillip another double whiskey and water. Phillip becomes even more agitated when he discovers, he left his fanny pack with his money and passport in the bathroom. Bolting from his chair, a fresh wave of anxiety overflows his entire body when he discovers it's no longer where he left it. It's been stolen.

Returning to his stool, he's frozen with worry, fear, dread, regret and a thousand other emotions he can't name. He's shaking so badly it takes both hands to get the whiskey to his lips.

Just about the time Phillip thinks he's going to explode, Captain Rikker comes back through the same door he had entered fifteen minutes ago. Phillip heaves a sigh of relief. Like an errant child, he confesses to Rikker his slip-up. Rikker listens with the strained patience of a disgusted parent. He's discovering the same thing Rolly had, *This guy's no damn good under pressure.*

With a calmer mind, Captain Rikker conceives a possible solution to at least get the missing passport back.

"Let's take a walk Phillip, I think I can come up with a possible good outcome."

They head down the street and hail a cab. "Take us to the radio station," Rikker instructs the cabbie.

There is only one radio station and it's blaring in every shop with the local musical favorites. Once there, Captain Rikker instructs the cabbie to wait.

"Wait here Phillip. You are about to learn how things get done in Santa Marta."

In five minutes Rikker returns ordering the cabbie to take them to the marina. The cabbie has his radio on. The voice of the disc jockey soon comes in with what sounds like an interruption for an emergency broadcast. Phillip doesn't understand Spanish but he hears his name mentioned.

Turning to Phillip, Captain Rikker asks, "Hear that? He just offered a reward of two-hundred-fifty American dollars for the return of your passport."

In fifteen minutes, the duo is dropped off at the marina. Captain Rikker spots Raphael. Pulling him aside, he explains what he's done.

"Phillip Hampton had his passport ripped off. I went to the radio station and for a few bucks they broadcast a plea to return the passport for a reward of two-hundred- fifty American dollars. They are instructed to return the passport to this marina, no questions asked." Raphael accepts the envelope promising to be the middleman.

Phillip is embarrassed as he always is when he's caught with his pants down. "Thanks Rikker. I owe you," says Phillip.

"That's okay we'll settle up later. Right now we have more pressing issues to deal with," says Captain Rikker.

As soon as they return to the boat, Captain Rikker gives them the details of how the exchange is to come about.

Hardly an hour has gone by before Raphael comes down the dock toward the *Polish Princess*. "*Buenos dias*. I have something here for you." With that Raphael hands over a passport.

Phillip can't be happier. In turn he gives Raphael an American twenty dollar bill.

"*Muchas gracias, Senor*," says Raphael with a smile from ear to ear.

With all of Phillip's nonsense out of the way, Rikker continues his briefing."We sail out of the harbor tonight at midnight and make our way down the beach a quarter mile. We will anchor offshore and wait for a barge to bring us our product. They'll load it, but it's up to us to do our due diligence and make sure we get a clean count on every kilo we're paying for."

In this part of the world, the tourists are not allowed on the beaches after dark. There are armed men preventing anyone not involved in big time drug dealing to wander around. Moonlight walks have to be limited to areas where drug dealing isn't permitted. In Santa Marta that amounts to hardly anywhere.

They decide to stay with the ship until it's time to begin the operation. Rolly and Rikker pass the time playing a game of cribbage. Phillip passes his time the way he usually does in a stressful situation—he drinks.

"Slow down on that stuff, Phillip. You're going to have to be sharp. These guys will watch for any advantage to scam us. If they spot what looks like an opportunity, they'll gut us," warns Captain Rikker.

Phillip throws back what he has in his glass, but complies by putting the bottle back in the cupboard.

"These people are gonna show up with probably six or seven guys to do the loading," says Rikker.

Speaking to Rolly, Rikker instructs, "I think you should play watchman. Keep an eye on who's doing what when it comes to unloading their barge and loading ours. Arm yourself with one of our automatic rifles and keep your finger on the trigger."

Turning his attention to Phillip, Rikker continues, "Phillip, you are in charge of packing this stuff so it doesn't shift around in the boat. We need to keep our load distributed evenly so we don't cause the ship to list. Also make sure we're getting unbroken packages. I'll stay up top and make sure the inventory is coming in as we've bargained."

The time finally arrives to get everything in position. The customs people, who take their job seriously during the day, are nowhere to be seen at night. The harbor is empty of boats except those doing drug business. The law, such as it is, is paid off by the drug lords to turn their backs on these things.

Under the cloak of darkness, the *Polish Princess* unceremoniously sails out of the harbor and slowly makes her way down the coast to the agreed location. The anchor is set. The wait for the barge is very short. Out of the shadows, the form of a floating crane slowly appears, making its way to the waiting vessel. It's a battered barge that has definitely seen better days. There are two large square blocks wrapped in burlap and secured with heavy twine on her deck. Behind these containers, as an integral part of the barge's deck, sits an antiquated steam-driven crane. In back of everything is a sixteen foot push boat with an outboard motor guiding this titan to the port side of the *Polish Princess*.

Just as Captain Rikker predicted, they arrive with a half dozen men on board. The lines that are necessary to fasten the two vessels to one another are quickly secured. Each man is fully aware of his responsibility to insure his part of the operation comes off with a minimal amount of confusion.

A short, stout man with a heavy Spanish accent sporting a large smile climbs aboard. He has an official looking clipboard in his hand with the other hand extended to Captain Rikker.

"Heyee Capitan, me hombre. Wee ready to do beesness no?"

"Yah Hector, I'm ready as soon as you are," says Rikker shaking his hand.

The steam-driven crane releases a whooshing sound as it prepares to transfer the two one ton containers of primo Colombian weed. There is only enough room to set one at a time in the open aft cockpit. As soon as the first is transferred, Rikker opens the bindings that burglarproof the giant box shaped bundles. He randomly pulls out a kilo, draws out a knife and makes a small slit. He soon establishes this is what he negotiated for. With little time to waste, he promptly sets up the assembly line using the laborers sent along with the barge. Each kilo ends in the waiting hands of Phillip whose task it is to distribute this loose cargo in such a way as to keep the ship stable.

An hour and a half later, four thousand pounds of packaged marijuana is spread through every nook-and-cranny of the lower deck. The money is exchanged and the *Polish Princess* is making her way north with a two ton cargo of contraband marijuana.

CHAPTER 39

The night rolls onward. The three men are still hyped up over their successful transaction and not interested in sleeping. The winds begin to pick up out of the east. Captain Rikker has been monitoring the changing weather conditions. His concern is for a tropical storm that's reported to be developing in the direction in which they're heading.

"Hells out for breakfast if we run into that son-of-a-bitch."

"What's the plan if we do?" asks Phillip.

"Pray," says Rikker.

None of them can imagine what it would be like to ride out a large storm in their craft. Living in Key West, Rikker is no stranger to the mighty force created by one of these storms. He is the only member of this crew who has been directly involved with the havoc produced by one of these instruments of Mother Nature.

The wind is currently at fifteen knots. The ocean's surface is now beginning to form chops. Captain Rikker has turned on the ship's two large spotlights illuminating the mounting disturbance. The choppy waters are soon developing into waves. The swells are slowly becoming larger, but still manageable, so far. Rolly and Phillip, for the moment, don't share the same concern as Captain Rikker—after all they're landlubbers.

By daybreak the storm has intensified. The swells are growing deeper and faster. All this spells trouble for this small craft and its crew. Phillip and Rolly remained in the wheelhouse with Captain Rikker throughout the night. The seeming sameness of the waves is creating a mesmerizing kind of fatigue. All three are showing signs of drowsiness. Rikker, in particular is aware of increasing signals of heaviness. His acuity in buffering oncoming waves is lagging, causing the ship to broach, turning on its side. Once that occurs, without a quick response, the end comes quickly.

Another concern is the amount of fuel used. Normally, he would avoid Haiti and refuel at the Caicos Islands. With these deteriorating conditions there is no other choice than to attempt to make landfall in Haiti.

The Haitian custom officials are notorious for corruption. Jean-Claude Duvalier, or "Baby Doc" as he is known after the death of his father "Papa Doc," is the unchallenged dictator.

"If we're forced to make land in Haiti, those corrupt bastards won't leave us enough for a cup of coffee," laments Captain Rikker.

The combination of the storm's sixty knot rage and the lack of sleep have allowed the ship to veer farther off course than Captain Rikker has calculated. Before he is fully aware of their position, land is sighted. With a quick check, he realizes he is already in Haitian waters, and offshore from the city of Tiburon. Captain Rikker hopes that due to the storm, entry formalities will be abated. In this dinky little town on the outskirts of the country he finds one full service marina willing to assist him.

It is all the captain can do to bring the vessel into a position to be fueled.

As they enter the marina, the winds shift allowing the *Polish Princess* to find some much welcomed calmer seas. They are met by a friendly Haitian introducing himself as Adlard. With a diminished wind, they manage to fill their tanks. Gladly paying in cash, they count their lucky stars the customs people weren't on duty. Within an hour they are back into the throes of the storm making their way toward the Windward Passage. This is the fifty mile strait between Cuba and Haiti.

The seas have swelled to ten to fifteen foot waves. Captain Rikker has released the boat's fore and aft anchors. He's hoping the trailing weights will help to stabilize the unsteady craft.

Adrenalin is substituting for sleep once again. Their undivided attention to the security of their cargo is paramount. The best they can do is to keep all the doors closed where eighteen- hundred kilos of stowed reefer are struggling to escape.

Finally, things seem to be getting a bit better. The wind has dropped from sixty knots to twenty. It looks like they have won the battle—that is until they become aware of a very fast and very official looking military vessel approaching off their port side.

"This ain't lookin' too good," says Captain Rikker not taking his eyes off this unwelcome visitor. What he sees is disturbing. It appears to be the blue and white alternating stripes and the red equilateral triangle with the white star of the Cuban flag shivering in the wind. The nearer this nemesis draws, the more perilous their situation.

"Boys, we're S.O.L. These assholes are gonna play for keeps," says Rikker with his eyes still fixed on the approaching vessel.

Phillip and Rolly are stunned speechless. By the time they process what is about to take place, it's already happening. A Cuban military boat is bobbing approximately twenty yards off the port side.

The command to board the *Polish Princess* is given. The rest is a very rapid downhill slide for her crew. They soon find themselves being patted down, their weapons removed and fettered with rough fitting handcuffs. They are removed to the Cuban ship and placed in a dark, holding cell below deck.

It goes without saying that within minutes of this invasion the cargo is discovered. Add to this the fact they have strayed into Cuban waters, and any hope for a speedy conclusion to this debacle goes down the drain.

Within hours, the three Americans find themselves led into the Boniato Prison. The hatred for Americans is evident as they are kicked and beaten for the slightest infraction. All prisoners are thrown into small cramped cells. In this particular scenario, the cell is designed for six prisoners. With the three of them being added, the number is now eighteen. There are six cots with mattresses that appear to be filled with leaves and straw. These are carefully guarded by prisoners who are capable of defending themselves against those more easily intimidated. The remainder have found wall space they can at least brace their backs against. At one end there is a squalid hole in the floor serving as a toilet. The floor has a rancid layer of sticky filth. Most of this is attributed to an overflow from leaky plumbing in a neighboring cell.

They have arrived in time for rations. In the broadest terms, it can only loosely be described as nutrition. Mostly consisting of rotten meat and what appears to be beans. The water ration is brown and obviously contaminated.

Phillip finds it impossible to eat any of this despite his hunger. Another prisoner willingly takes it off his hands, gulping it down as though he had won the lottery.

Captain Rikker and Rolly realize this may be all they're going to receive for the next twenty-four hours. Both manage to gag it down, minimally relieving their hunger and thirst.

Finding a space on the floor large enough to lie fully stretched out is impossible. They are nonetheless exhausted and find themselves dozing. Battling the storm had required all their energy, depriving them of much needed sleep. At this point, each of them could fall asleep atop a barbed wire fence and find it comfortable.

Phillip is the first to awaken. Earlier, in an attempt to get comfortable he had removed his shoes. Not seeing them where he had placed them, he begins to scan his surroundings. It only takes a moment before he spots them on a large grinning man sitting on one of the bunks. The unwritten rule in these facilities is any unguarded possessions are considered discarded. Since this fits that scenario, he appears to be very happy with his find.

The usual method in the Cuban legal system is to put an arrested person in prison until their trial comes up, which always takes more than a year. This is not the way any of these three had seen their lives going. There's no way to prepare to be in any prison much less one with a different culture and language. This wrong turn is going to bring long hard days ahead.

CHAPTER 40

Shelly may no longer have all the spare time she once had between filming movies. Her fame enables her to command a high fee for her escort services as she still has more than enough sex appeal and name recognition.

When she's not working, Shelly spends much of her time either drinking heavily or attempting to dry out. Arnie makes it his business to keep close tabs on her behavior. He has, unbeknownst to Shelly, gained an ally in Courtney. She gives him a run down on Shelly's condition before he dares book her with a client.

On this particular night, he has determined she's fit to work. He's booked her for an evening starting with dinner at Archie Tarpoff's and ending sometime later that night at the Hotel Olds. Still acting as her agent, Arnie escorts her to the restaurant and introduces her to the client. He's an important middle-aged man with a penchant for pretty young women.

Shelly knows the male psyche very well. She has spent the majority of her adult life fine tuning her skills, by which she's garnered a better than average living.

Arnie begins with, "Peaches, I'd like you to meet Clyde."

Extending her hand while arching her back and gently smiling in a very submissive way, Shelly keeps her eyes fixed on the eyes of her new paramour.

Arnie continues with the introductions. "Clyde, I'd like you to meet Peaches."

From the grin on Clyde's face, he could not be more pleased. He quickly stands to accept the hand of this famous sex object, considering her a privileged trophy he's just won. Putting his best foot forward, Clyde graciously pulls out a chair across the table from his own, inviting her to sit and at the same time handing Arnie an envelope in payment.

Clyde's grin remains as he reseats himself. Shelly in turn has still not taken her eyes off his since they met. Very gently, she reaches across the table and touches his folded hands. For Clyde, this touch goes through him like a jolt of electricity, but certainly much more pleasing.

The dinner is going very well as they engage in small talk about different happenings around the community. Shelly has learned to allow her clients to always have the last say and always agree with their sentiments. She established very early in this liaison that he is a man of very solid opinions.

Touching his arm, Shelly intensifies her gaze. "I can tell you are a good person, Clyde, and I consider it a pleasure to be in the company of a man with such strong convictions."

Clyde in turn knows he's not a good person, but talking as though he is and getting a good result is nearly as good as the genuine thing. To say the least, this evening is beginning on a very positive note.

Archie is making his rounds, stopping to schmooze with each of his patrons. It seems, he is very familiar with Clyde and is particularly struck by Clyde's date.

"Tell me, Clyde, who is this beauty you're with?"

"Archie, this is Miss Peaches O'Reddy," says Clyde obviously flattered by Archie's attention.

Archie pauses as if in thought for a moment before acknowledging the introduction. "Oh yes, I remember a few years back when you began your film career in this very restaurant," says Archie. Quickly summoning a waiter, Archie instructs him to bring a bottle of their famous house wine to the table. "Please accept this as a complimentary gift from me," says Archie, as he drifts off to another table.

Both are relishing their dinner and are feeling the effects of the drinks. In spite of her penchant for too much alcohol, Shelly intuitively knows how to move her client to the next level. By this time she has removed her high-heeled pumps and extended her foot under Clyde's pant cuff, gently massaging his leg. With all this going on beneath the table, Clyde interprets this as a very private and personal gesture. He then predictably says, "What do you say we get out of here and go to my room for a drink?"

"You've read my mind," purrs Shelly.

They finish the bottle of wine while waiting for the cab. The Hotel Olds is less than a half mile from Tarpoff's. The doorman attentively opens the door bidding them a good evening. Clyde reciprocates by pressing a tip into the doorman's hand.

"Thank you, sir," he says, as he continues forward to open the hotel door.

The elevator quickly shoots them to the penthouse on the tenth floor. No sooner are they in the room, than Shelly ravenously grabs him and kisses him passionately. She then methodically backs him toward a large French revival style bed at the same time beginning with his tie the process of disrobing him. Pushing him backward onto the bed, she sets about her own disrobing. Her career as a porn star has made this sort of intimacy a production. Each of her moves is choreographed as if it were being filmed. After a slow striptease, she likes to begin by giving her client a massage. This is all designed to produce an arousal within a man that his wife is reluctant to make.

This heightened desire is enough to cause a man to say things, to do things, to give things, to promise things he never would say or do without being in this aroused condition. Shelly is able to take her clients to new heights by fulfilling fairyland sexual experiences they may have only dreamed of. This kind of stimulation has proven strong enough to topple empires.

By midnight Clyde has been satiated. He has fulfilled many fantasies that came to light only with the aid of this fallen angel. As happens so often after one of these encounters, her client evidences a belief that this is beginning of a *real* relationship. They begin to refer to her by pet names such as "Sweetheart" or "Babe" with a belief that their encounter has left her with the same special feeling it has them. They always seem to forget they paid for this fantasy and that's where it remains—a fantasy.

Clyde is no exception. Going out of his way to accommodate Shelly, he makes a call to have his driver escort her home.

"I want to tell you, you are great. You're been the best thing I've had come along in a long time. Could I see you again?" questions Clyde.

Aware of this propensity for clients to attempt to date her outside of a business transaction, Shelly obliges politely, but succinctly, "I'm sure if you wish to contact Arnie for something to happen again, he can arrange it."

At this moment there is a quiet knock at the door. Shelly takes this opportunity to give Clyde a reassuring kiss and affectionately stroking his arm says, "We can do this again, Clyde."

Expecting it to be his assistant, Clyde opens the door. The assistant and Shelly have a moment where neither of them say a word, they stare speechless.

"Manny, I'd like you to drive Miss O'Reddy to her home," says Clyde in the usual condescending way he speaks to his underlings.

Waiting until they are well out of earshot, both Manny and Shelly stop and stare at one another again.

What the hell is going on? they think simultaneously.

Finally Manny musters up something to say. "Damn girl, it's good ta see ya. You're just as damn good lookin' as you've ever been."

They feel bound to their hippie pledge to live and let live but Manny can't help wondering how his friend's life took this turn. At the same time Shelly is wondering how Manny is connected to the guy she has just finished entertaining for the evening.

"How long has it been since we left the commune? In some ways it seems like just yesterday," muses Shelly.

"Well, let's see it was before McCarthy ran for president back in '68. That was when Phillip and I left," says Manny still trying to do some recollecting. "By the way how is Kate?"

Shelly is taken back for a moment. "How do you know about Kate?"

"I stopped by Die Landarbeiter once a couple years ago on vacation. So how is she?"

"Oh she's great. She's nearly lost all her baby teeth."

By this time they've reached Shelly's apartment.

"You wanna come in for a night cap? We can catch up on what's happened to the old gang," asks Shelly.

"That would be great," says Manny.

The whole apartment is sleeping. Courtney stays in a spare room when Shelly needs her to stay over. Going immediately to a cupboard, Shelly pulls down a fifth of vodka and two glasses.

"Vodka and orange juice okay?"

"Yeah."

While Shelly mixes the drinks, Manny looks at some of her pictures scattered around the room. There is one of Deidre and Shelly taken at Die Landarbeiter. There are also several depicting the progression of a baby to a time of school pictures. Manny assumes this must be Kate. He stares at the picture as though he's recalling a time that seems so long ago, but then being almost thirty, the elapsed time constitutes nearly a third of his life.

Handing Manny a drink, Shelly asks, "By the way, who is this Clyde guy you work for?"

The question hits Manny in an odd way. "Oh he's just one of the most influential legislators in the state of Michigan."

"That kinky son-of-a-bitch is a congressman?" asks Shelly. The smirk on her face says she is enjoying the irony of it.

The familiarity and commonality of their past relationship returns to a comfortable trust. This assurance leads Manny to dare ask, "How in the hell did you land in this business?"

"It's a long story. I can't even recall all the details. It just happened," admits Shelly taking a drag on her cigarette, quickly followed by a gulp from her glass. "How about you? How'd you end up working as this guy's pimp?

It's obvious to Manny, he may have peeled a scab. "That's probably as long a story as yours," he states agreeing to move on to other topics.

"I suppose you've heard about Phillip?" says Manny believing it will be more comfortable to discuss someone else's problems rather than their own.

"I haven't heard that name in years, and to tell you the truth, I could go longer without hearing that name again. But to answer your question, no, I haven't heard anything about him." Without waiting for an answer, Shelly quickly follows through with her own question, "Why? Who has he raped now?"

Manny knows what Shelly is referring to. It was no secret Phillip had a crush on Deidre during those years. It was also no secret Deidre had zero romantic feelings for Phillip. Many, including Shelly and Deidre, believed Phillip was responsible for Kate's conception. To have his name brought to light again, along with Manny's questions about Shelly's occupation, is enough for one evening.

"I think it's probably time for me to be going," says Manny.

A pajama clad female child suddenly appears in the room. Blinking as her eyes adjust to the brightness of the room, she crawls onto her mother's lap and draws her knees into a fetal position. She appears to be eight or nine years old.

Manny is quiet for the moment. "So this is Kate?"

Kate yawns, ignoring this early morning visitor.

Taking the opportunity, Shelly speaks for her. "Yes this is Miss Kate. She's very smart, beautiful and loves her mommy." Shelly is showering her with smooches.

Manny sits for the moment unable to say anything. Finally he gathers himself enough to say, "Hello Kate. I have to agree with everything your mommy said."

Kate is really too sleepy to engage in any late night exchanges, especially with people she doesn't know. Her response is to draw a little tighter into Shelly's lap.

"I think I'll leave for now, but I would like to have a better opportunity to kibitz with you." Pausing for a moment he adds, "Would you consider dinner tomorrow evening?"

Shelly also pauses for a moment. Manny reads into this that she's not sure. He breaks the pause with an additional assurance, "I promise I'll let all our sleeping dogs rest."

"I don't want to leave Kate. Would you consider coming here for dinner?"

There is no hesitation in Manny's voice. "What time?"

"Eight o'clock," says Shelly.

"I'll see you at eight."

CHAPTER 41

Manny begins his workday alongside Clyde Paderewski without a single reference to the night before. As with all of Paderewski's dalliances, they are expected to be forgotten, and never referred to again. In the tradition of the unwritten code within his job description, Manny is expected to lie, if necessary, to cover his boss's indiscretions.

"After all, the good I do within the Democratic Party far outweighs a few harmless transgressions," rationalizes Paderewski.

At least this is the justification he gives those in charge of covering his ass. This thought process is followed many other legislators as well.

The end of Manny's workday arrives with no last minute duties to hold him hostage. He's been looking forward to spending some time with his old friend. Remembering Kate is not even a preteen yet, he stops and buys a teddy bear as well as a bottle of wine for his hostess.

He spends the next twenty minutes driving across Lansing to Shelly's apartment. He's met by a scene he never anticipated. Coming out of Shelly's front door is a gurney, along with a team of attendants. They're making their way to a waiting ambulance.

Practically leaping from his car, hardly hearing the wheels bumping the cracks in the sidewalk, he makes his way to a motionless body. He's just in time to see Shelly in what appears to be a non-responsive state. Anxiously following behind them are Courtney and Kate.

"What happened?" asks Manny.

Not sure who this stranger is asking about Shelly, Courtney, responds, "Not now sir, we havin' an emergency don't ya see?"

Kate pulls on Courtney's arm to say something. Motioning her down to her level, Kate whispers something in her ear.

Standing upright, Courtney addresses Manny, "Miss Kate says you is a fren of Miss Shelly, so I can tell you dis much, Miss Shelly, she bleedin' bad. Now we gots ta be gittin' to da hospital."

Not to be put off, Manny quickly follows the ambulance to the emergency room at St. Lawrence Hospital. Courtney and Kate arrive right behind him. They all make their way directly to the emergency room. Shelly has already been met by a doctor and is on her way to surgery. Courtney wastes no time asking about an available waiting room close by.

Not sure what his position may be, Manny introduces himself to Courtney in the hopes of not being excluded from any forthcoming information concerning Shelly's condition.

For the better part of two hours, they sit together with very little exchange. At last, a surgeon still wearing his scrubs enters the room.

Pulling his surgical mask below his chin, he asks, "Who am I speaking with here?"

Courtney is immediately on her feet. "I'm Miss Shelly's nanny, Courtney Jones." Pushing Kate forward, she continues, "An this here be Miss Shelly's daughter, Miss Kate."

Not to be excluded, Manny also introduces himself.

Satisfied, the doctor motions for each to be seated and begins, "We found the source of her bleeding. She has a perforated ulcer. We managed to get it stopped for the present."

Without the slightest pause, he leads directly to his next concern. "Tell me, does she have a problem with alcohol?"

Courtney is the first to react. "Oh Lor', ah know'd it was gonna come to dis. Ah spend my time scoldin' Missy for all dat drinkin'. It kill my daddy, it gonna kill you too. Das what ah been tellin' her."

"Well it nearly has," continues the doctor. "She's not out of the woods just yet, but what we're going to recommend is a long term stay in our detox ward. If she continues to drink, she'll die."

Tears fill Kate's eyes at this blunt pronouncement. Courtney isn't doing much better. It's all she can do to keep from falling apart. After all, she has been Shelly's family since Kate was a baby. To receive this kind of news is devastating.

Manny is standing back waiting for an opportunity to intervene. After the doctor leaves, he approaches Courtney and Kate. He spends the next half hour filling them in on his and Shelly's long time involvement.

Kate is old enough to ask some questions of her own. Manny isn't sure how much Shelly has told her about her past and is not certain how to address them. But when she asks, "Do you know where my daddy went?" he is at a total loss. Looking to Courtney, Manny has a definitely perplexed stare.

Courtney comes to Kate's defense. "She been askin' dat question ever since she come back from her fren house. Her fren say cause she gots a daddy, dat Kate spose ta have a daddy, too."

Manny listens to this concern of Kate's with a compassionate ear. "Well let me tell you something, Kate. I may know the guy and maybe there's something I can do to help you find him."

****

The next few days are crucial for Shelly. Detoxing her while she is recovering from major surgery is, to say the least, a difficult balance of care. Nevertheless, within a few days, she begins to rally. She is far from a full recovery, but is becoming aware of the severity of her condition.

The doctor assigned to address her alcohol addiction is Dr. Bates. He's well known for his no nonsense attitude with alcoholics. He wants to have an intervention with as many friends and relatives as possible. In spite of Kate's young age, Dr. Bates has requested Courtney include her, as well as Manny.

The four of them encircle Shelly's hospital bed. Although she's puzzled what has brought them all together at the same time, nevertheless, she is happy to see each one.

"How are you doing today?" says Dr. Bates, methodically beginning the proceeding. He's an affable man, but to the point.

"I'm doing a lot better."

Not taking his eyes off her for a moment, he continues. "When you were admitted here last week, how mindful were you of the seriousness of your condition?"

"I remember a little of it," she sheepishly admits.

"Another five minutes of bleeding the way you were, this visitation with these people would be at the funeral home," says Dr. Bates pointing to Courtney, Kate, and Manny. He pauses for a moment to observe what reaction Shelly has to this pronouncement.

Kate is quietly taking this all in. She's old enough to understand the magnitude of death. She has been crying nonstop in her mother's absence. She's listening to Dr. Bates' words and looking at all the tubes coming out of her mother. Suddenly with tear-filled eyes, she sobs, "Mommy, please don't die!"

It's apparent this plea has an effect on Shelly. With all the motherly effort Shelly can gather, she flops the tubes aside and opens her arms to console her sobbing daughter. The embrace is the first contact mother and daughter have had in a week. This moment is more life-giving to Shelly than all the medicines pumped into her. Both are thinking of how barren life would be without the other.

Watching this bond between mother and daughter, Dr. Bates is satisfied with the way things are progressing. While Shelly's sense of confidence is at a low, he wants to explore a part of her psyche he suspects is out of kilter—that of her honesty.

"I want to ask you, Shelly, what you believe brought you to this end."

"I overheard somebody say it may have had something to do with drinking too much," she says.

"Maybe you misheard my question. I'll ask you once more, what do *you* believe brought this condition on?" restates Dr. Bates.

"I think it may be because I haven't been eating right and not getting enough sleep," states Shelly.

Focusing his attention on Courtney, Dr. Bates asks, "What do you make of this? Do you believe her lack of eating is at the root of her illness?"

"Tha ain't even da haf ah it," says Courtney. Turning to Shelly, Courtney carries on. "Reason you ain't eatin', Missy, ain't got nothin' ta do wif me.

It got ta do wif all dat booze you pourin' into tha poor ailin' body. I makes da same food for me an Kate an we ain't ailin'."

Dr. Bates picks up the conversation at this point. "You had a blood alcohol level above point five. That's enough to elevate your liver enzymes to a dangerous level, so we did a test to see where you are." Placing his hand on her abdomen, he asks, "Have you noticed that pouch on your belly?"

Shelly unconsciously rubs her hand across the bandaged area.

Making direct eye contact with Shelly, he goes on, "That's not belly fat, it's actually a distended liver from severe alcoholism." Dr. Bates doesn't saying anything more. Again he is patiently observing her reaction.

Quiet for a moment as this diagnosis begins to sink in, Shelly finally makes an assumption. "You're sayin' you think I have cirrhosis of the liver?"

"I'm not saying, '*I think*', I know for a fact that's what you have." He is quiet again. This last exchange slides down a little deeper into Shelly's psyche. This diagnosis hits Shelly hard. "Am I going to die?" questions Shelly. Her demeanor is changing bit by bit as Dr. Bates seemingly pounds more nails in her coffin.

"The answer is absolutely 'yes.' The other answer is absolutely 'no.' It's all going to depend on how badly you *want* to live."

Shelly finds herself in strange waters. She has always been of the opinion she could quit drinking any time she wanted. But something has changed. Lying in this hospital bed at this very moment, listening to the people who are focusing all of their attention on her need to stop her ruinous, soul-destroying alcoholism, she finds herself wanting a drink more than anything else. Facing her addiction in a life and death situation and still wanting to drink gives her pause. *Am I losing my mind? Why am I destroying myself? What the hell is happening to me?*

"I'm listening to everything you're saying, but now the only thing I know for sure is if you send me home today by tonight I'll be drinking."

There is a break in her voice. She stares blankly out a window into nothingness. "I can't do this. I know I can't. I'm too weak."

Dr. Bates sits up with a new energy. He's listening to an honesty in Shelly she has never admitted to anyone, not even to herself, much less to a room full of people she wants to think well of her.

"Now we're getting somewhere!" he exclaims with a sense of satisfaction. "No one is asking you to do this alone. What I am asking, along with these people who love you, is that you enter our rehab program. This is where you'll discover you're not alone. You'll find people who are willing to share with you a path to recovery."

It's evident Shelly is experiencing an internal conflict. "You're asking me to risk going through what life I may have left without my vodka, I don't know if I can do that," says Shelly.

"No, I didn't say that. You are misunderstanding. I didn't say for life. That's too big a chunk. For now you only need to do this one day at a time, and so far you've got a pretty good start on today" says Dr. Bates with a supportive smile.

Shelly's mind is grinding at the prospects. She reveals a daunting reality, "A life with my vodka may be miserable at times but at least it's familiar and damned predictable. It's been my friend when I needed one."

"And your worst enemy when it decides to turn on you. Remember you had one foot in the grave and the other on a banana peel when you arrived here," reminds Dr. Bates.

Shelly lets out a sigh. "What am I going to do with Kate… I can't afford to..."

Before she can finish any of her half sentences, Manny, who has remained quiet, steps forward. "Shelly, if you'll do this rehab thing, I'll help with whatever you need."

Shelly has a definite look of surprise. "Why would you do something like that, Manny?"

Remaining speechless for a moment as though giving it some thought, Manny ultimately says, "Cuz I want to."

Closely monitoring this conversation, Dr. Bates considers all things discussed relevant. "Shelly, I'll make a bargain with you. If you complete our rehab program and decide it's not for you, I personally guarantee we'll refund your misery."

Shelly looks at each of them. She sees the strain across her young daughter's face. Taking another moment, she ultimately says, "Okay, I'll give your program a shot. I got nothin' ta lose." This decision results in the closest thing to a smile Shelly has shown in days.

Kate's face brightens. She nearly smothers her mother with a hug. "Mommy, I'll be good for Courtney, I promise. Please get better and don't die!"

To say that none of this moved Shelly would be a lie. She is under the delusion if she could have just one drink, to clear her mind, she could make better decisions—like maybe to learn how to just drink socially. The more thought she gives to this whole affair, the more she believes Dr. Bates and all the rest of them have very radical ideas about her drinking.

Before these thoughts can wrap their tentacles around her mind too tightly, a male nurse comes in with a wheelchair. *What the hell have I gotten myself into?* Too sick to get up and leave, she gives in to his mobilizing and soon finds herself, IV and all, in a dayroom with people sitting around tables. These people are all in various stages of dealing with their recovery. Some are up and about helping with those who are not. Someone calling herself "Bea" asks Shelly if she'd like a cup of coffee. Before she can answer, it's poured and set on a table in front of her.

In another minute, someone is making an announcement Shelly had never dreamed she would ever hear. "Hi, my name is Bill, I'm an alcoholic. Welcome to the St. Lawrence Wednesday morning AA meeting."

To Shelly, this pronouncement is an openness she doesn't possess, and doesn't want. At this juncture, she would rather be sitting at Dagwood's having a few drinks with her friends.

She continues to look around wondering how she has managed to bring her life to this.

Over the next hour, as she listens to more than a dozen participants in her group tell their stories, she finds them touching parts of her life she had not imagined she shared with anyone. She can't believe the transparency these people are daring to expose. She has never once since Deidre died, confided anything troubling her to anyone.

Later when she's alone, she becomes aware of something in her soul awakening. Her own life begins flowing past her in segments. She finds it confusing to attempt to thread any kind of connection between these differing facets. *How did I go from a child, like Kate, to sitting here powerless over my life?* In one sense, she's looking forward to more awakenings, but for now what remains important is she didn't drink today.

CHAPTER 42

It's been nearly six months since Congressman Paderewski's office was contacted by Cuban officials informing him of the seizure of his boat and its captain. Phillip's father had also been contacted making it known Phillip was being held in a Cuban prison. Little mention is made of Rolly since he has successfully made himself into a non-person once again.

When the American press reported the Cubans had detained three Americans on espionage charges, Manny was not surprised to discover Phillip was among them. Phillip's life had taken a sharp turn. What had started as merely a recreational attitude toward drugs had escalated into a parley with the devil.

It took a while for all the information to reach the state department. It was spun and re-spun until these three American smugglers could be presented as victims of the evil Castro regime. The last thing Paderewski wants is for the details of smuggling and illegal drugs to land in the hands of the press.

"Those bastards would have a field day with that kind of information," laments Paderewski.

Manny has been in charge of setting up meetings with the Cubans to work out a deal. It's not a surprise when the negotiations begin to center around the Cubans suggesting a money settlement could be in the works.

"From what I've learned, they have no intention of returning my boat. Those Commies are more capitalistic than Batista could ever imagine. Rumor has it, they got a half-million in a cargo of confiscated marijuana. Now they're demanding a million bucks to get these guys' sorry asses out of prison," further bemoans Paderewski.

To obfuscate the source of these monies, they are filtered in from a dozen or more tax-funded programs and are then placed in an offshore account in the Bahamas. Within a few more weeks all the "i"s have been dotted all the "t"s have been crossed. An envoy sent to Guantanamo Bay is authorized to make the exchange. Of course, the Cubans are spinning this as a gesture of mercy from the glorious Communist party in returning these men to their families.

For both sides the moment of truth is at hand. A small military transport nears the Guantanamo compound. The three men are unceremoniously extradited. Each is well scrubbed, barbered, and clothed to appear as though they are merely returning from an extended vacation. The only giveaway for this ploy is they have each lost so much weight they appear more as well-dressed Zombies.

Phillip can't contain himself. As soon as he is in the compound, he drops to his knees and kisses the ground of the America he had spent much of his time criminalizing.

Later that day while waiting for their flight to Florida, Captain Rikker exchanges quips with a few of the military personal.

"Did you learn anything from this experience?" a sergeant asks him.

"Yeah, I did. I should have used a satellite navigator."

As for Rolly, he is happy to be free to resume his non-person portrayal. His plan is to disappear back into the masses and continue doing what he knows best.

Manny has arranged to be on hand when the military air transport lands in Key West. He has a packet of insurance papers from Paderewski for Captain Rikker to fill out in an attempt to receive compensation for the stolen *Polish Princess.*

Phillip is overjoyed to see Manny. He can't thank him enough for all he's done. He's agreed to go back home and take a job in his father's plant.

Rolly says a few hello's, a few thank you's, and is not seen again.

Word has reached Captain Tony's through the underground. The bar is in high spirits. The welcome for Captain Rikker is as ceremonious as if he were a visiting head of state. But as all things go, soon it is life as usual.

CHAPTER 43

During the thirty days Shelly has spent in rehab, Manny kept his word and did whatever was needed to make sure Kate and Courtney were taken care of. Over the last month, he and Kate have bonded. She hangs on him like she's known him forever. The difference in Shelly is profound.

She has been going to AA meetings at a place called the East Club. The irony of all this is at the first meeting she attended, who should be the one to welcome her but Mrs. Willoughby. It seems Mrs. Willoughby has been in AA for nearly a quarter of a century. Since everyone's last name is omitted for the sake of anonymity, Shelly now refers to her as Adele. Adele has agreed to become Shelly's sponsor.

Arnie is happy to see her sober, but she is reluctant to resume her escort job.

"Shelly you're one of my best girls. You know more in your little finger how this business is played than all these bimbos put together. Half the time these young girls I'm stuck with don't know shit from ice cream. I really need you back," complains Arnie.

"I'm not sure I can do that and stay sober," says Shelly. "The last thing I want is to get hit by that train again. Right now the most important thing for me is to stay the hell off the tracks."

Arnie hears something in her voice that's telling. It's a tone he never expected to hear from her. But with this new development, he also knows Shelly won't be pushed into something she doesn't want to be involved in.

"I can't wait forever. You know how this works. We have to be up and running when we get a client. Call me if you change your mind," sounds out Arnie, hoping she'll change her mind.

Manny is staying out of Shelly's business. Nevertheless, he makes himself available to Shelly in a very supportive way. Shelly has agreed to do ninety AA meetings in ninety days. Manny has volunteered to watch Kate in the evenings, allowing Courtney to have some time to herself. Shelly is starting to see Manny in a whole new light. She had always regarded him as Phillip's stooge. Today they are able to share conversations they never would have considered ten years ago.

It's normal for much of their talk to revert back to their days at Die Landarbeiter. On this evening, he has just returned from Florida and brings her up to date with Phillip's latest fiasco. She listens with a less than enthusiastic ear.

"That doesn't surprise me in the least. I never trusted him. As much as I love Kate, what he did to Deidre was wrong," says Shelly in her usual vitriolic delivery when a topic involving Phillip arises.

Manny usually becomes quiet when Shelly begins a rant against Phillip. She has always interpreted his refusal to support her opinion concerning Phillip as still wanting to protect Phillip.

"Why don't you admit it was Phillip who raped Deidre that night?" questions Shelly. "Don't you remember how he would stare at her? Deidre always felt it was Phillip!" Shelly says this with the conviction that comes from believing there couldn't possibly be another explanation.

"Don't get me wrong, I think Phillip is capable of a lot of things, but I don't believe he was the perpetrator," says Manny in a quiet voice.

"Drugs do weird things to people, Manny. You know that as well as I do. I don't think you can excuse him that easily," continues Shelly.

Kate interrupts this conversation when she comes bouncing into the house from play. She acknowledges her mother, but immediately jumps on Manny's lap. Shelly isn't sure she's comfortable with this strong attachment Kate's developed for Manny.

"Don't pester Manny like that, Kate," she finds herself saying.

"Oh she's fine," assures Manny, giving Kate a little hug in return.

Shelly is not quite sure how she should handle this situation. She has learned she needs to talk troublesome things over with her sponsor. The recommendation is to not make any major decisions alone. Adele has a good listening ear. She is encouraging Shelly to find a new vocation and has suggested Shelly look into a local cosmetology school.

Although the nature of this latest concern of Shelly's is different, she wonders if Adele is the right person to advise her. After all, she wouldn't know Manny if he came up and hit her in the head with a board.

Still pondering over this dilemma, she decides to consult the only person who will know what she is struggling with—Courtney. Since Shelly has returned home from rehab, and has no ready source of income, she has had to lay Courtney off.

Courtney is no more than a ten minute drive away. Shelly is debating whether she should call first or just drive there when her doorbell rings. Unaccustomed to having visitors, she can't imagine who it may be. Hoping it isn't Arnie, she peeks through a curtain and lets out a little gasp. Who of all people should be standing there but Courtney?

With the excitement of one who has literally had a prayer answered, Shelly throws the door open nearly shocking Courtney off the steps. "Courtney, thank God, you came!"

"My word chil, doan scare me like dat!"

Still mystified over such an eerie coincidence, Shelly stands stupefied with her mouth open, just staring. Courtney stares back unable to make heads or tails out of all this.

"Good Lor Missy, we gonna stan here gawken or you gonna aks me in?"

Catching herself, Shelly steps aside to let Courtney through the door. "Courtney, I was just on my way to see you when you appeared at my door," says Shelly.

Courtney has never imagined she would see this kind of life in Shelly. "Wha could be so dammable portant you needs ta scare da wits out me like dis?" says Courtney.

"I got some things I need you to help me sort out. Sit down and I'll make us some tea," says Shelly.

Making her way to the kitchen, she reaches up into the cupboard finding the stash of tea Courtney always kept on hand. It's suddenly occurs to her how strange it is that she had never made a cup of tea for Courtney in all the years she worked here. It gives her a moment of regret, but also pleasure in being able to do that now.

"What brings you my way?" questions Shelly while retrieving tea cups.

"Oh ah jus in da neighborhood doin' some dabblin' an thinkin' how ah needs ta stop by an see how you an Miss Kate gettin' on."

With a tray full of cups and tea and a plate of cookies, Shelly gingerly sets it on a coffee table she had seen Courtney use many times for just such an occasion. Stepping back for a moment, satisfied with her effort, she sits down in a chair across from Courtney.

From all this orchestrated hubbub, Courtney realizes something serious must be on Shelly's mind. Taking a sip of her tea, she looks directly across the table at what she has already perceived to be a troubled questioner.

"So wha be a troublin' you Missy? It ain't got nothin' ta do wif little Kate do it?"

"Well yes and no," says Shelly. "It probably has more ta do with Manny."

"Well les hear wha you gots goin' through tha pretty head o yourn."

"While I was in rehab, Manny spent a lot of time here. What did you make of him doin' that?"

Courtney suspects there's more to this question than meets the eye. "I can tell you dis much, iffen it worn't fer Mister Manny, Kate an me wouldna made it. He tooks good care ah everthing."

"I know all that. I guess what I'm concerned with is, Kate told me she and Manny have a secret. It scares the hell out of me. Do you have any idea what she may be talking about?"

Courtney is listening intently. "Miss Kate always tell me everthing she do. Ah doan let nothin' get by. Mus be it ain nothin' much or she'da spilt her beans by dis time."

"I hope you're right, Courtney," says Shelly.

Courtney can sense her answers are not giving Shelly the relief she's looking for. "Lemme aks you a coupla questions. Wha *you* think of Mister Manny?"

Courtney takes another sip of tea, purposely giving Shelly a moment to consider the question.

"He's a lot different than when he and I traveled with the same group. I didn't like him then, but now he seems so kind and considerate of me and Kate. It's like I'm waiting for the other shoe to drop or for the balloon to pop." Shelly considers her answer for a moment. "He could grow on me more if I'd let him but right now I'm not sure what the hell is going on with him and Kate."

"Ah do know dat chil been lookin' for a daddy a long time. Dis be da closest she come ta dat. Ah hopes you doan go ruinin' it over nothin'."

Something outside the living room window catches Shelly's eye. Manny and Kate are returning from Potter's Zoo. They're laughing as they evidently have shared something that caught both their fancies. Coming through the door Kate catches sight of her nanny. Running across the room, she throws her arms around Courtney.

"Courtney, I've missed you soooo much," cries Kate.

"Well Courtney, ah been a missin' you too. Dats wha bring me roun here."

Manny takes advantage of the moment to also give Courtney a hug.

"Oh mercy me. All dis huggin' gonna get me a cryin," says Courtney wiping her nose.

They all spend the next quarter hour going over things they want to tell one another. Kate is definitely enjoying everyone. Shelly's happier than she can remember being.

Soon Courtney is telling everyone good-bye with hugs going around again. When Shelly's turn comes, Courtney whispers in her ear, "Jus do wha you think be da right thing."

Shelly is determined to get to the bottom of this secret pact Kate says she and Manny have, so she takes a deep breath. "Okay Manny, Kate has told me that you and her have a secret. Are you planning to let me in on it someday? Well today is gonna be the 'someday.' I'm not going to spend any more time with my imagination taking me to a lot of bad places. So I want both of you to come clean." Shelly has a look in her eye that signals to them both she means business.

The two of them look at one another. Kate speaks up all excited, "Can I show her, Manny?"

Manny musters up a look that says he may be in for an uncomfortable time. "Okay, I think it's probably time she knows."

In a flash, Kate is out of her chair. She pulls Manny to the center of the room. With one hand she lifts Manny's hair off his collar, while with the other hand she points to a red birthmark along Manny's hairline.

"Look Momma, Manny's got the same birthmark as me! Manny says he thinks we're related. I think we must be cousins!" It would be hard to put a number on the enthusiasm this little girl is displaying over the possibility that this kindly man is somehow related.

Staring directly at Manny. Shelly remains speechless. The look on her face says everything. "You...You're..." It's all she can manage to say.

With all the determination he can muster, he looks at Kate's smiling face wondering what part of her life he needs to apologize for. Then looking Shelly squarely in the eye, he merely states, "Yes...Yes, I am!"

THE END